Praise

"This delectable story…is all about second chances and every girl's secret fantasy of marrying the perfect guy. Mulry creates a completely fleshed-out character in Bronte… She and the other characters make this charming book worth reading again and again."

—*Publishers Weekly*, starred review

"Megan Mulry's vivacious Bronte is every Englishwoman's nightmare—the straight-talking, hot-blooded, all-American girl who bags the Duke! Now, if only all English aristos could be as delicious as Max…"

—Hester Browne, *New York Times*
bestselling author of *Swept Off Her Feet*

"If you liked *Sex and the City*, you're going to love *A Royal Pain*… Filled with urban, rich, and royal characters, *A Royal Pain* is a wonderful debut that shouldn't be missed. I anticipate spectacular things from this author."

—Catherine Bybee, *New York Times*
bestselling author of *Wife By Wednesday*

"A fabulous debut! Megan Mulry brings together an iridescent American woman and her irresistible British gentleman with pitch-perfect dialogue and a keen eye for the dynamics of modern relationships. Equal parts romance and psychological drama, this book kept me up late and had me dipping back for more."

—Beatriz Williams, author of *Overseas*

A Royal Pain

MEGAN MULRY

sourcebooks
landmark

Published by Sourcebooks Landmark, an imprint of Sourcebooks, Inc.
P.O. Box 4410, Naperville, Illinois 60567-4410
(630) 961-3900
Fax: (630) 961-2168
www.sourcebooks.com

Library of Congress Cataloging-in-Publication Data

Mulry, Megan.
  A royal pain / Megan Mulry.
      p. cm.
  (trade paper : alk. paper) 1. Young women—Fiction. I. Title.
PS3613.U4556R69 2012
813'.6—dc23

2012020534

Printed and bound in the United States of America.
VP 10 9 8 7 6 5 4 3 2 1

HIGGINS [dogmatically, lifting himself on his hands to the level of the piano, and sitting on it with a bounce]: I find that the moment I let a woman make friends with me, she becomes jealous, exacting, suspicious, and a damned nuisance. I find that the moment I let myself make friends with a woman, I become selfish and tyrannical. Women upset everything. When you let them into your life, you find that the woman is driving at one thing and you're driving at another.

PICKERING: At what, for example?

HIGGINS [coming off the piano restlessly]: Oh, Lord knows! I suppose the woman wants to live her own life; and the man wants to live his; and each tries to drag the other on to the wrong track. One wants to go north and the other south; and the result is that both have to go east, though they both hate the east wind.

—George Bernard Shaw, *Pygmalion*

Chapter 1

A YEAR AGO, IF you had told Bronte Talbott she was going to quit her job and leave her life in New York for any reason, much less a romantic one, her answer would have been a quick and confident, "Bullshit." Bronte wasn't looking for anyone to sweep her off her feet. She didn't have any absurd ideas about her very own happily ever after. She had worked too hard and loved her job in advertising too much to throw it away for some guy. But that night at David and Willa Osborne's going-away party had been the beginning of a transformation that left Bronte almost unrecognizable to her former self.

She had walked through the packed front hall of David and Willa's apartment in Tribeca and seen Mr. Texas across the proverbial crowded room. Really crowded. Really smoky. Really loud. And he had looked up from his conversation as if her late arrival had triggered some unanticipated but welcome reaction, and he had given her a small, inviting smile that sliced through all the noise and peripheral distractions.

Slam.

She had met him a couple times before. Over the past few years, he had become a sort of bit player in their circle of friends. He lived and worked in Chicago, but he would fly into town for what he liked to call "the big weekends." He and David had hit it off after they'd worked on a financial deal together and discovered a shared love of the Austin music scene and alcohol.

At first, Bronte had written him off as a little too loud, a little too confident. He was from Midland, Texas, for chrissake. But in that moment of crosscurrent intimacy amid the melee, she had a little recognition of her own desire to ally herself with someone who might be a little too loud or a little too confident. For once, she wanted to be the one who didn't have to carry the conversation. Or the luggage, for that matter.

The rational, Gloria Steinem part of her railed (*My mother marched on Washington for this?*), but there it was. The shameful truth: a latent desire to be arm candy. To be taken care of.

"Hey," he said.

He'd left the conversation of which he had been, as usual, the center of attention and was standing next to her at the makeshift bar. Half-empty bottles of Belvedere Vodka and Johnnie Walker Blue and Myers's Rum were scattered across the black-granite countertop of David and Willa's narrow, modern kitchen.

"Hey," Bronte answered back as she poured herself a glass of red wine.

The two of them were temporarily alone in the relatively quiet space.

"So," he asked, "you think you'll go visit Willa and David in London after they move back?"

"I hope so. I've only been there once, but I loved it." She took a sip of wine and waited for him to carry on the conversation.

"What'd you think of the show?" he asked.

"What show?"

"The concert at Madison Square Garden!" He smiled. "I thought everyone here had been there."

"Oh, I didn't go."

Another friend, who was bombed, stumbled into the kitchen and pulled a soda out of the refrigerator, then weaved between the two of them.

"Hey, Bron," he slurred.

Bronte smiled as she watched the poor guy bump into the doorjamb on his way out, then she looked up to see Mr. Texas staring at her with something akin to interest or mischief.

"What could have possibly kept you away?" he drawled.

She looked into her wineglass, then back up into his eyes. "It was a flip of the coin, but I ended up choosing the Rothko show at MoMA over the concert. My cousin is moving to L.A. and it was our last chance to hang out before she moves."

"I don't think I would've missed that concert for anything, much less some grim museum exhibit. I've been to that Rothko Chapel in Houston, darlin', and I thought it was pretty lame."

Bronte laughed. She wasn't sure she had ever heard anyone dismiss Rothko. Or call her *darlin'*. If he had still been alive to meet him, her intellectual father would have absolutely despised this man.

"What kind of art do you like? The dogs playing poker?"

He smiled. "Yeah, I love that bull dog. The dangling cigarette. He's definitely got a full house."

"I know you are being purposely unintellectual," she said.

"Life is grand; why struggle with all those suicidal abstract expressionists?"

From anyone else, she might have been offended, but he had this uncanny way of making her academic interest seem, if not foolish, at least needlessly difficult.

"Yeah." She looked at him over the rim of her wineglass and wondered if he was drunk. He had a hint of mobility around his mouth, and his eyes were unsteady. But he seemed sober enough to keep his attention firmly on Bronte's lips.

"So, you want to go for a walk?"

She laughed again. "It's almost two in the morning. Where would we go for a walk?"

"I don't know. I was just thinkin' I could walk you home. You know, how one does."

He was ramping up the Texan drawl and she had to admit it was pretty damn sexy. She hadn't been attracted to anyone for ages. It felt good to have the warmth of his gaze on her. She'd been so focused on scratching her way to a level or two above entry level in the advertising business that her eye had simply been elsewhere. She was adept at compartmentalization. If she was focused on work, she was focused on work; she wasn't 90 percent focused on work and 10 percent focused on seducing someone.

Bronte had looked at these post-college years as the pay-your-dues chapter. She was willing to do just about anything to earn the respect of her boss and her colleagues, to prove that she wasn't some airhead who was working for a few years until she found a husband or hop-scotched to another industry. Whatever it took, she was going to be a kick-ass advertising account executive. She wasn't going to wait around for anyone to whisk her off her feet.

But.

This man was proving to be pretty awesome in the whisk department. Broad, blond, confident, jovial. He reminded her of Kipling's Kim, little friend of all the world. But big.

"Have you ever read *Kim* by Rudyard Kipling?"

"Is that like *The Jungle Book*? I've watched that cartoon with my nieces." His smile was inclusive and naughty.

Every guy who entered the kitchen to grab a beer saluted him with a mix of respect and camaraderie. A string of "Dude!" and "Hey, dude!" and "What a show, dude!" punctuated by high fives and emphatic nods constantly stalled their incipient conversation.

"Why are they congratulating you on the concert?" Bronte asked in one of the lulls.

He laughed. And it was as if a great bass guitar had strummed through her. "They're not congratulating me! We were just all agree-ing how great it was. Shared pleasure and all that."

He slowed his voice there at the end, and even though she knew it was some trick of seduction that he probably practiced (or no longer needed to practice because it came so easily), she still gave herself over to the warm flow of desire that it created.

"I like the sound of that," Bronte said softly.

Shared pleasure and all that, she repeated to herself in her mind. She would like to know more about "all that."

He reached out his hand and took Bronte's near-empty wine-glass out of her grasp. A sort of chauvinist gesture that she resented but also liked, hating herself a little.

"What if I want another glass of wine? What if I want the last sip in that glass?"

But he knew, and she knew he knew, that she would much rather abandon the dregs or the possibility of a future glass in favor of walking out of this party with this charismatic, larger-than-life, anti-Rothko hunk holding her hand.

He was pulling her in that direction when Willa and David entered the small kitchen, pretty much sauced and holding their arms around one another's waists. Bronte let her hand fall away from his.

"There you are!" Willa nearly sang.

She gave Bronte an emotional hug.

"Willa, I saw you for lunch today! You act as if I haven't seen you in years!"

"I know, but I'm going to *miss* you." Then, still holding one of Bronte's hands, Willa turned to the blond hero in close proximity. "And you! You have got to meet Bronte Talbott. She is fabulous." Willa's voice was a lilting mix of upper-crust British and drunk.

Mr. Texas smiled over Willa's shoulder and winked at Bronte in a conspiratorial way, then said, "Thank you for the introduction,

Willa. Bron and I were just gettin' acquainted. Please convince her that I would be a suitable escort to walk her home."

"Oh, Bronte! You must! He's simply so American, isn't he?" Willa grabbed his bicep as if he were a prizefighter. "All that might and muscle."

David rolled his eyes and pulled his wife's hand away from his friend's upper arm. "Really, darling, you must stop mauling our guests. Plus, I thought you wanted Bronte to meet Max."

"Well, I did. Who wouldn't want to meet the most eligible bachelor in all of England after all?" Willa gave Bronte a meaningful, if drunk, eye widening. "But if he doesn't have the decency to arrive on time, he's going to miss the catch of the day."

Bronte blushed, unsure if it was from being referred to as a catch or if it was from the possessive Texan hand that had just retaken hers.

"He's shit outta luck then!" The Texan drawl was back in full force, along with that firm hand. "Let me walk you home, darlin'. You must need to walk off all that Rothko, right?"

And she did need to walk it off. She needed to walk off a lifetime.

She felt like, up until that moment, her life had been a stressful balancing act of rebellion and conformity. Her appreciation of Rothko notwithstanding, Bronte craved people and ideas that served to disprove her father's despicable worldview that humanity was divided into two groups: one was made up of about a hundred intelligent people, and then there were the rest of the idiots. Lionel Talbott had been a brilliant academic who'd loathed his daughter's love of pop culture. In her early teens, her addiction to *Hello!* magazine had become almost feverish, especially in her father's presence. He had studied in England and had tried to get her to focus on Shakespeare and Marlowe.

What had started out as a mere act of rebellion on her part soon grew into a lifelong fascination. She would acquaint herself with

British history, all right. Starting with the torrid affairs of Henry VIII right up until the glamour of Lady Diana. She was especially fond of the brooding men who always had pressed linen handkerchiefs in their pockets and the stylish women who were born knowing how to wear a fascinator. Her father had despised Bronte's royal infatuations and had ridiculed her inconsolable adolescent drama when Diana died. Of course, his disapproval only served to solidify her attachment to all things having to do with British royalty (and occasionally Danish and French when marriages demanded).

In a perverse turn of events, she ended up reading Shakespeare and Marlowe in secret, while she flaunted the latest Regency romance or left steamy bodice rippers on the living room coffee table merely to antagonize her father. Unfortunately, all of those teenaged skirmishes culminated not in a mature evolution of mutual understanding between father and daughter, but in a final battle of the wills when Bronte refused to go to Princeton. That had been her anti-intellectual coup de grâce.

Up until now.

How her father would have sneered at this poker-playing-bulldog loving, brawny, blond Texan. Not that she was attracted to him for those superficial, anti-Daddy reasons, she hedged. But it didn't hurt. Mr. Texas was smart and well-educated and well-informed, and even after all that (the master's degree in international relations and the MBA in corporate finance from the University of Texas), he actually chose to toss all those diplomas aside and simply enjoy a great bottle of St. Estèphe or the perfect Dover sole.

"Means to an end and all that," he quipped when she pressed him for why he had gone to graduate school at all if he had no respect for higher education.

"Again with the 'all that,' huh?" Bronte said. "I sort of love how you are able to dismiss 'all that,' all that I have been brooding about for the past six years since graduating from college."

They walked on in silence for a bit. A nice silence, thought Bronte. The cool March air made her feel keenly alert.

"So is it just for the money?" she asked as they walked farther north up Hudson Street. They had crossed Canal Street and were making their way into SoHo. The three-in-the-morning streets were quiet, almost private.

"No such thing as 'just,' Bron."

He had started calling her Bron from the outset. Whether it was because that's how her drunk friend had addressed her or because he always assumed a level of heightened intimacy with everyone, she didn't care. She liked the sound of his warm, vibrating voice when he said her name.

She realized—without much perception, she later noted—that it didn't matter much *what* he said because that deep thrumming voice was seductive no matter what came out of his mouth. He could have read the directions for setting up her modem and she probably would have sighed and batted her eyelashes like a starstruck teenager.

But along with all that thrumming, sexy, deep *Bron*-calling, he was also just walking a girl home and holding her hand. He never got grippy or pawing or pushy or any of that.

He just held her hand.

No such thing as "just," she reminded herself.

"So if it's not 'just' for the money, what do you intend to do with all your filthy lucre when you've made enough?"

"Enough? Never enough!" he laughed. "And I'm already doing it... go to my favorite concerts, stay in kick-ass hotel suites at the Four Seasons, fly to London for the weekend to hang out with friends and drink martinis at Dukes and eat squab at Mark's, go skiing in Aspen, bonefishing in the Yucatán, hunting in Argentina, windsurfing on the Columbia Gorge. You know... live!"

Bronte so wanted to think of him as a pompous ass, but he made it all sound perfectly vital and joyful. *Who wouldn't want to go bonefishing in the Yucatán?* she argued with herself. Not that she would know a bonefish from a bone-in rib eye, but it all sounded so alluring when he said it in that carefree, optimistic drawl.

And she wanted to be a part of it all, laughing in the boat on the shimmering turquoise shallows as he caught the elusive bonefish and smiled that big Texan smile in her direction.

"This is me," she muttered as they arrived at the sidewalk in front of her modest apartment building in the West Village.

He kept her hand in his and leaned in to kiss her briefly on the lips, nothing demanding.

Just right.

"Thanks for walking me home."

"The pleasure was all mine. Are you around tomorrow, darlin'?"

"Sure." She suppressed another blush at his familiar use of *darlin'*. "What's tomorrow? Sunday? Yeah, I have to meet a friend in the morning, but after that I should be around."

"Want to meet at Balthazar for lunch?" he asked.

"That sounds great."

"All right then." He leaned in and kissed her again on the lips, lingering a bit longer this time.

"Mmmm," Bronte hummed as her tongue dragged slowly across her lower lip after he'd pulled away. She opened her eyes slowly.

"Good, right?" he asked, looking into her eyes until she nodded her agreement. "Right," he said with confident affirmation. "Okay, you get up to your apartment before I ask to come up there. And I'll see you at Balthazar tomorrow. About noon sound good?"

"Perfect."

"Perfect," he agreed, giving her another one of his trademark winks.

Bronte let herself into the vestibule and smiled over her shoulder as he watched to make sure she got through the second locked door safely.

She rolled into bed that night thinking that here was a man, a grown man, a gentleman even, who walked her home, kissed her good night, didn't seem to have a single urban neurotic impulse, and thought that she was quite perfect.

—⁓—

Max left a note on the kitchen counter, then pulled the door shut quietly behind him, not that there was any possibility of waking David and Willa anytime soon. He had crashed in their guest room shortly after arriving at two in the morning and then had woken at six thirty when the garbage trucks started clanging and crashing down the street. The flight from London had been one delay after another and he could have used a few more hours of sleep, but once he woke up, it was impossible. He read in bed for several hours, then decided to walk up to Balthazar, telling Willa and David in his note to join him there whenever they could.

He arrived at the height of the Sunday lunch crowd and spotted an empty seat at the bar. He smiled at the hostess as he walked by, then sat himself so he could look up at the mirror behind the bartender for a great view of the bustling brasserie. He ordered a spicy Bloody Mary and started scanning the reflected room. Back in the corner, he let his gaze rest on a particularly attractive woman. She was flushed and animated while she listened to a blond footballer type. She was entirely wasted on him, Max thought coolly. Even from this distance, Max could see how her erect posture and attentive look barely concealed a concentrated energy. The tosser she was with just looked like he was moving at half speed compared to her, nodding and smiling like a bobblehead in slow motion. Not that Max was being overly judgmental—what'd he care?—but clearly those two were doomed to fail.

"Do you know what you'd like?"

The barmaid was a tall, angular blond, and even though she was asking what he wanted to order for lunch, her mouth quirked in a way that suggested she might be able to provide more than what appeared on the menu. If only his brother, Devon, were with him, he thought with a wry smile, someone might have been able to follow up on her unspoken offer.

"Just lunch, I think." Max was a firm believer in the look-don't-touch school of flirtation. One thing led to another and then it just got messy. Devon, on the other hand, had an honorary degree in touch-all-you-want. And he always managed to skip away without a second thought.

Max ordered an omelet then resumed people watching. His eyes trailed back to the far corner to check on the tightly wound brunette, but the booth was now empty.

"There you are!" Willa sang, then grabbed her forehead as the sound of her too-loud voice exacerbated her hangover.

"A booth just opened in the back," David said, "Let's go sit."

Willa groaned as she settled into the booth between the two men.

"Ugh. I need a little something." She looked around for a waiter, then back to Max. "I always swear I will not get pissed as a newt and then I do this to myself. I swear—"

Max smiled as he snapped his fingers and waved at a passing waiter. He spoke quickly in perfect French and the busy Parisian nodded, took the order for two more Bloody Marys, and continued on his way.

"Why are you the only person I know who can do that without coming off like a total ass?" Willa asked.

"Animal magnetism?" Max said with a grin of self-mockery.

"You think you're joking, perhaps," Willa said, "but it's more than that. You just never come off as a pompous jerk—"

"Of course, we know better," David interjected.

"Very funny."

"No, seriously. It's a nice touch. You seem, I don't know, collegial somehow."

"Why thank you, Willa. I'm glad you approve."

"I do." She smiled up as the waiter set down the two new drinks. "Thank you." Her smile faded when she refocused her attention on Max. "But I'm still annoyed that you arrived too late to meet my friend. You two would be such a pair."

"And why is that?" The image of the brunette he'd been admiring in the booth where they were now sitting flashed in his mind. He may try harder to be prompt for someone like that.

"Because she is vivacious and smart and funny. And you are… well…"—Willa paused thoughtfully—"you."

Max smiled at Willa for the kindness. He had assumed she would round out that sentence with one of her typical most-eligible-royal-bachelor throwaway lines, and as much as he hated to admit it, he was pleased, even at the ripe old age of thirty-four, to feel that he was something more than the sum of his titles and holdings.

"Thank you, Willa. I think."

"You're welcome. I think."

They ate lunch then headed back to Tribeca, where they settled in to watch some college basketball and hang out on the enormous couch. Max had given them both a good ribbing about their absurdly large American life, but he secretly admired the sheer audacity of American design and, ultimately, the American psyche. While he questioned the disposable nature and planned obsolescence of many American enterprises, he loved the guts it took to think on a grand scale and just go for it. He came from a long line of men and women who prided themselves on preserving things. It was admirable. But it was also stifling.

"So what happens next?" David asked.

Max looked up from his novel. He'd never gotten attached to watching American sports, but for some reason, he always found it enjoyable to read in the same room while the television hummed and buzzed with commentary and prattle. He knew what David was really asking.

"There's not really much wiggle room, as you like to say. I finish out this semester, summer job in London, weekends at Dunlear being harangued by my mother, then return to Chicago next year to finish and defend my dissertation, and then… it begins."

"Come now, Max, it's not like you haven't seen it coming."

"Well, of course I've seen it coming. For most of my life it's the *only* thing I've seen coming. These years in Chicago have been such a blessed relief. I am just myself there, rising and falling on my own merits. In *that* Hyde Park, I am not the son of the Duke of Northrop, nor am I the Marquess of Dunlear, nor am I the seventy-fourth person in line for the throne, nor am I on the eligible royal lists—"

"I get it, I get it."

"—or any of that shit. But then I feel guilty for even thinking of it as 'that shit' because I really do want to succeed at it. To be worthy of it, I guess."

David looked at the television. "It's a lot. I'm not saying it's not. But you are clever." He turned and faced his friend, smiling because it was a huge understatement. Max Heyworth had been widely respected as one of the most gifted scholars ever since they'd been at Eton together. And not in the distractible, head-in-the-clouds stereotypical way. Max's mind worked in a methodical, precise fashion. His doctoral work on theoretical economics at the University of Chicago was more or less incomprehensible to the rest of his friends and family.

"Is he whinging about becoming the duke again? It's aeons away in any case. Get over yourself." Willa's posh accent derailed the serious conversation, and they all three started laughing. She sank into the couch next to David and put his arm around her shoulder to make herself more comfortable. "You really should have been on time last night, Max. My friend has been single for years—"

"Now there's a ringing endorsement," David said without looking away from the television.

"What in the world would I do with an American bird, anyway?" Max asked.

David rolled his eyes.

Willa pressed on. "You would love her, of course. And then marry her!"

"Oh, wouldn't that be the worst day of the duchess's life?" Max said. "Might be worth it just to see my mother's face when I come home with a *commoner*, and an American to boot."

David burst out laughing. "Who's she trying to set you up with these days? The twelve-year-old princess from Denmark?" Max rolled his eyes and David continued, "Or maybe the fourteen-year-old from Spain?"

"Just shut up, David," Max said.

"You're right; fourteen is way too old for you. Maybe there's a royal toddler in Monaco?"

Max started laughing despite himself and Willa began giggling too. "You know Sylvia's motto! It's just as easy to love a royal as it is to love a commoner, so—"

"You might as well love the royal!" all three of them chimed in unison.

Willa's laughter died down first. "Oh, that is the only thing that makes my hangover feel better... a good laugh. Thank you."

"You're welcome," Max said. "Always glad to be the brunt of your jokes."

"You're not the brunt!" Willa protested. "Your mother is!"

Max looked back at the book in his lap and felt the warm residue of humor slip away. "She's not entirely wrong, you know."

"How do you mean?" David asked.

"I mean, I am going to have to get married at some point—"

"Why 'have to'?"

"I mean, I want to, but I also have to, you know... eventually. Heir and a spare and all that."

"First things first," Willa said, "Just get a girl. That tends to be a good place to start."

"You make it sound like it's as easy as walking into the local pub and picking up a pint."

"Well..." David gestured toward Max as if he were exhibit A. "As Willa pointed out, you are *you*, after all."

"Exactly. You're pretty easy on the eyes, and don't try to deny it," Willa continued. "All that tall, dark, and handsome stuff is not to be tossed aside lightly. Think of it as a commodity, a bargaining chip"—Willa waved her hand in the air—"you know, some economic term that you can relate to... an option? A forward? Whatever it is, you need to *use* that shit."

"Charming, Willa," David murmured without looking away from the three-pointer that was being replayed.

"You know what I mean. He's too... good." Willa looked from her husband to their handsome friend. "You are, you know."

Max rolled his eyes to shake off the joke, but the pressure of reality was there just the same. After he finished this semester in Chicago, his fifth and final year was all that stood between him and a future that felt like a slowly constricting collar around his neck. The job in the City of London was already on hold the minute he returned to the UK for good. The obligatory weekends out at Dunlear Castle with his parents. The blind dates. It had never been stated outright, but the unspoken expectation was that Max would begin to assume more and more ducal responsibilities over the next ten years. His decision to attend graduate school had already caused a huge fracas between his parents, with his mother wanting him to begin living at Northrop House in London immediately after he'd gotten his degree from Oxford. Luckily, his father had supported Max's plan to buy his own place in Fulham, work in the City for a couple of years, and then attend graduate school in the United States.

Sylvia, Lady Heyworth, Duchess of Northrop, had finally relented.

It was the only time Max had ever heard his father raise his voice, and apparently it had had the desired effect. But the duchess wasn't happy about what she referred to as Max's years of "faffing about."

He shook his head and looked up from his lap to see Willa and David staring at him with genuine concern.

"You okay?" David asked.

Max gave his best all-is-well smile. "Of course! I mean, seriously, I have nothing to complain about. So my mother's a bit pushy... like that's news to anyone. I'm perfectly fine." There wasn't a hint of false enthusiasm. He had perfected that, at least. Keep everyone happy. No need to upset the applecart.

David looked skeptical. "Just get a girlfriend in Chicago to take your mind off things."

"Not likely, but I'll try."

Chapter 2

BRONTE HAD SLEPT LIKE a baby that night after Mr. Texas had walked her home from David and Willa's—and she slept well for many nights after. She slept soundly for months even, basking in the light of his attention, buoyed by his attraction and appreciation.

After he returned to Chicago, the long-distance phone conversations had been sublime. That voice. That urgency.

For the first weeks, they had spent hours every night sharing their life stories with each other. Later, all of those conversations melded together into a sort of first-blush-of-new-love montage in Bronte's mind. Everything mattered.

"My mother is a schoolteacher also!" he said.

"That is so funny. And your father is a wildcat oil driller? That is so cool. Does he write *wildcat* on his tax form under 'occupation'?"

"I guess, yeah," he laughed. "He probably does."

"Did you ever want to do that?"

"Of course, darlin'! What eight-year-old boy doesn't want to strike oil?! But then I think, in a way, I'm kind of doing the same thing in my business but just on paper. Trading has the same speculative edge, you know what I mean? Risky. I've already gone belly-up twice."

He said it as if it were perfectly normal to go broke. He was still a cowboy. ("Or still a boy," her mother had quipped with blatant disapproval when Bronte told her that particular story. For some reason, Cathy Talbott was not thrilled about Bronte's new boyfriend.)

Bronte had seen him as free-spirited. Bronte was sick of being judgmental. She loved how he lived at full capacity. Balls out, as he said.

Then, after they had succeeded in telling each other every possible detail of their lives, finding similarities and coincidences and meaning, they got into the habit of seeing each other every other weekend for lots of music and alcohol and sex.

Even months later, after the actual content had devolved into nothing more than loving murmurs, the sound of his voice over the phone was almost as sexy as the sex.

She remembered one night in July, at around two in the morning her time. Bronte had answered the phone to hear his throaty whisper, "Are you awake?"

"Barely, but talk to me while I pretend to sleep."

"I just got back from the greatest meal. I can't wait for you to get out here Friday night. I want to take you for dinner and watch you eat the best food you've ever tasted. I want to see your face when you bite into that crème brûlée."

"Mmmm," she hummed her appreciation through a fog of sleep deprivation. "Me too. I'll see you then." She said good night and rolled back over for a few hours of desperately needed sleep.

They spent that summer in a whirl: hotel rooms, concerts, expensive bottles of wine. Lots of those Big Weekends.

By early August, she was really beginning to fray.

"Are you there, darlin'?" he crooned into her answering machine as she ran to catch the call, fumbling with her keys in the lock before tripping over her dirty laundry on her way to the phone.

"Hey!" she answered, breathless.

"I'm thinking about you like crazy, Bron. Want to meet in Vegas this weekend?"

Did other people really just drop everything and go to Las Vegas for the weekend? She was starting to wonder. Bronte didn't know any. Was he suggesting Vegas so they could elope? Was he asking her to marry him after five months of great phone calls? And some pretty great weekend sex, she amended.

"Uh. What's in Las Vegas?"

She set down her huge bag. She was falling behind at work (from spending all her time at night on the phone with him and all her weekends traipsing around with him) and had had to carry a couple of presentation binders home with her.

"You know, the usual. A big, huge bed... and the Rolling Stones. Unplugged."

And a $500 ticket, she thought.

He wanted her with him, obviously... he was going crazy thinking about her, remember? But she was not in a financial position to buy a last-minute plane ticket to Las Vegas, nor, she suspected, her own concert ticket to a private, acoustic show with her good friends Mick Jagger and Keith Richards.

"I don't know," she hesitated. "I am really behind at work and I have a huge presentation next week."

"Did you hear what I just said? I have tickets to see Mick and Keith with like a hundred other people in a private club. It's a once-in-a-lifetime chance."

At the time, Bronte felt like every minute with him was once in a lifetime. His entire existence was made up of a string of once-in-a-lifetime moments. She ended up foregoing the trip to Vegas, but it made her realize how tired she was. She was sick of having to make what felt like life-altering decisions every time she wanted to hang out with him. It was all that urgency that made her contemplate a move to Chicago. She was simply exhausted trying to manage what amounted to two lives. Hers and theirs.

Then he told her he loved her. Really loved her.

It was the middle of August. They were walking around Millennium Park, enjoying a surprisingly fresh wind sweeping in off of Lake Michigan. And he was so gentle and tender. And he loved her. And then… she just went for it. Head first.

It was only *after* her feet left the emotional diving board that she discovered the pool was empty. In hindsight, it seemed glaringly obvious that his I-love-you declaration was nothing more than a reflex, a placeholder, a dating Post-it Note (Month Five: Say, "I love you"), whereas her I-love-you reply was meant to impart the weight and bliss of eternity. It was the first time she'd said it to anyone other than her mother.

Of course she was moving to Chicago. There was a man there who loved her. A man she loved. From the very beginning, she thought she was getting something that everyone else was too shallow to perceive. Beneath his bawdy jokes and big vodkas, she thought, he was really sincere. They shared a deep, quiet connection. The killjoy part of her brain sassed that the connection might be quiet because it was unspoken lust… or unspoken because it didn't exist… but she shoved that aside. It was her turn to have the great love chapter of her life. She had always dated artsy, intellectual types. As her college roommate used to jest, Bronte liked readers. And here, instead, was a broad-shouldered, high school football captain, card-carrying male. He read Tom Clancy, not Tom Wolfe.

So what?

He had always dated pert blonds; for the long haul, Bronte argued with herself, he wanted the artsy intellectual. It was a twisted sort of justice for them to end up together.

She tried to be rational, weighing the pros and cons of uprooting herself and moving to Chicago to be with him. Mr. Texas looked great on paper. He had his own successful investment business, came from a great family (parents who loved each other!), and had lots of funny, engaging friends.

They had not been dating long enough to warrant a marriage proposal, but she thought they might have a real chance. She didn't care if she ever got married, technically. If she was with the right person, she would know, and it would be right. Right?

If she moved to Chicago, she would finally be able to see how they would be together in real life, on a daily basis. If not, she was sure she would spend the rest of her life feeling like she hadn't tried hard enough to secure her own happiness.

She wanted to go for it.

By mid-September, certain that seeing each other every day would alleviate some of that crazy urgency and let them settle into a more normal relationship, she applied for a job at a fantastic boutique advertising agency in Chicago and got it. She wanted to surprise him.

He was surprised all right.

He was psyched she was moving to Chicago. He told her he was psyched.

"Yeah, I'm psyched."

But Bronte was never able to shake the feeling that he couldn't quite get himself fully behind anything that wasn't entirely his idea.

"Sure, that'll be great, darlin'." He sounded like he was watching television and having a beer while he talked to her. Half-listening.

There was no way any relationship could or should sustain the level of full-throttle intensity that they had shared those first few months, she assured herself. It was perfectly fine that he wasn't, you know, ecstatic. They were mellowing. They were both exhausted, she told herself when, occasionally, he was unable to talk as long.

She still slept like a baby, but a teething one. With the croup. And diaper rash. And colic. Once she got back in his arms, she reasoned, all would be well.

When she called her mother to let her know her decision, she wasn't surprised at the reply.

"Well. It's your life. You do what you think is best."

Bronte ignored the sledgehammer subtlety. Despite the soft,

controlled tone of her voice, Cathy Talbott might as well have screeched and flapped dragon wings that not in a million years would *she* move to another city without at least the verbal promise of a long-term commitment.

Of course, Bronte knew that quitting a perfectly good job, leaving a perfectly good, rent-controlled apartment in the West Village, and moving halfway across the country to "be with" a guy was probably not the smartest move.

At the very least, it was risky.

"A marriage proposal would be nice, for example," her mother lobbed.

But Bronte was liberated, wasn't she? She could pick up and move if she felt like it. She could adapt. Moving seemed like the only solution. How else would she know for sure if he was "the one"? All she had to go on was six months of panting, late-night phone calls and every other weekend spent in a mad rush of togetherness. And that was not cutting it.

And he loved her.

Suddenly, she was sick of her mother's wisdom. Wisdom was for the timid.

"Hey, Mom, that's my other line. I have to go. I'll see you this weekend."

It wasn't really the other line, but her friend April's desk was close enough that Bronte could give her the now-familiar rotational hand gesture for make-your-phone-ring-really-loud-right-now-so-I-can-get-off-the-damn-phone.

Apparently, that's what mothers were for, right? To make you question (to death) every (goddamned) decision you ever made in an effort to save you from going to all the trouble of making a complete ass of yourself. Or maybe it was just enlightened self-interest on the part of mothers everywhere to save *them* the hassle of having to pick you up and scrape you off and listen to all the heartache (again) when "the one" turned out to be "that piece of shit" and you were left without that perfectly good job, without that perfectly good, rent-controlled apartment, and (patently) without that boyfriend.

After more or less hanging up on her mother, Bronte went into her boss's office and collapsed with a melodramatic huff onto the chair across from the older woman's desk. Carol Dieppe swung her ergonomically correct, black mesh chair a half-turn away from her computer screen and raised one eyebrow.

"Please tell me you are not going to move to Chicago to be with this guy."

Bronte repressed a sigh and tried to look over Carol's shoulder and out across the midlevel rooftops of SoHo. This was more than just a perfectly good job she was about to give up; this was *the* perfectly good job. Carol had faith in Bronte. She had actually negotiated two years ago to take Bronte with her from their previous advertising agency, from which Carol had been vigorously recruited.

Carol was a successful, strong, kick-ass career woman. And she was forty-eight, single, childless… even contemplating that laundry list of antifeminist claptrap made Bronte feel guilty—but why?! Was *she* supposed to feel guiltier because she wanted all of that supposedly antiquated nonsense?

"Fuck. What am I supposed to say?" Bronte murmured.

"You're supposed to say, 'I'm not quitting my job and leaving New York until he goes to Harry-Fucking-Winston and rains rose petals down on Mercer Street outside this office window that spell out "will you marry me"… in fucking italics!' That's what you're supposed to say. But—"

Bronte couldn't help laughing. Carol smiled across the desk and softened her tone, picking up a pencil and holding an end in each hand as she rotated it distractedly.

"Look, Bron. I know you think I'm some dried-up old bitch from *Sex and the City*, but I promise you I want what's best for you

and"—Carol held up one hand to stop Bronte from interrupting—
"and… I know that what you want for you is not what I would
choose for me. I mean, I am not waiting for anyone—ever!—to
spell out anything in rose petals, but I know you have that dreamy,
romantic, blissed-out side of you that is waiting for prince charming… that is perfectly entitled to that… but I just don't think Mr.
Texas is your man."

Bronte sighed, audibly this time. "It's hard enough for me to
convince myself to leave all this behind, much less convince you, my
mom, my friends, and my landlord, but unless I move there, how
will I ever know if he's the one?"

Carol did her best cynical stare, then dropped the pencil on her
desk and raised her palms in an I-give-up gesture.

"I gather that is not a rhetorical question? Off you go then. What
more can I say? I don't ever want to say 'I told you so,' but if nothing
else, this is going to teach you one very good lesson."

"And what lesson would that be?" Bronte asked skeptically.

"Oh, just you wait and see."

Bronte forcibly ignored the ominous reverberation that followed
Carol's pronouncement.

After packing up her New York apartment and transferring the
lease to a friend of a friend (it's amazing how easily a perfectly good
life disassembles), the movers arrived and shipped the contents of
said life to an apartment across the street from *his* apartment. This
was one more layer of her idiocy: the thought that if she got her own
place, she wasn't *really* moving there just for him, but to have some
new, important life experience too.

Crap. Double crap.

After saying all the cheerful, tearful, I-hope-I-am-not-making-
a-complete-cake-of-myself farewells to friends and family, Bronte
hopped a flight to Chicago and then: The Bag Incident.

The Bag Incident transpired thusly.

Having just disassembled said pretty-perfect New York City life and made the great sacrifices of quitting job and leaving family and friends, but still feeling pretty heroic and grand-gestureish about the whole thing, Bronte landed at Chicago O'Hare airport. She made it through to baggage claim and, not seeing the promised welcome wagon of Mr. Texas anywhere in sight, set about the awkward task of hauling her bag off the luggage carousel.

It was an enormous, army-green duffel bag—looking back, it kind of screamed *refugee*—that was stuffed to bursting with every last-minute thing that had not made it into the final boxes that she'd shipped the week before. Then she turned and he was there—her big, brawny, blond dream, waiting for her, right across the security barricade and just outside baggage claim.

How sweet was that? Coming to the airport? He didn't need to do that in the middle of a busy workday, right? So Bronte dragged the massive duffel over to where he was standing, dropped the body bag on the ground with a thud, reached up to hug said dreamboat, and was greeted, instead, with a quick peck on the cheek and a terse, "I am in a no-parking zone so let's step it up, darlin'."

Those pearls of tender welcome were immediately followed by a quick pivot, the sight of a man's strong, wide back making its confident, blond way out of the airport, and a woman and her enormous bag—and unkissed lips—left standing in said airport.

Gutted.

She always thought of a Haida dugout canoe when she thought of that word. Perfect.

Fucking gutted.

He may or may not have come back to help carry the bag—her well-honed wolf whistle may have alerted him to his slight oversight—but that was irrelevant. The reality (why hello! Nice to meet you!) slapped Bronte so hard that she never really got over it.

He didn't give a rat's ass whether she was there or not. If she wanted to shack up for a while, that's cool, whatever. Move in with me. Move in across the street. That's cool. Wherever it leads. Yeah. Right.

Wrong.

In the end—for surely The Bag Incident was the beginning of the end—it wasn't even his fault. He had never said, "Move in with me and it will be hell-fire-kick-ass-knock-your-socks-off sex day and night followed by a lifetime of more excellent sex and marriage and children and more great sex." Bronte had simply hoped.

She had hoped hard.

She had hoped that because she was twenty-eight and smart and independent and tall and *all that*, and he was thirty-five and approaching a certain age and had always told her she was cool and how they were really great together and, yeah, well, you get the picture. One of his favorite compliments had always been to tell Bronte that she was "a bit of all right"—as in "you're a bit of all right, darlin'."

In real life, however, it turned out that the weight of any lasting commitment could not be borne by a bit of all right. It required a boatload.

By early November, after she had tried every desperate, craving, begging thing to keep them together, bitter understanding dawned. It turned out that all of his winking and thrumming and complicit Texan drawling was not in the least bit exclusive. Not that he was cheating on her, exactly—it was just that he made every woman feel like she was the only person in the world on whom he would bestow the shining light of his goodwill.

Unfortunately, Bronte did not grasp that germane fact until she had left her perfectly good life in New York and entered his world in Chicago. She was no longer the special weekend treat but the daily routine.

Was all that shit about getting the milk for free really true? No, in her case at least, it wasn't that—Bronte was already happily giving him the milk for free in New York and on sexy weekends elsewhere, after all—but when she was right there every minute of every day, asking about groceries and dry cleaning and whether he wanted to go to the movies on Thursday night? That just wasn't special enough. *She* just wasn't special enough.

Within days of moving to Chicago—within minutes, really—Bronte knew for certain that she had made the biggest, whoppingest, ball-out-of-the-park, shit-show mistake of her young life. The fact that *whoppingest* was not a word didn't stop her from using it (repeatedly) to describe the extent of her folly.

A mere eight months ago, she had been a chic, independent junior advertising executive, dating her long-distance dream man (successful, complimentary, magnetic, *all that*), while living the high life in New York City: at the top of her game, so to speak.

So.

To.

Speak.

The top of her game, in retrospect, was really her ability to sustain the belief that her feelings were shared when reality lent no such credence.

Mr. Texas had even had the gall to suggest they might want to continue "fooling around" after they broke up, you know, as one does. She had never gone for the friends-with-benefits idea and certainly wasn't going to start with, the bad boy from Midland. First of all, they were never really *friends* to begin with, and second of all, there was no *benefit* to spending time in bed worrying over why he never wanted to be *more* than friends.

She told him it was simply because he was a horse's ass. The truth was that his greatest crime was being a too-potent reminder of Bronte's emotional immaturity, but she would not come to admit that for ages.

He had been as ambivalent about breaking up as he had been about getting together. Her histrionics about the shattered pieces of her perfectly good life seemed nigh on hysterical compared to his blasé "Aw, babe, come on. It's just fading out."

Having no firm opposition against which to batter her breakup frustration was, at times, as depressing as the very failure of The Relationship. He did not even care enough to break up with fervor. In December, when Bronte finally accepted complete defeat, she told him, with a surprising absence of drama, that she would prefer if they never spoke again.

Bronte decided to render him permanently nameless, thus—retroactively at least—relegating him to that part of her brain reserved for The Purposely Forgotten: the bitch from tenth grade who lied and told everyone Bronte was sleeping around; the guy at Cal who had pursued her for months, finally seduced her, then never called again. Those types of people, in Bronte's opinion, deserved perpetual anonymity. Her joking epithet, Mr. Texas, was now his permanent soubriquet.

The lingering misery came more from Bronte's having to finally admit the extent of her own delusional stubbornness (real and vast), rather than trying to pin her heartbreak on his broken promises (essentially vague).

He loved her. So what, y'all?

January found her immersed in her new job by day and a fetid depression on nights and weekends. Carol's words were her constant companion: *Just you wait and see.*

Chapter 3

By the time spring rolled around, Bronte was feeling almost forgiving (of herself, for her own idiocy). It turned out that Chicago, the city, was really not to blame for her debacle either, at least not during the months between April and October. (November through March might have added to the depth of her wretchedness, but that was just sour grapes.)

With the birds singing and the buds just beginning to bloom on the tree-lined streets of her new, *cool* neighborhood (worlds away from his *supposedly* cool but really just antiseptic, middle-aged skyscraper neighborhood), Bronte was returning to her heretofore typical optimism.

These days, she was even starting to look at the bright side of her hibernation-cum-depression of the past few months: because all food had tasted like sawdust as a result of her self-loathing—she had lived almost exclusively on a menu of Grape-Nuts for breakfast, tuna salad (with Dijon mustard, no mayonnaise) for lunch, and the occasional salad for dinner—she was now the new-and-improved, super-skinny Bronte.

She had also managed to thrive at her killer job (what with all that free time in the evenings and on the weekends, she was like a goddamned drone). The small ad agency had a fabulous roster of clients, primarily in the fashion and travel industries, and she was just about to snag another hot new client, her fifth since moving. All of which meant if (when!) she moved back to New York, to her *real*

real life, she wouldn't have to do so with her tail entirely between her legs.

Relationship-wise? Yes.

Career-wise? No.

She tried to let all of that put a smile on her face as she strolled into her favorite used bookstore in Wicker Park and then wondered absently if she was too skinny. From the head-to-toe perusal she got from the Goth, pierced guy slumped over his comic book at the unvarnished plywood checkout counter, somebody seemed to think she was looookin' gooood.

Perfect, thought Bron. *Just what I need is to be attracting lascivious looks of approbation from pale, pierced twentysomethings.*

Great.

So it happened that she turned toward the science-fiction section with a bit more snooty-toss-of-the-head-toward-Goth-Guy than she had intended, which just goes to show that you shouldn't spend too much time dissing the Marilyn Manson checkout dude because your face may look bitter and pinched like that when you turn into the narrow science-fiction aisle and bump into someone actually worth smiling about. That would be the someone with the slow smile and the how-are-you, blue-gray eyes looking up from a squatted position near the bottom shelf, an open copy of *Hyperion* in his strong hand.

And *that's* the moment Bronte thanked her lucky stars that her college boyfriend actually demanded that she read *Dune*, *Shibumi*, and *Hyperion* to have true insight into the male mind. Because, thanks to that college boyfriend, she would now be able to say something witty about Dan Simmons and how she preferred his earlier work to his later terror stuff.

That was all great in theory. In reality, she stood there totally tongue-tied and just sort of stared.

Idiotically.

"Do you need to get past?" he asked politely.

Was that a British accent? Please. Yes, please.

"Uh…" *Bronte, come on, you can do this. He did not propose—he just asked if you needed to pass by to get down that part of the stacks.*

Another smile. "You all right, then?"

Definitely British. Definitely all right. (And way more than a bit of it.)

Air, please.

"Yeah, thanks. I've been spending a lot of time alone lately, so when I go out on Saturdays, it's kind of like I'm on parole."

Spending a lot of time alone lately? On parole? From the psych ward most likely. Are you kidding me? Oh, Bronte, tell me you did not just say that desperate sentence!

"So, yeah… excuse me… thanks." And with that, Bronte turned sideways (*am I emaciated?* she wondered again) and made her way toward contemporary fiction. She was going to need a heavy dose of Lionel Shriver or Ian McEwan to remind herself that there were absolutely no happy endings in this life. *Leave your bliss at the door, you optimistic fool!*

Okay, well maybe just a little Eloisa James thrown in for good measure. She tucked a couple of romances between the contemporary novels and headed for the exit.

Bronte ended up buying four books, gave the Goth teller a genuine smile for his troubles, and walked directly across the bright, busy avenue and into her favorite diner. A few minutes later, she was surprised to find herself to be nearly content, a huge mug of steaming coffee clutched firmly in her hands and an order of buckwheat banana pancakes on the way. The embarrassing loss of her powers of speech with *Hyperion* Man started to smack a little less. *Spending time alone?* Why not just wear a T-shirt that says *I Am Lonely…* or *Pity Me.*

The following Saturday, she returned to the bookstore around the same time.

Was she hoping to accidentally bump into *Hyperion* Man?
Duh.

She ignored the vampire at the cash register and made her way toward sci-fi and—la!—there he was, sitting cross-legged on the floor reading. It was like reverting to type, but in a good way. She *did* like readers.

He looked up then and smiled broadly. "I was hoping I might bump into you. Are you on parole again?"

"I am actually. Good behavior and all that. Especially on bright spring days like this, the warden thinks a bit of fresh air is good for the inmates."

"What did you think of the Ian McEwan?"

"The what?"

"The one you got last weekend, *On Chesil Beach*."

"How do you know what book I bought?"

"I asked the creep at the checkout counter."

"Isn't there some sort of attorney-client privilege at points of sale?"

"Not as far as the sales guy is concerned."

"Hmmm. I feel mildly violated."

His eyes sparked a happy flicker at the mention of Bronte's ostensible violation.

"Okay. So maybe by next week I will have sorted out my command of the English language. Until then." She smiled and moved past him, making a beeline for the romance section. No point in pretending her mind would be inclined to any other genre, what with that velvety British voice and those icy gray eyes to ponder.

And so it went for the next six weeks. Every Saturday at ten thirty, Bronte would make her way—casually, of course—into the science-fiction section, and every Saturday, the lovely young gentleman from England would ask about what she had read last week. By the third week, she realized he was buying the same books that she was and reading them over the course of the intervening week. Sort of an imaginary book club of two.

Without all those annoying discussions.

She liked the idea of him reading contemporary romance novels. One week, she chose a particularly erotic one and then felt compelled to offset it with a dismal dirge of a novel that had won all sorts of literary awards, just in case he thought she was merely depraved.

And then, every Saturday after her pass through the stacks, she would cross the street and sit at the same small table for two in the front window of the café with a clear view of the bookshop entrance. If he happened to walk out, and she happened to get another good look at him, then so be it.

Sometimes he waved.

Usually, she started reading one of the books she had just purchased and missed his exit from the bookstore altogether.

Then one morning in early May, she was turning the page of her latest penny dreadful and shaking her head with a final, self-deprecating snort, momentarily reliving her tongue-tied foolishness, when that deep, sweet voice asked, "Is this seat taken?"

And Bronte could do nothing but sigh inwardly with a victorious, *Yes!* As in: *Yes, there is a benevolent power in the force and I am not frigid or emaciated and I may make a new friend-who's-a-boy today who even pursued me all the way across the street from the bookshop.*

But of course it came out as, "Yes." In answer to the question, "Is this seat taken?" So she started laughing and then blurted out, "*No*, the seat is not taken. *Yes*, I would like you to sit there."

And so it began.

Bronte felt so rusty at being cheerful, much less flirty, that her halting speech and inept repartee actually made it easier for them to get to know each other. His name was Max Heyworth. He was finishing up his PhD in economics at the University of Chicago before heading back to England in July to be near his family and resume his career in mergers and acquisitions at one of the top firms in the British utilities industry.

"I finally finished my dissertation last week, the written part at least," he said, "and I have been thinking all these weeks that following you into this coffee shop today would be my just reward."

She liked the idea of being Max's reward, then felt a touch of melancholy that he would be leaving so soon. Two months was not much time for them to be together, but it was better than none at all. And as her friend April would have pointed out: since Bronte had failed so stupendously with Mr. Texas, she was no longer in the market for a life partner. She was now in the market for the perfect TM.

"What are you smiling about?" Max asked through his own smile, as he brought his coffee cup to his lips. *Strong, curving, kissable lips*, thought Bronte.

"I'm not sure I should tell you, since it will make me sound like a pretty cold customer, but in the interest of my newfound code of brutal honesty, here goes. I was just thinking that my friend April, in New York, has been slinging her own brand of self-help-hash lately, telling me that what I *really* need to get over my disastrous former relationship is a TM..." Bronte paused and looked into Max's mischievous gray-blue eyes. *Killer eyes*, she thought.

"And..." he prodded.

"And 'TM' stands for 'Transitional Man,'" she added in a rush.

A year ago, Bronte probably would have blushed at her own forthrightness, but she had decided months ago that she no longer blushed. Mr. Texas had seen to that. No more speculative moments of potential romance in the eyes of that handsome passing stranger on the way into Water Tower; no more hopeful reveries while watching babies in strollers and children flying kites near the Lincoln Park Zoo; no more mooning over the pages of the eligible royal bachelors in the pages of *Hello!* magazine. No more dreaming.

She was all about the facts these days. After her colossal misunderstanding of the most basic tenets of her relationship with Mr. Texas, she vowed that from here on out, when it came to men, she would actually listen to the words coming out of their mouths ("Sure, if you want to move to Chicago, you should." = "You're on your own, sister!") rather than the dream dialogue she was hearing in her brain ("Blah blah move to Chicago!" = "I really want you to move to Chicago so we can live happily ever after. I love you!").

She could do this. She could stand firm and cool. All it required was honesty. Brutal honesty. Even while he was looking at her with those dreamy, gray wolf eyes.

Steady girl.

"Yes," he replied matter-of-factly.

That was clear enough, Bronte thought. Then, "What had I asked? Sorry I wasn't listening."

"I think you asked if I wanted to be your Transitional Man, and I answered yes. Still yes." His eyes twinkled over the rim of his coffee mug as the reflecting sun caught the long window of a passing bus on Halsted Street and flashed across Max's face.

Nice.

Before Bronte could come up with a good retort, her cell phone started ringing. She glanced down, seeing Carol Dieppe's name on the caller ID.

"Do you mind if I take this, Max?"

"Go ahead. No worries."

She smiled and flipped open her phone. "This is Bron."

Max looked across the café table at the fabulous view of Bronte Talbott swearing like a sailor into her phone. Her long, straight, chestnut hair gleamed as she swung it carelessly over her shoulder to position the phone next to her ear. The curve of her jaw rested on the palm of her other hand. She started to twist a strand of her hair absentmindedly, and Max wondered how soon he would be able to do the same. His fingers were already itching to run endlessly through Bronte's hair, to caress the back of her long neck, to—

"No fucking way... he did not... are you going apeshit? Are you spending the whole weekend at the office?... Bullshit, he's just jealous... right... uh-huh... well, that's a load of crap and you know it... okay, I'll talk to you later. I'd love to run some of my ideas by you about a pitch I'm working on, no specifics..." Bronte was half-listening to Carol's response as she glanced up at Max, thinking she would sneak a look. But instead of the quick peek she had intended, she met a penetrating gaze that seared right through her. His eyes went a darker shade of steel blue and contracted for a split second when they locked on hers.

"Uh, yeah, I'm still here, Carol, but let me hop. I'll call you later this afternoon... okay... bye." Bronte ended the call and double-checked that the line was dead before she started talking about the person she had just hung up on.

She looked back up at Max with a sheepish smile on her lips. "So, by the way, as you might have just gathered, I like to swear. A lot. And most of my friends call me Bron."

"No problem on the colorful language. If you want, I can beef up your repertoire with some Cockney rhyming slang or the well-placed *shite*."

Bronte laughed and, for the first time in months, it felt like she had really laughed, instead of feeling like a cracking piece of glass.

"I am definitely adding *shite* to my bag of tricks," she said through her waning chuckle.

"So what's your pitch next week?"

"The ad agency I work for is pretty secretive about the whole thing, so I shouldn't really say, but it would be really great if we got the account. And that was my old boss from New York on the line, and it looks like she might have a spot for me back in New York, in a new boutique operation she's putting together with a couple of venture capital guys, so, just maybe, I can put this whole, sordid Chicago chapter to bed once and for all… present company excluded, of course," she added, still smiling.

"No need to make excuses. I love New York. I have enjoyed Chicago for other reasons." (Cue slow smile… and… there it is.) "But my days here are numbered. I am trying not to be too pessimistic—I mean, I really do love England, especially come midsummer. The gentle rain in July is, well, you should see it some time. It's beautiful."

Forcing herself to set aside the dreamy implication of a future that involved her ever stepping foot in the gentle rain, she plowed ahead: "So what should we do between now and then?"

Max gave her a mocking half-smile in response that nearly knocked her off her chair. Clearly, he had some things in mind.

Bronte pressed on. "The thing is, I probably seem really crass and pushy, and *American* in the worst possible way, but I just spent the last year building up to and then crashing down from this imaginary—or at least far more meaningful in *my* imagination than it was in *his* reality—relationship. And I have made this promise to myself that from here on out, I will err on the side of brutal honesty—lest I get sucked into another morass of second-guessing, unspoken hints, gestures, sighs, what have you…"

Just then, Max placed his cool, calm hand over Bronte's fidgeting one, and she couldn't talk anymore. She felt all her chaotic, nervous energy sputter and then slowly abate. She looked up into those astonishing slate-gray eyes and felt it physically: her shoulders eased and the weight of her anxiety slid away.

Not good, some hard-hearted alter ego grumbled deep in the back of her psyche. *Listen to what he's really saying. Don't be fooled! Run!*

No! I don't want to be his arm candy, she parried with her inner bitch. *I don't want to be rescued! He's just nice and there's a clear end in sight. I'm safe!*

But he just smoothed every conflicting inner quip flush away.

He stroked her like she was a nervous creature. A part of her once-burned-twice-shy conscience still bucked, but with a grudging capitulation: like an angry young horse that knows it is about to be saddled for the first time and concedes, haltingly, that it might not be all bad.

She brought her other hand over his and gently caressed the ridge of his knuckles as they rested over hers. She didn't feel like talking anymore. Her thumb moved slowly over each knuckle, loving the feel of the soft skin between each finger and the contrast of the rough, masculine texture of the hair on the back of his hand.

It was almost noon and the bright sun was streaking through the plate-glass windows to her left that fronted the café. Another bus sped by, shooting another flash of brilliant light across Max's eyes.

Heaven.

Bronte was going to hold on to this bit for as long as he'd let her. An involuntary hum must have escaped her because at that moment, Max looked at her with a questioning gleam in his eye. When Bronte continued to smile benignly, Max slowly turned her hand palm up on the table and began to trace slow circles there and occasionally up to her wrist and back. It was such a welcome novelty, just to be touched, to open herself to this; her eyes fell half-closed in a pleasant stupor.

It was just physical. Totally fine.

Another little hum of pleasure escaped through her slightly parted lips and Max let out a wonderfully deep, low chuckle.

"My younger sister always hums when she's happy. It's a nice habit. Letting people know you're content."

He slowly brought her hand to his mouth and kissed the center of Bronte's palm, then the pulse point of her wrist. She would have never believed that something so seemingly innocent could be downright erotic.

The waitress came over then and smiled conspiratorially at the two of them. They had finished their food and, before Bronte could grab her wallet, Max had already handed his Coutts Visa card to the waitress and preemptively launched into his don't-even-think-about-trying-to-pay-for-breakfast lecture, ending his diatribe with one eyebrow raised.

"I hate that you can do that, by the way."

"What? Pay for breakfast?"

"No. That." She tipped her head toward his. "The one-eyebrow thing. I tried for forever to do it… it's one of those you-either-can-do-it-or-you-can't type of talents."

"I suspect you have other talents."

They were making their way out of the restaurant then, and out onto the sidewalk, when Bronte looked up at Max. She had not realized how tall he was until this moment. In the bookstore, he had always been crouching or sitting down there near that bottom shelf, and at the restaurant, he had been sitting across from her, at eye level. She was nearly six feet tall and he was a good four inches taller.

"Well, that's a relief," she thought, then realized she had said it aloud.

"What? That you have other talents?"

"No. That you are taller than I am. I mean, it wouldn't have been a deal breaker, but April informs me that when looking for the ideal, er, Transitional Man, physical compatibility is near the top of the list of necessary prerequisites. Since soul-mate compatibility is irrelevant, the corporeal sort takes on, shall we say, greater importance."

Max laughed: a deep, rolling, joyful sound that coursed right through Bronte and settled somewhere deep in her belly.

"I say, Miss Talbott. I think you are planning on using me."

Good God. When he reverted to that faux-formal Brit-speak it was sexier than the naughtiest, most graphic pickup line she had ever heard. His arm settled easily across her back and around her waist, his hand coming to rest on her hip as they moved in tandem down Halsted Street.

Her head leaned on his shoulder momentarily and she marveled at how terrifically natural it all felt. No false hope. No empty promises. No more sawdust for food.

"I lost some weight recently, due to the, uh, recent unpleasantness, so you'll have to pardon the slightly protruding hip bone. Buckwheat banana pancakes are a very good sign that I'll be back up to my fighting weight in no time."

"I think I can make do with things as they are."

"That's good to know."

With the hand resting on her hip, Max's thumb found its way up under Bronte's T-shirt and traced the upper ridge of said hip, leisurely caressing the indentation, then sliding back up around, meandering under the waistband of her jeans.

She was toast.

Whether it was the hiatus in her sex life or the hot, English, 100-percent-male specimen currently taking his time mapping a few mere inches of her body, she was a goner.

After walking around Wicker Park and Bucktown for the rest of the afternoon, pretending to pay attention to the shops and parks and noisy teenagers and arguing parents and street musicians, and laughing more than she had in months, they stopped for a coffee at the sidewalk café that had just opened on Division Street. Bronte was overcome with the sense of promise that pervaded the universe. She was, as Carol would say, totally blissed out.

They settled into a free table out on the sidewalk and Bronte put her elbows up, resting her chin in her hands. She was so happy just to gape at him. Max trailed his fingers along the back of her hand and down her neck, then across her shoulder, then put his hand down on the table and looked out to the street. Bronte almost felt bereft when his hand moved away.

"I think—"

"I think—"

They both started and stopped simultaneously. Max turned back to look into her eyes again, his lids intensifying. "You first."

Bronte swallowed. "Well. It's been a grand day so far, and I was just starting to think about later and—"

"Yes."

"Excuse me?"

"I said yes. Whatever you want to do, wherever you want to do it, however many times you want to do it. My answer is yes."

"Just like that?"

"Just like that."

"You don't want to know more about me? Or where I grew up? Or my favorite movies? Or how many brothers and sisters I have…"

"No. I mean, yes, of course, eventually, that would all be splendid information, but for now, no. I am not particularly interested in any of that. All of you is sitting right here. I know what you like to read, after all. And that other information is just, well, as Martin Amis would say, the information."

"Nicely put. I could not agree more. I mean, gentle rains and all that sound delightful m'lord, but why bother?"

Max winced for a split second, then grabbed Bronte's hand and leaned across the narrow table for a kiss. The first kiss he had been anticipating for the past four hours, the past six weeks. The kiss he could no longer delay. His tongue trailed tentatively across the seam of her inviting lips, then ventured into the warm welcome of her luscious mouth.

Bronte simply gave in. Her eyelids became unaccountably heavy and she emitted an unconscious mewl of pleasure. He tenderly withdrew a few inches, his eyes clouded over with desire, barely able to focus.

Bronte whispered his name, "Max." An invitation. A new statement of fact.

The moment hung there: weightless, timeless. Bronte brought

her tongue to the corner of her mouth, to relive the feel of his in that same spot only seconds before. Max leaned back into his seat and put the palms of both of his strong, beautiful hands flat onto the table.

"We should probably go, Bron."

"Where?"

"Somewhere with a bed?"

"Okay."

Max smiled and pressed on. "I was just kidding about the bed part. Well, sort of; I mean, maybe we should start on a couch and work our way up. I think you might live in this neighborhood…"

Bronte replied dreamily, "You're right. I think I might."

"Shall we go there? Or would you rather hop in a cab and go to my place in Hyde Park?"

The tiny, piercing voice of the savvy single woman in her balked at the idea of having some guy she'd never really met into her apartment, let alone diving into bed with him after a few hours hanging out on the near west side of Chicago. She tried to rationalize that she'd kind of known him for six weeks, or six Saturdays, as it were. Maybe it wasn't so slutty and tawdry after all.

The other, visceral, gut-knowing part of her accepted the fact that she was going to attack him one way or the other, and it might as well be at her place right around the corner rather than his grad-student studio apartment twenty minutes away.

What was the best way to run a three-minute security check on a guy to make sure he was not an axe murderer?

"You're worried I'm an axe murderer?"

Bronte looked at him askance. "That's a worry."

"What? That I might be an axe murderer?"

"No. That you can answer my unasked questions… I'll have to work on cloaking my pedestrian thoughts a little more thoroughly."

"Not at all. I will tease them out of you one way or another. Might as well stick to Plan A: Brutal Honesty."

"Okay, then yes, it did just, for a split second, cross my mind that all of your sexy, British wonderfulness might be a fabulous ruse and you are really a homeless vagrant, come to seduce me."

"Let's see. That very last part is true by the way." Max ruminated, theatrical index finger tapping one cheek. "References? A dance card? Letters of credit? I've got it: a mutual friend! Isn't there some damn thing about six degrees of separation? Surely, between the two of us, we know someone in common—someone who can vouch for us to one another. Do you know anyone in the economics department at the University of Chicago?"

"Alas, Milton Friedman and I have lost touch. Chicago is probably going to be a dead end, since I know about seven people here— six of whom I work with and one of whom I never wish to lay eyes on again. What about New York City advertising agencies?"

"Sorry, no. Not that I can think of. Where did you go to college?"

"UC Berkeley. What about you?"

"Oxford."

"Of course you did."

"Very funny."

"It's just that, does every highfalutin Brit go to Oxford or Cambridge?"

"Who said I was highfalutin?" Max asked with more force than he had intended.

"No one, Mr. Sensitive. But wouldn't you agree that British PhD candidates at the University of Chicago are not that thick on the ground, if you get my meaning. A self-hating intellectual, perhaps?"

"Something like that," Max conceded.

"All right then. I was not a total slacker at Cal—there has to be some highfalutin Brit who has crossed my path. Let me put my thinking cap on and—" Bronte snapped her fingers and smiled with enough wattage to disrupt the grid. Max could not have been more pleased.

"Who?"

"David Osborne? He was at Oxford, then I met him through one of my cousins who was in the same training program at Morgan Stanley and now he's back in London—"

Max was whipping out his cell phone and scrolling through his saved numbers, then he looked up and punched the green "talk" button with a victorious jab.

"David? Then step out of the pub if you can't hear me, you stupid toff… No, I'm not back in London yet… stop your yammering and listen… no, I won't be back in time for that party. Tell me what you know about Bronte Talbott… mm-hmm… mm-hmm…"—broad smile—"… yes, nice bit of crumpet that, eh?"

"Give me that phone, you pig!" Bronte said, laughing as she wrenched the phone out of Max's hand and continuing to laugh into David's ear. "So what do I need to know about this Max Heyworth character, David? Mm-hmm… originally from Yorkshire, mm-hmm… well, that's not a lot to go on, but I was really just trying to rule out axe murderer, so I guess your drunken acknowledgment that he's a stand-up guy will have to do…" Bronte could no longer concentrate on the rest of what a very inebriated David was yelling into the crackling transatlantic connection (something about Anne Boleyn winning the Nobel Prize), what with Max's index finger tracing the edge of her other ear and her trying weakly to swat him away. "Right, right, David; that's all for now. Send my love to Willa."

Max was grinning stupidly as Bronte handed him back his phone. "Any other flammable hoops for me to jump through?" he asked, one eyebrow raised.

"Of all the bad omens…" Bronte murmured, her laughter fading.

"Are you kidding? What could be a better omen than the jolliest person we know being our mutual acquaintance? And if you know anyone jollier, I demand an introduction."

"I won't dwell on it, but I met my ex at David and Willa's, at a huge party after some big concert a little over a year ago."

"I was there!" Max said.

"No. You were not. I would remember."

"Seriously, I was. Maybe that's why I thought you looked familiar when I saw you that first time in the bookshop. That was a crazy scene—David's apartment was thronged, right?"

Bronte nodded.

"My flight from London was delayed, so I didn't get there until after two in the morning, but I swear I was there. I stopped in New York on my way here actually, after my spring holiday. Oh my God, I bet you're the one Willa wanted to introduce me to. Too bad you went home with the wrong guy."

Bronte covered her face with her hands. "You have no idea."

He pulled her hands away so he could really look at her. "On the other hand, you wouldn't be sitting here now, in possession of your Brutal Honesty Manifesto no less, so maybe I should be thanking that scoundrel for luring you to this dark world of wind and heartbreak, eh?"

"Don't even think about it. I am not one of those people who stays friends with ex-lovers—a sad fate, I fear, that you will one day share… or maybe you will be the exception, since you do seem particularly… amiable."

"Well, thank you, kind lady."

"I am starting to adore when you go all *royal* on me." Bronte was distracted by the loud siren of a passing ambulance and missed Max's momentary grimace.

As they lingered at the café table, Bronte pressed her thumbnail against her lower lip and contemplated the reality that Max had been at Willa and David's party. She wondered if this was a second chance of sorts. She wondered if, this time around, it was possible to be totally up-front from this very first day, to be honest to the point of crass, to avoid all of that crazy devolution into crushing hope that had ensured the failure of her previous relationship.

"Look, Max. Here's the deal. I want to be all casual and modern and all that, but the reality is that I am not all that sure I can do it, unless we have a pretty ironclad understanding. I love the philosophical idea of entering into a sexy friends arrangement"—she smiled at him—"but the truth is that I will probably become cloying and desperate and… you'll find me wanting. So I think if we deal with all of that from the very beginning, then we can, you know, make do."

He looked at her as if she had two heads.

Then he smiled some wonderful ancient smile that could have soothed medieval kings and seduced daughters of foreign enemies. Bronte wavered in her conviction and thought, for a tiny moment, that she might dive into his arms and betroth herself to him right there on Division Street, intellectualized parameters be damned.

No! her wiser inner-self screamed. She had sworn off gut instincts. Gut instincts had moved her into a shitty studio apartment in Chicago. Gut instincts sucked.

But this Max—he seemed to be well-versed in the language of blatant honesty. Bronte thought it may have been his sheer command of the King's English. Something about the very primacy, the way he made use of each word of the language, made her feel that he had a clearer understanding of… well, everything.

"So let me get this straight." Max smiled across the café table into Bronte's sparkling eyes. "You think if we set out, from the very beginning, to be… I'm sorry, Bronte, but I cannot bring myself to use that tawdry phrase that is constantly bandied about… I shan't ever be *anyone's* fuck buddy…"

He said the last two words as if they had been scraped off his tongue. He would never utter them again in his life.

Bronte laughed and reached one hand across the small distance to grab one of his hands in hers. "Of course, that's not what I'm suggesting. I hate the friends-with-benefits bullshit. I'm just saying, let's try to be honest, realistic, and not try to pretend that there's some grand future, some wonderful tomorrow that involves me... and your gentle British rains. It's just so much easier for me—not that *that* is your job, you know, to make my life so much easier." He smiled at her forthright enthusiasm, then she continued apace, "I mean, let's just call it what it is. You are in town for, what? Eight more weeks? We are obviously—I mean, I suppose I should say *I* am obviously taken with you and look forward to spending as much of your free time with you as possible." She smiled again and reached out her other hand to enclose his hand firmly in both of hers, as if they were making a pact. "But, I mean, *really*, what's the point? Let's just have *so* much fun! Don't you think?"

Max looked at this incredibly beautiful woman and wondered what had happened to make her so skittish, so totally unwilling to just move forward at a normal pace with a (relatively) normal guy in a normal romantic relationship. But, as it was, he supposed it was worth it to play by her strange rules of engagement: no mention of lasting tenderness, no long-term plans, no future. And certainly no mention of his title. If an eight-week affair with a run-of-the-mill graduate student made her jumpy, he could only imagine what a potential future with the nineteenth Duke of Northrop would do to her precarious equilibrium.

"All right, Bronte. I accept your terms."

He said it in a way that had Bronte worried he was going to add, "And I raise you!"

Instead, Max reached across the table and held Bronte's cool cheek in the palm of his hand. "Let me head home for a little bit, then. Can I pick you up around seven thirty and we'll go to dinner and a movie? Some people might call it a date, but we don't have to call it anything."

Bronte looked at him strangely. In the romance-novel part of her brain, she had simply assumed that she and Max would end up (that day, damn it!) in bed together in a tangle of false promises and condoms.

"Oh. Okay. Yeah. That sounds… great," she said, recovering. "I'll be ready at seven thirty. Will you pick me up at my place or shall I just meet you at the theater?"

"I'd rather pick you up, if it's not too old-fashioned of me?"

"Too old-fashioned sounds ideal."

Two hours later, Bronte was spending way too much time wondering what to do with her hair. If she put it up again, that would be the fourth attempt in as many minutes. She growled at her reflection and brushed it straight.

"No false promises," she chided the overly optimistic alter ego who stared back at her—especially promises to herself. *But he's British*, her hopeful self protested. *He's charming and dashing and gallant and… everything!*

She turned away from her foolish self and switched the light off in the small bathroom.

She had showered and changed into her favorite pair of jeans and a long-sleeved French boat-neck shirt. She was wearing a new pair of huge gold hoop earrings that she had treated herself to a few weeks ago. Something about them made her feel all Foxy Brown. Even though her appearance was about as un–Pam Grier as possible—skinny, tall, and pale—good jewelry could work miracles. *And every woman deserves a little Foxy Brown*, she'd argued with herself the moment before she'd slapped down her credit card and splurged.

The doorbell rang and she grabbed a lightweight khaki jacket from the front hall closet and opened the front door.

Max looked a little too big for the entrance, which was really the bottom of a stairwell. And then he smiled, a big, glorious smile that had Bronte repressing the briefest thought that he might not only be too big for her little apartment, but maybe too big for her entire world. She'd already burned through her lifetime supply of larger-than-life men. But her palpitating heart hadn't gotten that memo, so on it hammered its happy beat.

"Let me see you," he said, gesturing in a small circular motion as if he were choreographing *Swan Lake*.

"You want me to spin?" Bronte laughed.

"Yes. Please." He looked a little sheepish, maybe worried that he had already trespassed into forbidden, unnamed regions of the sexy friends road map.

Bronte let her arms come away from her sides and turned slowly, keeping her eyes on his over her shoulder. "Okay?"

"Very." He leaned in and kissed her turned cheek, no hug or embrace, just a lovely, tender kiss that made Bronte want to fall into a puddle right there in the cramped entryway.

"Let's be off then," he said, then took her hand and spun her lightly back around.

After that night, and for four consecutive nights after, he picked her up at seven thirty. On the dot, as her mother would say. Not that she was telling her mother or anyone else that she was seeing someone… because she wasn't. He was merely an interlude. And he was fantastically prompt.

Then, Thursday he called her at work.

"Hey, lovely."

Bronte did not want to begin to contemplate what that little "lovely" did to her pulse—very accelerated—but she certainly wasn't going to tell him to quit it.

"Hey, you," she answered. "What's up?"

"I was thinking tomorrow night we might go out for a proper meal."

"What does 'proper' mean?" Bronte joked. She was sitting at her desk overlooking a small park. The tiny pink buds on the trees were joyful and life-affirming, making their annual triumph over grim winter, but she found her mind—already!—in a constant state of relating everything back to the weeks until Max's departure.

Buds led to full-blown blooms, which in turn led to the thick, leafy trees of high summer. When he would be gone.

"You know, a nice bottle of wine… snooty waiters… you in a small dress."

"Aaah, that kind of proper. I love that kind of proper! Do you want me to make a reservation somewhere? Should we try to be mindful of the cost or just live a little?"

"I'll make the reservation, and I think we should just live a little. And I don't want to go if we are going to argue about the bill. It was my suggestion; I want to pay."

"I told you—"

"Fine," he interrupted, "then we won't go."

Bronte had made financial parity one of the nonnegotiable demands of her sexy friends doctrine. All of that fiscally irresponsible jet setting with Mr. Texas—initially with her pretending she could keep up on her own comparatively small salary, sometimes with him paying exorbitant sums with openhanded generosity and love, and finally with Bronte feeling like a ridiculous circus clown pulling out her empty pockets and tilting her head with that exaggerated, freaky, grease-makeup frown—had made her vehemently opposed to any of that grand gesture crap.

Max had bristled at that part of their deal way more than she would have anticipated. She had seen his tiny studio apartment down in Hyde Park near the UC campus and it certainly didn't look like he had a ton of dough to spare. His clothes were immaculate, but she assumed he was just naturally fastidious. He didn't have a car. He was a student for chrissake. He didn't need to be saddled with the expense of entertaining her.

"No need to get peevish," she laughed. "I suppose it won't kill me to let you buy me dinner. Just don't get cocky."

"Too late for that, I'd wager."

Bronte laughed again then told him she'd see him the following night. *The following night*—she turned the words over in her mind after she hung up the phone. She was hoping that the intervening week of heavy petting at the movies and in the park and at Navy Pier and anywhere else they could get their hands on each other meant that she was no longer a flat-out slut for wanting to actually have *proper* sex with him after their *proper* meal.

What would Kate Middleton do? The silly rejoinder popped into her mind. She'd been so immersed in all the royal wedding commotion the year before—for work, of course, keeping her finger on the pulse of contemporary culture and all that. At least that's what she'd told herself. The truth was that Bronte simply loved all of the fairy-tale romance mixed with modern glamour and a real-life happily ever after. The footage she had seen of Charles and Diana's wedding had seemed surreal, with the virginal Diana looking like a newborn calf being led to slaughter. Kate, on the other hand, looked like a woman who was about to get exactly what she'd always wanted—while wearing killer clothes.

Royal gazing had been one of Bronte's favorite pastimes since she was a teenager. A harmless habit. But with the onset of her own happily *never* after, Bronte had forced herself to remove all the royal tabs from the top of her computer screen and all the royal watchers from her Twitter stream. She'd thrown in the towel on romance altogether. Tough-as-nails single gals in Chicago did not have time to lurk around the Internet checking the length of Pippa's coat or whether Eugenie was wearing her hair down or in a chignon these days. (Three-quarters length and down, of course. Pertinent facts had a way of filtering into Bronte's psyche, as if by osmosis, via the collective unconscious. Some things just couldn't be helped.)

As Bronte sat at her desk daydreaming about what Kate would wear on her first proper date—and whether or not she would take it off after dinner—she overheard Cecily's side of one of her frequent conversations with her best friend, Giacomo Pietrello, and nearly fell off her chair. After Cecily hung up, Bronte marched into her boss's immaculate office.

"Are you insane?"

"Probably… but about what in particular?" Cecily grinned.

"About choosing not to take *perfectly good* Valentino castoffs, for example." Giacomo was one of Valentino's top designers in their New York atelier. "You are not the only size eight in the world who might benefit from such manna from heaven, you know? You might think of the little people every once in a while!" While Bronte was venting her sartorially jealous spleen, Cecily had picked up the phone and hit her speed dial. She spoke in quick Italian, laughed, and hung up.

"A little red dress is on its way. It will be here tomorrow afternoon in time for your *proper* date." Cecily raised one eyebrow then flipped her hand toward the door with a smile. "And you are a size six, not an eight. Now out!"

Bronte tried to remain calm, but it was impossible. Even Kate would have let the same little squeal of delight escape at the thought of an honest-to-goodness Valentino red dress to call her very own.

And, oh, how Max ended up loving that little red dress.

It was hard to say which one of them had been more flummoxed by the other's transformation. Having only seen each other in a parade of T-shirts and jeans for the previous days and weeks, when Max opened the door to Bronte's flat and saw her in the little red Valentino dress, he clasped both hands over his heart, as if to stave off an attack. Bronte was similarly stunned by Max in full, debonair splendor. His broad shoulders and trim waist were even more appealing in his perfectly tailored navy suit, a few curls of brown hair touched the collar of his crisp white shirt, and he had finished it off with a pale-green Hermès tie. (They were going to have fun with that tie later, Bronte promised herself.)

Max hired a car and driver to chauffeur them around for the night, and Bronte winced slightly at the needless expense. He called her out.

"If you are constitutionally unable to enjoy spending a little bit of dosh on a night out, we need to have a talk."

She laughed and decided, for one night at least, to let go of her financial hang-ups. "Fine! All right! I give in. Go ahead and spend. I'll do my best to turn a blind eye to all this wild extravagance." He obviously wasn't the starving student she thought he was if that suit was any indication.

Max looked out the window of the relatively grimy dial-a-car and hid his amusement at Bronte's idea of extravagance. She was in for a few surprises when she came to London. And it was definitely *when* she came, because as far as Max was concerned, there was no *if* about it.

They arrived at a small French restaurant and Bronte gave a brief note of thanks to the powers that be that she had never been wined and dined by any Texan suitors at this particular establishment.

"Since you have rescinded financial equality," Max said after they were settled side by side in an intimate booth and looking over the outrageously expensive menu, "I was thinking maybe I should just take the reins altogether. I think I'll order for you, feed you, intertwine my arms through yours as we drink a memorable bottle of Léoville-Las Cases…"

He brought his water glass to his lips and watched her face transition from brief, affronted shock, to humor, to something seductive and willing.

Right before he took a sip, he said, "Oh, Bron, please don't look at me like that until we're finished with dessert."

"Okay," she purred with false compliance. "Whatever you say, Your Grace."

He almost spewed his water at her offhand remark, but instead pretended it had gone down the wrong tube and brought his napkin to his eyes to conceal his surprise.

She patted him on the back gently. "Are you okay?"

"Yeah," he sputtered, "fine, just excited I guess."

Bronte finished rubbing his back then put both of her hands in her lap. "Me too. And nervous all of a sudden."

He took one of her hands in his and gave her an encouraging smile. "Don't say that. It's one of my favorite things about you. You are never nervous."

Her blood sped at the idea that he already had a *favorite* thing about her—one of many, apparently—then she swatted herself back into reality.

"Everybody's nervous sometimes." Bronte reached for her water glass. "Even Kate."

Max looked at her with confusion. "Who?"

"You know, the Duchess of Cambridge."

If he had been drinking water that time, Max would have spewed that mouthful for sure. The way Bronte had phrased the sentence made it sound like *you know* the Duchess of Cambridge. Whom he did, in fact, know.

He paused again, waiting for the other shoe to drop. Either Bronte had spent the past two days scouring the Internet and knew all about his family and connections and had decided to taunt him into confessing, or she just happened to be stumbling blindly into it.

Bronte burst out laughing. "I mean, of course you don't *know her* know her. But you know what I mean. She's always so authentic and calm and pretty and smiling and, you know, perfect."

How the hell was he supposed to reply to that? Silence was always one of his best allies.

"Oh forget it. You men are all the same, pretending it's all silly princess worship or whatever. Still, I bet it's hard work being perennially cheerful all the time, and I certainly wouldn't want to do that in a million years."

Well, Max thought, *that wasn't an acceptable alternative either.* He smiled suggestively. "I'm sure her position has its… advantages, wouldn't you say?"

Bronte took the bait. "Oh, all right. William is pretty cute, I'll give you that."

Max didn't know whether to laugh or cry that the future king's cuteness was at the top of Bronte's list of royal inducements.

"And?" Max prodded.

"Oh. Fine. One might also become… fond of… the clothes. And maybe the jewelry."

Max smiled and Bronte gave him a small punch on the arm.

"What are you smiling about? I am not horribly shallow. Every girl likes clothes and jewelry."

He raised an eyebrow. "So Kate is just like every girl, then?"

"Yes," Bronte agreed, then shook her head. "No! You are twisting my words. She may *have been* like other girls—past tense—but she can never be like other girls again. That's the part that I think is weird and sad."

Max watched as the waiter poured a bit of wine for him to taste. He sniffed it quickly to make sure it wasn't rancid, then waved the waiter to fill both glasses. He hated all that pompous swishing and gurgling nonsense.

"Well, you probably know more about it than I do," Bronte said. "Willa has some royal friends, I think. You must have met your share at Oxford, right?" She tasted the wine and let her eyes slide shut at the pleasure of it. "Yum. That is some good wine you chose."

"Thanks," he answered quietly. Now what? Did he just blurt out that he was probably one of the royal friends to whom Willa had been referring? He knew he was slipping dangerously close to prevarication.

She was waiting for him to answer.

"Yes. I guess I have met my share."

"And?"

"And what?"

"And everything! Are they happy? Are they snooty? Standoffish? Rude?"

A slow smile came to Max's face as he thought of his father, his aunt, his grandmother… and his mother. In that order. "I suppose, yes."

"What do you mean 'yes'?" She took another sip of wine. "Mmmm. This is *particularly* delicious."

He loved seeing the color rise in her cheeks as the wine hit her system. The skin across her neck and chest was turning a pale pink, probably from the alcohol, but maybe from the company—he hoped.

"Up here," she joked, pointing his gaze back up to her eyes and away from the plunging V at the front of her dress.

"Sorry. I mean, of course I'm not the least bit sorry. You look gorgeous, by the way."

"Why thank you." She bowed her head slightly as she took the compliment. "Without sounding too corny, you make me feel pretty."

She might as well have stuck one of the gleaming knives into his chest. His heart simply stopped for how badly he wanted to make her feel stunningly beautiful every minute of every day for the rest of her life.

"So?" She nudged him with her elbow. "Go on, give me some royal scoop."

"Bronte, the thing is—"

At that very moment, the overly attentive waiter loomed over them and cleared his throat as if he were about to begin Hamlet's soliloquy. And before Max could tell him to hive off, he launched into his well-rehearsed spiel with the grand conviction that the dinner specials took precedence over Max's conversation. Bronte reached under the table and grabbed Max's hand in hers, trying to prevent herself from bursting into laughter. The waiter was such a narcissistic idiot.

Max squeezed her hand back and watched as her eyes gleamed with humor.

"...the dory is then lightly breaded in a subtle blend of hand-shaved fennel..."

On and on he went, describing every ingredient of every dish. When he finished, Max was quite certain the aspiring thespian took a tiny bow.

"We'll need a few minutes to process all that, I think," Max said.

"I quite agree." The waiter nodded and exited stage left.

Bronte pulled her napkin up to her face and proceeded to laugh until she cried into the fine white linen.

"Oh... God..." she finally gasped. "How could you keep a straight face?"

Max had one arm around Bronte's shoulder, and his other hand lightly traced the stem of his wineglass. He looked into her face and rethought his decision to tell her anything at all about his ducal future. She was so joyful and vital. What was the point of undermining that? If things proceeded according to Max's wishes (as they usually did), the two of them would have a lifetime to fulfill the expectations the outside world would impose upon them. For the next few weeks, he just wanted to be with the woman whose eyes could sparkle like that with sheer, unadulterated joy.

The rest of the meal sped by in a blur of suggestive banter punctuated by jammy wine, under-the-table hand-holding (and thigh-holding... and inner-thigh-holding), and rich food (some of which he actually did feed her from his own fork).

They decided to give up on dessert altogether.

"Since you refuse to obey my request that you cease looking at me with that open, smoky look in those misty green eyes of yours, I am forced to put an end to this date."

Bronte gave him a little pout and unconsciously wiggled in her seat. "An end to the dinner portion of the date, you mean?"

"Yes," he said in a low voice very close to her ear. "And stop moving your hips against the banquette like that or we won't even make it back to the car."

Chapter 4

BRONTE'S APARTMENT WAS CLOSEST, so they opted for that. After a quick ten minutes of mauling each other in the back of the Lincoln Town Car, they tumbled through the front door of what Max referred to as Bronte's lower-ground-floor flat.

"I love telling people I live in a basement… it's positively medieval, don't you think?"

Max stood in the small living room and ran his fingers absently across the back of the pale-green velvet sofa as he watched Bronte make her way around the charming apartment, turning on a lamp, unlocking and opening the French doors out to the small, intimate garden at the rear, which was just starting to come into bloom.

"And this," Bronte said, gesturing Max out toward the garden, "is what makes it all worthwhile."

As she turned back to see if he was coming out to join her, she bumped directly into his solid form, both of her hands flat and firm against his muscled shoulders, then moving, more slowly now, down over his chest. Max's arms circled her small waist as his mouth captured hers in a fierce, possessive kiss, totally unlike the more exploratory variety they had shared up until then. This was the knowing kiss of more to come. This was a kiss full of promise.

Bronte gave herself up to it entirely. Her tongue caressed the underside of his tongue; she nipped at his lower lip; her hands made their way up his neck, skimming over muscled shoulders, then finally, her fingers dug greedily into his thick, brown, wavy hair.

The strong cords of his neck flexed involuntarily at her touch. Her lips moved to his neck as his hands made their way under the hem of her very short red dress. Then he pulled her flush up against the length of him, his erection firm against her belly, sending shocks of warm anticipation between her legs.

"I think I may be panting," she whispered into his ear.

"I am totally in favor of panting," Max breathed huskily, and then repositioned his hands to a tight hold around her waist, easily lifting her up and swinging her back into the apartment and onto the oversized velvet sofa. She kicked off her high-heeled shoes, then propped herself up on her elbows to watch as Max whipped off his suit coat, loosened his tie, and nearly tore his white dress shirt as he pulled it over his head. Bronte could not help the lascivious grin that stole over her face at the sight of his miraculous stomach.

"Well, if you aren't the cat who got the cream, miss."

"Yes, sir. Get your ass over here." With that demure invitation, Max and his rock-hard torso were lying along the length of Bronte's body in moments.

"Do you want to get rid of this bothersome bit of a dress or shall I?" asked Max peevishly. "I need skin… now… badly…"

"I think you should. I'm feeling rather self-conscious of my skin-niness all of a sudden."

"In that case, maybe a slower approach is in order." Max gave her hips a firm yank, moving her entire body far enough down the couch to have her fully reclined, putting her arms above her head, and clenching her wrists gently but firmly in his grip.

"How am I supposed to touch all that fine flesh of yours if I am in a half nelson?" Bronte whined.

"First of all, this is not a half nelson, and second of all, I need to—how shall I say—narrow your focus for a few moments to relieve you of this absurd body image situation."

"As you wish, m'lord."

"And stop calling me that," Max replied tartly.

"I can't help it if I have a thing for Regency romances... just play along, you big spoilsport. This is a fantasy I've been fine-tuning since middle school. What's it to you if I like to imagine you as some rakish duke or fallen-away marquess? I mean, you have to admit your accent is deliciously *plummy*."

"Very well then," Max growled. "I am a fallen-away marquess."

"Oooh! Yay! That's the spirit!"

There, he thought to himself. *Technically I've told her the truth.* Then he started in on a loving disputation of Bronte's misguided view of her stellar body.

She gasped as his left hand held her wrists while his right made a slow trail along the side of one breast, through the red silk material. One of his legs moved firmly between her thighs, exerting pressure and heat there. His thumb grazed her nipple, and her back arched in response as her breasts responded to his touch.

"So beautiful," he half whispered, half moaned right before he slid the plunging V-neckline aside and took the taut nipple into his mouth, through the sheer-lace fabric of her bra. His free hand was making a slow, determined path up the inside of her thigh as his mouth made its way over to the other breast. Before Bronte realized what he was doing, he had lifted the hem of the dress and revealed her pale, smooth stomach.

"God in heaven."

Max just stared at her lovely waist, and below, as he taunted her with slow back-and-forth caresses across her lower abdomen. A single finger, tantalizingly close to the top of her white sheer-lace underwear, caused the most delicious, involuntary quiver to ripple across Bronte's skin.

Max lowered his mouth to her navel and let his tongue dart in, then around her center. The heat between her legs was infernal; her underwear was a confining, wet bother.

"Please. Max. Please," she begged in a voice that was not entirely her own.

"Please what, Bron?" he taunted, continuing to bring his tongue farther down, now nipping at the edge of her underwear wolfishly. He suddenly moved so he was kneeling on the floor next to the sofa, and Bronte had a momentary panic that he was going to leave her in this state of intense desire and she would somehow be stuck in this exquisite torture for all eternity.

He was going to play her like a harp, he mused. He pulled her outstretched hands even farther over her head and used his other hand to run long, smooth strokes along her endless legs as he breathed hot, demanding breaths across her tiny underwear, which really did nothing to conceal the triangle of silky brown hair beneath.

Bronte was desperate. Her fingers were flexing and unflexing with desire: to scrape her nails against his rippling back, to drag her fingertips lightly across the hair on his chest, to feel the hard evidence of his desire in her palm. The deprivation was becoming so intense she could barely tolerate it.

"Please, Max. I am desperate to touch you."

He merely chuckled and let his hands loosen away from her wrists, and then used both of his hands to slowly peel off her dress and the offending scraps of bra and underwear, taking his time down her legs, then tossing the tiny panties aside carelessly. He worked his way back up her legs, kissing the sensitive skin behind her knee, rubbing her thighs more deeply, and slowly parting her legs as his head began to approach her warmth.

"Oh, God. I can't," she whimpered.

Max laughed again, low and male this time, the smell of her desire so close, nearly sending him over the edge. "Then you are in luck, because I can," he stated matter-of-factly, then his tongue dragged a slow, languorous path.

Bronte nearly pitched off the couch, as if she had been stuck by a cattle prod, and grabbed Max's thick head of hair frantically with both hands. Whether it was to prevent or encourage him, she had no idea.

"Easy, Bron," he cooed, giving her another incendiary lick and then another, until he was moaning his own pleasure as he brought her precipitously close to her release.

"I can't... I just can't do it this way... it's too intimate..."

He was relentless. Demonically, gloriously, perversely, fantastically relentless. One stroke of his tongue was inside her, the next a tender tease, then his teeth grazed her and she screamed a dry, raspy cry.

"Max," she begged feebly.

Then he slowly put his thumb with exquisite pressure right below her entrance, as his tongue penetrated in and out, over and over, until she couldn't stop, she couldn't... her head was flailing from side to side, her hands had a death grip on his skull, he did something miraculous with his lips and then she exploded, with a kaleidoscope of color and fragments of sound and light breaking all around her.

It was pure: unlike anything she had ever experienced before. She thought she might have been idiotically calling out, "Max I can't" at the very moment he manifestly proved she could.

When she started to come back to herself, she raised her head slightly and opened one eye to see Max's head in the same general location but turned sideways, with his cheek resting against the tender skin just above her thatch of hair, looking up expectantly, waiting adoringly for her to return to earth. Her frenzied attack on his hair had left it boyishly disheveled, a few brown locks dangling into one eye.

He smiled, unwilling to break the wonderful silence with a silly quip or retort. She met his gaze for a few long seconds, then let her head flop back against the sofa cushion with one arm cast limply across her eyes.

"Fucking. A. Where have I been all my life?" Bronte sighed.

"With the wrong guys."

"Very funny."

"I didn't mean it as a joke."

When he spoke, his voice vibrated through her womb, mirroring the reverberation of her orgasm.

The physical sensation was stellar, but the gravity in his tone shook Bronte from her stupor. "I'm not laughing. Come here." She pulled on his hands and urged him back onto the couch and along the length of her naked body. He nuzzled his head into the crook of her neck in a heartbreakingly tender motion, then he gripped her hair fiercely, propping his elbows on either side of her and forcing her to look directly into his eyes.

"Okay, so this is how this is going to go," Bronte began, trying to assume a tone of authority, despite his position over her and the aftermath of her pleasure still pulsing through her.

Max smiled a wide, toothy grin.

"What? Why are you smiling at me?"

"Because I—" He caught himself, then clearing his throat he began again. "Because I think it is adorable how you think you can manage everything… anything…"

"That makes it sound like I am a controlling bitch, when in reality I'm just trying to let you off easy. Establish a few ground rules. Lay of the land and all that. Just that we should keep it casual. You know. No strings attached." She tried to accelerate her speech so it wouldn't be so obvious that she had never talked so carelessly to any man.

Despite her cavalier talk with April and Carol about TMs and sex with Mr. Texas, in actual fact, she had only slept with three men (soon to be four, she conceded) in her entire life. And one of them was that bastard from Cal who had never called her again, so that barely counted. But something about Max trusting that she was sexually liberated and breezy and uncomplicated made her want to really be that way.

"In case you haven't noticed, I have what might well be the hardest cock of my life pressed up against you, so I'll pretty much agree to anything you say. But I'd much rather quit the jawing."

"So much for my worries about being too forward," Bronte replied dryly, moving her hips against his.

"Since it is brutal honesty you are after, Bron, I shall feel quite within the bounds of your... constraints"—he tightened his hold on her hair momentarily for effect—"to speak plainly for the duration of our... what? ...arrangement?" he asked with one raised eyebrow.

"Yes!" she agreed, then, as if just remembering something, she added, "I'll be right back!"

Bronte wriggled out from under him, trotted into the bathroom, and then returned a few seconds later with an unopened box of one hundred condoms and a very naked Max waiting for her on her bed.

"What the hell is that?" Max asked through a laugh as Bronte hopped onto the bed and sat up on her knees next to him.

"So here's the deal. I have always been a sort of belts-and-suspenders kind of gal about birth control. I've been on the pill for years—"

Max looked momentarily taken aback at the vision that conjured of Bronte sleeping with every unprotected male in her path.

She laughed and continued. "Not like that! It wasn't to do with sex—I mean, it's kind of useless as a prophylactic, really—well, whatever, for girl reasons." She looked flustered and rolled her eyes. "Moving on! So anyway, I am in Costco, like four months ago, and I just stood there staring at this, er, product, and thought, 'I wonder if I will ever have sex again. Ever.' And then I thought, 'Fuck that. Not only will I have sex again, I will have it hundreds of times. I will use every condom in this goddamned box.' I am an optimist for chrissake. This, my new sexy friend Max, is the symbol of the human spirit. This is Hope."

"Yes! I like the way you think, Bron. Better yet, why don't we make it our goal, our mutual endeavor, to dispense with the entire contents of that Box of Hope by the time we part ways in July?"

"Now you're talking!" Bronte said.

But something dreadful clanged against her chest when Max managed to say "part ways" with a smile on his face, even though she had to admit to herself that she was the one who had thrown down *that* gauntlet. And she wasn't about to mess with a good thing now.

Everything always went pear-shaped after eight weeks anyway, right? This way, she would get all the hot, new, you-are-the-best-thing-since-sliced-bread sex she could stand, long before it turned into that's-not-how-I-like-my-bread-sliced.

Max grabbed the cellophane-covered box out of Bronte's hand and tore it open.

"A hundred condoms in fifty-six days... I'm liking the odds."

He pulled one out, tore the edge of the wrapper, and had it on in seconds. Bronte squirmed with delight, giggling like a schoolgirl as his strong arms tossed her down on her back then rested firmly on either side of her head as he was poised to enter her. "Any last words, m'lady?"

"Speechless, m'lo—"

He drove into her then with one powerful thrust before she could finish her sentence, her head flying back in a paroxysm of sheer delight. Max marveled at the sinuous beauty of her neck and let the rising surge of his own desire crowd out the already-looming menace that was July 15.

If she was somehow attached to the pretense that they were only indulging in a short-term dalliance, he would humor her for the time being. Come July, Max vowed to himself, she'd be disabused of that notion entirely.

By the following weekend, it was looking like they were going to burn through the Costco jumbo pack long before the designated eight weeks were up. Bronte felt like a rabbit on goddamned Animal Planet. And whatever great sex she thought she had been having with those *other guys* was nothing more than some weak approximation of the real thing: namely, Great Sex with Max.

The other odd novelty was that all of this fucking did not seem to be distracting her from the rest of her life. In fact, she felt more focused at work, more inclined to cook a good meal, more likely to return the long overdue phone call to her mother. Just more adept at life in general.

She was downright competent.

Unlike the other times in her life when she had been consumed by the first blush of romance (when she had lost sleep, pined, swooned, missed deadlines at school or at work), this time around, she felt perfectly grounded.

Things were looking up. Maybe there was something to this casual sex after all.

By the third week, they were practically an old married couple. They weren't living together, per se, but the fact that Max never spent the night at his own apartment anymore started to register somewhere in the back of Bronte's mind. *Too much too soon?* she wondered, only to dismiss the thought with the bittersweet reality that he was on his way home in five short weeks. It was partially devastating and wholly liberating. Not that Bronte wanted him to go—but as far as Transitional Men went, he was the cream of the crop.

Jump-started me sexually? Check.

Reminds me constantly that I am smart, funny, and luscious? Check.

No pesky emotional hangover? Check, check, check.

By the end of week seven, Bronte was not feeling quite so jaunty about the entire arrangement. That said, she certainly was not moving to England, not that he was asking. And he certainly wasn't staying in the United States, not that Bronte was asking. Who was she to ask that? Or vice versa?

And so it went, with all that glorious fucking and (she hated to admit) loving that Max and Bronte found themselves in the middle of week eight like two angry wolves on a windy hilltop.

Well, to be fair, he was being his normal, sweet self, while she was the one spoiling for a fight. Bronte had convinced herself that getting into some stupid breakup argument a few days before he left would be a hell of a lot easier than finding herself clutched on to his leg and being peeled off by airport security as he tried to board his plane at O'Hare.

He had just gotten home (uh, to Bronte's apartment) after a long day of packing up and/or throwing away the bits and pieces of crap that had accumulated over the past five years in his modest apartment. Max had defended his dissertation two days before, and his mind was still a cluttered mass of fragmented phrases like "total endogeneity" and "aggregate risk," and all he wanted to do was toss Bronte into bed and keep her there for the remaining six days until he was, quite reluctantly, going back to England. He had decided to tell her the truth about his family at some point that last week, but she'd turned so churlish these past few days, he kept putting it off. He needed her to be more understanding, not less, when he tried to explain why he had purposely not told her what was obviously going to be something of paramount importance to both of them.

Max had convinced himself it was probably too soon to propose marriage to Bronte before he left—the royal info was bad enough; he didn't want to frighten her off altogether—but he wanted them to be moving toward that eventuality, one way or another. He could probably squeeze out a year or two more in the States before his parents flatly demanded he return to England, but more than that was highly unlikely. Eventually, Bronte would need to agree to move to the UK. He wanted to begin laying the groundwork gradually and then propose, but first things first: he couldn't very well propose much of anything until Bronte knew what he was really proposing. Namely, a life as a duchess.

"Don't do it, Bron, please," he whispered in her ear as he came up behind her and began kissing her neck, nuzzling his way past all that delicious, long, brown hair and working his hands under her T-shirt and leisurely across her smooth abdomen.

"Don't do what?" she simpered with false sweetness as she tilted her neck a bit and continued to stir the homemade sauce of fennel sausage and broccoli rabe she was making for the pasta.

"Don't pick a fight so you can say this was all going to hell anyway." More kisses on the nape of her neck. "Don't do it. Don't pretend this"—more kisses along her collarbone—"whatever we have going on here, is some eight-week fling that we can ignore after next week." Hands now gliding effortlessly along the bottom of her bra, her breasts tightening, almost painfully, in anticipation. "That line of thinking, as you would say, has been a crock of shit," whispered between kisses, "since sometime in the middle of week one."

Bronte decided to turn down the stove and avoid further discussion right at the moment. What was the point of spoiling a festive romp with nay-saying and bitching about pesky concepts like *reality* and *the future* for chrissake? She turned to face him, pressing her chest against his, feeling the consoling power of how hard he was against her and the instantaneous warmth that triggered in her.

She had to confess, to herself at least, that all of this everything-will-have-run-its-course business was turning out to be quite the—what was his phrase?—crock of shit. Shoving that thought aside, Bronte gave herself up to the rapidly overpowering desire that was coursing through her.

By the time she realized what was happening, they were on the floor of the living room, with Max having taken off Bronte's shirt and bra. He was caressing her breasts and stomach while she lay there like a goddamned odalisque. He never seemed to tire of these small journeys across her body: just now he was trailing a finger along one rib and up toward the breast he was sucking, alternating the near-painful force with little conciliatory licks, which only made her want more of the near-pain, and so on.

She arched her back and flung her arms above her head, then collected herself, as much as possible given the circumstances, and brought her hands back down to his shoulders and maneuvered him onto his back, straddling him on all fours. She wanted to take him in every way imaginable.

She wanted to be so completely full, so *done*. There must be an end to the joy, mustn't there? If she simply gorged herself on him for the next week, surely she must tire of him, mustn't she?

It wasn't even a coherent thought, but the joy the idea brought her must have shone in her eyes, and Max smiled up at her from the floor, as he fidgeted carelessly with her nipples. She swatted him away playfully, then stood for a moment to get her pants and underwear off, and pulled his pants off while she was up. He rid himself of his *More Cowbell* T-shirt.

Staring down at his fabulously long, lean, hard body was, well, breathtaking. He had his hands clasped behind his head with a what-me-worry? expression that categorically erased any other thoughts from her mind. It was a simple moment. No psychological man-at-my-feet bullshit—just the opposite, really. She was about to make him a *very* happy man. She swung her long hair in front of one bare shoulder in a gesture she knew he adored and slowly prepared to take him.

He was so hard and ready she could not resist slowly kneeling down between his legs and looking up under hooded lids with a wicked smile. He rolled his eyes in a mute thank-you-Jesus and reached his hands down to push his strong fingers into her scalp. Massaging, stroking, guiding, fingers tracing the nape of her neck as her lips and tongue began savoring, always as if for the first time, she thought, the delectable joy of him in her mouth.

Those Catholic-girl hang-ups had died a very happy death in the past eight weeks. For some reason (okay, for many reasons), she had always steered clear of the Big Bad Blow Job. She had been amazed in college by how many women—intelligent friends of hers, no less—were more than happy to go down on a guy without thinking twice. Laughter rang through the corridors of Berkeley at Bronte's expense when she confessed with drunken conviction she would much rather screw a guy than give him a blow job.

Much rather.

So it was all really an unexpected and very happy turn of events for everyone concerned when Max began to chip away at Bronte's aversion. He had started by simply being naked all the time, or at least as much of the time as possible, because, as he rightly suspected, much of her reluctance stemmed from a girlish avoidance of "down there" that had naturally evolved into "I'm just not good at it."

"After you get used to having it around, you know, you'll want to get better acquainted," Max had joked one morning, standing behind her, both of them stark-naked and fresh out of the shower, his warm, smooth cock nestling snugly against her backside. She couldn't help reaching around to grab his ass to pull him even closer, massage a bit, then give him a quick spank. "Enough of that, Romeo. I am actually going to work this morning."

"I know, I know. And I too am venturing afield. I only have three classes left and Dr. Hedges wants to go for lunch today. I'm not suggesting we pursue it now, just planting the idea, so to speak." He turned and left the bathroom and, as she reached for her toothbrush, she felt the absence of his warmth almost as much as she had felt the presence of it.

Not good.

All of the sweet memories of the past few weeks were starting to splinter and crowd around her mind in a dreamlike montage: snippets of conversations, the feel of some part of his warm body coming into contact with her hip in the middle of the night, the feel of his tongue on her, the feel, as now, of him deep in her mouth. Deeper and deeper she wanted to take him. She wished she could open her throat even more, the possession of it, the thrill of his response, a response to *her*, a joy from *her*, the feel of his tension in one of her hands, her delicate touch, then firmer, wanting him to know how much it all mattered to her, how much she lov—

And then he arched and came in her mouth in the most crushing, salty, wet rush, as she sucked again, pressed harder into him with her hand and smiled to herself and to him. As she tenderly pulled away, she licked her lips for the mere pleasure of it and looked up at his utterly satisfied expression. Eyes half closed, mouth half open.

"So much for your prior concerns about that particular activity," he joked in a husky, low voice. He pulled Bronte up along his body and began caressing her back as he relished the very languid feel of her long, graceful form draped down the length of his. He held her tenderly, almost cautiously, protectively, then started to let his hands wander down along her back, the sides of her hips, her thighs. He trailed his hands lazily around her body, stroking her, up and down and in, loving the shape of her ass.

"Mmmm," she purred.

"Mmmm-hmmm," he moaned in reply, giving her a good grab on one cheek, then resuming his gentle tracking. Farther down with one hand, now, then the other hand coming up her back to trace the outline of one shoulder blade. His other hand was perilously close now, then, "Oh, Max," as one finger, then two began a slow, methodical rhythm against her slick opening.

She was so becalmed, like a blanket on him. She loved the

relaxation, but her legs were starting to quiver, and she knew she couldn't stay merely receptive much longer. Her upper thighs started to tense in an uncontrollable way, the heat and moisture in her building to an almost unbearable pitch.

"Oh, Bron, you are so wet, so ready, from having me in your mouth, so good…" His voice trailed off as his mouth captured hers in a plunging, maddening kiss and his fingers found the exact spot to trigger her response. She grabbed on to him, as if on to a raft, for dear life in a terrible storm, pulling away from his kiss and nearly sobbing into the crook of his neck, grabbing him with her teeth, her sweat and saliva—and perhaps tears—mingling with his salty, masculine scent.

She didn't know how long they wallowed there, like castaways flung onto the middle of the living room floor. She opened her eyes and saw that the fading, early summer sun had turned to dusk, and the warm hues of gold and amber were reflected across the ivy-covered garden wall.

She wondered vaguely if the broccoli rabe had overcooked into bitterness by now and started unenthusiastically to peel herself off of Max when his phone trilled a bizarre, unfamiliar ringtone.

"Damn. That's my mother," Max ground out, as he scrambled awkwardly out from under her, fumbled into the pocket of his discarded jeans for his phone, and hit the talk button. "Hello, Mother… yes, I can hear you, but it's not really a good time… I'm sorry, I didn't mean to interrupt you while you were speaking. What's happened? Are you all right?"

Abruptly, Max got up from the crouching position on the floor where he had recommenced petting Bronte's arm in his initial belief that he'd be able to give his mother a call back later. He cradled the phone in the crook of his neck, pulled on his jeans distractedly, and moved out to the garden, leaving the French doors ajar so Bronte couldn't *not* hear him.

"Just tell me… you're not making any sense. Mother, put Devon on the phone, please. Hi, Dev. I couldn't understand her. That's not possible... oh, Jesus... where should I go? All right, I'll be there in two hours. All right... okay, hang in there, Dev; I'll be there as soon as I can. Can Mother come back to the phone? Mother? I am on my way. I will be there by morning... I know. Me too."

Bronte had thrown on his oversized T-shirt and stood hesitantly, arms crossed, in the half-open doorway to the garden. Max stood stock-still with his back to her. Every inch of his body was so familiar to her now. Every nuance of every muscle along his spine, the beautiful curve of his hip, the wide shoulders, the turn of his upper arm, the warm, male smell of earth and faint bay rum that seemed to define him.

She stepped quietly out into the small garden and rested her cheek against his back as she snaked her arms around his bare waist. He slipped his phone down into his front pocket, then covered Bronte's hands with his own. It seemed like a long time that Bronte just stood there, relishing the feel of the warm strength of his back against her cool cheek. She could have stood there forever.

"I won't pick a fight. I promise," she whispered.

"My father is about to die."

"Oh, Max," she gulped. "I'm so sorry."

He turned slowly into her arms and kissed her so tenderly, so deeply, so completely, her knees were useless.

"What can I do for you?" she asked.

"I don't know... there is going to be so much familial turmoil. This is not how I wanted this to happen with you and me. I thought we'd have so much more time... I don't know if you should come with me now or in a few weeks."

Sweet Jesus. Bronte thought she could help him finish packing up his apartment for fuck's sake. Why the hell was he talking about her going to England? He was obviously in shock. He didn't know what he was saying.

"First things first, Max. Where do you need to be in two hours? Where are you meeting your mother tomorrow?"

"I need to be at a private airfield near O'Hare in two hours. A car is coming to pick me up at my place. Will you come help me get my shit together?"

"Of course. Let's grab whatever you have here and we'll head over to your apartment."

"Maybe you should pack a bag and just come with me now, Bron... I think I want you with me," he stated matter-of-factly, his spine going slightly rigid beneath her palm. This wasn't going in the order he had intended, but his feelings were the same: they were meant to be together.

"Max... you don't want me there..."

"Of course, I want you there, Bron." His voice was still gentle, but there was also an edge of rising impatience. "My father had a massive coronary less than an hour ago and my mother is virtually incoherent. One of my sisters is backpacking around Australia; the other is on vacation in Prague with her useless husband. My younger brother, Devon, is alone and trying to keep his shit together until I get there."

"Max... I wish I could, but please... I can't just *not* show up at work tomorrow... I can't just drop everything and wander off..."

"Bronte!" His voice exploded. "It is not wandering off! This is important. You're my—" He paused, as if he couldn't complete the sentence. "I guess I am not used to having to ask for things in this way—maybe I am not doing it right—but I really need you right now... I am asking you..." His voice quieted as he looked at her.

She tilted her head and gave him a questioning look.

"All right"—his frustration was palpable now—"I am not asking you. I am telling you. I need you. You need to come with me. This is so much more important than showing up at your job tomorrow."

Wrong answer. She felt the hairs on her neck bristle. Even if he was right—and boy, did that romantic side of her want to dive right in: he wants you! he is begging you to go with him! he needs you by his side!—it was still all wrong. Because she knew (or thought she knew) where those eager cravings of hers led.

To perdition.

She could not, she *would not*, let herself be stirred by the promise or threat of so-called once-in-a-lifetime opportunities.

She looked down at the slate of the garden floor and loosened her hold around his waist.

"I just can't, Max," she whispered. "I'm sorry. You'll see, you have your family there, you will want your space, you won't want me underfoot—"

"Stop it!" he shouted with uncharacteristic brutality.

She felt it like a punch in her stomach. He never lost his temper. That was her job.

His arms fell from her waist and he walked back into the apartment. He continued speaking, without looking at her, while he began to gather up his things.

"You might not have wanted to pick a fight, but you got one." He wasn't yelling, but the steady, controlled anger was almost worse. "Don't you *dare* tell me what I want or don't want. You are the one who doesn't want to be there with all that messy emotional distress and all those uncontrollable feelings flying everywhere and all that godforsaken *not knowing*. If—no! *when* my father dies, probably while I am completely and utterly alone on a plane over the Atlantic Ocean trying to get to him, I will become responsible for all of them. And all of his business dealings. And my mother's grief. And the grief of every other person who has come to rely on my father's kindness and generosity over the past sixty-four years."

Max finished putting on a clean button-down shirt, slipped on his shoes, and stuffed the last of his things into his overnight bag.

"Spare me your cool distance and emotional fortitude for now, okay, Bron? I've had quite enough of you thinking you know what's best for *us*." He spit out the last word. "If I wanted space, you would know it. Because I would tell you *I needed space*." His teeth were clenched through the final syllables. "Because that's what intelligent, mature adults do, Bronte. They say what they mean to say." Max tried to control his breathing, but she could see that his chest was heaving despite the effort.

In the face of her continued silence, he began again, more calmly. "I'm going to leave now. Are you coming with me or not?"

Even though he was on the other side of the apartment, she felt like he was physically pummeling her with every word.

"This is it," he said with deadly precision. "This is not some cooked-up emotional test or scheme for me to manipulate you. My dad is going to die. I have to go. I want you with me. I can't make it any clearer than that. It's now or never, Bron. Is it all... or not at all?"

Bronte blanched at the oddly familiar ultimatum, then realized it reminded her, for a terrifying second, of her father. She knew it wasn't Max's fault, necessarily, but the damage was done: there was no way in hell she was ever going to be propelled into action by the demanding threats of a man who thought he knew what was best for her. Lionel Talbott had spent too many years making her feel like she wasn't entitled to her own opinions... to her own mind. Even the vaguest hint of Max trying to wield the same arrogant power made her withdraw. She shook her head in a slow, silent no.

"No? Fine then. But just so we are clear, this is all you, Bron. I am not being overly demanding or cruel, or any of that. You know you can do whatever you set your mind to. You of all people. You know. This is the fork in the road and you are walking away from me... not the other way around."

Max turned toward the door and dragged one hand through his thick hair. Reluctantly turning back toward Bronte, his expression defeated, his voice empty, he said, "You know what? You are probably right. Clean break and all that. That is what you wanted all along, right? No muss. No fuss."

She was frozen to the spot where she stood, standing there in the middle of the room like an idiot in nothing but his oversized T-shirt. She wanted to pull him into her arms so badly, but it felt impossible. She knew she was watching him slip away, and she was utterly paralyzed to do anything to stop it.

He took a deep, long breath, deciding whether or not to speak, then continued, almost against his will: "I love—I loved you, Bronte. I mean, flat-out loved you. Wasn't it obvious?"

And with that fucking neutron bomb, he walked out of the lower-ground-floor flat and out of Bronte's life.

Chapter 5

BRONTE STOOD IN THE center of her living room until her legs were too tired to hold her any longer, and then she sort of crumpled into a heap on the carpet, curled up like a baby right there in the middle of the floor, with his T-shirt stretched over her knees in a little cocoon. How the fuck did she go from the eternal optimist to the woman who just let the best man, who loved her—who actually really *meant* he loved her when he said he loved her—walk out her door?

As she faded in and out of a half-conscious, dismal approximation of sleep, her mind tripped haltingly back, conjuring a confrontation from nearly a decade before.

—✺—

Spring had tried to come early. It was barely April in New Jersey. Bronte always recalled how the bright-yellow buds of forsythia outside the kitchen window were so idiotically cheerful in the midst of all those grim, bare branches. She stood in the kitchen with her mother's hand resting lightly on her shoulder as the two of them stared at the piece of paper on the worn Formica counter.

The ivory vellum with the embossed orange and black logo may as well have been radioactive. Bronte didn't want to actually touch it.

"I never thought I would really get in," Bronte said quietly.

"It's so exciting, Bronte! We are so proud of you!"

Bronte despised when her mother used the royal *we*. Her father rarely left his home office upstairs, and when he did, it certainly wasn't to show any team spirit with his wife. As far as Bronte was concerned, her parents were not a *we*.

"Mom. I don't want to go to Princeton. I want to go to the University of California at Berkeley."

"Oh, honey, you are just saying that to be... contrary."

"No, I promise, I'm not being contradictory. I just can't stay in New Jersey. I can't. I only applied because I knew how much it meant to you, and Dad, I guess. But"—she shook her long hair, trying to shake off the whole situation—"I never, ever thought I would get in."

"Bronte. Please. You have straight As and nearly perfect SAT scores. Why would you be so down on yourself?"

She turned to look at her mother.

"I am not down on myself, Mom." Bronte almost laughed at the irony. "I—I'm embarrassed to tell you, but at this point, I guess it doesn't really matter... I wrote my entire application essay about how much I disrespect my father and the entire world of East Coast academia, how hypocritical, arrogant, out of touch—you name it—all those ivory-tower assholes are. Completely removed from the rest of the world, creating Central American nations with their rich friends. Washed-up spies and politicians grazing off the fat of ill-gotten endowments."

"Oh, Bronte, you didn't." Her mother brought her hand to cover her mouth in near-horror.

Bronte barked a sardonic laugh at her mother's dramatic response, then picked up the piece of paper with her thumb and index finger as if it smelled.

"And look what they do? I insult them, ridicule them—*hate* them!—and they want me! Do you see how perverse this all is?! I can't, Mom; I just can't. Not to mention the goddamned money."

"Please don't swear, dear."

"Oh, Mom. You have no idea. I curse more than you will

ever know. I swear almost every other word. I love swearing. That 'goddamn' is the least of your worries. Mom, Princeton will cost a fortune. I don't want you to have that kind of debt… financial or otherwise…" Bronte added.

"Oh, Bronte, have I ever made you feel beholden?"

"No, Mom." Bronte sighed and tried to ratchet her voice back to a normal level. "Because you are a saint. Because you work like a beast to make sure we can live in this sweet ranch house and I can go to the best school and that lazy son of a bitch can sit upstairs and write or do whatever it is he is supposedly doing in there—"

Bronte thought she must have blacked out for a second before she realized her mother had slapped her quickly and firmly across the cheek.

Tears sprang to both of their eyes: Bronte's were tears of shock; her mother's were tears of rage.

"Please don't ever speak about your father in that way, Bronte. I won't have it."

Bronte felt her blood drain straight down to her toes.

"Mom…" The tears didn't fall and her voice was even. "I love you so much. But I don't love him." She accidentally dropped the acceptance letter from Princeton onto the kitchen floor, her grip loosening in a moment of forgetting, but she didn't bother to pick it up.

She stared down at the typed letter for a few seconds, then, when she looked up from the familiar, yet suddenly unrecognizable, faux-brick linoleum floor, she saw that her father was standing in the doorway to the kitchen, just over her mother's shoulder.

Bronte's mother turned swiftly to see her husband.

"How long have you been standing there, Lionel?"

"Long enough. She's going to Princeton."

Bronte laughed, softly at first, then to the point of hysteria. She watched as her mother fought the constant battle: stand by her man or soothe her frantic teenager.

Bronte often felt guilty for forcing her mother to have to make that choice, then she merely felt resentful that her father, the supposed grown-up, needed so much of her mother's soothing. Lionel Talbott remained leaning against the doorjamb, arms crossed in an arrogant posture that let Bronte know he was waiting for her histrionics to subside, but he wasn't happy about it.

Bronte finally came back to herself from a few minutes of half laughing, half crying.

"Whatever, Lionel," she said with a dismissiveness that only a petulant seventeen-year-old girl could muster. She loved how much he hated that she called him by his first name. "Are you going to put me on a leash and walk me over to campus? Sit next to me in my freshman English class and watch as I take notes on Chaucer? Correct my grammar? You know what Lionel? Fuck you."

"Bronte!" her mother screamed.

"Mom, seriously. This is totally between him and me." Bronte avoided referring to her father directly whenever possible. "He doesn't give a crap about me or who I am or what I like—"

"The Royal Family and fashion magazines and shoes you can't afford, Bronte? Are those aspirations?" He spoke as if she were bringing home the neighbors' pets and dissecting them in the basement.

"No, they are not *aspirations*, Lionel. But they're not despicable either! You are so lofty in your worldview, aren't you? So far above the rest of us. Discussing Gilles Deleuze and the Lake Poets, the Bloomsbury Group and the Baroque. But you know what, *Lionel*? Those people had *lives!* They left their homes and did something, made something, had something to *show* for themselves. Other than a split-level ranch in New Jersey and a wife who did every *fucking* thing for them."

"We will not pay for you to go anywhere but Princeton. Am I making myself clear?"

"Who's 'we'? You?" She laughed in disgust. "You haven't earned a fucking penny in years." She looked at her mother for confirmation, but Cathy was in some sort of shock, shaking her head and crying softly.

"I am going to get as far away from here as possible. I have three months left of high school, and if you want me to move out, I am sure Aunt Patty would take me in. Otherwise, back the fuck off."

"Bronte"—his voice was just this side of rage, but perfectly controlled, as he moved across the small room and put one arm protectively around his wife's shoulders—"you will devastate your mother if you turn down this opportunity."

"Really?! How do you figure? The way I see it, the one who will be devastated is *you*! All that transference! All those *aspirations*!" She nearly spit the words at him. "Those are your aspirations, Lionel. Not mine! I love it down here with the television-watching, gum-chewing masses."

She wished she could have controlled the volume of her voice, but she was nearly shrieking. She hated how he seemed to make her loss of temper his small victory.

Cathy was sobbing outright by that point.

Lionel had a strange, detached, bitter grimace playing across his face.

Bronte forced herself to calm down and decided to retreat from emotions and continue in the easier realm of practicalities.

"It's better this way. I will defer my enrollment at Cal for a year."

Her mother looked momentarily optimistic, then defeated as Bronte continued.

"I'll find an apartment share and go live in San Francisco and wait tables for a year to establish California residency. Then I'll go to Cal as an in-state student, so I can afford it without bankrupting you. And it will be mine. My education. Mine to use or squander."

Lionel shook his head in disapproval.

"What?!" Bronte fumed. "It's not as if the University of

California hasn't produced its fair share of academic excellence. You are the worst kind of snob. You disgust me."

With that, Bronte turned sideways to walk past her father without having to actually touch him.

She went up to her room, grabbed her backpack, threw in a couple of T-shirts and a pair of jeans, went into the bathroom to get her toothbrush and hairbrush, and walked back downstairs. She stood near the front door, watching across the living room as her parents spoke quietly in the kitchen, her father in the highly unusual role of comforter, gently stroking her mother's arms.

"Mom. I'm going into the city for a couple of nights with Janice. I'll be back for dinner Sunday night."

She wasn't waiting for her mother to give her permission—if Bronte was going to be this new independent, kick-ass woman of the world, she figured she had to start now—but she had hoped her mom would at least look up and nod that she had heard. Instead, Lionel turned to look at Bronte as her mother buried her face into the front of his shirt. His threat was no longer veiled.

"Be home by five o'clock on Sunday, Bronte. *Or not at all.*"

Bronte wanted to stomp her feet and smash one of those hideous antique Meissen bird figurines that her grandmother had left to her mother. How did Lionel always end up making her sound like the moody, immature burden, and himself the wise protector?

Lies.

Bronte took a deep breath as the desire to break things abated. "I'll see you Sunday then." She turned, nearly composed—she congratulated herself—and walked out the front door.

No slamming.

Looking back, she thought that "or not at all" may have been the last thing Lionel Talbott had ever said to her directly.

For what turned out to be the remaining year and a half of his life, her father and Bronte tread a careful dance, avoiding one another across a continent and competing to see who could be kinder and more devoted to Cathy Talbott.

—⁓—

Sometime near three in the morning, back in the foggy present, Bronte was so cramped and cold there on the floor that she forced herself to get up and move into bed, pulling the neck of Max's shirt up around the middle of her face, torturing herself with the intense smell of him.

She brought the covers over her head and wished for oblivion. When her alarm went off a few hours later, she mused that she now knew how it felt to be hit by a train.

She went into work armed with a triple-shot, twenty-ounce latte and tried to get her mind around the very sharp, very broken pieces of what the fuck had just happened. Unable to help herself, she decided to spend a little time Googling one Max Heyworth from England. In their frenzied courtship (of sorts), neither of them had given a damn about the "information," as Max had so eloquently put it that day at the sidewalk café.

She didn't care a fig what his family business was; he didn't care what hip clients she was after. (She *did* land that new swanky hotel group she had been pursuing when they first met, she reminded herself, and she *was* on her way to landing a fabulously chic shoe store). But none of that had mattered. They had just wanted each other in the here and now (the here and *then*, she corrected), with none of the other supposedly pertinent details.

Now that he was totally AWOL, however, she felt starved for pertinent details. Maybe there would be a grainy black-and-white photo of his rugby team at Oxford. Maybe he had won a prize for the best sheep at the county fair when he was twelve... she would like to see what he looked like when he was twelve, come to think of it. She would like to see baby pictures of Max, come to think of it.

Oh for fuck's sake, this was a veritable disaster.

A Google search on "Max Heyworth Yorkshire" brought up a fish-and-chips shop, an auto mechanic, and a list of self-catering cottages near Castle Heyworth, then a mishmash of everything from Yorkshire pudding recipes to ancestry links. All of a sudden, Bronte remembered the snippets of David's drunken, incomprehensible recitation of Max's bona fides. Just for the hell of it, she typed in "Maxwell Heyworth Anne Boleyn Nobel Prize"... and up popped several links to Sophia Heyworth and her second cousin, Anne Boleyn, and then links to a newspaper article about a political spat from a few months ago between one George Heyworth, the current Duke of Northrop, and a Nobel Prize–winning agronomist.

Farther down, there were seven links to a decade-old obituary of the seventeenth Duke of Northrop. Bronte felt the tingle of anticipation crawl up her spine, then took a fortifying slug of her latte and clicked on the *Times of London* link.

"Holy. Mother. Fucker."

She had not meant to say that one aloud, but all of her work colleagues were now well acquainted with her guttersnipe vocabulary, so nobody much cared. The seventeenth Duke of Northrop was one major twentieth-century dude. Born during World War I, a major during World War II, he grew up in a large family in Yorkshire, had six brothers and four sisters, and was survived by three sons and four daughters—the eldest of whom, George Conrad Stanley blah-blah (seven middle names later) Fitzwilliam-Heyworth, the eighteenth Duke of Northrop, was fifty-four at the time of writing (ten years ago) and was the father of two sons, Maxwell and Devon, and two daughters, Claire and Abigail.

Fuck. Fuck-fuck-fuck. Fuck-fuck-fuck-fuck-fuck-fuck-fuck.

Max was a fucking duke? Technically, according to the *Times*, he was only a marquess—a fallen-away marquess, she remembered with a bittersweet smile—until his father left this world and he took on the title. Bronte recalled one of the acronyms she had committed to memory in the early years of her adolescent fascination with all things royal: *DMEVB*—duke, marquess, earl, viscount, baron.

She thought over all the stupid, offhand comments she had made to Max about how she loved when he went all royal on her. Or—oh God—all the times she had been flipping through *Hello!*, ranting about how idiotic all those women were who fawned over William and Harry. Oh dear God. Or how she wouldn't want to be Kate in a million years. She had probably insulted some member of his immediate family. And now that she allowed herself to sink into the full depths of her shame, she realized she had interrupted him numerous times when he was probably on the verge of telling her that very fact.

She sank lower into her chair and began clicking on the copious photographs of Max that had appeared in the press over the years. At least her postbreakup stalking wouldn't be relegated to a few grainy shots of a twelve-year-old boy and a blue-ribboned steer.

He was fucking everywhere.

She clicked on a photo of him—looking quite dashing, she hated to admit—at the Henley Royal Regatta. She pulled her chair closer to her desk and hunkered down. Formal shots at Ascot. Buckingham Palace. Sandringham. Hunting in Scotland. Tabloid shots on holiday in Spain. At a corporate event at the National Gallery. A formal family photo—Max's father looked really nice, thought Bronte, and now he was sick and Max was on his way back to them… and away from her.

Bronte was overcome with a mix of sheer glee (look how gorgeous he is, and he loves me) and sheer horror (look how gorgeous he is, and I totally screwed up).

"Hello?" she barked rudely into the incessantly ringing telephone on her desk.

"Hi, Bronte, it's Sarah James. Is this a bad time?"

Sarah James was the überglamorous, pretty young thing who had started the hottest new line of shoes since Louboutin. Her family was a reigning member of the Chicago old-school elite, and she was the sparkly little gadfly in their ointment. Despite all of that, or because of it, she was a savvy, no-nonsense businesswoman and she admired Bronte's efficiency, not to mention her swearing.

"Hey, Sarah. I'm sorry. I didn't mean to be such a churl. Just a little hiccup on the romance front. End of the affair and all that. Nothing that will prevent me from making every person in the free world adore every delectable creation that comes out of your atelier." Bronte shut her Internet session down and focused on her potential client.

"Well, that's why I'm calling really. I have been putting off making a final decision on the ad agency for the big launch because I think I want to move to New York and really be there full time to get this off the ground."

"Classic. Chicago is going to be the death of me, I swear it. Good luck in New York without me. I totally understand your reasons for not choosing BCA." It wasn't that BCA didn't have lots of national and international clients, but Sarah had made it very clear that she wanted to work hand in hand with whichever agency she finally chose. If she was moving to New York, Bronte simply assumed Sarah was going to hire a New York agency.

"No, Bron, listen. Would you want to go?"

"What?"

"Do you want to move back to New York? I don't care how you swing it: if you ask your partners here if they want to open a New York office-of-one, or if you want to start your own agency, or if you want to go in-house with Sarah James—though I doubt that would be the best long-term solution for you—"

"Sarah, this has been twenty-four hours from Mars... I don't even know where to begin..."

"Your British ship has sailed, I take it?"

"Mm-hmm." *More like the fucking royal yacht* Britannia, Bronte thought as she absently twisted a long strand of her brown hair and swiveled her chair around to look out onto the summer treetops and across the park to the facade of the Newberry Library. "You know what, Sarah? I think a victory march back to New York City is very much in order. My landlord is going to kill me—I have only been in my apartment for six months—but fuck it. This city has always been a holding pattern for me. Let me talk to Brian and Cecily about how they want to do it. I do not want them to see me as poaching, so it is probably best if I stick with them and open a BCA office in New York. Let me go talk to Cecily and figure out what's the best way to move forward. Want to meet for lunch at Le Colonial at noon? I will need a glass of wine by then for sure."

"Sounds great… are you humming?"

"Yes, hard to believe given my lovelorn state, but I really think we are going to take Manhattan, Sarah. See you at lunch."

Brian Coleman and Cecily Bartholomew were the dynamic pair that started BCA in the late nineties and turned it into one of the hottest, hippest advertising agencies in the Midwest. They left Quaker Oats and McDonald's accounts at the big firms to branch out with their own special brand of intimate customer attention and creative, unique, glamorous ads. Brian was the visual genius and Cecily was the brass-tacks negotiator.

Their business partnership spread seamlessly to their personal partnership in a way that Bronte could only wonder at. They had gotten married a year after they met at Ogilvy. All that time together seemed admirable, if inconceivable, to Bronte's jaundiced eye.

On the other hand, spending every minute of her life with the future Duke of Northrop at Dunlear Castle seemed perfectly conceivable. She shook herself and knocked on Cecily's door.

Bronte sat across from her boss, looking over the immaculate etched-glass tabletop balanced on polished chrome struts and the lone Apple wireless keyboard and mouse that made up the entire contents of her work surface. Bronte had a complete déjà vu moment from that day in Carol Dieppe's office in New York almost a year ago.

"Hey, kiddo, what's up?" Bronte loved how Cecily called her *kiddo*, somehow infusing it with filial respect rather than patronizing dismissal.

"So here's the deal, Cecily. You know I've been working on Sarah James for months now, and I think I've snagged her."

"Fabulous. That has been your baby all the way. You sought her out; you pursued the account. Congratulations. So why do I get the feeling this might not have a happy ending?"

"Well, you're kind to compliment me on my perseverance, but you of all people know she wouldn't have even taken my call, much less listened to my pitch, if it didn't come on BCA letterhead, with your strength behind me."

"Mm-hmm." Cecily started to swivel slowly back and forth in her chair, kind of like a leisurely shark, Bronte thought, then shook her head again to dismiss the predatory image.

"So… fuck…" Bronte grabbed her long hair into a tail and shoved it behind her back. "Sarah wants to move to New York; she wants to move *me* to New York and have me focus all my attention on the launch. She offered me anything I want… in-house, BCA New York office, my own office… oh and by the way, Max flew back to England yesterday."

Cecily's chair stopped moving and she rested her forearms on her desk, meticulously setting aside the keyboard and mouse, as if they represented a world of clutter in her otherwise pristine existence.

"You don't seem like the backstabbing, poaching kind, Bron, and I can see you are trying to do the right thing here. But what is really going on?"

Bronte covered her face with her hands, then rubbed her eyes.

She didn't even feel like crying. She was so far beyond tears at the moment. She was just exhausted all of a sudden. Utterly and completely depleted.

"I want to go home. I want to get back to New York."

"Oh, Bron. I need to talk to Brian, but I am 99 percent certain that he and I will be in complete agreement on this. I would love for you to open the BCA office in New York, and if you can get that talented bitch Carol Dieppe to jump ship and join you, we will pay you a hefty bonus. Go for a walk. Go shop. Go have a fancy lunch. Get out of the office for a couple of hours and then meet me back here at four."

"Cecily, you are the fucking bomb. Why don't we all move to New York?"

"Thanks for the invite, friend, but if I wanted to live in that rat-infested stink hole, I would. In the meantime, I will take my townhouse on Astor Place over your bedsit in the West Village any time. Now get the hell out of here."

Bronte went back to her desk, grabbed her bag, and headed out of the building. A good dose of retail therapy on Oak Street was just the thing. She checked her cell phone to see if she had missed any calls while she was in with Cecily and saw there was a call from her mother. Ugh, she would return that later.

She made up her mind to call Max's cell phone, just to make sure he had arrived in one piece, she told herself rationally. She pressed the preset and listened to the line click and crackle as it connected to a foreign trunk line. The long beep of the European ring made her heart skip a beat. Once, twice. Then a polite recorded British voice informed her with clipped formality that the call could not be connected; please try again later.

He'd pretty much told her she had totally let him down; she wondered if maybe she should let him be. On the other hand, even her supposedly hard heart could not bear the memory of his sweet innocent expectation that she would, of course, head back to England with him to help him during his difficult time. If only for a week or so.

Oh God, what had she done?

What had he done? How could he not tell her he was a duke—or going to be—for fuck's sake?

She scrolled down through her phone list until she came to David and Willa's home number in London. She hesitated with her thumb hovering over the talk button, then bit the bullet and pressed it.

Again, the long beep tone of the British phone system heightened her anticipation, and then the phone was answered with an abrupt, "Huh-*loh*?"

"Willa, is that you? It's Bronte Talbott calling from Chicago. I hope I haven't caught you at a bad time."

"Hey Bron, perfect timing. David and I are just sitting down for an after-work cocktail and planning an outing for next weekend. I think we might head down to Dunlear to welcome back Max Heyworth. David said he vaguely remembered a late-night phone call at a pub a month or two ago and mentioned that you two had crossed paths in Chicago. Did you hit it off?" Willa laughed carelessly, the ice in her drink tinkling happily in the background as she took a sip.

"Uh, you could say that."

"He was the one I wanted to set you up with in New York, remember?"

"Yes. I remember." *You could have mentioned he was a fucking duke,* Bronte wanted to add, but refrained. She kept trying to convince herself that it really didn't matter if he was royalty or not. It really didn't. (But it did.)

"Well, he belongs in England, that one, so you'll have to come here if you want him in your clutches, but be prepared to queue up behind every chit in the peerage, if you know what I mean, eh?"

Oh. God. This was truly misery. "Yeah, about Max. His father is really ill so he had to fly back a few days early. I think he's there now, but I only have his US cell phone number and it's not working and I'd really like to make sure he got home but I don't even have a phone number for him in England because we got in a fight right before he left and I thought it would be all so cut-and-dried and it isn't at all but now I think I've fucked it all to hell and he won't want to hear from me anyway but he wasn't totally up-front with me either"—she gasped for breath—"but I have to at least let him know that I am not the stone-cold ice princess he left standing in the middle of our living room yesterday afternoon."

"Fuck's sake, Bron. Bad as all that, huh? You should be careful with your heart when it comes to those royal types—they're used to getting what they want and, well, David's getting mad at me with his eyes now so I am passing the phone over to him." Bronte could picture Willa widening her eyes and mouthing "*What?*" at her exasperated husband.

"Hey, Bron, David here. Where do you want to begin?"

Bronte settled herself onto a shady bench in the park, the morning sun dappling in and out through the trees over her head. "As absurd as it sounds," she began, "I honestly didn't know about any of that duke crap until this morning. I am so up shit's creek, David. He actually asked me to come back to England with him while he sorted out all this dismal shit with his family—his father had a heart attack yesterday... would that sort of thing be in the news there? Never mind. What I mean is, in a nutshell, I think we both thought it was going to be this two-month-long, no-strings-attached fling while he defended his dissertation and we set about the happy task of mending my broken heart one kiss at a time. But, David, the damnedest fucking thing is I think he fell in love with me and I fucked it all to pieces."

"Listen, Bron, I mean this in the nicest possible way, but you have a bit of a bad habit of thinking men are in love with you when, you know, they just might want a good shag… again, no offense—" Bronte heard Willa grabbing the phone out of David's hand and then a loud slap.

Bronte felt like she too had been slapped.

"Please pretend my caveman husband did *not* just say that to you," Willa pleaded. "What he was trying to say in his pathetic, illiterate fashion was, you might want to be patient on this one and see where the chips fall. If there is truly something real and lasting with you and Max, good shagging aside, it will all rise to the top once he sees his way clear of his father's illness. If it's meant to be and all that. Just sit tight, Bron. Who knows? Maybe his dad will be just fine and Max can go back to being a relatively anonymous marquess for another twenty years."

"Oh good God. So he really is already a marquess?"

"Well, Bron, I mean, it's a courtesy title really, kind of a polite placeholder until he becomes the duke."

"Oh, fuck."

"Well. In any case, here's his British cell phone number and his parents' number at Dunlear Castle…" Bronte took out her small silver pen and miniature pad of paper and jotted down the numbers, trying not to dwell on the word "castle" as it careened around her skull like a pinball in a metal bucket.

"All right, then. Thanks, Willa. I don't know where any of this leaves me, but I can at least get in touch with him if need be. And tell David thanks for the caveman advice, but for the first time in my ill-fated love life, I may have finally underplayed my hand."

"Oh, Bron—"

"Never mind. I am going to beg off if you don't mind. I'll be back in touch soon, and if you happen to see Max before I talk to him, please, *please* do not mention this conversation. Ciao."

Bronte hit the off button on her phone and simply stared at the screen. In a moment of weakness a few weeks ago, she had foolishly changed her screen saver from a black-and-white photo of a Zen rock garden to a goofy picture of Max and Bronte on Navy Pier with the Ferris wheel in the background all golden and sparkling from the reflected sunset. They looked like two ridiculous tourists: he with that goddamned *More Cowbell* T-shirt on, and Bronte gazing up at him like some lovesick fool, and the old Japanese man who was taking the picture repeatedly telling them to get closer, and Max pulling her tighter and tighter around the waist until she was practically dry-humping the side of his jeans and gasping for air, and they were both laughing and it was so good.

And she was such an idiot.

What an idiot.

She looked down at the small pad in her hand and realized the numbers were starting to smudge as two stupid, slow tears dripped from her cheek. Wiping her face resolutely, she punched in Max's British mobile phone number and waited for the call to go through. It went immediately to voice mail, and his voice on the outgoing message was quick and sounded more British somehow. It sounded so formal.

"This is Max. Leave a message."

She was still savoring the sound of his voice when she realized the beep had already sounded and she was in that silent void, recording empty air into his voice mail.

"Uh, Max, it's Bron... Bronte. I got your UK number from David and Willa. I hope that's okay. Um, I just am kind of in shock. I mean, fuck, it's not about me, I get that. So, anyway, I hope you got home safely and that your father is okay, and if you want to talk, you know my number and well, I'm rambling so... I miss you. It's not so cut-and-dried... I'm sorry... but you could have told me about all the royal stuff... brutal honesty, remember? I guess it doesn't matter now... but I hope you are okay... okay... bye..."

She cut the line then took a deep breath to regroup, gathered her courage, and dialed the number for Dunlear Fucking Castle.

One ring. Two rings. Three rings. "Dunlear, may I help you?"

Staff. Duh.

"Yes, please. My name is Bronte Talbott and I am calling to speak to Max... Heyworth, please."

"Is he expecting your call?"

"Not exactly, but—"

"I am sorry, miss, but I have been asked to take messages just now. May I please have your information and I will pass it on?"

Bronte breathed out slowly in an attempt to stifle the urge to rip someone's throat out with her new werewolf claws.

"My name is Bronte Talbott. *B-R-O-N...*" As Bronte methodically spelled out her full first and last name, she felt herself slipping into a morass of loss and self-pity. By the time she had given her cell phone number, she did not think the woman on the other end of the line had much more patience than she did. She didn't bother with any message and just asked the maid to make sure she told Max that she had called, maybe placing a tad too much emphasis on *make sure*, resulting in what may have been a little harrumph from the maid, who was obviously insulted at the implication that she would not, of course, pass on the message.

Bronte ended the call and then smiled ruefully. *So let me get this straight*, she thought to herself, with a wicked sense of divine retribution being hurled her way from Mount Olympus, *yesterday at this time, I had a first-class, VIP, all-access, backstage pass to the heavenly body and intricate mind of one royal Max Heyworth, and now I have... nothing.*

Fucking brilliant. Just fucking brilliant.

She shook off the bitterness and put her phone back in her bag. Bronte crossed the park and set about discovering the calming effects of high-end retail therapy on Oak Street along with an inner pep talk. She did *not* have nothing. She had her own life, which she had built. An education, which she had paid for. So what if he was basically the perfect man?

Fuck. All right. Let's try that again.

She started to feel the wave of depression and self-pity that had defined the previous months, after she'd broken up with Mr. Texas. She clenched her fists and tensed her arms, as if she could ward off the encroaching misery like a sorcerer casting out a demon.

"No!" she barked out loud, then smiled at the older woman who passed her on the sidewalk, who was now probably wondering whether Bronte was sane. *No*, she repeated to herself silently. It had been a measly eight weeks with Max. It wasn't *nothing*, but it didn't have to be *everything* either. Bronte would have to carve it out like a lump. Or, barring that possibility, at least lock it up tight. The whole deal. It had to be objectified, that eight-week interlude. She had to distance herself from her own desperation.

If she granted herself even the slightest crack in that fortress of denial, she would be a wreck. There was no way in hell she could stop at a quick reminiscent thought of his sparkling gray eyes… without letting her mind wander to the wit and depth that resided behind them. And the man he must be when he was really in his element. In a castle. Strong. Authoritative. In some enormous Elizabethan four-poster bed… sexy as all… fuck.

Then again, it must be something miserable and pale, that life, if he wasn't even willing to share it with her in the retelling. He must be bogged down with a string of meaningless ribbon-cuttings and charity fund-raisers. What a bore. (*Did a duchess get to wear something new to every event?* her treacherous mind wondered idly.)

"Stop it," she muttered to herself. The saleswoman at Jil Sander was giving her the fisheye.

After a few mind-numbing hours pawing cashmere and silk and leather at Hermès and Jimmy Choo, Bronte met up with Sarah James at Le Colonial.

"You look really bad, Bron."

"Gee, thanks, Sarah," Bronte said in a deadpan voice as she cast a jealous stare at her friend's perfectly coiffed blond hair, sexy figure, and impeccable wardrobe.

The waiter opened the bottle of Chablis that Sarah had ordered and poured a taste for her. Bronte set down her shopping bags and hung her purse on the back of her chair. Sarah spoke in perfect French to the tall, handsome waiter, and then he poured the crisp wine into Bronte's glass, topped off Sarah's, and set the bottle in the standing ice bucket near the table.

"I hate that you are all international like that."

"I am not 'all international like that,'" Sarah replied, but she smiled and took a sip of the expensive wine. "Well, maybe just a little. I may have inherited a bit of a penchant for the finer things in life from my grandmother, but there are worse legacies. Who am I to complain?"

"You're right," Bronte said as she raised her glass. "I'm not complaining."

Bronte sipped her wine and continued to look across the narrow table at her elegant friend. She silently marveled at how Sarah had retained an air of grateful innocence that was completely at odds with her cosmopolitan adolescence, when she had lived in France with her wealthy grandmother. "Don't change a thing," Bronte added. "All that breezy sophisticated ease is going to make you a star."

"Well, I don't know about that," Sarah said. "I mean, I hope people love my shoes in New York as much as they seem to like them here in Chicago, but you know, who knows?"

"I do. You are going to kick ass, Sarah. Seriously."

"What did Cecily say? Was she furious?"

"No. She sort of assessed the situation like she does, then saw the beauty of it. She wants me to open BCA in New York."

Sarah raised her glass. "Here's to you and your victorious return to Gotham."

Bronte raised her glass and smiled, then started crying involuntarily. "Oh my God." She put the wineglass down and brought the napkin up from her lap to dry her eyes. "Oh my God. This is so unprofessional. I can't believe I am crying right now."

Sarah reached across the table and held Bronte's free hand in hers. "It's okay, Bron. You can't be a machine all the time. From the first time we met, I had hoped we'd become friends. Are you sad about your British chap? You knew it was coming, didn't you?"

Bronte took a deep breath and a deep gulp of ice water. "Of course, I knew it was coming. That was the whole point. Transitional Man. No heartbreak. But—" She closed her eyes and tried to let the emotion fade a bit. "But I guess I just didn't anticipate the… reality."

"Yeah. Reality can be… not what we anticipate," Sarah said. "I don't know if you know much about my family. I mean, I know you know about my dad and the stores and all that, but when my mother died, well, I kind of came to accept that reality is not to be trifled with."

Bronte smiled and took another sip of wine. "I told you I was going to need a glass of wine."

"I know. That's why I had it cooling when you arrived."

They talked for a few minutes about what they were going to order for lunch, then spoke to the waiter and got back to their discussion.

"So tell me more about the British guy. Couldn't you try to do a long-distance thing?"

"I don't think so. He asked me to go back to London with him."

Sarah nearly choked on her sip of wine. "What? Did he ask you to marry him? Oh my God. Are you in love with him?"

Bronte laughed. "Sarah, you are like a puppy! No, he didn't ask me to marry him. Really. How old are you?" Bronte held up her palm face out. "No! Don't answer that; I know I am only five years older than you are, but you make me feel ancient. It's not something I want to dwell on right now. We will market the hell out of your youth and exuberance, but just now it makes me feel grumpy."

"I'm not sure being what my dad would call a dingbat is really a marketable skill."

"That's a laugh."

"Well, you know what I mean. I never even went to college."

"You know more about shoes than most scholars know about Shakespeare. That counts."

"I know, I mean, I am proud of what I've accomplished, but the point is, oh, I don't know what the point is!" She laughed and waved her hand. "I just want to hear more about the romance."

"Well." Bronte exhaled slowly and decided to keep the bulk of the royal details private. "The bottom line is that he lied to me and that was really the only thing I had told him was my total freak-out, crazy-making, do-not-go-there red flag." Bronte knew it was a broad interpretation of the truth, but it helped to cast a little blame at his feet. "From the first time we got together, I told him that I had just gotten out of a hideous breakup and the only way I was going to heal, or whatever"—Bronte rolled her eyes at the foolishness of such a thing ever being possible—"was that I needed him to be totally honest with me."

"Was he sleeping with someone else?"

"God, no. Nothing like that."

"Then what? I thought you told me that you sort of loved how he didn't care about your parents or where you grew up. That you two were sort of in a romantic vacuum."

"I guess that was all partially true. But the thing he didn't mention was bigger than any of that."

"What's that supposed to mean?"

"He's a fucking royal duke." So much for discretion.

Sarah clapped her hands together and grinned with delight.

"How could you possibly have that reaction?" Bronte asked. "He totally lied to me. That is not just some detail he forgot to mention—that's actually who he *is*."

"Oh my God, is it Harry?"

"Of course it's not Harry!"

"But isn't he the only royal duke?" Sarah put a finger to her lip. "Wait, I don't think he's even a duke yet. And Andrew's too old for you—"

"What the hell are you talking about?"

"I mean, your guy may be royal and he may be a duke, but I don't think he's a royal duke."

"Are you fucking kidding me? What difference does any of that make?"

Sarah gave Bronte a taunting smile. "Exactly. What difference does any of that make, Bronte?"

"You are evil." Bronte took another sip of wine. "Look. I guess he is technically still a marquess, I guess, and his grandmother was related to the Colin Firth king, so that's why he's royal. I don't fucking know. It's a courtesy title or something." Bronte waved her hand again, as if those were considerations she'd never have to entertain again anyway.

"Oh, this is just too good."

"Sarah."

"Seriously. You had an affair with royalty."

"And that is good because?"

"Oh, stop it with that. Just admit that it's every little girl's dream come true, you shrew. Admit it!"

Bronte smiled. "Okay, I admit it. He was pretty amazing. But"— her face fell again—"he was amazing when he was just a British guy finishing up his doctoral work at the University of Chicago. Why wouldn't he just tell me the truth?"

"What truth, Bron? You think I want to tell some guy who asks me out, 'Oh, hey, by the way, I stand to inherit a massive fortune from my grandmother. And my father. And my mother's estate.' It's ludicrous. The last thing I want is to be liked—or disliked—for *that*. That's not who I am. And you provided the marquess"—Sarah shivered and smiled—"I'm sorry, but it is divine. Anyway, you provided him with the perfect petri dish to see if you loved him just for him. It sounds like such a cliché, but isn't it what we all want most of all… just to know if someone loves us, for no reason whatsoever? They just do."

Bronte stared into her wineglass. "Yes."

Sarah smiled.

"But no!" Bronte cried.

Sarah frowned.

"I mean, I can see how he wanted that," Bronte said, "but it was so obvious from the first moment, from the minute I practically tripped over him in the bookstore, that I was perfectly crazy about him. Seriously, I don't think it would have made any difference to me one way or another if he'd grown up above the fish-and-chips shop or in a huge castle."

"Oh! Did he grow up in a huge castle?"

"Stop that!" But Bronte smiled despite herself. "Yes. Huge. There are pictures online. If anyone cares to look at such a thing."

Sarah's eyes widened. "What is his name, Bronte? Holy crap. This is unbelievable."

"Forget it. It doesn't matter. It's over. It has to be over."

"Why does it have to be over?"

"Because we both failed each other. No one's to blame. We both just… it wasn't right. I can't be a…"

"Duchess?!"

"Oh God. You are impossible."

Sarah made eye contact with the waiter as he refilled their glasses. He asked if they wanted another bottle when their meals arrived, and Sarah's *bien sûr* practically made him blush with pleasure.

After he had left the table, Bronte asked, "Do you even know the effect you have on men, Sarah?"

"What effect? I'm totally clueless. You know that."

And Sarah was, Bronte marveled. She just smiled and sparkled and spoke perfect French and thought the best of everyone and was completely unaware of the joy she engendered in others. *Someday,* thought Bronte, *someone's going to quietly knock your (expensive, silk) socks off.*

"Never mind all that," Bronte said. "Let's talk about work for a while. I can only handle this emotional crap for so long."

"Okay, for a while only. Then I want to get back to the *duke.*"

Bronte rolled her eyes and then launched into a string of ideas about how best to position the Sarah James store in New York, where it should be, how they should create the brand around Sarah's personality. They spoke over lunch and well into the second bottle of wine.

"I still don't understand why it's all so impossible, Bron."

"Nothing's impossible. Your ad campaign is going to be a huge success. What are you talking about?" Bronte ate the last bit of pasta and rested her silverware at the side of the plate.

"You and the duke. Why is it so impossible?"

"Sarah. Look at me. I am not a duchess, for chrissake. It was an affair. A perfectly wonderful"—she stopped and looked down at her lap to control the emotion, then brought her eyes back up to Sarah—"affair. And now it's over. I am just being a grown up. Everything has a beginning and an end—that's what my mom always used to say. And it's true. It was great while it lasted. And now it's time to move on." Bronte reached across the table. "I'll be fine. Let's focus on making you a star."

The two of them were laughing and flushed when they finished lunch and stepped out onto Oak Street. Bronte toddled back to her office and hugged Cecily with buzzed enthusiasm. As expected, Brian was equally pleased with the idea of launching a satellite office of BCA in New York. Unlike Cecily, he welcomed the chance to spend a few days each month in Manhattan. Brian promised Bronte that he would give his full support to all the new projects, especially Sarah James, for whom he had developed a grudging respect after Bronte had convinced him that she was far more than a pampered heiress. They spoke for a few more moments, then Cecily put Bronte into a cab and sent her home. She slept for eighteen hours straight and woke up feeling ready to face the rest of her life.

Alone.

Fortified, she amended.

Fortified.

After a few days of cell-phone silence, Bronte realized her disappointment at not hearing back from Max was tinged with a strange relief. It had all come to a fulcrum point when Max asked her to pack a bag. She tried to pretend that she could not have possibly realized the enormity of what he was asking at the time, but even then, she knew. She had been scared fucking witless. She was your basic, run-of-the-mill coward.

What if she had said yes and then it didn't work out?

Better to lick her wounds and settle for the really *good* they had already had rather than risk it all on the possibly *great* they might (or more likely, might not) have in the imaginary future. She knew all about imaginary futures, she reminded herself, and if she could not make a go of it with the easygoing Mr. Texas, she certainly was not going to get the brass ring with a fucking duke. (*No! He was just sweet Max*, the hopeless-romantic voice in the back of her head pleaded. She told that voice to sit down and shut up. He was royalty, damn it. And a bit of a duplicitous royal at that.)

It was much easier to distance herself from the whole mess if she built up this (patently false) historically revisionist depiction of Max as the scheming, unattainable, lofty noble instead of the tender, delicious, devoted lover he had, in reality, proved to be.

Yet again, Bronte realized how easy it was to disassemble her so-called life. The landlord's son was moving back from Colorado and the little old lady had been secretly hoping the downstairs apartment would free up, as much as she loved having Bronte there. Within two weeks, Bronte had hired movers, signed a lease sight unseen on a one-bedroom apartment that had miraculously become available in her old friend April's Gramercy Park doorman building (with coveted key to the park included), and negotiated a kick-ass raise.

To top it all off, Carol Dieppe's negotiations with the venture capital guys who had approached her about starting her own agency had come to a screeching halt when one of them had asked Carol if she was willing to drop her pro bono work for Human Rights Council. She refused. A few days later, Bronte was able to convince both April and Carol to jump ship and open BCA NY with her.

Then, about a week after he'd left, in the midst of all that chaos, Max did return her call. She was in a meeting at work and didn't have her cell phone when he called. She returned to her desk to discover his voice mail.

"Hey Bron, it's me. Max. Thanks for your messages. Yes, I made it back in one piece. Everything's pretty bad here, but my dad is hanging on, so who knows? So… well, you have my UK number now if you ever need to get in touch. Take care of yourself, Bronte." He sounded conclusive. He sounded tired and defeated and so far away. Not just geographically far. Far from her. She cried and played it over and over to hear his voice and imagine him speaking directly into her, reliving the warm caress of his breath against her ear.

But she didn't call him back. He hadn't really asked her to, and even if he had, what could she say? She was no closer to diving into the deep end of the relationship pool than she had been the day he had left, and he'd been heartbreakingly clear that that's where he was… and where he wanted her to be. In the deep end.

When she read about his father's death a week later, a few days before she left Chicago (it was just Google alerts, not stalking, she rationalized), she wrote him a condolence letter. Her mother's enduring influence—etiquette—made it impossible for her to let the sad event pass with no communication whatsoever. She was formal in her tone, relying on the solemnity of the occasion to maintain a cool distance through her words. She wanted him to know she cared but not to feel like she was trying to weasel her way back into his good opinion. An opinion she sought, but could never quite believe she deserved.

What would have been the point of hinting at something more? Of suggesting they get together if he was ever in New York? She didn't even bother telling him she was leaving Chicago. She knew she couldn't offer him anything, really. She was sure that he was simply too *good* for her. Not in any holier-than-thou, haughty way. Not because he was royal, whatever that meant. He was just a better person. He knew things. Things like how to speak honestly about his emotions. Like how to express sadness and loss when his father was about to die. Bronte didn't think those things would ever be made available to her. He was right: they had been so good together. They had even loved each other. But she convinced herself it was what Max would have called a one-off. Better left in the perfect world of memory.

Ever the gentleman, Max did send her a letter in reply about a month later, as formal and distant as her own. Almost a mirror image of hers, she realized. He was not going to tread into the dangerous language of a potential future. Why should he? He'd already gone there and gotten a sad glimpse of the emotional wasteland and cowardice that rested in Bronte's heart.

So, other than the enormous, catastrophic cock-up that she now referred to (to herself only, of course) as The Deal with the Duke, things were actually looking up. Having already learned not to go around telling all her friends about the hot new guy she happened to be sleeping with, she didn't have any explaining to do when she rolled back into the Big Apple that summer. Only Sarah James and a few of her friends at BCA even knew he existed, and even then, they only knew him as her British fling. At the time, they'd all joked that Bronte was certainly keeping a tight leash on her new boy toy and they all knew he was scheduled to go back to England mid-July regardless, so no loose ends to explain on that front either.

It all went quite according to plan, in a way—or so Bronte tried to convince herself. Her Transitional Man had served his purpose and she had successfully catapulted right back into her chic little New York world. The fact that she now knew she could, when presented with the challenge, burn through a hundred condoms in fewer than eight weeks didn't hurt her confidence either.

At Christmas, Max left what was to be his final message: a simple holiday greeting wishing her well. He may have left the same message for his valet. Concise. Formal. As far as Bronte could tell, his passion had cooled and everyone was back on track.

Or at least he was.

Chapter 6

Max stared at his father's fresh grave. It seemed simultaneously appropriate and demented that the funeral would take place on one of the most glorious days of summer. The leaves were sighing contentedly in the background and the swallows and starlings were so cheerful that Max wanted to laugh out loud from the simple joy of it. Or get his shotgun out and kill some birds.

The early light of summer glinted off the beveled glass windows of the nearby family chapel. The funeral ceremony had taken place inside those thick medieval walls, but Max's father had insisted on being buried outside, rather than in one of the family crypts.

"I certainly don't want to spend eternity in that dank place if it comes to that," his father had joked with Max just a few days ago, the supplemental oxygen giving his voice a reedy quality.

That had been one of the good days, when the doctors at the hospital had been sure His Grace was on the mend. Max had spent hour after hour sitting in his father's hospital room, mostly reading or staring quietly out the window. It was an odd balance, to ask the in-case-you-die questions without seeming to hasten someone's departure. By the second to last day of his life, it seemed that George Heyworth was quite certain about his imminent departure and wanted to take advantage of that small window of opportunity.

"Max. I think we both know what's coming." He had waited until Sylvia had left the room. She was a cold stoic in so many areas of her life, but in this episode, she had turned mildly hysterical. At one point, she tried to blame one of the visiting physicians for the fact that George had had a heart attack in the first place. Max and George had finally convinced her to return to Dunlear for a few hours of rest.

"Yes, Dad." He pulled the vinyl hospital chair closer to his father's bedside.

"You are going to be fine, Max. Really fine."

Max stared at the linoleum floor, his eyes resting on the speckled turquoise.

"Max?"

"Yes, Dad?"

"What happened in Chicago?"

Max looked up quickly to see his father's knowing glance. His father kept staring at him.

"I don't know... I mean, I thought I knew. I thought I fell in love."

His father's smile widened and caused a crease around his eyes. He'd always been a hopeless romantic. *One would have to be hopeless to fall in love with Sylvia Beckwith*, Max thought ruefully.

"Where is she then?" his father asked.

"It's not always a two-way street, is it, Dad?"

His father's brows knit. "That's impossible."

Max burst out laughing and a nurse gave him a stern look as she passed the open doorway and shushed him.

"It feels good to laugh with you, Dad."

"Tell me about the girl."

Max looked at him again. Of course his father didn't want to spend his final hours talking about the irrigation negotiations or the renovation of the medieval refectory at Dunlear. He wanted to hear about the girl.

"I don't know what to tell you, Dad. I guess I just thought what you did. That of course she would love me if I loved her. But when I asked her to come with me, as soon as Mom called to tell me you were... ill..." Max stopped for a few seconds to keep his thoughts straight. The endless hours in the hospital had curdled his brain a bit. "Well, she simply said no."

The oxygen tube distorted his father's expression somewhat, but Max still recognized the look of disappointment.

"What?" Max laughed. "She said no; what was I supposed to do? Drag her here by her ponytail?"

His father's breath was strained again. It was becoming more of an effort to speak. "She has nice long hair, then?"

Max smiled again but repressed the bark of laughter that would have come out if that shushing nurse hadn't been nosing around still.

"Oh, Dad. She is lovely." Max allowed himself that brief honesty. "And smart. And funny. And kind of fierce and independent."

"Sounds like your mother." George winked, knowing the comparison would drive Max crazy.

"She is also quite affectionate," Max said, effectively insulting his mother.

"Now, now, Max."

"Fine, I won't waste our time on that." Max started to feel the double barrel of loss push into his sternum. His father was slipping away before his eyes, and Bronte was already gone. When she had mentioned, on her uncharacteristically brief voice mail, that he *might* have *mentioned* that he was a *duke*, he knew they were through. "I don't think she was too happy to learn I was the next Duke of Northrop."

"Now, that really must be impossible. What woman doesn't want to be a duchess?"

Max smiled again as he looked at the floor. "I may have found the only one."

His father wheezed a bit. "Of course, she secretly does."

"Father. Really. It is the twenty-first century. I honestly don't think any woman *secretly* does anything. She is quite forthright. It's one of the things I really love—loved—about her."

"So what did she say when you told her about the title?"

"Well... I never actually told her."

His father started to laugh but it turned into a raspy cough and then a hard racking attempt to catch his breath. The bossy nurse came quickly into the room with a scowl for Max and a soothing word or two for his father. She adjusted his oxygen levels, checked his IV and vitals, then tossed Max another disparaging gaze as she left the room.

"Max."

"Yes, Dad?"

"That's not the type of information a girl wants to happen upon willy-nilly."

"I've gathered that now. But it's a bit too late." Max straightened his shoulders. "But enough about her. I think it was all a bit of a flash in the pan."

His father looked at him for another long minute. "I am glad I got to see the look in your eyes when you talked about that flash in the pan."

"Me too," Max said.

And then two days later, his father was gone. The hospital personnel had been efficient and kind—especially in the face of Sylvia's histrionics. And three days after that, here he stood with the summer wind lightly caressing the leaves of the alders that surrounded the centuries-old churchyard.

Everyone else had finally gone back into the castle to rest for a few hours before dinner, so Max was blessedly alone for the first time in as long as he could remember. He kept looking at the perimeter of grass where the gravediggers had done a very neat job of edging the hole into which the casket had been lowered. The bright green turf fluttered in the light breeze, and then it simply ceased and the black hole began. A perfect delineation.

Over the past two weeks of his father's brief recovery (and then rapid decline) from the heart attack, everyone had been watching

Max. The press and representative members of the Royal Family had all been there, if respectfully distant. Those types of inquisitors were almost easier to deal with. The family had a press secretary, and protocol dictated nearly all of Max's actions in any case.

The more difficult observers were closer to hand. His mother kept looking at him with a cruel demand in her eyes, as if to say, *I told you to hurry up and get married… now your father will never have the comfort of knowing the line is secure.* His sisters had looked to him for strength and direction. It was surprisingly easy to act like he knew what he was doing. He was good at logistics. So was Devon. His younger brother looked to Max as an adjutant would look to a superior officer: mostly to make sure they were on the same page, to keep their mother from becoming hysterical, to keep their sisters comforted.

But most of all, his immediate family looked to him because they wanted to make sure they were relieved of the burden of having to handle the brunt of what was coming down the pike. That Max was on it. Because Max was always on it. He could handle it. Just like his father used to handle it.

Max had a momentary recollection of when the family had moved from Yorkshire down to Dunlear, after his grandmother had died. George's father had asked them to move in and begin taking on the ducal responsibilities in the late eighties. The family had been like a little troupe of (very well-to-do) tinkers. Displaced. His father had seemed particularly mindful. Max remembered how his dad kept asking the young ones (Max, ten; Devon, eight; and Abby, six) how they were adjusting. How they liked their new home. If they'd found any good hiding places.

Max scowled.

His father could not have cared less about securing the line. His mother was an idiot. She was more concerned about where to seat the queen's representative, the Duke of Gloucester, at supper that night than about Max's marital happiness. Max felt the familiar resentment bubble up and did his best to toss it aside. For whatever reason, his father loved his mother—*had loved*, he corrected—but that was a love that somehow skipped a generation. Sylvia, Lady Heyworth, the Duchess of Northrop, had no love for her eldest son. And the (lack of) feeling was mutual.

Max looked up to the sky and watched as the flock of starlings was spooked and flew away in a sweeping arc from the cemetery where he stood. His father would have loved that. Bronte would have loved that. The temporary, ephemeral, beautifully orchestrated moment. And then nothing.

His father would have loved Bronte.

And, damn it, that's what finally made him cry after all. He had withstood all the cool, empathic glances of his relatives and the well-wishers in the chapel and then out here in the beautiful open air. He hadn't even felt the slightest press of emotion. It was logically too soon to miss his father—he'd been alive three days ago, for goodness' sake—but missing Bronte was starting to ferment.

He smiled bitterly as the tears slowly rolled down his cheeks. At least he could stand there, unassailed, and weep for the loss of a woman who had revealed a part of him to himself that he'd never been able to admit was present, or perhaps a place into which he had never allowed himself to admit anyone. She had slid into his soul through a strange alchemy of bitter humor and raw vitality. It wasn't the sex. (Of course it was, but not in the way it sounded.) He hadn't told anyone about her.

Max had kept her as some sort of secret. At the time, he'd thought he was savoring those first few precious months of private intimacy in anticipation of what he'd thought was going to be a lifetime of shared public happiness. Now he regretted that he hadn't relayed every anecdote to Devon or Willa or David, so he could call upon them and ask them to tell him (over and over) that it had been real. That she had been real. Of all the people he could have shared his feelings with, why had he chosen the one who was now there in the ground at his feet?

He reached into the inside pocket of his gray morning coat, pulled out the perfectly pressed linen handkerchief, and rested it slowly against each of his eyes. Willa and David had been the last to leave him alone at the graveside. Willa had looked like she wanted to say more when Max thanked them for passing along his contact details to Bronte a few weeks before. He probably appeared barely interested, as his attempts to avoid thinking or talking about Bronte led him to appear wooden when her name came up. As much as he thought he was "processing" his father's death in a healthy way—and that may have technically been true—if he was honest, the effort it took to stay in control of that particular grief meant that everything else had to be very carefully carved out, wrapped up, and put away. Especially thoughts of Bronte.

To people on the outside—the press, his family—it was justifiably difficult to balance his life in the face of the unexpected loss of his father. If he confessed that he was more likely to have a nervous breakdown at the loss of a woman he'd only known for a few months, they really would have had him committed.

So he allowed himself to mourn. And if he was mourning the loss of Bronte as much as the loss of his father, then that was his business, and no one else really needed to know. One was the loss of what might have been and one was the loss of what was. Neither was more or less real to him at that moment. He figured he could wring it all out together and be done with the whole bloody mess in a few months' time.

Two weeks later, he received the condolence letter Bronte had written. It gave him the courage to let her go altogether. It was so devoid of any true feeling. So perfunctory. He replied to every condolence letter he had received. By hand. Eight hundred and twenty-three to be precise. He replied to Bronte's just as he replied to the queen's. Politely.

By Christmas, the combination of sexual frustration and desire had started to push him to the breaking point. He had finally confided in Devon, who was beginning to worry about the cause of Max's perpetual irritation. In a moment of pique, Max had been uncharacteristically short-tempered with a group of labor leaders who were representing the agricultural workers at Dunlear Castle. After Max had clenched his hand into a fist and slammed it on the negotiating table, Devon had hastily called the meeting to an end, citing a family emergency, and then summarily punched Max in the face once everyone else had left the room.

With Devon furiously grabbing the lapels of Max's chalk-stripe suit jacket, Max had finally collapsed into a chair and told him the whole sorry story about the *chit* from Chicago.

"So let me get this straight," Devon said. "You fall madly in love with this woman and now you are letting her go?"

"Damn it, Dev, you sound just like Dad. I can't very well make her love me."

"Of course she loves you!" Devon waved his hand in the air. "You are the lovable one, remember? I'm the rat bastard around here."

Max smiled as he poured them both a few fingers of scotch. They had gone back to Max's house in Fulham after the labor meetings had ended so disastrously. Devon took one of the glasses from his brother and continued speaking.

"Seriously. So what? So you didn't come right out and tell her that a future with you would be full of flashing paparazzi cameras and prying reporters. That's not irreconcilable. Call her now. It's Christmastime." Devon tossed his phone at his older brother. "Quit being a puss."

"Shut up." Max caught the phone but stared at it without dialing the number he'd never forgotten.

"Just do it."

Max took a fortifying slug of scotch, then dialed the number. It went straight to voice mail and her message was damnably short. He was recording dead air before he'd even considered what he might say. "Merry Christmas, Bronte. I hope… you have a wonderful year ahead." Click.

"You're going to have to call her back. Tell me you did not just leave that stilted piece-of-shit message on her answering machine! That was a joke, right?" Devon was laughing.

Max whipped the phone back at his younger brother.

"Ow!" He scrambled to protect his face.

"Serves you right, you pushy bastard. I wasn't prepared to talk to her. I need to think about the best way to go about it."

"For another six months? Time's a-wasting, Max."

"Just shut up. I want to get foxed."

"That I can do!" Devon stood up and retrieved the nearly full bottle of scotch. "Let's get despicably drunk, shall we?"

"Perfect." Max held out his glass for a refill and the two brothers proceeded to get hammered. Max was passed out cold a few hours later when Bronte returned his call.

The fact that he let it go to voice mail struck Bronte as some sort of petty retaliatory gesture for her not having picked up his lame Christmas greeting. She left him a mirror version of the message he'd left. Empty and meaningless. And she began to feel more and more grateful that she'd escaped with her heart (barely) intact from a man who could run so hot and cold.

Chapter 7

HAVING JUST GOTTEN HER hair done and looking like a goddamned shampoo commercial, Bronte was humming one of her favorite New York tunes and feeling like the city was her oyster. She gave her long, dark mane an extra sassy swing as she headed out onto Madison Avenue.

Damn that guy was good. No matter how hard she tried to brush, treat, blow, condition, or deep-fry her hair on her own time, it never felt as good as it did after two hours at Frederic Fekkai. What was up with that?

As long as she didn't factor in her nonexistent love life, the year that had passed since her move to New York had been very, very good to Ms. Bronte Talbott, if she did say so herself. The Sarah James flagship store and atelier had swooped into Manhattan like a heat-seeking missile. Everyone was crazy about her barely-there, sky-high styles, and Sarah herself was the perfect It Girl to embody the whole brand. She didn't need to promote it: she lived it.

Bronte glanced up to see which cross street she was on and realized that the Sarah James store was only two blocks north. She decided to pop in unannounced and check in on her favorite client and closest friend. As the sparkling, seemingly endless early June day was starting to wane, Bronte thought she might even convince Sarah to join her for a celebratory cocktail. The Council of Fashion Designers of America had surprised them all by shortlisting Sarah James for one of their prestigious CFDA awards, and the presentation ceremony and ball were the following night at Lincoln Center.

A couple of beautiful people were coming her way, Bronte noted absently, as she rummaged through her too-big satchel to retrieve her ringing cell phone. The woman was a tight little colt of a thing with a short blond bob, classic retro wayfarers, and Sarah James kitten heels clicking in time on the sidewalk, and the guy was in a great, classic blue suit, and had his arm hung loosely around her shoulder.

Bronte pulled herself up short and turned to face the Barneys window, lifting one knee to support the bottom of her bag. She attempted to dig deeper into her godforsaken garbage pail of a purse, murmuring a steady stream of "fuck-fuck-fuck-fuck-fuck" as the phone continued to ring and she continued to be unable to extract it from the quagmire that was the inside of her bag.

As she shook the long wall of her gleaming hair out of the way with an impatient toss, she looked up into the plate-glass window of the department store to see Max's reflection staring at her back. She gave up on finding her phone and slowly turned around.

Thank God I am looking fucking hot, she thought stupidly. Her phone beeped one last petulant time to let her know she had missed the call.

"Hi, Max."

"Hi, Bron."

Did he have to say it in that deep, familiar way? Ugh.

He raised his sunglasses up on his hair. His killer hair. What? Did she think that after less than a year, he wouldn't still have the best fucking hair in history? That he would have gone prematurely gray and bald due to her absence? His hideously perfect blond, nearly preteen companion was looking doe-eyed, moving her glance from one of them to the other, when Max came back to his senses, partially, and said, almost dismissively, "Oh, this is Lydia. Lydia, this is Bronte Talbott."

"Nice to meet you, Bronte," Lydia said formally and a bit shyly, looking up to Max as if for guidance.

"Nice shoes, Lydia," Bronte commented dryly. "I was just on my way to see Sarah James as a matter of fact."

"Ah," Max said, "so you won that account after all. Congratulations."

"Yes," Bronte answered, surprised that he would even remember. "Sarah opened her shop on 68th and Madison last year."

Max turned to his companion. "Do you want to go shoe shopping, Lyd?"

What the hell? Bronte thought. *Did he think I could just bump into him and act all normal?*

"Sorry," Bronte cut in, "it's a business meeting. We're going over some advertising budget numbers for next year. Maybe another time." Bronte gave the petite woman a tight smile, then turned to face Max.

Bronte lifted her oversized black sunglasses onto her head and caught Max's eyes. Big mistake. His gaze pinned her tighter than a butterfly in a lepidopterist's glass box. Not good. Definitely not good.

"Okay then," Bronte snapped after that eternal stare, returning her sunglasses to her face: mortal combat required the proper body armor. No way was she going to survive those gray-blue eyes boring into hers right out here on the open battlefield of Madison Avenue.

"Great to see you, Max. Lydia, a pleasure."

Bronte turned to go. Max gave her his best half-smile and reached tentatively for her upper arm—to stall her, touch her, she didn't know what—then he thought better of it and looked heartbreakingly vulnerable for a split second. He put his sunglasses back on and made a gesture with his hand that was part salute, part wave.

Bronte continued apace, trying to regain her composure as she made her way north on Madison Avenue. She still hadn't succeeded by the time she barreled into Sarah's store and continued upstairs to her office, ripping the door open unceremoniously and throwing her enormous bag onto Sarah's gorgeous white calfskin couch.

"Well, well, well," said Sarah. "If it isn't my brilliant advertising agent."

Sarah then turned to her assistant, Julie, with whom she had been looking over some letters and last-minute speech adjustments for the CFDA awards (on the million-to-one chance that Sarah James the person actually received an award on behalf of Sarah James the brand) and told Julie she could go home for the day.

Bronte sat on the couch, one leg crossed over the other and kicking quickly, quickly, quickly.

"It's times like this I wish I smoked, because all I want to do is rip open a pack of cigarettes and chain-smoke like a fucking dragon lady."

"Hmmm," Sarah offered noncommittally as she took a bottle of Veuve Clicquot out of the small refrigerator at the back of her cluttered private workroom/studio and began to uncork it.

"Only you," Bronte said through a bitter laugh, "would have Veuve Clicquot at the ready at a time like this. You are truly the best woman on the planet."

POP!

Bronte smiled warmly despite herself, grateful that even the most chaotic emotional upheaval could still be soothed by the sound of a cold bottle of champagne being uncorked.

"Talk," Sarah barked unceremoniously as she handed Bronte an immaculate Waterford crystal flute. "As my grandmother says, everything's better with the merry widow."

"Who the hell is the merry widow?" Bronte asked.

"The champagne! Veuve Clicquot is French for merry widow."

"And of course you would know that." Bronte took a grateful sip. "Sarah, you are such a paradox. This office, or studio, or whatever you are calling it these days looks like a tornado just blew through, yet you have spontaneously produced a perfectly chilled bottle of the best champagne and two immaculate glasses from which to drink it. All I can say is, thank fucking you."

"Keep going."

"So, as you may or may not have gathered, that little fling with the duke has been rather difficult for me to, well, compartmentalize… this champagne is particularly restorative. I can't thank you enough."

Bronte sank deeper into the luxurious couch and took another sip, closing her eyes half-mast to further appreciate the delicate snap and flavor. When she reopened them, she saw the pink, orange, and purple sunset starting to color the sky behind Sarah's silhouette through the fabulous studio windows that made up the west wall of her second-floor space.

"Go on."

"I feel like I am at the best possible shrink appointment in Manhattan: champagne, sunset, and I can dump my heart out onto your beautiful carpet. So… whatever… I don't really even know where to begin, but suffice it to say I thought it was completely over with a capital *O* and I just bumped into him on Madison Avenue with some little blond British bimbo hanging from his arm and he looked at me like… as if… you know… as if we had been drinking coffee this morning and he was on his way home from work and what's for dinner, darling? For fuck's sake, here I am having the best fucking year of my career"—Bronte raised her glass to Sarah, which Sarah returned in kind with a wink and a wry smile—"and I'm feeling like I am all that and a side of fries, shaking my booty right out of Frederic Fekkai and hacking through this urban jungle with a goddamned, motherfucking Prada machete for chrissake. And then I bump into him and I am… fuck… slammed. I was a fricking deer in the fricking headlights. All my mojo was utterly fucking AWOL."

"Who is he, Bronte?"

"Max. His name is Max. What's he even doing in New York? I hope he's not actually living here. That would be just fucking perfect. I would bump into him and his bit of fluff at every fucking crosswalk. How can I be so mature in other areas of my life and so fucking juvenile about this? Oh, Sarah. He was so damn good in bed. That's the worst part. I didn't really even care about little Blondie... I almost blurted out something along the lines of, 'Want to meet up for a quickie while you're in town?' I mean that's just lust, right? Nothing more than animal magnetism, right?"

"Ummm. Not sure I'm really the one to ask about the animal stuff. I'm pretty much a grab-the-animal-magnetism-where-you-can-find-it-and-never-let-go kind of gal. But if you are more of the take-it-or-leave-it variety, then maybe a quickie would be the right thing for you."

"Of course, I would grab it and wrestle it to the ground if I had the courage, but the bottom line is I am your basic commitment coward. And I don't even mean long-term, connubial commit-ment... I mean even committing to *considering* connubial has me running for the proverbial hills. But this guy, I mean, I could really hunt him down and tie him up and hold him hostage in my apart-ment for a really long time before the police came. I mean, I think he would really like that."

Julie tapped on the door and then poked her head in. "Sorry to interrupt. Bronte, there's a really hot British guy named Max Heyworth downstairs asking to see you."

Sarah smiled broadly and said, "Please send him up."

"No! Fuck you, Sarah. Please don't! Julie, please don't let him up! I'm a mess," Bronte cried.

"You're going to have to see him at some point, Bron," Sarah said gently, "and he obviously wants to see you if he followed you up here."

Bronte's head swung around to Julie. "Is he alone?"

Julie smiled and leaned her head further into the office. "Yes. Tall. Dark. British. And totally alone," she said in a loud stage whisper.

Julie hovered at the door until Sarah put on her best fake-bitch face and said, "What the hell are you waiting for, then? I am your boss and I told you to send him up. Do it!" Sarah winked and Julie smiled as she shut the door and went to get Max.

"Oh, but you are so evil," Bronte growled. "You were supposed to be my friend, to protect me! Batten down the hatches and all that. You will pay so dearly for this. I think your heels might accidentally break off on your way up the podium stairs to accept your CFDA award tomorrow night, you little—"

Sarah purred as the door opened: "Hello. You must be Max." She reached out to shake his hand then forged ahead. "What a pleasure to finally meet you. I've heard so much about you. Care for a glass of champagne? Bronte and I were just toasting my nomination for the CFDA accessories award tomorrow night."

Sarah turned casually back to the cabinet where she kept the Waterford champagne flutes, poured Max a glass, and handed it to him with her best air-hostess smile. Bronte rolled her eyes, then turned her head back to look at the brilliant colors of the sky, her crossed leg resuming its quick, annoyed kicking.

"So," Sarah prompted.

"Thank you for the champagne, Sarah," Max began graciously, raising his glass. "Congratulations on your achievement." Max took a sip of the cool, sparkling champagne, then held the flute by the stem between thumb and two fingers and rested the base in his other hand. He slowly turned his head enough to look at Bronte through heavy lids.

She refused to look at him.

He returned his gaze to Sarah and gave her his best ducal smile. "Sarah, would you mind terribly if I had a word alone with Bronte?"

"Absolutely not a problem! Let me just grab a few things and I will be out of your way in two shakes. Take your time. I have a million things to do downstairs so no rush whatsoever—"

"That's enough, Sarah!" Bronte snapped.

"Bye, you two," Sarah cooed as she shut the door firmly behind her. The background music of the hip shoe boutique wafted through the closed door, the muted voice of Morcheeba coolly encouraging everyone to be themselves.

Before Bronte could prepare herself, Max was sitting next to her on the buttery-soft, white leather couch. Dangerously close.

"Where's your… date?" she blurted.

"Jealous?"

"Probably. Pathetic, I know, but probably."

"Good to hear, because when I saw you on the street just now, looking this smoking hot"—his eyes traveled briefly down her body then back up to her eyes—"I thought you had to be seeing someone and my thoughts turned to murder."

Bronte's heart plunked right down into her stomach, her eyes closed miserably, and her head sank back onto the couch. Morcheeba was now on about how we all want some success but it's never around. How fucking true, thought Bronte.

Max just sat there staring at her. Drinking her in. He was speechless. What had he expected? That she would be holed up somewhere waiting for him? Well, maybe not in a cave, but he certainly did not anticipate this confident, sexy, fierce woman. She was so tense, he thought he could touch her with one finger and watch her explode.

Bad idea.

His mind immediately leapt to all the places on her body he remembered doing exactly that. She still sat with her neck stretched taut and her eyes closed in contemplation. He thought of the first time he had made love to her, with her neck stretched in ecstasy.

Lou Reed was up next, his übercool I-love-yous seeping through the door. *I am going to kill Sarah*, thought Bronte viciously. She heard the delicate clink of Max's glass being put down on the glass coffee table in front of the sofa, and she continued to sit there like a statue, unable to move, eyes closed. She nearly threw her own glass out of her hand when she felt Max's index finger trail down her exposed neck.

She was wearing a stiff-collared white shirt from Anne Fontaine that should have screamed Victorian schoolmarm, but had always made her feel rather naughty. Her short, navy, Marc Jacobs skirt had been another treat, she now realized, in the ongoing, self-prescribed treatments of retail therapy in which she had indulged since moving to New York.

After that, David Bowie and Freddie Mercury were screaming about giving love a chance. Bronte was going to see to it personally that Sarah was burned at the stake for the crime of playing DJ for young lovers.

"Aach, Max. Please don't do that."

He pulled away his hand abruptly and Bronte opened her eyes to look at him.

"What are you doing in New York?"

"Business. We have some investments here and my cousin wants me to sit in on some meetings. Strictly silent partner stuff. What about you?"

"I live here."

"Since when?"

"Since about two weeks after you left me." The words fell flat. "I mean, since two weeks after you left. I mean… well… you know what I mean."

"But… why didn't you tell me?"

She shook her head. "I don't know… I just couldn't see the point. You deserve so much more than I…" She stumbled over her words, then sighed. "I'm sorry, Max. I am so sorry. About your father. About everything."

"It's all right, Bron. I'm not here to badger you. It was all too much too soon for us, I guess." He didn't believe that for a minute, but if it was going to calm her down enough to get her back into his arms, he'd say whatever she needed to hear. "Maybe it is good we had the year apart. I had to spend endless months with the solicitors and the land agents and the stewards and my mother and sisters and brother and cousins and, well, perhaps we both needed that. But that's all behind us now."

She looked out the window and tried to hear his words, but the heat of his body was so close it was hard to concentrate. And he kept switching tenses. Was he saying it was all in the past? Herself included? Or was he saying his obligations were behind him? She felt so muddled.

He spoke slowly and gently, looking at his hands in his lap. "I suppose I could have called or pursued you, or whatever after all that settled, but it seemed like you and I were some sort of embalmed memory... that you had gotten your wish and I really was just the Transitional Man. So, after a few months had passed, I sort of figured the ball was in your court, you knew how I felt... how I feel... and that you were finished with me."

Bronte thought she might throw up.

She very carefully placed her champagne glass down on the coffee table next to Max's, then roughly wiped away the single tear that was trailing down her left cheek. She hated herself.

"Good God, Max. You make me sound like a beast. You know it wasn't like that. I was a wreck when you left, but I had just gotten over being a wreck when I met you and I just couldn't go there again. I called David and Willa the day you got back to England—as I had mentioned in my message, that's how I got your numbers—and I left you a message at your home, your *castle*, I mean, with that bitch of a housekeeper, and your message back just sounded so... far away. So cordial. So finished. I listened to that message over and over, searching for clues... should I call him? Does he still want me after I let him down? How could he?"

Max felt the heat of renewed possibility burn in his chest as Bronte continued.

"Of course, if I was a mature woman, I would have picked

up the phone and we would have struck up a perfectly friendly conversation, but I'm not mature. Especially where you're concerned... I'm like twelve. And then David and Willa made it pretty fucking clear you were one big royal deal back in jolly old England. I won't even go into the whole duke situation. I mean, give me a fucking break. How could you not tell me that? What would you want with some—"

"What the hell did David and Willa tell you?" he interrupted. "I asked them about you at my father's funeral and they were rather tight-lipped about everything. Said you had called for my numbers, almost as a courtesy. I assumed you had asked them to fend me off. What a fucking mess." Max's shoulders slumped forward and he ran one hand through his hair in an achingly familiar gesture. It was all Bronte could do *not* to rub her hands along his weary back.

"I want to put my hands in your hair so badly my fingers are cramping," Bronte whispered haltingly.

Max turned to look at her, mystified. "Then why *aren't* you? What do you need from me, Bron, to make it all right for you? Do you want a ring? Do you want a proposal? As far as I'm concerned, you already left me standing at the altar."

"That's a load of crap and you know it, Max. We *never* talked about the future—"

"Only because it was one of your stupid stipulations—"

"We never talked about kids, where we would live, how we would live, what the fuck? I mean, seriously! Just like that, *poof*, we get married and all that shit just miraculously works itself out? And I would be a duchess? A duchess who says the word *shit*."

"Pretty much. Yes."

"Even now you're acting like I've rejected you and you've never really even asked me to do anything specific except pack a bag and hop on a private plane with you a year ago. What are you really after, Max? You want the whole deal? Or do you want to have some more great sex—it was great, wasn't it?" Her voice cracked and he nodded. "Because if that wasn't great, then I am really *really* in deep shit. Because I thought it was the greatest—"

Max's patience snapped. He grabbed Bronte's head in his hands, pressing his palms against her cheeks, strong fingers pushing against her scalp, and gave her a good shake.

"Listen to me right now, Bronte Talbott. You know exactly what I want. I want you. I don't give a crap about any of that other *shit*, that's all your *shit*."

"Being a royal duke is your shit, not my shit—"

"I am not a royal duke!"

"You are royal. And you are a duke, aren't you?"

He gripped her harder. "Yes, but no!" He shook his head, flustered. "Bronte! Stop! I haven't been with anyone since I was with you. I can't even look at another woman without thinking of you. I came to New York on business and was going to fly to Chicago for a couple of days and try to accidentally-on-purpose bump into you. I am desperate for you. Even sitting here right now, it is torture not to rip that sexy-as-all-hell school mistress getup you've got on right off your smoking hot body. Let's go get married right now. Let's get in a cab and go to City Hall and get married. I want to be with you all the time. I want to hear you say fuck-fuck-fuck-fuck-fuck every time you are looking for your cell phone in that absurdly large bag of yours. I want to watch your face when I make you come—"

"Stop! Just stop it!" She shook her head out of his hold, pushing his forearms away with her own. "I haven't seen you, or even talked to you for that matter, in nearly a year, and just like that I'm supposed to drop everything? You are related to the *queen* for chrissake. That is not nothing—"

"Who's your great uncle's daughter?" Max blurted.

"What?"

Slowly, he repeated, "Who is your great uncle's daughter?"

Bronte looked out the window, knowing where this was leading. "I don't know. Brockhurst somebody, maybe."

"Well, that's how I am related to the queen. It's so tangential… it matters, of course it matters." He swept his arms toward the cityscape outside the window. "Out there, it matters. But in here? With us? Come on. I loved that you loved me for me in Chicago. It was just us. The two of us. Alone. No great uncles or even siblings or anything… remember?"

She bit at her bottom lip. She wanted to dive into his arms, of course she did. But Chicago with Max had been a complete vacuum. If her passion for the Texan couldn't survive the comparatively mild demands of daily life, how would her relationship with Max endure the scrutiny of… she couldn't even get herself to say it out loud. Royalty. Tabloids. Absurd. Speaking of which… "And what about your blond—"

"Bronte," he interrupted with a small smile. "I just proposed to you." He let his index finger run the length of her jaw and watched as her body gave her away, the muscles rippling at his touch. He felt a wave of joy surge through him. In that moment, he knew she was his, not that he was going to say that to her. Until she arrived at that conclusion of her own volition, hurrying her along would only prove counterproductive.

He got up slowly and pulled one of his shirt cuffs so it was even with the other at the edge of his suit coat.

"I will be in New York for a few more days. I'd love to see you. You can reach me at this number if you want to see me." He placed a small calling card on the coffee table next to her champagne glass. "No ultimatum. No threat. Just the truth." He leaned down, his lips very close to her neck but not quite kissing her, and whispered, "I love you, Bronte."

By the time Bronte had recovered her senses, all she caught

sight of was his retreating back as he turned out of Sarah's office. After Sarah showed Max out, she closed the front door to the shop and slid the lock home. She came up the stairs, peeked into her office at Bronte, and clicked her iPod remote to cue a woeful post-breakup ballad.

"Very funny," said Bronte through the tears that were now streaming unabated down her face. Fat, messy, sniveling, splotchy tears this time.

"Oh, Bron, it can't be that bad. He's hot as hell but there are other fish in the sea. You could have a new hot date every weekend."

Bronte didn't have the courage to blow her cool-girl cover and tell her friend that she hadn't even kissed anyone since she'd been with Max.

"Sarah, I think he just proposed to me... I mean, I don't think he did. He did. And I just sat here like a gaping fish that has flopped ashore, gasping for air. What kind of idiot doesn't accept a marriage proposal from the Duke of Northrop?"

Sarah's jaw dropped.

Then she screamed.

"Are you telling me that your Max is Sir Maxwell Fitzwilliam-Heyworth? The Duke of Northrop? Oh, Bronte!" Sarah actually squealed with glee. "This is simply too delicious! I've heard his younger brother is quite the tasty morsel. Do you think you could introduce me someti—"

"Earth to Sarah! Grow up! On the one hand, you are a successful businesswoman who quit school at seventeen to design shoes and eight years later here we sit in your shop on Madison Fucking Avenue. On the other hand, you have the emotional intelligence of an eight-year-old."

"That's right. And that's why I surround myself with brilliant, mature women like you to help raise my *E-I-Q*."

"I am not a mature woman, by the way. Sophia Loren is a mature woman! I am only five years older than you. Back off on the mature angle, thank you very much."

"At least you're not crying like a big bawling baby anymore."

Sarah's accompanying smile did have a wonderfully calming effect on Bronte's frayed nerves. Having spent her entire short life bucking every expectation that had been made of her, Sarah was not really the emotional eight-year-old that Bronte accused her of being. In fact, Bronte's utter lack of trust in the male of the species held her place far more securely in the emotional immaturity hall of fame.

Sarah refilled their glasses of champagne and passed Bronte's flute back to her.

"Let me gather up all my crap and we can go get a drink-drink at that sexy new bar around the corner. Okay?" Sarah leaned away from her desk and began sorting through the papers she wanted to take home with her that night.

Bronte let her mind wander as her tears abated. She had recently read an obituary about a novelist who wrote primarily about what would now be referred to as her dysfunctional family. Back in the seventies, an interviewer had asked about her inspiration, and she had remarked—rather blithely, Bronte thought—about her father's rages that would sometimes last for three days at a clip. Bronte had to turn the page of the paper before the red heat of anger, shame, and embarrassment washed over her, right there on the Lexington Avenue subway.

Her own father's rage had seemed like a constant hum in the background of her life. Percolating. Occasionally shutting off and on like the central air-conditioning in her apartment, but only in order to maintain the same constant temperature of antagonism, resentment, and fury.

Lionel Talbott had died of an aneurysm during Bronte's freshman year at Cal, when, after a year and a half away, Bronte had finally come home for Christmas. She had gone through all the motions of grief, but ultimately Bronte had been relieved he was gone; there had just been too much about him that she despised for her to pretend otherwise. She had headed back to Berkeley nine days after the funeral and resumed her classes without even telling her roommate what had happened.

Her mother, on the other hand, had been devastated.

Bronte was an only child, and she and her mother had always been painfully close—an intimacy that was partially fostered by the need to bolster one another against the constant negativity that Lionel's grim presence rained down upon them.

He had never beaten them or anything. *He was an academic, after all*, Bronte thought snidely. He was far too intelligent to bother with physical abuse; it would be like asking a surgeon to use a blunt instrument. He was just mean.

Bronte's mother was one of the top English teachers in the New Jersey public school system, but her father had never ceased to remind her that she was only a "schoolteacher," not a "professor" like he was. The fact that he had not professed jack-shit for nearly ten years before his death didn't seem to bear close inspection, at least to his way of thinking.

After the Princeton showdown and Bronte's subsequent departure for California, however, Cathy and Lionel Talbott had mended much of their broken relationship. Bronte didn't like to look too closely at the fact that her absence may have accounted for her parents' renewed happiness.

Eleven years on, Bronte still battled with those unresolved feelings. Should she feel sympathy for him, for what was probably a legitimate chemical imbalance? Should she try to imagine the Rhodes Scholar full of promise that he had once been? The one her mother first fell in love with? Fuck that. Everyone thinks they're fucking top drawer when they're twenty. The trick is to get on with your life.

On her more spiteful days, Bronte wished that he had lived to see the anti-intellectual path she had chosen. Ever since she was a thirteen-year-old girl flipping greedily through highly-prized issues of *British Vogue*, *Hello!*, and *Harpers & Queen*, she couldn't wait to get into advertising, an industry her father had always held up as the pinnacle of bourgeois mediocrity. He would have probably said, "It is the sine qua non of capitalist groupthink being imposed upon the masses." Or some such pedantic rubbish.

She had told her father that she was going to make lots of money encouraging people to buy things they didn't need. In fact, she wasn't only going to encourage them, she was going to make them feel downright evangelical about products that had no lasting value whatsoever. But the real reason, when Bronte was perfectly honest with herself rather than motivated by spite, was that she truly believed that everyone deserved to have a little personal fantasy. And if a silky shampoo could make a woman feel like a princess, or a certain stylish shoe could make a man feel like a prince, then what was the harm? Wasn't everyone entitled to that little, temporary fairy tale?

Sarah was one of the few people who understood Bronte's ambivalent feelings about her dead father. Something about the way Sarah simultaneously loved and defied her own father had triggered a confession reflex in Bronte one night between her fourth and fifth margarita at Tortilla Flats. The irony of it all, of course, was that despite her father's ceaseless bombardment of negativity and pessimism, Bronte was a card-carrying optimist.

When she had first arrived in California, she had been like a pig in shit. All that endless sunshine and good vibration crap was right up her alley. She may swear like a goddamned pirate, but even that was just because she liked the *energy* that went into it. It made her feel alive.

Once her father died, she was free to be the Pollyanna she secretly was. To go after her own personal fairy tale. She had decided she would prove to him posthumously that a person could be smart *and* happy.

Which was all well and good in the abstract.

But when sticky emotions got involved, or other people's incomprehensible needs started to squeeze out the sides of the relationship sandwich… well, suffice it to say, Bronte didn't like that part. She'd had a couple of casual boyfriends in California, but anytime it started to get even remotely serious ("Hey, let's drive down to L.A. and you can meet my parents…"), Bronte quickly lost interest.

She had seen a therapist for a couple of years when she moved back to New York after college, but he was such a weasely Freudian that she had finally called it quits (he was turning into one more demanding relationship, after all).

And then she met Mr. Texas.

And then Max.

"I am as clueless about men and relationships as I was when I was thirteen," Bronte croaked. "I apologize, Sarah; that makes you way older than I am in the emotional intelligence department. I would be happy to introduce you to Devon Heyworth if I ever get the chance. Thanks for the champagne, doll, but I am just not up for going out."

With that string of non sequiturs, Bronte picked up her absurdly large bag, took Max's card off the table, and headed home to her apartment to sleep on her satin pillow so she didn't mess up her Fekkai'd hair for tomorrow's final pitch to W. Mowbray & Sons and her big night at the CFDA awards with Sarah.

Chapter 8

SATIN PILLOWCASE OR NOT, Bronte did not get the sleep of the just that night. She went over her Mowbray presentation at least seventeen times, then tried everything in her insomniac's bag of tricks: eyes open, eyes closed, palms flat on the bed, legs crossed, legs uncrossed, arms across her chest, lying on her side, lying on her other side, getting up for a glass of water, putting those idiotic fuzzy little socks on because her feet got cold when she got the glass of water, eyeshades, white-noise machine, silence, window open, window closed, trying on sexy Josie Natori satin pajamas, pretending that Max was caressing said satin pajamas, getting distracted by said fantasy of Max and the pajamas, dozing for a few minutes after said distraction.

At four thirty, she finally capitulated and decided to start her day.

Today would be a new beginning, she decided. She was going to nail the Mowbray pitch to the fucking wall, look like a goddamned supermodel at the CFDA ball, and meet some anonymous Prince Charming on the dance floor and invite him back to her place to screw. She knew there were women out there who were perfectly capable of such things… why couldn't she be one of them?

She would *not*, on the other hand, allow herself to indulge in her mushy adoration of one particular duke who would only come to despise her after her hipster veneer cracked and exposed the affection-starved, possessive, compulsive lover she knew lurked dangerously close to the surface. If he pushed too hard, he would see her for the desperate, weak, craven woman she was where he was concerned—and what could be more repellent than that?

She stripped her bed with a bit more force than necessary and then made it up with an insanely expensive set of French sheets—retail therapy extended far beyond mere clothing, she'd discovered over the past year; high-quality home goods were beautifully rationalized away as a form of healthy, nurturing, self-esteem-building.

She took extra pleasure in the fact that she could luxuriate in a deep, steaming hot bath, on a Thursday no less. She headed out of her apartment at 6:00 a.m. with a laundry bag to drop off with the doorman for pickup later and reminded herself again how much she loved her life—*this* life—not the imaginary life of a duchess or, as her mother would say, some such nonsense.

This was the fabulously organized, clean, independent life that she had been planning for since the very first time she had read Simone de Beauvoir.

This was the life that served as an iron-clad refutation to depressed, insulting fathers everywhere.

As the debacle with Mr. Texas proved, straying into the murky waters of grasping devotion was just plain cloying.

She walked the twelve blocks to her favorite diner in the East Village. She armed herself with her morning essentials: crisp copies of the *Post*, *Times*, and *Journal*; an enormous, steaming cup of coffee; and an order of poached eggs and dry whole-wheat toast. She hardly ever made it out of her apartment or to the office before ten, so the world that populated lower Manhattan at six thirty in the morning was a novelty.

There seemed to be a hushed sobriety about the place, as opposed to the mid-morning fracas she normally encountered the other times she'd been there on Saturdays and Sundays. Instead of the usual forty or more chattering weekend customers she was used to, there were only four other people in the diner at that hour.

No background music.

The dull clank of industrial white restaurant plates being stacked somewhere in the back behind the grill. Bronte stared at the sweating water glass with crushed ice on the upper-right-hand corner of the white crepe paper placemat over the gray-and-black boomerang Formica tabletop.

She opened the silverware that was tightly wrapped in a white paper napkin and lined up the fork and knife on the left and right of the placemat. The series of movements forever reminded her of a guy she had dated for a while a few years back. He was one of those three-shrink-sessions-a-week New Yorkers who viewed every random act as a launching pad for profound navel-gazing. Because Bronte was a no-shrink-sessions-a-week New Yorker by that time, his profound interest in himself (thinly veiled as merited introspection) started to grate.

One night at a bustling restaurant on Eighth Avenue in Chelsea, when he saw her straighten her fork and knife methodically (as she always did), he had his ah-ha moment and declared, "*That* is why you need to see a shrink." Needless to say, that was their last date.

Bronte welcomed the arrival of her poached eggs, doused them with a generous portion of hot sauce, and set about rereading her W. Mowbray & Sons presentation notes for what seemed like the hundredth time.

Mowbray was a classic British menswear manufacturer that had been in business since 1854. The brand had always sustained a firm following with the upper crust through its bespoke division, and in the late 1950s, it had cofounded the British Menswear Guild with several other quintessentially British brands, such as Church's Shoes and Hilditch & Key. The consortium's goal at the time had been to export the idea of Britishness—the keyword that was the linchpin of Bronte's proposed advertising campaign.

She had already succeeded in selling the pitch to the company's ad buyers, marketing department, and board of directors. That morning at eleven, she was making her final presentation to the CEO and two of his majority shareholders who were flying in from London to help him make the final decision.

Following on the success of Sarah James's transformation from small-time Chicago storefront to international household name, Bronte had signed on four new major accounts in the fashion industry since opening the New York offices of BCA. When she heard that Mowbray was considering a similar rebranding in anticipation of its entry into the US market, Bronte picked up the phone and started harassing the CEO, James Mowbray. His great-great-grandfather had founded the business on a lark when he decided he wanted his own clothes made his own way.

No rags to riches story here, more of a riches to riches. The founder William Mowbray was a viscount and a close friend of Queen Victoria and Prince Albert; spent weekends at Pembroke Lodge with Lord and Lady Russell; frequently corresponded with an elderly Wordsworth and an aspiring Dickens; and happened to take a very keen, hands-on interest in his sartorial decisions. He hired four tailors to roam the Continent in search of the best fabrics and the finest techniques, then proceeded to set them up in a lovely village in Somerset to see to his personal tastes and, eventually, the particular requests of a few well-chosen friends. Over time, the scope of his influence widened, then transformed into a full-blown industry.

Bronte's proposed campaign managed to transform all of that lofty, unattainable "Britishness" into something perfectly attainable to anyone willing to spend $400 on a meticulously made collared shirt. Much as Ralph Lauren's original ad campaign had offered ready access to the elevated world of polo players and Palm Beach playboys, so Bronte's "Britishness" campaign would do for Mowbray: it would allow the common man to own a tangible piece of the elite.

The irony was not lost on Bronte that the entire campaign

served as a microcosm for her relationship with Max. In fact, when she finally pierced the veil that was James Mowbray's outer office and convinced him that it was in his best interest to hear her pitch, she was tempted to ask him if he knew one Maxwell Fitzwilliam-Heyworth. But then she thought she would have sounded like one of those idiotic people who, upon meeting someone from Arkansas, says, "Oh! I know someone from Arkansas!"

Ridiculous.

And what if he *did* know him? What was the punch line? "Oh, this one time, in Chicago, he and I used a hundred-pack of condoms in record time."

Bronte thought not.

She put some cash on top of the receipt for her breakfast, placed the salt shaker on top (as if it would blow away?), and decided to linger a bit longer over the newspapers. It was only eight o'clock in the morning after all; normally she would just be getting into the shower.

She flipped open the *Post* to Page Six and tsk-tsked in dismay. There in all of his tailored glory was the Duke of Northrop and *Lady* Lydia Barnes leaving La Grenouille after a "fabulous lunch," gushed the insipid Lydia. The picture must have been snapped mere moments before they came upon Bronte swearing endlessly into her bucket bag.

From the way Page Six swooned over these members of the British aristocracy, you would think the colonies had never left the benevolent protection of King George III. Who was probably Max's great-great-great-great-great-great uncle, thought Bronte dismally. Goddamned star-fucking *New York Post*. At least the gossipmongers had the good sense to mention Lydia's Sarah James shoes, Bronte reluctantly conceded.

Bronte slapped the paper closed in disgust, left it on the table, and collected the rest of her things. She headed out of the diner and hailed a cab to take her to her office in Midtown.

By mid-morning, the early summer weather was starting to heat up. She had gone over her presentation one final time in front of April and Carol. They rolled their eyes repeatedly, having already heard the absolutely, positively perfect pitch in every stage of the Mowbray pursuit.

Finally, Carol cut her off and said, "I have more important things to do than watch you preen!" She patted Bronte on the back much like a high-school basketball coach might before the big game. "Go get 'em, Bron. You've got it in the bag."

Mowbray had set up a small corporate office on Fifty-First Street, so Bronte decided to cover the four blocks on foot. She had her laptop and three extra hard copies of the presentation packet to give to James and his colleagues, and she had slipped her wallet and cell phone into her leather case rather than lug what was now officially The Absurdly Large Bag (preferably said with a haughty British accent).

She made the walk at a leisurely pace so she wouldn't show up with a glistening sheen of sweat on her brow, then turned into the revolving door that led into the center of the multistory atrium lobby of the building. She checked in with the security guard, put on her visitor pass, and headed for the elevator bank that led up to the Mowbray offices.

She rechecked her appearance in the golden reflection of the inside of the elevator doors and thought at least she didn't have anything to complain about in that department. She had decided to stick with the sassy-schoolmarm aesthetic she had going yesterday, today wearing an even starchier white broadcloth shirt with an even stauncher collar, clunky gold necklace and bracelet, and snug black pants and maybe-a-tiny-bit-too-high-for-daytime black pumps that, nonetheless, made her legs go to epic lengths.

She took a deep breath as the high floor approached, exhaled with concentration, then, once the elevator doors had opened completely, stepped out into the lobby with a smile for the charming receptionist she had met during her two previous visits.

"Hello, nice to see you again. I am Bronte Talbott from BCA here to see James Mowbray, please."

"Yes, of course, he is expecting you. He is just finishing up his ten o'clock meeting. If you'd like to take a seat, I will bring you to the conference room in a moment, Ms. Talbott."

Bronte waited in the lobby of the modern, immaculate offices of W. Mowbray & Sons and began to abstractly contemplate the rest of the day. After she slam-dunked this pitch (no point in false modesty when you were talking to yourself, she reasoned) she might just ask James Mowbray if he had any interest in escorting her to the CFDA gala that night. What better way to do a full, one-hundred-gigabyte memory wipe of one British dream man than to substitute him with another equally charming British dream man?

As if summoning the substitute dream man into existence, the receptionist's phone rang and she picked up the call with a smile and a glance toward Bronte. She replaced the receiver after a few seconds, then rose from behind the desk, coming around front and quietly gesturing for Bronte to follow.

"Right this way, Ms. Talbott. Mr. Mowbray is available to see you now."

Bronte always entered a state of heightened awareness at times like these; she was reminded of football players, helmets in hand, walking ape-like down the darkened tunnel leading out to the overbright stadium, the swell of the crowd rising in anticipation— that moment of darkness and inner quiet, and a little fear, quickly shaken off and tossed (until the next time) into the rapid current of forward action.

In what Bronte had initially mistaken for a moment of complimentary weakness, her father had once likened her to a shark. (*Good*, she'd thought, *killer instinct*.) Then he had gone on to elucidate: blind, constant, relentless forward motion, water over the gills... or death.

Bronte did live in a world of swirling, infinite motion. She frowned momentarily, then brought herself briskly back to the present. She took a few deep breaths as she stared down at the immaculate, soundless, gray carpet that passed beneath her feet on the way toward Mowbray's conference room. She shook the mild annoyance she felt at the thought of her father's noncompliment and entered the conference room with what could only be described as a swagger, reaching her free hand out to clasp James's with genuine warmth.

"It's such a pleasure to see you again, Mr. Mowbray." She beamed.

"As it is to see you, Ms. Talbott. And, please, do call me James." For fuck's sake, did he have to sound exactly like Max? That British purr was deadly.

"Please, call me Bronte. Please." She smiled, genuinely as it happened.

"All right then... Bronte. We are all looking forward to hearing your pitch and moving forward with our final decision on the campaign."

"As am I," she said through a soft laugh. "Oh, and before I forget, I do have—not that this is meant as any inducement, or anything"—soft laugh—"but my client Sarah James has an extra ticket to the CFDA gala tonight at Lincoln Center if you or one of your colleagues would like to go."

"It turns out we decided to purchase our own table—as it happens—with the British Menswear Guild. So we will look forward to seeing you there. But I do appreciate the offer... genuinely." He smiled. *Was that an extra moment in the glance? Nice.*

"Ahem." A deep voice sounded from behind the door.

James held Bronte in his smile for half a second more, then let his glance slide over her shoulder to where the other people stood.

"Bronte Talbott, please allow me to introduce you to my most trusted colleagues"—professional smile—"and silent partners: my sister Gwendolyn Tate and my—what is it technically, Max?—my second cousin once removed, Max Heyworth."

Then, there was that wonderful, hideous moment when the air left the room, her breath left her body, and she turned in flash-frame slow motion to see Max, previously concealed on the other side of the door that James had opened to let her in.

Wooosh!

Okay, at least the return of oxygen is something to be grateful for, Bronte thought as the color drained then returned to her face.

Max smiled his best you-can't-escape-me grin and reached out his hand, leaving it up to her to say whether or not they knew each other.

"Of course, Max. It has been a while. How are you?"

Of course James's second cousin once removed would be Max. It wouldn't be a three-hundred-pound septuagenarian with hairy ears, would it? Of course not. And her absurd invitation for James to join her at the CFDA ball tonight? *Fabulous*, she thought bitterly.

"Quite well, thank you. And you?"

Pissed off like a motherfucking alley cat. "Very well, thank you."

Bronte felt the pressure of James Mowbray's gaze as he looked from her to Max with a curious interest. "Aaah, so you two are already acquainted. Excellent." Mowbray's expression looking more resigned than celebratory. A moment later, he squared his shoulders, as if to clarify it was still *his* company the last time he checked, and broke up the little reunion. He put his hand near, but not on, Bronte's shoulder and gestured toward his sister.

"And this is my sister, Gwendolyn Tate… technically Lady Francis Tate, but we will dispense with the formalities."

Gwendolyn Tate was a lifesaver, and Bronte would never forget it. She briskly informed her male relatives to stop ogling the lovely Ms. Talbott and kindly allow her to set up her presentation and begin the pitch. While Max and James were turning to take their positions back at the other side of the long, highly polished mahogany conference table, Gwendolyn gave Bronte a conspiratorial secrets-of-those-who-know-how-to-handle-arrogant-British-males sisterhood wink, then told her how much she had enjoyed the information she had seen so far of the BCA pitch.

"Ms. Talbott—"

"Please call me Bronte."

"Yes, then, Bronte, I have looked through all of the mock-ups for your print ads and am very much looking forward to seeing your presentation. It is most likely I who will be overseeing that aspect of the American launch, so I am particularly keen to get to know you better and ask a few more questions. Shall we begin?"

By that time, Bronte had opened up her laptop and connected it to the USB cord that fed into the projection system in the conference room. She double-checked that her remote control was working and moved over to the screen on the far side of the room to begin her PowerPoint presentation.

"The main push, as I see it," she began easily, "is the fortification of the brand. While Mowbray may be a household name among your loyal British clientele, it is still a somewhat rarified one here in the United States." *Click.* "The message needs to be both bold and traditional, and after speaking with James at length about your intentions here in the US market, I believe this is the best course." *Click, pause, click.* "I think we should play on the American perception of the romantic British heroic ideal—Byron, Mr. Darcy—brought with confidence and cool into the twenty-first century." *Click, pause.* "The way to visually convey that would be through a series of eight to ten very recognizable, let's say iconic, mid-twentieth-century British images in black and white." *Click, pause, click, pause, click.* "Then to superimpose very bright, contemporary images from your latest collection over those original ones. This image…"

Bronte knew the pitch cold and hit it on all cylinders, despite the fact she could not hear the sound of her own voice. By keeping her focus almost entirely on Gwendolyn Tate, she was able to remain professional and on task for the full thirty minutes. On the few occasions she forced herself to glance in Max's general direction—he *was* in the room, for God's sake—she was miraculously able to remain calm, letting her gaze slide coolly away from his dubious stare.

Bronte finished up by speaking about estimated budgets, timelines, and some relevant magazine deadlines. After a few final questions from James and Gwendolyn (thankfully, Max kept his mouth shut), Bronte wrapped with a pert, "Thank you again. BCA would be proud to partner with W. Mowbray and Sons."

She shook hands again with James and Gwendolyn, and reluctantly with Max, then turned to gather up her laptop, undo the patch cords, and put her extra presentation papers away. The other three headed for the door.

Bronte was sliding her computer back into the sleek, navy leather case she adored—more recent retail therapy at Bottega Veneta—when she accidentally dropped her small remote control on the floor and it skittered under the conference table. Thinking she was alone, she squatted unceremoniously, butt in the air, trying to retrieve it when she heard the door close solidly behind her. She bumped her head on the underside of the conference table with an undignified thwack accompanied by the obligatory, "Fuck."

Max was standing right behind her.

Alone.

"Could you not stare at my ass, please?" Bronte, on all fours, looked back up at him over her shoulder and turned bright red, immediately reminding herself, and him, she suspected, of all the fun they had had in exactly that position many times before. An instantaneous pull of sexual tension crackled between them.

She turned quickly, remote in hand, and sat cross-legged on the floor, pulling her hair around and in front of one shoulder (in a practical, not sultry, way, she assured herself). Her black fitted pants stretched to accommodate the unbusinesslike position. Max sat down on the floor in front of her and smiled suggestively.

Bronte was not amused.

"So did you know I was going to be making this pitch when you *accidentally* bumped into me then followed me into Sarah James yesterday? Is this some sort of joke to you? I know my $150,000 salary is probably like the equivalent of, what, your mother's Bentley? But it provides quite a satisfying well-rounded life for little old me. So if you are going to dangle this account as some sort of carrot—"

"Hold on, Miss Paranoid. I had no idea you were making the pitch until you walked in this room and started hitting on James." Deadly smile. "My aforementioned cousins, James and Gwendolyn, merely asked me to sit in as a favor. I was in New York for a meeting earlier this morning to go over some labor negotiations and project finance on another deal. James was already one hundred percent in your court, but didn't give me any details other than he worried that the ad exec might be a little too, what was the word he used… fiery. Yes, that was it, fiery."

"I like that. Fiery. I might have to use that in my bio. Nice picture on Page Six, by the way."

"Listen, Bron, about yesterday…" He paused for an eternity. "Aren't you going to interrupt me?"

"No, actually, I'm trying to turn over a new leaf. In my vain attempts to embrace Brutal Honesty, I think I may inadvertently frighten people. I'm trying to be more open, more patient." She punctuated that last bit with her best Pollyanna smile.

"Very well." He stared at her, first quizzically, then almost scientifically, narrowing his gaze. After another nearly excruciating silence, he added, "I, well, don't you want to say something?"

"Not particularly."

"Jesus, you are a tough nut, lady."

"Oh, that reminds me, there is one thing I meant to ask you. Should I refer to you as 'Your Grace' or is that only in Regency romances?"

"Bronte, stop it."

"What?"

"Never mind." Max got up and stretched his legs. "By the way, I am joining James and Gwendolyn at the CFDA awards tonight, so I will keep an eye out for you and Sarah James. That part I *did* know about when I saw you at her place yesterday, but I've been having a hell of a good time since then imagining what you will be wearing and how tall you are going to be in a pair of her shoes. Didn't want to spoil my anticipatory fun, now did I?"

Bronte growled as she got up, ignoring the hand he offered. "I am going for my fitting now if you must know."

"Say no more. I want to be surprised."

"Don't you want to escort me, Prince Charming?"

"Alas, I can't. I already have a—"

"I was only playing along, Max. Please. Whatever. I will see you there. Or not. Whatever. Please tell your cousins it was a pleasure and I will be available for any follow-up questions they might have."

Bronte had finished gathering up her stuff and was headed toward the door. Max crossed his arms in front of his chest, leaned his hip against the side of the conference table, and watched his future wife strut away in a fabulously sexy huff.

And then he smiled, really smiled, for the first time in almost a year.

Chapter 9

IT TOOK EVERYTHING SHE had not to stab repeatedly and maniacally at the elevator button in the Mowbray reception area. Bronte gave it one firm push, leaned up on the balls of her feet then back down again, and smiled in a friendly way toward the nice receptionist. She smiled back. The seconds plodded on. The elevator dinged then opened. Still no maniacal pushing.

Yet.

The elevator doors closed.

"Fuck-fuck-fuck-fuck-fuck-fuck-FUCK!" With a satisfying jab at the L button punctuating each exclamation, Bronte felt her frustration begin to slip away in time with the descent of the elevator. *Damn him*, she thought to herself. He was so fucking smug. So perfectly composed. Not a care in the world. Mr. Cool Breeze. Fuck.

Bronte went over the scene in the conference room and her mood started to improve. The pitch had gone perfectly. Gwendolyn practically gave her the thumbs up. James was on her team from day one. Max would *never* do anything to mess with her job, no matter what she had implied in her little snit when she was alone with him in the conference room.

Better to shake it off. She had done her best. Either BCA got the account or they didn't. It was out of her hands. The elevator doors opened and she headed out onto Park Avenue, the warm summer sun smoothing her jagged nerves.

She reached for her cell phone and called Cecily in Chicago.

"Hi, Cecily, it's Bronte. I just got out of the final pitch to Mowbray and I think it went really well."

"Oh, we all knew it would. Well done. Are you ready for the CFDA awards tonight?"

"Yes. I'm on my way to Valentino now to pick up the dress."

"Perfect—oh, there's Mowbray on the other line. Great work. Call me tomorrow, Bron." The line went dead and Bronte walked the few blocks to Valentino, thinking that she should have been feeling far more victorious than she was.

By six o'clock, she had rebounded completely. Decked out in an haute couture floor-length black Valentino satin gown, Bronte felt utterly invincible.

Three hours later, she was making a beeline for the ladies' room. She locked herself in a stall, lowered the toilet lid, and sat down, deflated.

Dress or no dress, she was a mess.

She had laughed, and mingled, and smiled, and made small talk, and poked at her dinner, and whooped when Sarah James won, and she felt like her face was going to crack right off. She tried to stop herself from hyperventilating, hands hung limply between her knees, chin on her chest, when the high-pitched giggles of two women floated into the bathroom.

"But, Lydia, you're so lucky. He is absolutely scrumptious."

"Oh, Pen, stop. He's not scrumptious. He's a grown-up. The good news is I think he's going to give me the keys to his place tonight."

"Eeeeeee! Lydia, aren't you excited? You are going to have a blast. Mmmm, this lipstick is to die for. Do you want to try it?"

"Sure, pass it here."

Bronte couldn't stand another minute of their inane chatter. She made her way out of her stall and over to one of the wash basins, hoping that Lydia wouldn't recognize her from their brief introduction on the street yesterday.

No such luck.

"Ms. Talbott, is that you?"

"Yes, Lydia. Hello."

"Pen, this is the woman I was telling you about, who has done all the fabulous ads for Sarah James. Ms. Talbott, please allow me to present Lady Penelope Blandford. Penelope, Ms. Talbott."

"A pleasure to meet you, Penelope. If you two will excuse me."

Bronte emerged from the bathroom with far more force than she had intended and barreled straight into Max's all-too-familiar chest. She had already seen him once or twice—okay, about seventeen times—across the ballroom, but the effect of the Duke of Northrop in a perfectly fitted tuxedo at very close range was nothing short of devastating. He had clearly been waiting patiently to escort Lydia and Pen back to the ballroom and was disconcerted to have Bronte lurch into his arms instead.

"James says he gave you the good news this afternoon about the Mowbray campaign," he blurted, hoping to adopt a business-casual tone, when, in actuality, he came off sounding like a stilted, arrogant prig bestowing his patronizing good wishes upon her.

A silence fell around them.

Max was finished accommodating her paranoia any longer. Her upper arms were resting securely in his grasp and apparently she was saying something, but he failed to parse the words through the fog of his own longing.

"…yes… he called… he… we are really grateful for the opportunity to…" Then she simply stopped talking and breathed, a whisper, "Max…" swaying helplessly toward his warmth.

Just then the bathroom door swung open with a giggly, frothy commotion: Lydia and *Lady* Penelope emerged, both showing the effects of not a little champagne. Even though the feel of Max's hands on her had brought about a distinct thaw, much about Bronte's demeanor this evening had screamed pure glacier. Lydia's giggles quickly faded into an awkward silence as the pretty young thing looked askance at the duke and then at the pillar of ice that was Bronte, and then back to Max.

"Excuse me, Max…"

"Lydia." Max had released Bronte's arms but kept one warm hand at her lower back, his thumb touching bare skin where the dress plummeted provocatively. "Please mind your manners. Bronte, please allow me to make a formal introduction. Lady Lydia Barnes, Miss Bronte Talbott. Bronte, please meet Lady Lydia Barnes, my sister's daughter."

Lydia made a small, contrite curtsy and Bronte just stood there feeling like a ten-foot-tall American brute. Penelope made a little hiccup-giggle that broke the moment, and Lydia asked Max if he would mind if she spent an hour off on her own checking out all the movie stars and then head home on her own. Max gave his young niece a quick peck on the cheek, handed her the keys to his flat, and told her to enjoy herself. "But mind the champagne, Lyd!" he called after her.

Then he turned the full weight of his attention back to Bronte.

He put his other hand on her forearm to guide her toward a private-looking area a few yards away, and Bronte gave a silent prayer of thanks for her full length gloves. His warmth at the small of her back was intoxicating enough; she wasn't sure she could have handled his touch against her bare wrist.

As they sat down on a modern, kidney-shaped sofa in a shadowed alcove, Bronte was momentarily consumed with the idea that she was going to faint. Her four-inch heels were starting to dig into her ankles and she hadn't eaten much since those poached eggs fifteen hours ago, come to think of it.

"Have you eaten anything recently?" Max asked, his hand gently rubbing one of her glove-clad arms.

"I hate that you can do that."

"Do what?"

"Answer my exact thoughts. Here I am pondering the straps of these infernal shoes, which are, at present, digging into my ankles mercilessly, wondering how you can look so fucking hot in that tuxedo and whether or not I remembered to eat today, and then you go and do *that*... that..."

"Oh, Bron..."

"Please, Max, I don't know how this all got so fucked to hell. You were supposed to be my TM, remember? Not some perfect dream guy... and a fucking duke no less... what's up with that? How are there still goddamned dukes running around? Are you an imperialist invader? Do you pillage?"

"You I might pillage. But as a rule? No."

"And that offhand remark, that's exactly what I am talking about... you might pillage me... where do I go with that?"

"Back to my place?"

"Stop the banter."

"It's not banter, Bron. I'm crazy about you. My brother finally had to take a swing at me after I practically screwed up some of the most delicate negotiations yet with our agricultural unions and all because I am trying to respect *your* wishes. To pretend that everything that transpired in Chicago was some sort of alternative universe. That all the time we spent together, all the time we spent in bed, never happened. That you are now some hotshot advertising powerhouse and that I never had my tongue—"

"Stop!" Bronte actually put her hands over her ears, which in hindsight was probably a mistake because the motion of her upturned arms strained the already crushing bodice of her dress, forcing her breasts together and up and nearly out of the tight silk fabric.

Then, as if in slow motion, Max leaned forward and lightly kissed the swell of her left breast, the back of his head and his thick dark hair sweeping under the sensitive part of her exposed upper arm. Excruciatingly erotic.

Bronte's eyes eased shut and her head fell back—she couldn't fight it any longer. She felt her naked upper back make contact with the cold, high-gloss, white enamel wall behind her and she gasped. Max captured her lips with his as her hands made their way into his thick, achingly familiar hair and the corded muscles at the nape of his neck.

God, this was so good, she thought. It didn't matter if they were in her Wicker Park basement apartment or Sarah James's cluttered office or in this shadowy alcove at Lincoln Center: his lips felt so good on her, everywhere now, on the column of her neck, across her collarbone, back down to the rise of her breasts. Murmuring sweet words and Bronte's name, like a chant, the heat of his breath against her skin mesmerized her.

"Please, Bron. Let me back in. I promise…"

Red flag. Fire alarm. Ice water in the face.

Bronte's eyes opened with a flash as she pushed him back into an upright position.

"You promise what, Max?" Her breathing was ragged and shallow as she tried to get more air into her lungs. "I am still that same hard-hearted, stone-cold bitch you met in Chicago, remember? I don't believe in anything. I used to believe. Before I let myself get duped. Before I made a complete fool of myself and gave it all away to some asshole who didn't give a shit about me. So d-don't go around p-promising—"

"It is not like that, Bron," he said softly and soothingly, as if she were a frightened animal—she *was* a frightened animal, terrified actually—as his masculine, knowing index finger tentatively, longingly, traced the edge of her bodice, dipping into the fabric and across her bare nipple.

"You are a menace…" Bronte tried to sound dismissive, but it came out on a husky whisper that had exactly the opposite effect on Max.

"Quite."

"Max," she whispered desperately, as her head began to tilt back again, her seditious body wanting to give him everything. "It's like you are some sort of ghost lover. I forget who you are when you touch me like that. I mean, not that I forget…" She was unable to suppress a moan as his tongue and lips and teeth tugged at the upper edge of her bodice. She vaguely remembered that the dress was on loan and bite marks at the seams might be hard to explain.

"Mmm-hmmm," Max murmured encouragingly.

"It's more that all the externals fall away and it is only you, only the essence of you and the essence of me, when we are together. Do you really think that would stand up to the weight of our real lives?"

"I am sure you are making perfect sense," he whispered gently as he placed a tender kiss near Bronte's ear. "But at the moment, the words are not registering in my brain." He nipped at the pale, exquisite line of her jaw. "Good God, you are phenomenal."

"Max, I don't think I can hold off any longer… empty promises or not."

"None of my promises were ever empty," he whispered intimately through her hair, the heat of his warm, moist breath sending electric jolts all the way out to her fingertips and toes. "I'm the one who wants to marry you, remember? It's me, Max. Stop confusing me with those other guys. Or that other *guy*. I never did any of that to you."

"Where can we go?"

"Anywhere… my place… your place… a hotel… I will do whatever you want, wherever you want, as long as we are together."

She placed both of her palms on Max's cheeks and kissed him soundly, almost matter-of-factly, on the lips. As if to say, "Get ahold of yourself for now and let's get the hell out of here." He helped her up from her half-sitting, half-reclining position and twined his fingers through hers as they made their way back into the ballroom.

All of a sudden, it was just Max and Bronte walking around Chicago on a spring afternoon, hand in hand, without any of the external complications of families, work, obligations, and duty that had plagued them for the intervening months. They were both oblivious to the stares and comments that began reverberating through the room as Max-and-Bronte, the unit, made their way through the crowd.

Max kept Bronte firmly in hand, the two of them laughing and rushing down the long, wide piazza, past the fountain, and on into the cool, sparkling Manhattan night.

Paparazzi bulbs were flashing for some nearby celebrity who was also leaving, the lights vaguely registering in Bronte's subconscious mind. The two of them were like a juggernaut, an unstoppable train. Max hailed a taxi, pulled the door open, then hauled Bronte in, all in one smooth motion as he kissed her full on the mouth.

He yanked the cab door shut and the taxi took off for Gramercy Park. The flashbulbs of the receding photographers were the last thing she remembered before Max was undoing the zipper on the side of her dress and running his hands and mouth hungrily across her body.

Who am I to deny a starving man? she wondered as she savored the feel of his lips against her rapidly heating skin and frantically beating heart.

Chapter 10

BRONTE OPENED ONE EYE as her hand roved across the empty space and rumpled sheets next to her. Clearly she had imagined her fairy tale departure from the ball last night and Max was still a neatly compartmentalized Chicago memory.

"Hello, gorgeous."

Max's English lilt sent delicious shivers down her spine as she snuggled deeper into her voluminous white bedding and smiled behind the sheet, pulled up over her nose, bandit-style.

"Hello, handsome. What've you got?"

"Triple-shot latte for you and the *Post*, *Times*, and *Wall Street Journal* for us."

"Mmmmm. Coffee in bed. You are something else. How did you wake up so early?"

"I am invigorated."

"Really? I'm exhausted." Bronte reached over to her bedside table and placed her coffee down, closed her eyes, and started to curl deeper down into the bed. "Mmmm. What is better than this? Waking up to a hot man and a hot coffee and then dozing back to sleep for the rest of the morning. I've just decided I am going to give myself the day off. I scored a big account yesterday, by the way. I think I need to celebrate."

Max whipped off his now-rumpled tuxedo pants and white dress shirt—an outfit he had somehow transformed from early-walk-of-shame to slightly-scruffy Clive Owen—then crawled back into bed with Bronte, bringing her in close for warmth and just to feel the curve of her body against his. She started to breathe evenly, drifting back into the first stages of sleep with an angelic little smile on her lips and that soft humming exhalation that was so her.

He felt the stirring of desire return, then relaxed into the rhythm of her breathing, forcing himself to enjoy the very nearness of her, the reality of her creamy flesh in his arms, the gentle rise and fall of her shoulder. The pure joy and gratitude that he had her back, and this time he swore it was for good.

They had spent the entire night in a physical and emotional ebb and flow—the first rushed moments of their arrival, tearing at one another's clothes, barely making it to the bed, then Bronte laughing and sending Max into the bathroom to get the condoms out of the medicine cabinet.

When he opened the mirrored door, he saw the still-shrink-wrapped box and smiled to himself. Then, as he was closing the door, he noticed a three-by-five-inch snapshot taped to the inside of the cabinet door and stopped short. It was the two of them in front of the Ferris wheel at Navy Pier. He was still staring at it when Bronte made her way in to use the bathroom, giggling and trailing her touch along Max's naked back as she walked by. She caught his look.

"What?" she half-laughed, half-spoke.

"Nice photo, Miss Stone-Cold Bitch."

"Oh. Yeah. Well, what can I say? Maybe I have a soft, warm center where you are concerned."

She tried to scoot past him, but he turned and caught her in a warm embrace, kissing her with a possession, a gratitude that she couldn't even fathom. She pulled away with a happy gasp and chided, "Get back to bed and let me use the bathroom."

The rest of the night had been a mix of dramatic crests and peaks, punctuated by hours of intimate conversation about everything from

Max's childhood to Bronte's anger toward her father to how Max wanted ten children (or at least wanted to spend the rest of his life trying) and on and on until the early summer dawn began to creep through the window of Bronte's bedroom.

Bronte fell back to sleep after the early-morning coffee delivery, then woke a few hours later, disoriented but utterly rested. She stretched out her arms and legs to their full extension, making herself into an attenuated *X* in the middle of the bed. She lifted her head slightly to see Max in her living room, talking quietly into his cell phone, standing stark-naked in front of the large window overlooking Gramercy Park.

He ran his free hand absently through his thick, dark hair and turned slowly; the mere fact of her quiet awakening had registered in him somehow. He smiled just for her as he continued the business conversation he was having, with his brother, Devon, apparently.

"I know I said I'd be flying back today, Dev, but I bumped into Bronte and I think I am going to stay in New York for a little while longer… yeah, it's all good…"

What constitutes "a little while"? Bronte wondered to herself.

"Yes… mm-hmm… of course I will definitely be back in time for the final negotiations… yes… yes… just send any new contracts or demands straight to my private email and I'll be fully prepared…"

His smile widened as he continued to look at Bronte, and he walked slowly toward the bedroom. "Oh, sorry… is that better? Can you hear me now?" he asked as he turned back toward the front window and continued his conversation for a few more minutes. He finished the call, put the phone down on the coffee table, and made his way back into the bed.

"What time is it anyway?" She had no idea: Bronte had no clocks in her bedroom, relying instead on her cell phone as an alarm, and clearly *that* had never made it out of the evening bag that had been carelessly tossed on the kitchen counter when they fell into the apartment last night. She thought she had heard its muffled ring several times through the haze of sleep, but had happily ignored it.

"It's almost noon, you heathen. I finally got up around ten o'clock to make some calls before the offices in London closed altogether. Your phone has been ringing incessantly, by the way."

He had gently turned her onto her stomach and was drawing abstractly on her smooth back: down her spine, over her beautiful round ass, lightly between her legs, then trailing up her back, along her shoulders, then back down again, as if he were taking a stroll in the park. Her face was turned away from his, and she forced herself to bite her lower lip to prevent herself from moaning.

He was lying on his right side, his head resting in the palm of his right hand, while a single finger, sometimes two, from his left hand continued to make an aimless path around her rapidly heating body. It reminded her of the way he sometimes ran his finger up and down the stem of his wineglass, as he had often done in Chicago when they would eat dinner and have a normal conversation about their day. Innocently possessive.

But now she was the stem of his wineglass and there was nothing innocent about it. She was melting under his touch and he was talking about cell phones and offices and words that were no longer registering in her mind at all. She must have let out an involuntary groan when he stopped his ramble and straddled her from behind, half-kneeling around her upper thighs in a playful way. He leaned down to see her face and asked what she was thinking about, the strength of his desire obvious against her. She groaned again, deeper. *More Max*, she thought.

"Oh, Max, how can you possibly touch me like that and not know what I'm thinking about? I can't think of anything. I'm a puddle."

"Touch you like what?" he asked with more than a hint of mischief in his voice. He leaned away from her again. "Like this?" he teased as he slowly trailed a single finger between her legs. She was pinned to the bed in the most elemental and satisfying way. If he weren't sitting the way he was, her legs may have quivered or rippled in response, but as it was, the weight of him only intensified the center of her desire. There was no radiating pulse, only the hot deep center… and he was there.

"Or like this, you mean?" he asked, his finger slowly entering.

Bronte exhaled through her teeth, almost irritably, but with the most intense pleasure.

One finger, she thought dismally. *He could do this to me with one lazy finger?*

Her eyes rolled back and her lids fluttered as his finger withdrew and entered again. "Or that?"

"Mmm-hmmm," Bronte tried feebly.

"Was that a yes?"

"Mmm-hmmm," Bronte tried again.

"I think I need a more concrete response, Bron."

Her fingers were now clenched desperately into fists around the folds of the pillows and sheets within grabbing distance. "Please…" she whispered.

His finger was leaving her again, he was teasing her, rubbing his erection against her in a maddening way, taunting her, making her beg, and she didn't even care. She wanted to beg for it. And as that thought crossed her mind, she felt the moisture between her legs intensify. She wanted him so badly, her body wanted him so badly.

"Say it, Bron." He was lying along the length of her back now, his voice so close to her ear, it was almost as if it was coming from the inside of her head.

"I'll say anything, Max."

"Say you'll marry me, Bron."

"Put it in, Max."

"You have such a way with words, darling."

"*Please*, put it in."

He was moving cruelly, gently, sliding up and down, closer and closer. She was so ready for him. Nothing mattered. She was his already; whether she pretended she could avoid it or not, the reality trumped her feeble psyche.

"Yes, Max, I will marry you. But *please*—"

He had reached his hands around her hips to tilt her up to him, and on her final *please*, he thrust into her, both of them gasping with pleasure and satisfaction, as if they were consummating their love for the first time, as if they hadn't been rolling and panting and screwing like minks the entire night. He brought his hand under her body and touched her, again almost carelessly, because *of course* he knew her body like he knew how to tie his shoes, or how he liked his coffee… he just knew.

She came with such force, his hands gripping her: strong, possessive, inexorable. She was past speaking as he pulled out and firmly turned her over to face him, her hands flung wide, a fabulous vacant grin on her face as she slowly returned from the particulate world of her release. She sensed his hesitation before moving back inside her.

His arms were firm now, his hands gripping her hands.

"Look at me, Bronte. You're still on the pill, right?" His voice was almost fierce in its command, the deep resonance startling Bronte out of her dream state.

"Yes…"

"Do you mind if I don't use a condom? Just this once, as a little… prenuptial celebration…" He was poised above her, his arms straining, neck muscles taut.

"Yes. It's all good," she whispered, reaching her hands out of his grasp, to wrap them around his neck, to pull him closer. She had a momentary flash of worry—all that skin-on-skin business sounded dangerously close to baby making—but then reminded herself it was only a gesture really. She was protected.

She kissed him with all the love and depth and meaning that

coursed between them as he entered her, joined her, so slowly, with such sweet torture.

"You're coming with me, Bron…"

"Oh, Max, I'm spent… I can't…"

Then he started to move so deeply, so methodically. She had been so throttled by her last orgasm, she would have thought it was impossible to go there again… until the heat began to pool, the urgency rising. He was looking at her with such beautiful intensity, bringing her with him, the pleasure increasing again. He was gazing at her, loving her. He brought his mouth down to hers and kissed her, his tongue trailing like a feather across her lower lip, then dipping in, then trailing across her upper lip. She felt the pull, the need for him building inside her, until something raw and deep exploded through her.

Her moan of pleasure was lost in his kiss as she arched up to meet him for one final joining, then his face pulled away and he gasped, eyes lightly closed, growling in pure male satisfaction. He turned his head slowly to one side, his beautiful profile a silhouette above her, as she trailed one finger down the taut cords of his neck, flexed in his moment of sheer ecstasy.

She watched him intently, placing the palms of her hands lightly on his chest, pressing her thumbs against his hard nipples, as he thrust a few more powerful strokes in time with his final aftershocks. His body subsided, his comforting weight slowly coming down along the length of her grateful body. He nuzzled into her hair and she could feel his smile against the sensitive skin of her neck. She had a moment of clarity, without any of the panic she would have imagined, when she felt the unfamiliar sensation of her own moisture as well as his begin to ease out of her.

All this no-condom business was quite fine in theory— although Bronte was certainly too neurotic to make a habit out of it in practice—but just this once she was glad. It felt like the physical consummation of their words. It meant something beyond the biology. At that moment, Bronte really believed that they were actually a part of one another on some elemental level.

They both lay there. Quiet. Regrouping.

"Now that was a proposal," she finally declared.

His laugh was deep and low, rumbling through her neck. "I thought you'd go for something a bit more, well, straightforward, eh? No embarrassing billboards in Times Square or hot air balloons or anything." After another companionable silence, he lifted his head and looked at her with the alertness of a child. "I have an idea!"

"What?"

"Well, shall we do it today?"

"As far as I can recollect, we've already done it several times today."

"Very funny, Bron. I mean, shall we get married today?"

"Wouldn't want to rush into it or anything would we, Max?"

"Why, yes, I would. You're more skittish than a yearling at Tattersalls and I don't want you getting out of this bed only to forget—or talk yourself out of—the reality of what just happened. I asked. You accepted. End of story."

"I don't think Tattersalls still sells yearlings!" she laughed. "And what do you mean by 'end of story'?"

"They do still sell yearlings and you know perfectly well what I mean. No messing about."

"Won't your family expect a royal wedding of some sort? Horse and carriage and all that?"

"Probably, but I don't—"

"What do you mean by 'probably,' exactly? If I am going to be a, what, a *duchess* for chrissake—which reminds me, can duchesses say 'for chrissake'? Don't answer that. I mean, I need to know a little bit about what's expected of me."

Max rolled onto his back and smiled up at the ceiling. Bronte felt an immediate chill at his absence. *Great*, she chided herself, *he moves three inches away and I miss him*. This is going to be hell. She sat up to grab some of the sheets that had pooled at the end of the bed in the midst of their lovemaking and stretched her back as she reached down the length of her legs, letting her head rest there across her knees to get a full stretch, her forehead just below her kneecaps. Max rested his hand at the small of her back.

Aah, she thought, *contact*.

"What is it, love?" he asked quietly.

Bronte felt the tears come and made no attempt to stop them. "I just can't be held accountable for my actions, Max. I'm going to cling to you—"

"Oooh, I like the sound of that—"

"And I am going to wonder where you are all day, and I'm going to want to screw all the time—"

"It gets better and better—"

"And it's not *funny*," she said with a bittersweet smile, turning to look at him, her cheek resting against her legs as the tears simply ran down and her words were spoken through strained, swollen vocal chords. "What happens to me when—" She was starting to choke on her sobs.

Max sat up quickly and held her.

"Stop, Bronte. Just stop. Ssshhhh. Look at me." He was gentling her—just like he had said: a yearling at her first auction.

"What happens when—when you don't love me anymore?"

There.

She said it.

Now he knew her for what she really was: a paranoid thirteen-year-old girl trapped in the body of a woman.

Pathetic. Needy. Unlovable.

"Oh, Bron. You are daft. And I mean that in the most respectful way. Maybe I will do the Times Square billboard bit, just for the hell of it. As far as I can tell, I will never stop loving you. I don't know where you get these notions. Speaking of how you became you, I would very much like to meet your mother… perhaps we could take her out for dinner tonight."

Oh dear God. He was not getting any of this.

"Did you hear what I just said?" She swiped at the tears that were starting to abate as they left a salty itch along their path. Her despair was quickly turning to annoyance. "You are not listening to me. I will become cloying—"

"I love that idea—"

"I will become jealous—"

"Of whom? I will be with you all the time."

"Ugh. You're just not being realistic. You work in some very important capacities, I suspect, from the bits I've gathered eavesdropping on your conversations. I will want to work… don't you want to argue with me about that?"

"No. I love the idea of you being all schoolmarmy-sexy and clicking that remote control with your little bossy jabs and all those slavering toffs knowing that you are coming straight home to me. What else?"

"Bossy jabs?"

"Well, admit it. You were a bit annoyed that I was there yesterday at Mowbray and you were a bit hard on the remote control there a few times. Right?"

She was shaking her head and smiling despite herself. "What about your mother?" Bronte asked.

"What about her?"

"What if she hates me?"

"Luckily, she is not the one marrying you, so it's of very little relevance. What else?"

"Where will we live? What if I don't want to move to England? You can't very well abandon the duchy or dukedom or whatever you call it… wouldn't that be like abdicating or something?"

Max slowly raised one eyebrow and gave Bronte his best half-smile. "Are you saying you don't want to move to England? I suspect you are just playing devil's advocate. But for the sake of argument, let's spend a few years in New York if we want, or part of the year, or whatever. Keep this great apartment if we want. And as for the *dukedom*"—he nearly pursed his lips when forced to say the word out loud—"we are well into the twenty-first century, and just in case you missed the headlines when you were in grade school, the House of Lords was more or less purged in the early 1990s so, as Bertrand Russell once noted, a title is probably most useful for getting hotel rooms. What else?"

"Max, I can't just roll over tomorrow and become a duchess. It can't be that easy."

"Easy? Since the moment I walked out of your apartment in Wicker Park until the moment I bumped into you on Madison Avenue, this has been the worst time of my life. I lost you. I lost my father. I almost lost my mind, for that matter. I don't think any of this has been easy." He pulled her back from her forward position, tucking her in close so his back rested against the headboard and she was cradled in his arms. "All of the royal obligations or whatever you are imagining are no different from your work obligations. You'll see. You just treat it like a job to a certain extent. It can take up as much or as little time as you want. My mother has a social secretary who helps arrange ribbon cuttings and that sort of thing, but you'll see how you want to do it. You don't need to obsess about it. I promise. Plus, all of that is external. As long as the two of us are united"—he held her tighter—"none of it will matter in the way you think."

She leaned into him, trying to get herself used to the idea. All of it. The idea of leaning on him most of all. Her worries about running her day-to-day life as a duchess were nothing compared to her real terror about giving him her complete trust.

"It's not about that, though, is it, Bron?"

She shook her head no and buried her face into his strong, warm chest.

"So be as demanding, needy, craven, desperate, or jealous as you want and we can simply compare notes at the end of each day. I'm not going anywhere. I promise." He smiled at how fatuous the words sounded but lifted Bronte's face so she was forced to look him straight in the eye. "Get it?"

She nodded and let her head fall back to the comfort of his shoulder.

"So let's have dinner with your mom tonight, Bron."

"Oh, all right. But we're not getting married today. That's just too ridiculous. Plus I don't think my mom would ever forgive me. Let me call her about dinner."

Bronte kissed his chest and neck a few more times for good measure, then got out of bed and pulled on a flowing kimono-style robe, tying the sash loosely around her waist. She walked through the living room and into the small kitchen to retrieve her evening bag, grabbed it, and headed back toward the bedroom, unzipping the black, beaded clutch and pulling out her phone.

She pushed the button to turn it on.

"Fuck. What the hell am I doing with twenty-seven voice mails?"

"Um. I might know a little something about that…"

Bronte looked up slowly from her phone, tilting her head slightly to one side. "What little something would that be?"

"Now don't get upset, because I had nothing to do with it…"

"Oh for fuck's sake, what?"

"Go look at the *Post*…"

"Oh perfect. Did Sarah James get falling-down drunk and end up at some after-party getting hog-tied by Leonardo DiCaprio? Or did—" She stopped when she saw Page Six, left open on the coffee table. She sat down in slow motion on the edge of the couch.

"The Stars Were Out for CFDA," the headline blared, listing name after name of all the nominees and winners, including Sarah

James. The accompanying photo, however, took up almost a third of the page, showing Max and Bronte clear as day, holding hands like idiots and gazing at each other adoringly. "Prince Charming and Cinderella Leaving the Ball," the caption read. It elaborated: "Bronte Talbott, of BCA, seen here leaving the CFDA gala on the arm of the Duke of Northrop. He wore Mowbray; she wore Valentino."

"Well, at least they plugged Valentino. Sarah will be pissed they didn't credit the shoes, but they were fucking killing me so it serves her right." Bronte looked up from the living room and caught Max's eye. "What?"

"Are you upset?"

"Well, surprised maybe... I'm usually the one to the left and in the shadows, so it's more odd than upsetting, I guess. But, and I'd better get used to saying this anyway, we are getting *married* for fuck's sake, so people are probably going to know about us. Right?"

"Oh, Bron, you are such a romantic," Max replied with false sweetness.

"Very funny. Let me call my mother and put her out of her misery. She must be going nuts not hearing from me..."

She tapped the phone and brought it to her ear, swinging her hair out of the way, crossing her legs, and leaning back into the sofa.

"Hi, Mom, yes... I know if you... yes, they credited it correctly. Yes, he's right here actually and he wants to have dinner with you tonight... no, with me there also, Mom. You sure you don't need to check your calendar or anything? I'm just joking; don't get upset. All right... right... okay... I said, okay! Relax... so why don't we come out to New Jersey? Well I do. You don't need to redecorate the house for fuh—for goodness' sake—we'll just swing by and pick you up around six o'clock tonight and then we can go to dinner at that great Lebanese place over in Hoboken. It's perfectly fine, Mom; he doesn't eat with the Queen every night, only every other Thursday. Well, of course he heard me say that—he's sitting right here... believe it or not I think he likes that about me... Mom... Okay... Good, sounds great. We'll see you at six... love you too."

Bronte tapped the end button on her phone and looked up at Max again. He was smiling wickedly.

"I hope you are happy," she said. "That's one down and twenty-six to go. Who next? Carol and April..." She scrolled to her work number and brought the phone back to her ear.

"Yes, it's me... yes, I saw it, Carol... I know, great plug for BCA, right? Well, the Cinderella stuff I could do without, but he's pretty fucking hot, right?" Bronte winked at Max then returned her gaze to the paper. "Okay, sure... and by the way, I am taking the day off today..." After the pause of Carol's reply, Bronte laughed, a spirited, deep laugh, and Max contemplated the happy prospect of an afternoon spent with him lying in bed watching her juggle twenty-seven ten-minute phone calls.

He settled in with a paperback and simply savored the sight and sound of her: the fabulous resonance of her voice, the pitch of her laughter, the pause of her breathing, her conspiratorial glances at him. There was nowhere else he would rather be.

Four hours later, after they had showered and called a car service, they were headed to Max's apartment so he could change out of his Clive Owen day-after outfit. The car waited out front as the two of them went up the elevator of the beautiful prewar building on a tree-lined street on the Upper East Side.

"Why would we keep my apartment when you have this one?"

"Because I don't own this one. It's just a corporate flat for Mowbray. But nice, eh?"

The elevator doors opened onto a small landing with two identical doors, and Max headed to the right, ringing the bell and waiting for Lydia to open the front door. She pulled the door open slowly, with a hungover, unpleasant smile and then pulled the door wide to let them in.

"Well, if it isn't Prince Charming returned from the ball."

"Watch it, Lydia," Max said with a warning glance. "You don't look like you heeded my words of caution, so why don't we both call a cease-fire? Isn't it time for you to be getting back to England anyway?"

"Of course, it is time for *us* to be going back to England, Uncle Max. *We* are supposed to be going back tomorrow, remember?"

Max ignored her, walking directly down a long hallway: crown moldings over pale yellow walls; parquet wood floors that had been polished and repolished for decades; to the right, a lovely antique chest of drawers with an enormous bouquet of exotic flowers spraying about five feet into the air.

"Nice place."

Lydia turned back after shutting the front door to face Bronte. "So you and Max had an overnight playdate?"

"Are you being rude or merely impertinent, Lydia?"

"Neither. Just trying to make conversation. My grandmother called about fourteen times today looking for him and I just let it go to the answering machine, but truth be told, she sounded a little peeved. She's a bit highly strung, you know."

"Really. Are you trying to head me off at the pass or what?"

"I don't know how we got off on the wrong foot, Ms. Talbott, but I'm just trying to pass the time. Oh, hi again, Max." Lydia smiled her best cherubic, eighteen-year-old, peaches-and-cream smile. Bronte wasn't sure if she was a bitch or just bitchy.

Max had changed into jeans and a pale blue Oxford shirt and was reaching to put Bronte's hand in his when he turned to Lydia and paused with his other hand on the doorknob.

"If you must know, Lydia, Ms. Talbott and I are engaged to be married, so I suggest you cut the just-trying-to-make-conversation jag and keep your trap shut. If you dare tell your mother or grandmother the news before I have had the chance to do so, I will make your existence an utter misery. I will *not* be returning anyone's calls this evening. And you *will* be returning to London tomorrow, with or without me on the flight. You are perfectly capable of traveling on your own, and my baby-sitting days are over. Try not to make a fool of yourself if you go out this evening... and close your mouth."

With that, Bronte and Max left the apartment and closed the door. The elevator was still on their floor, opening quickly after they pressed the call button. They heard Lydia storm off down the hall as the elevator doors came to a close.

"Maybe she's just young and insolent, and not really mean."

"Of course she was being mean. Her mother is mean, my mother is, well, not mean exactly, but let's just say she tends to *participate* to the point of manipulation."

"Fabulous. This is going to be quite a treat."

"I don't expect you to be best friends with my mother, Bron. Let's just enjoy dinner with your mother and leave mine out of it for the time being."

"That's all well and good for the next three hours." Bronte strode across the sidewalk and into the waiting Lincoln Town Car, then resumed her train of thought. "But what happens when you decide to bring the little lady home to meet the masses?"

"Devon and Abigail are stupendous. The four of us will form a majority, as it were, leaving Claire and her idiot husband to mop up after Mother."

"Oh, Max, it can't be as Gothic as all that. Really."

"It's hardly Gothic, Bronte, it's just my mother. Her father raised her to believe she was entitled to everything the world had to offer, with no particular effort on her part. She doesn't have a maternal bone in her body, except as it relates to buying the most expensive clothes for her to wear in the *happy family* photos that are then immaculately arranged in sterling silver frames on the shelves of the library. Her role, and I have to reluctantly admit she performed it admirably, was to love, honor, and cherish my father.

Anything beyond that was, well, just beyond her purview. Children, logistics, details of any kind really were just annoyances that, were she to ignore them long enough, simply went away. While my father was alive, that was all well and good, I suppose. It's not the marriage I want"—he put an extra pressure on Bronte's hand that rested in his—"but I guess she gave him some sort of emotional ballast, since he did everything that might have naturally fallen to any other woman in her position. He ran the estates, ran the businesses, ran our education, ran, ran, ran… and she just stood by and looked beautiful and, as she often reminded us, went to the gargantuan trouble of birthing four children as part of the bargain."

Max paused for a long while, staring out the window as they made the approach to the George Washington Bridge, the Palisades looming in the early evening shadows, hazy copper light dancing on the Hudson River.

Bronte stared lovingly at his profile, recalling the moment earlier that day when he was above her, and reached out her hand to caress his cheek.

He turned and looked at her, then smiled shyly. "What?"

"I don't think I've really told you how much I love you. I do. Really love you, that is." She brought her lips to his in a tender, delicate sweep, then pulled back slightly to look into his eyes. "You know that, right?"

"Yes, but I certainly like hearing it. A lot." He brought his hand up to her cheek and kissed her solidly, gently pushing her head back against the seat of the car. She began to groan, then pushed him away.

"Mmmm. You are so good… but now is not the time. We're only about fifteen minutes from Mom's and, as much as I'd love to see that kiss through to its natural conclusion, I don't think now is the time. Did I just say that? So anyway, continue with your mom. Where does she spend most of her time now that your father is… gone?"

"London, mostly. She left Dunlear a few weeks after my father's funeral and I don't think she's even been back once. I do truly believe that she loved him—always true to him *in her fashion*, as Cole Porter would say—but now that he's gone, I give her two years, three at the most, until she's found another man to look after her. She just doesn't *do* alone. She's got her house in London, her dower house on the grounds at Dunlear, and another property in Lincolnshire that her father left her, so not to worry about the duchess. She'll probably resent you most of all on the basis of semantics. After we're married, you will be the duchess while she will technically be the dowager duchess. That said, even then I wouldn't recommend referring to her as the dowager. Ever." Max turned to Bronte and smiled again, but with a bit more tightness around his mouth.

Chapter 11

THE CAR STARTED TO slow down as it entered the tree-lined streets of Englewood Cliffs, coming to a stop in front of a 1970s ranch house. The home Bronte grew up in was straight-down-the-line, middle-class fare: set back about thirty feet from the curb, one-car garage to the right, six steps up to the front door approached by a curving path from the driveway. Freshly cut lawn, mature shrubs running neatly along the home's perimeter, a single shady tree in the front yard.

Bronte took a deep breath, closed her eyes, and let her head slip back to rest on the fake leather headrest. She wanted to cry. Or at least not get out of the car.

She adored her mother, she really did. Cathy Talbott was just… needy. As a friend had once pointed out, "She loves you… *to death*!"

"What is it, Bron?" Max's voice was much closer to her than she had expected, and intimately low. She turned her head toward him, still resting on the headrest, and opened her eyes slowly to look into his.

"It sounds so mean… then I just add guilt to my original feelings… but I'm just tired of how much my mom loves me. Isn't that ridiculous? Even saying it out loud sounds so ungrateful. I love her—you will love her…"

Max squeezed her hand and smiled, encouraging her to go on.

"She is truly lovable, and supportive, and smart and every good thing, but she really wants *in* on my life… does that make any sense?

And I don't really... I'm not a really good sharer... and now with you and our *big news*, everything just feels sort of crowded."

"Shhhh. Bron. Let's go have dinner with your mom. It's just dinner. We are not getting married." Her eyes widened at the words. "I mean we are not getting married this minute, so let's take it a little at a time."

One of his fingers circled the center of her palm in the most calming way. Normally, she would have snapped back with an angry, are-you-shushing-me barb, but instead all she wanted to do was curl up like a cat onto his lap. Was that a good thing or a bad thing? Capitulation or comfort? Was she being paranoid or rational?

Her eyes were starting to drift closed, enjoying the rhythm of his gentle touch, when there was a smart rap on the window behind Max, her mother's beaming smile coming through the tinted glass.

"Game on, m'lord," she muttered so only Max could hear. He kissed the palm of her hand where he had been touching her and opened the door with his best smile for Cathy Talbott.

"And you must be Maxwell Heyworth!" Cathy gushed before he was even fully out of the car. Max smiled again, about to speak, when Cathy plowed on, "And here comes Bronny!"

Bronte just looked at Max with a slight widening of her eyes, as if to say, "Don't even think of *ever* calling me Bronny!"

"And you must be Mrs. Talbott. Please call me Max; only my grandfather called me Maxwell, and only that when he was utterly incensed."

"Oh, Bron, isn't he charming?"

"Mm-hmm," Bronte agreed as she made her way up the front path.

"'Utterly incensed,'" her mother chimed. "That British accent is wonderful."

Max was smiling one of those smiles that made a little crystal *ting* sound accompanied by a little comic-strip star when depicted on a toothpaste commercial. *How did he do it without seeming like a complete ass?* Bronte wondered idly as she opened the front door into her mother's living room.

Bronte tried to see her childhood home through Max's eyes, tried to see it as a perfectly normal suburban house: neat, modest, unremarkable in a pleasant sort of way. Cathy Talbott had always kept an immaculate home—the ferocious cleaning worked as some sort of martial perimeter against the constant unpredictability of her husband's mood swings.

At the time, Bronte had thought it a colossal waste of time: because her father had not been able to get mad about the decrepit state of their home, that just led him to seek out new indignities and sociopolitical affronts further afield. Maybe if Cathy *had* let the house fall into a state of inconsistent carelessness, Lionel could have focused on the ring left by a water glass on the antique coffee table, instead of having to cast about for new frustrations on which to cut his teeth.

Bronte felt the pressure of Max's hand as he gently reached for her lower back.

"Relax," he whispered warmly through her hair. And, miraculously, she did. Her shoulders settled down, her feet felt firmly planted on the living room carpet, and she closed her eyes momentarily. Her mother had gone into the kitchen to get them something to drink, and Bronte began to wonder if it was really possible that Max was right.

That they were right. Together.

That "relax" spoke volumes.

Throughout her relationship with Mr. Texas, she had forced herself to swallow all the bitterness that had welled up whenever *he* had told her to relax. Whenever *he* had told her to relax, it really meant calm down and shut up. He always denied it, but Bronte never really gave up on that deep-down conviction that she knew the difference between relax (fuck off) and relax (lean on me).

On the contrary, the same small word from Max was a salve. He wasn't trying to shut her up; he was trying to soothe her, to assuage her worries. The hand on her lower back wasn't a patronizing pat-pat; instead, it was like a conduit that alleviated her worry, a physical draining away.

How? she wondered.

"What did I do to deserve you?" Bronte smiled as she turned to look in his eyes and felt a jolt—first of joy, almost immediately over-shadowed by doubt that was fueled by years of skepticism and fear.

Before he could answer, Cathy was coming into the living room with three glasses of iced tea on an antique silver tray.

"So tell me about yourself, Max. Where did you grow up? Brothers and sisters? Favorite color?" Cathy set down the tray and handed Max a tall cool glass with a little embroidered linen coaster underneath.

Bronte had a momentary glimpse of her mother as a person: here was a woman who had always loved small, beautiful, seemingly insignificant things. Who even used linen cocktail napkins anymore, for goodness' sake? Who washed them, ironed them, stored them in layers of white tissue paper, and then, on top of all that, remembered to retrieve them when the rare occasion actually presented itself to use them?

Cathy Talbott always had a proper linen handkerchief in her purse. She ate off of French china. These weren't expensive habits, she used to say in her own defense when Bronte would accuse her of being a totally antiquated woman. These were moments—opportunities really—to be civilized.

"...Yorkshire, until I was ten, then my parents moved to Hertfordshire. My father died about a year ago and my mother has moved to London for the most part, so I guess Bronte and I will have to decide where we want to stake out our home base." His glance to Bronte was a visual caress. "And my favorite color is definitely green—exactly the green of Bronte's eyes, as fate would have it."

His wink was quick, just for Bronte.

"Mom, I think you may have just gotten more information out of him in five minutes than I got in months of close contact in Chicago last year."

"You never were very good at asking questions *and* waiting long enough for people to answer, Bronny."

"That is so untrue!" Bronte's eyes darted quickly to Max, and then back to her mother. "Max and I had a mutual agreement when we first met, right Max?"

"Well, it was more of… Bronte's idea than mutual, but of course I was willing to go along with it, in the interest of fostering our—what exactly, Bron?—relationship, I suppose, in Chicago."

"In any case"—Bronte squinted briefly at Max then brought her attention back to her mother—"we were trying to really get to know each other without all of the peripheral who-what-where-when type of white noise. All that do-you-know stuff becomes sort of tiresome. On the other hand, had I known that the 411 on Max was more like Gibbon's *Decline and Fall of the Roman Empire*, and less like my-mom's-a-retired-schoolteacher-and-I-grew-up-in-New-Jersey, I might have been a tad more… penetrating."

"I have parents!" Max said in mock defense. "I grew up… somewhere. And I take exception to that decline-and-fall part."

"Mm-hmm," Bronte agreed skeptically while taking a sip of her iced tea.

"No need to squabble, Bron," her mother added lightly.

"Yes, Bron, no need to squabble," Max concurred through a delicious smile that should have been illegal (for how indecent it made Bronte feel), but that her mother found perfectly amenable.

"Moving on," Cathy continued with renewed cheer, "Bronte, you will be delighted to hear that I have finally gone through your father's things."

Bronte's face clouded. "After ten years, it's about time you got rid of all of Lionel's junk."

"Well, first of all, I still dislike the fact that you refer to your father by his first name—even all these years later it still sounds disrespectful—and second of all, yes, as a matter of fact, I actually began to go through some of his papers and journals after Christmas last year and I have a few I'd like you to read."

Bronte had been shaking her head in the negative before her mother even completed the sentence. "No interest."

"Bronte," Max blurted out before he thought better of it. He had been trying to stay out of it, but he hated to see Bronte so embittered.

"Yes, Max?" she replied archly, wishing more than ever that she could raise only one of her damn eyebrows.

"Nothing, darling," he replied, all ease and accompanied by that menacing, perfect-son-in-law-to-be smile again.

"Mom, I have nothing whatsoever to say about 'Dad' and his 'work,'" Bronte said, using her index fingers to make mocking quotation marks around her words.

"I am not going to give in on this, Bronte."

No longer Bronny, she noticed, as her mother continued in her best schoolteacher voice: kind but utterly unyielding. "I have come upon something that is quite remarkable and I would very much like your opinion. If you must, simply ignore the fact that your father wrote it and give me your unbiased opinion. I am of a mind to pass it on to an editor friend of mine for possible publication."

"Sincerely, Mom, I am not trying to be a churlish adolescent, but you are delusional. His 'writing'"—again with the mock air quotation marks—"was acerbically dry and painfully self-important. It's hard enough to get people to read something well-written and cheerful, much less something pedantic and bitter."

"It's a satire, dear." Cathy might as well have said Lionel had also worked part-time running pony rides at preschool birthday parties for all Bronte was able to process the idea of him having a satirical bone in his body.

"I would love to read it," Max lobbed casually.

"I already feel ganged up on, and we haven't even been here an hour!"

"No one's ganging up on you, Bronny, and Max, thank you, I certainly appreciate the offer."

"My pleasure."

"I am not sure if Bronte has told you much about her father, but I am afraid he did not age well."

"That's an understatement, Mom. He was not a bottle of wine for chrissake."

"Now you *are* sounding like a churlish adolescent, Bronte," her mother sniped. "As I was saying, he did not age well because from a very young age, he had been led to believe that he was a gifted thinker and writer. Unfortunately, the prizes and accolades of adolescence and young adulthood rarely prepare anyone for the realities of rejection, both in the world of publishing and in the world of tenured professorships. The more he read that was substandard and pedestrian, the more arrogant he became. And the more he read that was truly intelligent and inspiring, the more quickly he would be beset by immature fits of dark professional jealousy."

"Mom, I can't believe you are still defending him. He was an ass."

"Bronte tries to upset me with her colorful language, Max, but I chose long ago to ignore it completely. Perhaps you will be able to cure her of the lazy habit."

"I find it quite adorable, actually." Max smiled.

"Well, that's only fitting, I suppose. In any case"—Cathy slipped a strand of her hair behind her ear in exactly the same way Bronte always did when she was attempting to steer the conversation back on course—"I don't think I am being unduly defensive, if you will, when I say this is a wonderful read. It's an incisive look at the contemporary American family, sort of *A Confederacy of Dunces* meets *Anna Karenina* in North Dakota."

"It's been done, Mom. Jonathan Franzen wrote it already; it's called *The Corrections*. American readers have had it up to here with dysfunctional families and the misunderstood academics who are torn from their fabric."

"I've read *The Corrections*, Bronte, and this is not it. I think if you can tear yourself away from the familiar comfort of your filial disdain, you might be pleasantly surprised." Cathy stared at Bronte a few seconds longer than necessary, then turned her attention to Max.

Bronte sat quietly for several minutes, looking out the front bay window as the early evening light came through the branches of the big sycamore in the front yard. Her mother and Max were talking pleasantly about England and the latest Booker Prize kerfuffle—both of them chuckling at the irony of all those Oxford and Cambridge types being accused of producing nothing but inconsequential boredom.

Was Bronte frozen in a state of adolescent malaise where her father was concerned? It wasn't as if the mere memory of him smacked of bitterness; it just felt like a betrayal—to herself, to her mother—to simply toss aside a lifetime of protecting oneself from all that petty meanness. *Was it a familiar comfort or a familiar bitterness?* she wondered sadly. What a waste if that was all it was. So he was a pompous jerk; so what?

She glanced away from the window and back at Max; her stomach lurched—love? terror? He was gesturing wildly with his hands as he was describing how his younger brother, Devon, used to run up behind the horse that Max was riding and jump up on its bare back, the two of them whooping and screeching and looking like nothing so much as the itinerant Romany gypsies that still came to Dunlear to trade horses.

Max proceeded to do a wonderful impersonation of his mother—or what Bronte assumed was a wonderful impersonation, because she had never encountered the original—his voice raised to a feminine octave, strained and clipped with lofty disdain.

"Please refrain from your carnival antics when we have company, children," he crowed. When Max and Devon were twelve and ten, he explained, they were ill equipped to deal with the subtle nuances of their mother's idea of what constituted "company." More or less throwing his mother under the proverbial bus, he continued apace.

"How were we supposed to know the difference between Reggie, the Duke of Wellington, and Reggie, the nice man who trained the horses between indiscretions with the local physician's assistant? Our father never seemed to differentiate, and we were simply young and eager to show off our grand skills!"

Cathy was wiping at the tears of mirth that had formed at the corners of her eyes as her laughter subsided. "Max, you really shouldn't mock your mother, even though you are quite good at it; it's very cruel," she said, but she smiled good-naturedly, and Bronte was glad. "Parents everywhere suffer, you know, trying to appear supremely consistent and reliable; meanwhile, their children lie in wait, gleefully anticipating their missteps: 'You said—' or 'You promised—' It is an endless, and necessarily losing, battle"—she turned meaningfully to Bronte—"to live up to your own child's infinite trust."

Bronte looked down into her now-empty iced tea glass, rattled the remaining ice for a second, then returned the glass carefully to the lovely round serving tray. "Point taken, Mom. Where is Dad's manuscript?"

"Come along, Max. I am sure Bronte will want you to see her childhood room, where she dreamed of her escape from this painfully mundane existence."

Her mother's complete absence of malice would never cease to amaze her. Coming from anyone else, that comment would have struck Bronte as petty or spiteful, whereas Cathy Talbott was simply stating a fact: Bronte *had* spent hours, years really, planning her escape from this mundane existence.

Max and Bronte were on their way back into the city after a festive dinner at the little Lebanese restaurant in Hoboken. Cathy and Max had split a bottle of white wine as Bronte meditated on the completely unfamiliar (yet comforting) joy of watching two of her favorite people genuinely enjoying one another's company. Mr. Texas had always found Cathy a bit grating.

"Whenever we go to visit her house, I feel like I am about to break something," he'd remarked defensively after one particularly chafing visit.

Bronte smiled sardonically to herself at the now-glaring irony, seeing that *she* was the one who ended up broken and she would have been wise to heed her mother's barely concealed skepticism of Mr. Texas, the good old boy.

"What are you not really smiling about?" Max's arm was loosely resting across Bronte's back, his middle finger grazing her upper arm.

"Just remembering other maternal visits with other men."

"Good, as long as that bitter grin is never the result of one of my visits. Your mother is an angel, by the way."

"Well, if she likes you, of course, that is certainly the case. If you happen to, shall we say, question her authority, she's somewhat demonic in her affect."

"I'll keep it in mind."

"I think *you* would have to grow horns and a spiked tail and carry a red pitchfork for her to even begin to contemplate your less-than-perfectness."

"It's nice to know I have someone firmly in my camp."

"What do you mean by 'someone in your camp'?"

"I mean, the way you've been talking about our life together, you make it sound like an uphill climb… in the snow… both ways."

"As my mother made perfectly clear over dinner, I tend to be difficult."

"Now, that's an interesting point." His hand was wandering

again. "I think you have this view of yourself as one tough customer, as the saying goes, but in reality I think you are really all warm and soft and gooey inside." His hand was moving up under her shirt, then trailing one mischievous finger along the waistband of her white jeans. Her entire abdomen rippled in response.

"Well," she sighed, "I think you're the first person to think so. Unless you mean soft as in soft in the head."

"Very funny, you self-deprecating wench." He pulled his trailing finger from her waist, brought both of his hands up to her cheeks, and turned her to face him.

She tried halfheartedly to look away, but he held her gaze and the air seemed to suddenly quiet around them. "I like when you call me 'wench,'" she whispered. "It makes me feel like I am the tavern maid and you're the local gentry."

"Look at me, Bronte. See me loving you right now. There is nothing else. I don't think there's anything you could do to drive me away—not that I want you to try, mind you—but whatever's gnawing—"

She simply closed the distance of a few inches between them and captured his mouth in a kiss of depth and passion.

After that, neither of them knew what happened.

When the driver rapped his knuckles twice, sharply, on the Plexiglas divider, Bronte felt as if she were coming up from an early diving expedition, with a monstrous diving bell being unscrewed with wrenches to let the decompression begin, ears popping. Her eyes were dark with longing as Max slowly took his hands out of her tangled hair, where he had apparently been gripping her in a mindless thrall.

"Holy fuck," Bronte muttered.

"My thoughts exactly."

Max slowly got out of the Lincoln Town Car on the street side, walked around the front of the car in a daze, then leaned into the front passenger-side window. He'd never broken his old habit of paying London cab drivers from the sidewalk.

Bronte leaned down toward the floor of the backseat and retrieved the burgundy canvas tote bag her mother had given her to carry the nine composition books that contained her father's novel. She quashed a momentary impulse to accidentally-on-purpose forget the bag in the dark well under the front seat.

Max had opened the door to let her out and was gazing down at her bent back. "Don't even think about it, Bronte."

"Whatever do you mean, Your Grace?" She got out of the car and tossed the tote bag casually over one shoulder, carrying it with two fingers like her long overdue dry cleaning.

"You know damn well what I mean. If you are going to dismiss your father's writing out of hand, at least let me take a look at it. And no leaving it in the back of an anonymous dial-a-car."

"Oh, very well." She smiled and said good night to her doorman as they passed through the lobby of her building and headed up to her apartment. As soon as the elevator doors began to close, Max pressed the full length of his body up against Bronte, pushing her forcibly back against the elevator wall.

"Now where were we?" Max's voice was a low growl.

"Here is good." Bronte brought her lips up to his and lost herself again in the depth of their kiss. There was no preamble, no recon- nect; it was like plugging into a full-on electrical socket. The elevator doors opened at the ninth floor and Bronte's eighty-four-year-old neighbor was standing there waiting to get on. Bronte and Max awkwardly disentangled themselves from one another then made their way past the wide-eyed, but hardly surprised, Mrs. Johannssen. Max held Bronte's hand as they walked down the short hall and into Bronte's apartment.

"I like how you like to hold hands," she said.

"I am certainly glad to hear it, Bron."

"No, I mean, I like the heat and the whatever that was in the car—what was that by the way? I don't think I've ever been quite so bowled over by a kiss… something in that Lebanese wine?" She put the tote bag with her father's notebooks down on the kitchen counter and turned to see Max right behind her, then her hips were wedged against the counter with the weight of his torso pushed against her.

"I don't know what that was in the car either, but I think we need to do a little research." He lifted her up onto the counter and set about investigating.

Within a few minutes, she was arching into him, overcome by the power of her climax. Her head fell forward into the crook of his neck and she was unable to stop her quiet tears. It wasn't even sobbing… it was more of a cleansing release. The crisp smell of the starch in his shirt, the hint of bay rum that he must have put on when he went back to his apartment to change before dinner, the strength of his arms supporting her now-limp body: the solace these things offered terrified her beyond measure.

He began to stroke her long hair methodically, gently. "Are they tears of joy or abject terror?"

Bronte pulled away from the safety of that crook with great reluctance. "Fifty-fifty I think."

She tried to laugh, but it came out as something approximating a seal bark, which, accompanied by the tears and runny nose, must have presented quite the sexy picture. "My emotions just feel shockingly huge sometimes."

"Maybe we should lay off the hot sex for a while? Let things calm down a bit."

"Yeah right, like that's going to happen. You just made me come with a hot breath and a quick wave of your hand over my jeans, and you think we'd be able to lay off the hot sex?"

Bronte wiped her dwindling tears away with the back of one hand, then reached across the sink and tore off a piece of paper towel to dry her nose. "I think it's just going to take some getting used to. I'm not really, you know, in touch with my feelings, like you are. I kind of, well, as you of all people know, I have spent much of my adult life ensuring that those feelings remain pretty well off limits. And the fact that you can simply glance at me—I mean literally, there was one point tonight when you looked across the table at the restaurant and I felt a wave of, well, lust I suppose, but it's not even horny really, it's just this visceral need to be physically connected to you and, yes, that scares the living crap out of me."

"I wish I could say I was disappointed but I am, in fact, down-right delighted."

"You are a beast."

"No. I am merely glad to see that we are both suffering from the exact same condition. Let's get a good night's sleep and address all of these messy feelings in the morning, shall we?"

She wrapped her arms around his neck and her legs around his body, then gripped. He carried her over to the bedroom and the two of them collapsed in a heap. *Good night's sleep*, Bronte thought ruefully. *As if.*

Chapter 12

LATE SATURDAY MORNING, WHICH was, in fact, early Saturday afternoon, offered a bright new day: perfect for solving the world's problems in general and Bronte's commitment phobias in particular. The city street sounds were making their way through the open window into Bronte's bedroom: the muted screech brakes on Park Avenue, a distant horn beeping several blocks away, a short burst of siren. Bronte rolled over onto her pillow and tried to fall back to sleep.

"Enough sleep for you, miss."

"Aaaargh. You tax me all night long then pester me awake all morning. When do I get a break?"

"Never. Today is the first day of the rest of your life and we are going out to celebrate. First, I want to eat delicious food—hot coffee, crusty bread, fluffy eggs. Let's go to Pastis then walk around for a few hours."

"Are you nuts? The West Village on a Saturday is like Disneyland for chrissake. Let's go over to Brooklyn and walk around in Prospect Park. There's a show at the Brooklyn Museum I want to see and we could hang out there for the afternoon."

Max bowed formally. "As you wish, my lady. Now get your lazy bum into the shower and let's make a day of it."

They took the subway out to Brooklyn and had pints of beer and fish and chips on Atlantic Avenue, then walked around the tree-lined streets of Brooklyn Heights and Cobble Hill, talking over their plans for the next few weeks.

"I have to be in London to resume some negotiations by next Thursday, but would prefer to arrive a day or two earlier to collect myself and go over all the paperwork beforehand. Is there any way you could follow a few days later and we could spend the weekend at Dunlear, then head back into London for a few days? Surely Sarah James needs a little boutique on Bond Street, eh? And Mowbray must need a hands-on visit from their new North American advertising executive."

Bronte was marveling, and not for the first time that day, how entirely possible everything seemed when Max stated it as a quick trip here and a quick visit there, lickety-split... London... the weekend... Dunlear...

"You are not really even listening to me, are you?" he asked.

"I am... it's just that, ugh, I sound like a broken record, but it all *is* happening too fast, Max. I want us to be together, obviously, but let's keep a little perspective in terms of the timeline."

"How long does a little perspective require these days, exactly?" Max waited silently then proceeded apace. "Days? Months? I am not even going to acknowledge the idea of a little perspective on an annual basis."

He turned to look at her as they were walking down a quiet side street, making their way back into the city.

"Max..."

"Bron?"

"Well, a yearlong engagement is not unusual, so you don't need to make it sound as though I am some sort of heartless bitch because I need a little time to get used to the idea."

Max dragged his fingers through his hair slowly, contemplating how best to move forward. "Bronte... I am not splitting hairs or being rhetorical. I am legitimately asking: what is the idea, *exactly*, that you need the time to get your mind around?"

Her silence was not the answer he was looking for, but she could not get the words out. She was afraid she would sound like a squeaking little bird if she continued.

"Max," she started, then cleared her throat, buying some time and trying to sound in command of her very out-of-control emotions. "You're... I mean, I am..."

"Go on."

"Okay, fine. I'm all for it," she rushed out in a stream. "Let me talk to Carol and Cecily about taking a few days off the week after next. I mean, it's awkward, though; you must see that."

"Actually, I really don't. In fact, I'm doing my best not to be reminded of standing in your basement flat a year ago and asking you to come with me to my father's deathbed"—he held a hand up quickly to prevent her protest—"and I don't want you to think I am bringing that up as some sort of emotional blackmail. Honestly. I just don't get it." He stopped short and put his hands on her shoulders, forcing her to look at him. "Look at me, Bron. It's me. Again. What's up? Why delay at all? I know you don't want a big splash of a wedding, so it's not like you need the year to pick out china and reserve the best hotel ballroom. I know you don't want to get married in a church and I am going to have to fight like hell to make that happen. My mother's going to go berserk; we might need to invite the family vicar as a courtesy, but I think even you in your atheistic zeal can accommodate that. So that only leads me to believe one of two things: one, you are petrified of marrying *anyone* and hope to put it off as long as possible—in which case I will push even harder to make this the shortest engagement in the history of the Heyworth family—or two, you are having doubts about marrying me in particular, in which case we need to thoroughly revisit—"

"You know it's not that," she blurted, "so just stop with the organizational flow chart. It's not a labor negotiation for chrissake. It's just me. Not wanting to be the idiot... I... I live in fear of loving you so much that I am no longer good at anything else."

He kissed her tenderly after she finished speaking, trailing his thumb along the line of her jaw. "You have no clue how much I love the sound of that. I know it is despicably caveman of me to relish the idea of you adoring me night and day, to the exclusion of everything else, children underfoot, smiling at me across the dinner table and all that. I know it's horribly egomaniacal, but it's so madly sexy."

"Oh good God. You are a madman. Children? Let's try to get through Marriage 101 first, okay?"

"Just letting my imagination get the best of me."

"Max, you are so good. So strong and dear." He started to make a self-deprecating smirk and she cut him off. "I'm not flattering you. I mean, you are all those things so naturally. I can't help but envision a slow water torture of my own encroaching invisibility. It's your world I will be entering, your family, your country." She looked to the sky through the swaying leaves above them, then back into his eyes. "It's not just procrastination or delay for its own sake. It's a matter of finding my place in that world that so thoroughly belongs to you. I don't want to sound like some late-for-the-party feminist, but I have always dreaded my erasure... my loss of identity... it sounds like such a cliché but I feel it so sharply."

"Bronte. I understand what you are saying, but—"

"It's not about understanding me or supporting me, or carrying me through a rough patch. It's about me... ugh... it's about me staying strong and good... not only for me, but for us."

"All right then. I see where we are headed." Max's voice had a military quality that was bizarrely satisfying. He wasn't being bossy; he was being fabulously pragmatic. "You are coming to London next week. My treat, by the way. I know we haven't dealt with the whole financial side of things and I suspect that that's part of what you're spinning on about in some sort of roundabout way, so let me just lay that piece out on the table, so to speak. Buying last-minute transatlantic airline tickets is certainly not in your budget, and since I am practically forcing you to do so, I think it's only fair that I underwrite that particular expedition."

She *had* been worrying about the money, but she had had no idea how to broach the subject without sounding like she was adding that to the already increasing pile of what he considered her baseless worries. "Money had crossed my mind."

"The vulgar truth about my family's money, Bron, if you must know—which, obviously, you must—is that the Heyworths have been making the stuff hand over fist for the past six hundred years. I would not say it in such a cavalier way except I seem to be pressed for time where you are concerned. Sign a prenup if you want, if you're worried people will think you are marrying me for the dosh, or don't sign one if you don't want to. I don't care either way. My solicitor, and my mother, come to think of it, will be delighted if you sign, but do what you want. Either way, I will fully expect to pay for everything from here on out, and for you to bank everything you make in your own name."

"You see, like even that. *Wham. Bam.* Problem solved."

"Would you rather I stood here wringing my hands and gnashing my teeth in anticipation of all the hardships that await us? Ridiculous."

"I know you're right. And I think I would like to sign a prenup. Or fuck, I don't give a shit. I'd like to sign something that says I don't want any of your money if we split up, which seems patently absurd since I have no intention of ever parting from you."

"Well, now that's more like it." Max leaned in and kissed her on the tip of her nose, a punctuation mark of sorts.

They resumed walking up the street and were headed toward the subway.

She slowed and took a deep breath. "Let me talk to Cecily and Carol later today and maybe I could fly over with you on Tuesday.

Then I could work at Mowbray in London on Wednesday, Thursday, and Friday of this week. If it's an all-expenses-paid lovers' tryst, I don't see how anyone at BCA is going to care one way or the other."

"Let's walk across the Brooklyn Bridge, shall we?"

"Oh, I love that idea. It's not too windy and the sun is starting to set. It sounds downright romantic."

Bronte flipped her hair over one shoulder and smiled up at Max. Her heart skipped a light riff, and she was pretty sure the terror was abating and the warm peace of true affection was taking the lead.

Who was Bronte trying to fool? This was the fucking best. She and Max had spent an hour in the brand-new first-class lounge at Virgin Atlantic's Newark terminal, then boarded the plane and hunkered down for the overnight flight to London. The cabin lights were set at a perfectly calibrated wattage… soothing but with plenty of task lighting for the other passengers who wanted to get some work done or read during the flight.

Bronte and Max were holding hands under the shared blanket that lay across them. The residual smell of their delicious dinner mingled with coffee grounds and the vague overtones of one of the flight attendant's light perfume.

Max's hand felt like a treasure in hers. He was starting to doze, but his head was turned toward her, and when he would open his glazed eyes, half-awake, she thought he gave new meaning to the word *dreamy*. His smile was half-cocked and his wolf-gray eyes sparkled like a little boy up to something, or that same boy falling asleep in the back of a car on the way home from a long, fulfilling day.

She squeezed his hand lightly as her own exhaustion crept up on her, even as she tried to fight it off, loving the intimacy of watching him fall asleep in the dark halo around them. She took her other hand out from under the blanket and reached over to touch his hair, softly repositioning it behind his ear, then sleep overtook them both.

She was startled awake three hours later by turbulence, while Max continued to sleep peacefully. She tried to get back to sleep, but her heart was beating so quickly it seemed ludicrous to lie there in that position, pretending to doze. She worked herself up into a sitting position as quietly as she could and looked around the cabin to see if anyone else was awake.

There were two businessmen a couple of rows back who were working on their computers, and another woman who was reading, but other than the steady burr of the engines, all sign of human existence was drowned out. She looked down at Max asleep as she fought back the panic that was still bubbling from whatever menacing dream she had been having when she was jerked awake. She took a few deep breaths, closed her eyes, and then started to come back to herself.

For as long as she could remember, she had never woken up with a clear head. She usually needed at least an hour to feel like her eyes were no longer covered with a gauzy film. Carol always joked about her rearranging early-morning client meetings to accommodate her non–morning person persona.

She had tried everything to combat it—early to bed/early to rise, no caffeine/tons of caffeine, yoga/no exercise—and it was always the same. She basically had no idea where her psyche went or what went on there during those deep nocturnal wanderings, but wherever it was, it was very, very far away and it took a while to come back from.

She made her way up to the first-class bar area and asked for tomato juice. The adorable Australian steward smiled and handed her the drink, then she got herself situated on a comfortable seat and started to read the romance novel she had picked up at the airport.

She clearly needed something to take her mind off the upcoming meeting with Max's entire family, and as much as she was now reconciled to reading her father's novel, she wasn't about to dive right into it. Unfortunately, the historical romance novel she had haphazardly chosen at Newark was all about evil stepmothers, duplicitous stepsisters, and hard-to-handle rakes, so she couldn't help her mind wandering to her own version of the evil mother-in-law-to-be, along with her multigenerational coven.

Little Miss Menace, Lydia, had returned to London as per her original schedule, so she had had four days to pave the way for a prickly welcome on the part of Max's mother, and Max's older sister, Claire, Lydia's mother. Bronte was starting to think of those three Heyworth women as the witches from *Macbeth*: agents of chaos.

Devon, on the other hand, was clearly in her camp. Max had passed the phone to her a couple of times over the past few days as he was talking to his brother. Devon's enthusiasm was contagious and he was patently relieved to know his brother had not been living in some imaginary world populated by The Perfect Woman Who Got Away.

"I can't tell you what a pleasure it is to know you are actually a real person, Bronte. Max has been diabolically ill-tempered ever since he got back from Chicago."

"Oh, Devon, I can't wait to meet you in person. I am a real person, but I am definitely a *nervous* real person these days."

"Nothing to worry about. If Max has been telling you gruesome tales about how our mother wanted to bake us into pies and sell us at fairs… well, that part *is* true, but the other parts about being tied to the rack in the dungeon at Dunlear… well, come to think of it, that part is sort of true too—"

Bronte's laughter bubbled over and Devon started to laugh along with her, then he continued.

"The thing is, Bronte, you can't let them see you falter. If you are feeling shaky or out of place, by all means, give me a quick signal— tug on your ear, what have you—and I will immediately whisk you out to the gardens for a stroll if Max is detained. All joking aside, get ready to put on that Teflon raincoat and let it roll right off your back. Those women are three generations of Heyworth bitches."

Bronte started laughing again to hear Devon's aristocratic chivalry and royal charm punctuated at the tail end by his version of a Snoop Dogg slap down.

"Oh God, Devon"—she wiped at the tears of laughter at the corner of one eye—"I am so looking forward to hanging out with you over a few pints. I just had a vision of bringing little hostess gifts to your Mom, Claire, and Lydia: little pink T-shirts with *Heyworth Bitches* spelled out in tiny rhinestones across the chest… and I could greet your mom as 'Yo, bitch'—"

By that point, Devon and Bronte were both laughing hysterically and Max had come back into her living room, looking a bit miffed to be left out of the joke.

"I wanted you two to get acquainted, not get on like a house afire for chrissake. Pass me the phone."

"All right, Devon," Bronte gasped through her settling laughter, "Max has just come back into the living room, and apparently he is the only person allowed to make me laugh that hard. Can't wait to meet you in person next week. Here's your brother." She widened her eyes with a smile of exaggerated innocence as she handed the phone back to Max.

Clearly, Devon was not going to present a problem.

Bronte had also touched base with a very contrite Willa and David, sharing the happy news that she and Max were engaged, but that they were keeping it quiet until Max had told his family in person. And that believe it or not, she had *not* imagined it this time around.

"Bronte, we are utterly disgusted with ourselves," Willa dove in. "Please come 'round for a kitchen dinner one night while you are here. It was beastly what David said—" The phone was wrenched from her hand, dropped, and then David got on the horn.

"David here, Bron. Quite a cock-up over here at The David and

Willa Show. Still can't believe I said that crap about you and Max last year. I mean, what an ass I was! I hope you will forgive us and that we can all still, you know, put all that 'thinking men are in love with you—'" Phone grabbed. Scuffle.

"Willa again here. He cannot be trusted, Bron. He is such an ass, but I am married to him so I don't know what that makes me. An ass's wife, I suppose. In any case, please tell me you and Max can come for dinner, okay?"

Bronte was smiling broadly as she finally made her way into the conversation. "Willa, it was such a crazy way to start a relationship— the whole I'll-never-see-him-again-so-why-bother-telling-anyone-about-him thing was really idiotic, so no worries about David basing future results on past performance as far as I was concerned. Your ass is an investment banker after all—his pragmatic honesty is one of the things I admire most about him. So, yes, of course I would love to come 'round, as you say."

They made tentative plans for Thursday night, barring any unforeseen complications with Max's meetings that day.

Bronte looked down at her third tomato juice and decided to give up on reading her novel. She made her way quietly back to her pod next to Max and tried to force herself back to sleep for the next hour or two of the flight.

―⚬⚬⚬―

A few hours later, Max awoke feeling rested and ready. He heard the flight attendants trying to be quiet in the galley, noticed the sun beginning to come through the edges of the window shade across the aisle, and felt the steady thrum of the 747 engines pulsing through his body.

He held still while he looked at the gorgeous sleeping beauty who was breathing evenly a few inches from him. The past week had been overwhelming on so many levels. The main thing was that he had succeeded in convincing Bronte that everything was going to be smooth sailing this week, when in fact he was dreading every minute of the upcoming family gathering.

His mother was just the tip of the iceberg. Her glacial response was to be expected on some level. After seeing to her husband's happiness, her only other concern was making sure each of her children had a "proper" marriage.

Claire had fallen into line—and look where that had led. A wanker of a husband who slept around. Max found the whole scenario utterly ridiculous. The women of England had finally crawled out from under centuries of oppression, and Sylvia had to go and throw it all back in the crapper.

Max's father, George, had been nigh on obsessed with ensuring absolute equality when it came to providing for his four children. He had no time for sexist policies that favored sons or the firstborn. That innate egalitarianism had been passed down from his own father and mother.

George's father, Henry, had married the royal princess, Augusta Pauline, the very mild seventh child of George V. Everyone knew her simply as Polly. It had been a love match: a perfect joy for both Henry (who lived to protect and adore the ethereal Polly) and for Polly (who lived to admire and adore the strapping Henry). Everyone smiled benignly at the idea that their ten Heyworth offspring, wild-eyed woodland creatures left to roam free over the endless acres of Castle Heyworth, were also royal by Polly's blood. Royalty didn't seem to bear much significance to Max's grandmother. Her country habits and instinctive modesty were passed down much more than any conscious acknowledgment of elitism or regal entitlement.

Henry spent most of his life as the "spare," only to be surprised somewhat late in life with the ducal title. As it turned out, Henry's elder brother, Freddy, had been born and raised to be the duke, had married and prospered accordingly, and had had a houseful of children; alas, all six were daughters.

So, when the rugged, frugal Henry became the seventeenth Duke of Northrop in 1968, he and Polly were mildly disapproving of his older brother's rather fun-loving handling of the finances. There was never any malfeasance of any sort, but according to the freewheeling Freddy, the idea of fiscal responsibility was something you read about in the *FT*, not something that you ever applied to your own habits.

Upon inheriting the title, Henry promptly sold off the race cars, dismantled the recording studio, and turned the major rooms at Dunlear Castle—including the salons, reception rooms, and art galleries—over to the National Trust. Henry and Polly Heyworth were the new breed of duke and duchess: practical, considerate, no-nonsense.

Henry's years as a field officer in Africa during the Second World War had ensured a sense of leadership and confidence that easily translated to his parenting. His second eldest son, George, had been the spare to the spare, so he had even less intention of ever taking over the lofty responsibilities that attended the title. George lived a carefree childhood in the wilds of Yorkshire in the postwar 1950s and was devastated when his older brother died in a car accident in the early 1960s. When George's father became the seventeenth Duke of Northrop, George finally had to accept that the title would one day be his, but given his father's obscenely hale constitution, he had little thought of that turn of events coming to pass anytime soon.

For nearly twenty years, Henry and Polly Heyworth trimmed the sails at Dunlear Castle and ensured the ongoing prosperity of the Heyworth family. Their large family was well-provided for, and Henry rarely treated the dukedom with anything more than passing respect, a form of practical modesty that he passed on to Max's father, George.

After his parents moved to Dunlear Castle, it was decided that a rather young, shy twenty-one-year-old George was to stay at Castle

Heyworth in Yorkshire to oversee the running of that large property. Like his royal mother, Polly, George preferred the wild solitude of the country and hoped to raise his own family there when it came to that. Despite the blood in his veins, George Heyworth never really felt he was cut from royal cloth, preferring a long walk in the woods to any awkward social obligation.

It was this seed of social insecurity, perhaps, that led George to choose Sylvia Beckwith as his wife. She was dreadfully pretty, of course, but more to the point, she was *aspirational*. Her sister had married an earl.

Her entire family excelled at propriety.

Sylvia was utterly dedicated to the appropriateness of everything: education, etiquette, friends, interior decoration, even the cars they drove. The irony that George was the royal one but Sylvia knew more about the peerage was not lost on either of them. She didn't really *do* anything per se, but she was the supreme arbiter of taste. And because George would rather haul bundles of rough switches on his bare back than decide who was to be invited to the next house party, he proposed marriage to Sylvia.

After Claire was born—and oh how Sylvia had cursed her own treacherous body for not delivering a male baby first—she proceeded to suffer several miscarriages. After eight years of near constant anxiety—punctuated by intermittent weeks or short months of ecstatic, tortured hope—she finally produced Maxwell Fitzwilliam-Heyworth.

The strain she must have been under to fulfill what, to her mind at least, was her singular, primary responsibility must have been quite heavy, because once it was lifted, she managed to pop out Devon and Abigail in very rapid succession. After Abigail's birth, Sylvia's responsibilities now utterly and completely fulfilled, she left the raising of the three younger children almost entirely in the capable hands of her extensively researched and lengthily interviewed nannies and tutors. By the time Max's father discovered that Sylvia's aptitude for decision making and delegating formed the basis of her motherhood plans for the three young ones, it was far too late to consider the long-term consequences that parenting-by-proxy may have on actual children.

Claire, on the other hand, was always the exception. Those eight long years of Claire's being an only child, with her mother's ever-growing fear that she might be *the* only child, had forged a bizarre intimacy between Sylvia and Claire. Sylvia doted on Claire in the extreme, carefully choosing every outfit and writing out weekly menus for her every toddler meal.

Such deep attachment might have been endearing, had it not been such a marked contrast to how Sylvia treated her subsequent three children. It was as if, having suffered through the intensity of those intervening years with only Claire and the constant threat of no more children, the duchess had permanently exhausted her parenting resources.

Sylvia was always concerned with Claire far more than she was with the others, which, Max supposed, was understandable on some psychological level, but their mother-daughter relationship never really contributed to what one might call overall family harmony. While Max's father was still alive, Sylvia was always able to couch her favoritism in a supportive-if-sexist vein: to wit, the boys were born knowing how to take care of themselves, and Abigail was always being taken care of by the boys.

George always agreed with Sylvia in theory, but he often spent extra time with his Three Musketeers, as he dubbed the younger siblings, when Sylvia began taking the teenaged Claire to London for extended shopping and museum visits.

And so the contemporary family dynamic, like so much of the Heyworth family history going back as far as Henry V, was set in very ancient stone. Within weeks of George's death, it was no longer a matter of Sylvia couching her feelings in any way whatsoever. Because she no longer needed to even pretend to appease her husband's nebulous feelings of something-amiss-in-the-sibling-equality-department, she was free to ignore Max, Abigail, and Devon quite categorically.

During Max's early twenties, his mother had finally turned her attention to her eldest son. She wanted to get down to the business of brokering an excellent marriage for Max. She had been quite adamant about the importance of Max finding a suitable bride, and quickly. After his father's death, she changed her tune. With Max a confirmed bachelor about town, and relatively young and bookish at that, she soon realized that she could be enjoying her time as the Duchess of Northrop for many years to come.

Enter Bronte Talbott, upstart American. Stage left.

Max continued looking at the planes of Bronte's fabulous face and sighed as he contemplated the arctic gleam that would appear in his mother's eye when she would be introduced to her usurper. It wouldn't occur to her that her dear, devoted husband had left her one of the wealthiest women in England. It wouldn't occur to her that her son was going to be deliriously happy each and every day of his wedded life. It would never occur to her to actually share in the patent abundance.

Max must have sighed more audibly on this last thought because Bronte slowly opened her glazed green eyes, particularly seductive in the reflection of the growing dawn as more passengers began to open their window shades across the aisle.

"What are you sighing on about?" she asked as she drew her hand out from under her blanket and caressed his cheek with her index finger, then let her hand wander down toward his chest.

"Don't start something you can't finish, Ms. Talbott," he whispered as he grabbed her hand and placed it back on her own side of the sleeping pod. "I've already warned you that I have no interest whatsoever in joining the mile-high club."

"Neither do I, Max. I just wanted to touch you first thing in the morning. You don't need to make everything about sex, you know."

"Well, when you are lying eight inches away from me and making all of those kitteny, wake-up noises, it's quite difficult to make it about anything else."

"Nice try." Bronte wriggled herself into more of an upright position. "I saw the Max-look-of-worry cross your face right as I was waking up. What's up?"

"I don't really want to dwell on it, and I know Dev has been really great about keeping things light and all that, but Bron, my mom is a real piece of work."

"I know I'm American," Bronte began defensively, "but I wasn't raised in a barn, you know. I think I can see my way around a four-course dinner, and I'm sure I won't be too much of an embarrassment for you."

"You see, that's exactly what I mean." Max was now also attempting to sit up and have a proper conversation eye-to-eye. "It has absolutely nothing to do with you, American or otherwise. She may pretend or grasp, or what have you, that you are American or working or lascivious—"

"Lascivious!?"

"I mean it doesn't matter what absurd notion she latches on to," he said, raking his hand through his hair in frustration. "Please. What I mean is this will be entirely about *her*… she will do every damn thing to make it about my father's death, or my sister's near divorce, or your nonroyal blood—none of it will have any basis in truth. And when you saw that—what did you call it again?"

"The Max-look-of-worry…"

"Yes, that. In any case, I was contemplating my mother's, well, let's face it, what promises to be her hostile response to our happy news."

"And you are just now contemplating this?"

"Well, not just now. I mean, I told you she might not be thrilled—"

"Max, you have a PhD in complex economics for chrissake.

Please don't be obtuse. Just admit there exists a galactic gap between not thrilled and *hostile*. What the fuck?"

"Bron—"

"Did you purposely wait until we were making our approach into Heathrow to tell me the... the... the fucking severity of the situation? What are we really talking about here? Does she even know we are coming?"

A split-second shadow of hesitation passed over Max's face.

Bronte deflated. "Or should I ask, does she know *I* am coming?"

Silence.

"Max?"

Chapter 13

"WOULD YOU LIKE COFFEE before we serve breakfast, Mr. Heyworth?" the attractive Australian steward intoned politely.

Bronte simply glared at the poor attendant mercilessly, as if to say, "You will keep on moving down that aisle if you know what's good for you, Crocodile Dundee," then turned her attention back to her wayward fiancé.

"Max? Care to elaborate?"

"My mother… I mean, obviously she knows about us. Lydia's been home for days, and I'm sure she has told her…"

Bronte refused to dignify that hanging thought with a response. Max plowed on.

"Sylvia has never taken much of an interest in me, Bron. I don't mean to sound maudlin, seriously. It was probably the best for everyone involved. You'll see how her field-marshaling of Claire's life has turned out. Well, you don't know all the particulars yet, but trust me, *not well*. And the mother-son détente has always served both of us quite well, thank you very much. But she can be quite a cur if things don't go her way, and I guess I have just put off thinking how it will feel to have the Klieg light of her dissatisfaction shining right on me… on us…"

"Klieg light? You make her sound like an armed guard looking to stop a prison break. Holy fuck. This is… this is…"

"Calm down, Bron darling. I promise, it's just—"

"Stop. Please, Max, just stop. I need to think for a few seconds."

Bronte tried to busy herself with folding and putting away the mangled sheets and blanket that Virgin Atlantic had supplied, but she was making a mess of it and taking out her frustration with her now less-than-perfect fiancé on the innocent linen. She finally resolved the sheet situation by shoving the whole unruly mess into the footstool contraption, whipping her hair back into a ponytail, and putting her sleeping pod back into the full upright seat position.

Nothing like a little mindless bustle to take your mind off things.

She rubbed the palms of her hands along her linen khaki pants—*comfort*, she had thought when she chose to wear them on the flight; *idiocy*, she now thought as she looked at the wrinkled lower half of her body. *I won't be deriving any much-needed confidence from my appearance, then.*

And, as fate would have it, she smiled at that. He was already in her head. When would she ever have tacked on that useless *then* to the end of a perfectly good sentence? In a reworking of her favorite Steve Martin one-liner about the French, she thought, *Man, those Brits have a word for everything.*

Max cleared his throat.

"So what's the smile for, then?"

Bronte theatrically erased any trace of a smile.

"I have no idea what you're talking about."

"That"—he touched the edge of her lip with the lightest caress—"right there at the corner of your mouth."

He knew it was one of the most sensitive parts of her body, and he was quite prepared to lure her out of her dread with some good old-fashioned flirting.

"Don't even try it, Max. It's such a novel sensation, me being truly and justifiably pissed at you. Let me savor it for a few minutes at least."

Max frowned boyishly.

"And don't try that either. I don't give a fuck if you feel guilty or ashamed of yourself, because you damn well should."

Bronte crossed her arms in front of her chest.

Max trailed a finger down her neck and she tried to shake him off with a shrug, then swatted at him when his touch moved down her shoulder.

"Cut it out!" she half-whispered, half-groaned.

Max smiled, got to his feet, then leaned over his seat to whisper into Bronte's ear.

"This is so not a big deal, I swear. I'm going to the loo and you had better be done with your snit by the time I get back or I will have to resort to extreme measures. And I am warning you, if you require a proper spanking in the airplane lavatory, I will provide it."

Whether it was the heat of his breath or the naughty, suggestive laugh that undercut his words, Bronte realized—for better or for worse, ironically—that she would never be able to stay angry at Max for long. She looked away as he headed toward the first-class bathroom so he wouldn't see her grin.

Bronte decided to try her hand at freshening up before they served breakfast, and to apologize to that nice Australian steward while she was at it. She headed back to the other bathroom and waited for the "occupied" light to turn off, hoping there wasn't some hairy beast of a man taking his time in there.

While she waited, her eye wandered to the nearby magazine rack and the most recent copy of *Hello!* magazine. Something about that exclamation point always made her smile. She grabbed it and began flipping through the pages to pass the time. She was daydreaming that she would probably see her own face in those pages sometime soon when, about three-quarters of the way through, she found herself—Valentino properly credited—skipping across the Lincoln Center esplanade hand in hand with Max as he tugged her along.

"Good God," she muttered.

The very handsome and not at all hairy-beast-of-a-man who had been taking his time in the bathroom, had, of course, emerged in immaculate splendor at that exact moment and gave Bronte's mussed, disheveled appearance a quick head-to-toe perusal.

He caught sight of the magazine image and caption, then added, "You might want to stick with Valentino." He somehow managed to accompany the near insult with the world's sexiest, albeit utterly inappropriate, wink. Then he was off down the aisle resuming his seat.

Bronte tucked the magazine under one arm and shook her head in disbelief.

About five minutes later, she plopped back down into her seat and slapped the copy of *Hello!* onto Max's chest as if it were a subpoena. "News travels fast."

"What now?"

"Just a rehash of the picture from Lincoln Center that was in the *Post* last week, but I suppose I should have paid more attention when you gave me the 411 on your celebrity status over here. Well?"

"Celebrity status? You must be joking, Bron."

"Look, all I'm saying is please prepare me for the inevitable. I get it—you're royal, you're a duke, you're an eligible bachelor. You are *somebody*. But are you, say, the Brad Pitt of London or the little-known but much-adored second cousin of Jude Law?"

"Very funny."

"Believe it or not, I wasn't even trying to be amusing. Max?"

"Well, I'd say probably more toward the second cousin variety, but occasionally certain family connections crop up and one of us turns up in the news for a few days. But you don't need to worry about paparazzi trying to catch you topless on the prow of a yacht. We don't have a yacht, for starters, but the topless bit—"

"Okay!" Bronte interrupted. "Let's get a few things clear, Max. If it wasn't my ass on the line, I would probably find your cagey humility perfectly sexy, but as it stands, I'm on the verge of dumping you for that flirtatious bathroom hog a few rows back."

Max's head whipped around to check out the smarmy bastard across the aisle and two seats behind him, then turned to Bronte with a grim look.

"Very well," Max said. "There's no way to predict how it will all spin out, but just to give you the back story, our family has been well out of the spotlight for many years—with only the occasional mention of Sylvia's hat at Ascot or a snap of Claire at the ribbon-cutting for the children's hospital near Dunlear. Basically, my father and grandfather were particularly adept at imparting a healthy sense of our own irrelevance."

Bronte's smile made it easier to proceed.

"So, you three would have that in common," Max continued with a self-deprecating grin. "Basically, I think they will leave us alone as long as we're not out clubbing until three in the morning or puking in Leicester Square."

"How attractive."

"We'll just keep a low profile, Bron. There are two charities that I am particularly involved in, and all the business stuff, of course. No one is going to leave you in the lurch. My mother's secretary is wonderful. I've already scheduled a meeting for the three of us to meet. She can walk you through the early stages of what's involved."

Bronte felt her chest constrict.

He sensed her anxiety and squeezed her hand tighter. "Bron, look at me. Nothing has changed. Just think of it as a business. That's all it is. I have offices in London and out at Dunlear. Would you be so worried if I had inherited a real estate investment finance business from my father?"

She shook her head. "I guess not. But it's not the same, Max. It's just not."

"It is, Bron. That's exactly what it is. A job." He paused for a few seconds. "Just one we can never quit," he added quietly.

He looked up at the overhead compartments to gather his thoughts, then stared back into Bronte's eyes. "I think this is why I never told you back in Chicago. It was wrong; I know it was. You were right to be pissed. But—" He exhaled. "But the ducal responsibilities really do not have to take over our lives. You are so efficient. You can juggle more crap in a single hour than most people can deal with in a week. I have three stewards who oversee all the buildings and lands. I know it might be disconcerting for you personally. I mean, you're gorgeous and they're all going to want to take pictures of us at parties and write about what you're wearing for a few months maybe..."

"Max," she whispered, "that sounds terrifying."

"But you already do that. Think about it. You do that for Sarah James and you know tons of people in that world already. I mean, you don't say 'fuck' in your press releases. It's not like you've ever tripped over a red carpet."

The weight on her chest was now starting to feel more like the anvil that Wile E. Coyote used to drop on Road Runner. "I have, actually. It was more of a stumble, but still. It was at a Valentino show last year."

"Oh God. I am going about this all wrong. Just forget about it for now. One thing at a time. Let's get through dinner with my mother. After that, the rest of it will feel like a cakewalk."

"I've never actually done a cakewalk."

"Very funny." He leaned in and kissed her, slowly at first then with a rising passion. He pulled away from her reluctantly and his lip quirked up on one side. "Just remember, *that* is what we need to keep as our priority. Okay?"

"Okay," she sighed. "All I'm saying is forewarned means fore-armed. I can handle whatever comes our way as long as you give me a little heads up. All right?"

"Of course. I just didn't want to worry you—"

"See," Bronte interrupted, as she placed the palm of her hand on his cheek. "Like that right there will be a real problem moving forward. You know me well enough to recognize that ignorance is most definitely *not* bliss where I am concerned. Just give me the worst, then let me rail and stuff sheets into idiotic hassocks for a few minutes and I'll be good to go. But if you casually introduce me to someone whom you just happened to have slept with once or twice way back when and just kind of *forgot* to tell me, not good to go."

"Is that hand on my cheek a show of intimacy or are you about to slap some sense into me?"

Bronte drew her thumb slowly across his lips and replied softly, "Definitely the former."

It was a relatively quick ride from Heathrow to the mews house in Fulham that Max had purchased soon after he came down from Oxford. He moved to London after he'd secured his first job as a minion at a large steel conglomerate. The house had needed a ton of work, and his dad had loved coming into town and helping him fix it up on weekends. The two of them had ripped out decades of lino, as Max described the linoleum floors to Bronte, and layers of flocked wallpapers and stripped the whole structure down to a beautiful, rustic simplicity.

Bronte was so taken aback at the combination of charm and sophistication that she dropped her bags just inside the front door and gasped at the beautiful living room.

"Oh, Max. I never was able to picture how you actually lived. This is so fantastic!"

She began walking through the room, lightly touching her index finger along the dark mahogany antique drop-leaf table that doubled as a collection spot for keys and mail.

"It's not much really. My mother still chides me for living in the stables."

But Bronte could tell he loved it. The living room had an enormous window that faced back out onto the quiet cobbled mews, happily framed by the ancient wisteria that was a riot of green and purple. The morning light cast a luminous glow on the rough-hewn, wide oak floors.

After all that linoleum was pulled up, the wood floors were in a beautiful state of well-worn age: scuffs and scars from centuries of use, bent nails, and the hint of sanded away bits of paint and glue from the passage of many years. The large beam that ran across the center of the punched-up ceiling had a similar patina of comforting wear.

The furniture was a mix of well-worn, unpretentious antiques and casual upholstered seating. Two enormous white sofas with inviting down cushions faced each other in front of a fireplace with a deep interior blackened from use. A set of narrow stairs led away to the right, and two sets of welcoming French doors led to the back half of the ground floor.

Bronte continued to make her way through Max's world, loving everything about it. The back portion of the little house had been completely gutted so it was a single room that ran the full width of the building. A modern stainless-steel kitchen took up the entire wall to the right, with a multitiered, stainless-steel industrial work surface on oversized wheels serving as the kitchen island. A well-loved farm table, probably about ten feet long with ten mismatched wooden chairs set convivially around it, took up the rest of the room.

"And now for one of my favorite parts," Max whispered hotly into Bronte's ear as he guided her with the warmth of his hand at the small of her back out into an intimate, overgrown, walled garden.

"Oh, Max!"

He leaned in to kiss her and she felt herself give way to a sense of relief greater than she could have anticipated. For some reason, she had been having all sorts of miniature anxiety attacks about Max's house being cluttered with minor Rembrandts and early Van Dycks carelessly hung in the guest bathroom, and she had been envisioning herself sleeping under a cavernous, maroon-velvet tester bed.

As it turned out, it was quite the contrary. She had stepped into a garden idyll. She was about to have what amounted to a lovely stay in what felt like a little country house, that just happened to be tucked away on a private little side street right in the middle of London.

The tiny whispering sound of the nearby climbing-ivy leaves rustling was crisp in her ears; her senses were in a state of both jet lag–induced exhaustion and heightened physical awareness. This kiss, the smell of summer in the air, the distant sound of a foreign siren with its unfamiliar high-low-high-low pitch, the feel of Max's unshaven cheek against the soft pads of her fingers.

She pulled away for a second, getting her bearings.

"It's like déjà vu all over again… the two of us back in the walled garden at my old place in Wicker Park."

His arms were loose around her waist, his hands clasped at her lower back.

"Why do you think I was so at home there?"

He began to kiss her again; it felt like a welcome-home kiss, then turned deeper and more demanding until he withdrew and dragged her up the narrow stairs to the loft-like master bedroom. The open space consisted of painted-white wood floors and an enormous white platform bed. And not much else.

Just after Max did away with the crumpled excuse that passed for her linen pants and she wriggled out of the rest of her clothes, she glanced up at the hard wall of his stomach and chest—his face momentarily covered by his disappearing shirt—and trusted it would all turn out right. When the heat and texture of his strong torso came into full contact with her smooth, sensitive skin, she inhaled as if she hadn't breathed for endless minutes. The sheer physical relief of contact.

It would all work out.

She hoped.

A short two hours later, the noon bells chimed from a nearby church tower and Bronte opened one eye to see Max standing at the sink in the bathroom across the room. He had a white towel wrapped securely around his waist and the muscles in his back tensed and relaxed as he reached to turn the water spigot on and off between strokes of the razor against his face. She must have shuffled the sheets because he caught her gaze in the reflection of the mirror and smiled.

"Good afternoon and welcome to London, lovely."

"Why thank you, sir. What's on the docket for today? Are we going to meet up with Devon? Go out for lunch? While away the hours here in bed?"

"You are such a temptress, but alas, no to that last proposition. I had hoped our earlier activities might have satisfied you"—raised eyebrow—"for longer than a few hours. Apparently not."

"Quite satisfied, thank you." Bronte had made her way out of bed, padded over to the bathroom, and hugged Max from behind.

"Hive off, Bron! Into the shower you go. I've got a surprise for you." He reached back and gave her bare bottom a quick slap. "We are expected at two o'clock in Mayfair."

Bronte reached in to turn on the shower within the clear-glass enclosure, then turned back to look at Max. "Your mother already?"

"Not yet. This is more of, well, a little pregame pep rally. We'll be having dinner with Mother tonight."

Bronte groaned as she entered the shower and pulled the glass door closed behind her. "Is our appointment today more business or pleasure?"

Max's smile was deadly as he raised his voice slightly to be heard over to the shower spray. "Pure pleasure for you, I hope."

"Mmmm, I'm liking the sound of that."

Bronte let the scalding water run over her exhausted body. The flight had been luxurious as flights go, but she was still covered in a residual coating of airports, airplanes, and taxis. She took a deep breath of the moist, hot air inside the shower, then felt the pressure of Max's gaze upon her.

Opening her eyes and looking suggestively over one shoulder, she asked, "What?"

He was frozen in place, his wrist limp, fingers lightly holding the razor over the edge of the sink. "Uh…"

She turned to face him full on, slowly realizing he was enjoying the sight of her glistening, wet body.

"You sure you cleaned behind your ears?" she teased.

He was in the shower within seconds.

—m—

The extraordinarily clean couple was drinking strong coffee half an hour later under the large, white, café umbrellas in the outdoor area in front of Bluebird in Chelsea. Max was reading the *Independent* and Bronte was reading an email on her phone about the latest sales figures from Sarah James.

Even though Max had only been half-joking when he'd suggested one reason for a London visit would be to scout out a stand-alone boutique location for Sarah's flagship store in the UK, it turned out that Sarah was actually quite taken with the idea and wanted Bronte to do some forward recon while she was in town. To that end, Bronte had set up an appointment to spend Thursday morning with a commercial real estate agent who would take her around London to look at a variety of potential locations.

Mowbray, on the other hand, was not going to be a legitimate business visit. As much fun as it would be to meet all of the Mowbray employees and to see the historic London headquarters firsthand, W. Mowbray & Sons had their own British ad agency, so Bronte's visit didn't have really anything to do with the US BCA campaign that she was going to be frantically putting together over the next six months. She was all set to see James Mowbray Friday morning, to meet his staff and to get a real, hands-on feel for the history and sense of place that she was sure the mid-nineteenth-century offices would exude.

She clicked out of email and started to scroll through her to-do list, then momentarily looked up at Max. He was wearing a pair of classic aviator sunglasses, and as a double-decker bus went by, she was reminded of the first time she'd sat across a table from him, the two of them having coffee and pancakes on Halsted Street in Chicago.

He finished the article he was reading, shook his head dolefully, then glanced up from the paper as he turned the page.

He caught Bronte's look and perked up. "Hey."

"Hey. I was just thinking about how I have spent the past year savoring the eight short weeks we spent together in Chicago. I kind of honed and polished every memory."

"Sounds delightful, all that honing and polishing."

"Very funny. I mean it. All of a sudden, it's just a relief, really, to think that I can glance up and see you all tall, dark, and handsome anytime I feel like it."

"Better and better. Do go on."

"You are such a conceited horse's ass. Seriously." But she smiled as she said it.

Max's tone turned serious. "Bron, all conceit aside. Your good opinion matters more to me than you can ever imagine."

Even in the midst of the buses, taxis, and clinking china and silverware of the bustling café, there seemed to be a sudden vacuum around them.

Bronte swallowed carefully.

"I love you, Max. Not to worry. You have secured my affections."

Max had laced the fingers of his left hand through Bronte's right and was smiling magnificently across the table at her.

"Well, if it isn't Max Heyworth!" said a very plummy, British-accented female voice.

Bronte and Max looked up, startled, and Bronte instinctively tried to pull her hand out of Max's grasp, only to feel his hold tighten possessively on hers. Neither of them was in favor of public displays of affection—despite what the CFDA paparazzi may have snapped that fateful night last week—so Bronte was a little surprised that Max was very decidedly leaving said affection on very public display.

This should be interesting, she thought ruefully.

Max oozed Etonian formality and charm. "Lady Claudia Seeley, please allow me to introduce Ms. Bronte Talbott. Bronte, Lady Claudia."

He did not stand or make any pretense of intending to do so.

The perfectly groomed Lady Claudia was a very well-maintained woman of a certain age. Bronte suspected she was in her mid-sixties, but she didn't have a stray hair or ounce of fat in evidence, nor a wrinkle in sight. In addition to the little cairn terrier she had tucked under one arm, she was also sporting an enormous blue crocodile Hermès Birkin bag, definitely *not* a knockoff, and wore what Bronte had to enviously confess was one of the most fabulous white Chanel pantsuits she had ever laid eyes on.

Bronte tried to get a glimpse of her shoes without giving her a totally obvious once-over, but the sharp matron caught her out.

"They're Sarah James, darling. Are they not divine?"

Lady Claudia took a moment to turn one foot this way and that, and despite Max's obvious lack of patience with this woman, Bronte fell instantly in love.

"Would you care to join us?" Bronte blurted, as she wondered if her knuckles would crack under the pressure of Max's death grip.

"Why, aren't you just so *American*?! All of that immediate intimacy that is so utterly lacking here in mother England. Perfectly charming. I'd love to."

And with that, Max let go of Bronte's hand and went back to reading his newspaper.

"Since Max is clearly in a sulk about some silly accident of birth—his horrid mother is my sister, but please don't tell anyone—I shall pretend he is not here and you and I can have a perfectly enjoyable discussion about the more important things in life. Namely, shoes."

Bronte looked from one to the other, deciding to see if there was really any bad blood, caught the slightest hint of a smile on Max's face, and, taking that for reluctant but tacit encouragement, decided to dive into the fabulous world of Lady Claudia Seeley.

"Well, first of all," Bronte launched breathlessly, "your bag is absolutely to die for. I have never seen the crocodile in blue and I might very well have stopped you on the street, regardless of your mixed blood."

Lady Claudia's deep, throaty bark of a laugh was remarkably similar to Max's, and even he was smiling as he continued to pretend he was mired in deep contemplation of the business section of his newspaper.

"Mixed blood? How perfectly true! Oh, Max, where did you find this gem of a girl? Has she met your mother yet? But of course not: I know you have always sworn you would never introduce any woman to that shrew unless you were on your way to the altar."

Bronte smiled benignly and glanced at Max.

He looked up at his larger-than-life aunt and couldn't resist. "We are having dinner with Sylvia tonight."

Then he casually returned his attention to the newspaper.

Max had to admit, silencing Lady Claudia was tantamount to stopping the tide, so he took a satisfying moment behind the invisible wall of his reflective sunglasses to enjoy the blessed quiet.

"Roasted pumpkin and goat cheese salad?" the no-nonsense waitress snapped, holding the plate slightly aloft with a take-it-or-leave-it gesture.

"That's mine." Bronte raised her hand slightly.

As the waitress set a plate of eggs Benedict down in front of Max, Lady Claudia found her voice and nearly sang, "And a bottle of the Laurent Perrier rosé and three glasses, please."

The waitress nodded and went to fetch the expensive bottle of pink champagne.

"What are you celebrating, Aunt Claudia?" Max asked disingenuously between bites of egg and brioche.

"As if you don't know, Maxwell." Lady Claudia raised her eyebrow.

"Aaah," Bronte confirmed as she swallowed, "so the eyebrow-raising comes from your mother's side of the family, Max!"

"Absolutely, dear," Claudia interrupted as Max continued to eat as if he were at a table for one. "And so does drinking champagne at lunch. So has he already proposed or is he waiting to see if you will still have him after enduring the trial by fire also known as Sylvia, Duchess of Northrop?"

Bronte nearly choked on her salad and reached for her water to clear her throat and buy some time.

"Don't look at me, Bron," Max grumbled. "You are the one who invited her to join us."

Chapter 14

"WELCOME TO LIFE IN the lion's den, Ms. Talbott."

"Please call me Bronte. You know how *overly* familiar we Americans are."

"Well, if the two of you are going to be hush-hush over the details," Lady Claudia proceeded as she took a small brown nylon packet out of her stupendously fabulous purse, "and since I don't see a ring on your finger"—the little contraption opened origami-like into a portable, stylish, square dog bowl—"I will have to accept that your introduction to the duchess this evening is merely the launching of Max's first salvo."

She then proceeded to carefully pour some of her Evian water into the bowl and slipped it under the table, where the perfectly behaved terrier was sitting contentedly at her feet.

The champagne arrived and was poured, the sparkling pink liquid bubbling and popping festively in the early-afternoon sun.

Lady Claudia raised her glass.

"Take those damn sunglasses off, Max, and pick up your glass of champagne."

Max obeyed, albeit slowly.

Bronte looked from one to the other, reached for her glass, picked it up, then waited.

And waited.

Finally, Lady Claudia inhaled as if to speak, when Max forestalled her almost-toast.

"Lady Claudia, let us raise our glasses to my *fiancée*, Bronte Talbott." His eyes narrowed for a split second as if daring Claudia with a look, then he continued, "If you breathe a word of this news before I have a chance to tell your sister in person, I will not be as charitable as my wife-to-be: I will no longer consider your blood *mixed*; instead, I will assume that the same malicious brew that flows through my mother's veins also courses through yours."

"Now, Max—" Bronte tried gamely. She had never heard him quite so firm.

"Really, Max, I am Lady Claudia Seeley," she said in lofty defense. "Don't you think I have better things to do with my time than ruin my sister's day?" She turned to look in the metaphorical middle distance, then returned her gaze. "Well, when I put it that way, I don't have much better to do, but I assure you I won't celebrate her *demotion* until after you make it public."

Lady Claudia turned to Bronte with what appeared to be renewed, and far shrewder, interest. "You, my dear, may have bitten off more than you can chew, but let the feast begin! Cheers!"

"Cheers… I think." Bronte took a very careful sip of the perfectly delectable rosé. "Mmmm, isn't that delicious?" She smiled despite herself.

"Yes, dear, very. And don't you have quite the winning smile," Lady Claudia said as she put her glass down with precision then turned the force of her full attention on Bronte, ignoring Max completely. He merely put his mirrored sunglasses back on, picked up his paper, and muttered something along the lines of "here we go."

"So, tell me, dear. Where did you grow up? Who are your parents? How did you and Max meet? Was it romantic?"

Bronte laughed and couldn't help feeling like she and her best friend from sixth grade were about to dig into a brand-new clandestine issue of *Seventeen* magazine at the foot of her bed.

"My mother lives in northern New Jersey, about twenty minutes outside of New York City. My father died over ten years ago and I have no brothers or sisters." She made a show of inhaling for breath, then plowed on. "Max and I met in the science-fiction section of a second-hand bookstore on the west side of Chicago and"—dramatic intake of breath—"he fell madly in love with me and I haven't been able to get rid of him since, so I finally gave in and accepted one of his persistent proposals of marriage." She filled her lungs while reaching for her champagne, then proceeded to drain the entire flute. "Aaaah. Delicious."

Lady Claudia stared in utter amazement. "You dare to make fun of the irreproachable Master Maxwell? It gets better and better. I can't tell you how pleased I am that I decided to walk dear little Amis down the King's Road today! To think I might have gone into Hyde Park and, oh, it's all just too divine." Claudia savored another sip of champagne. "Oh, Max, admit it, your mother is going to go into fits. Well... no need to cause the lovely Ms. Talbott—I mean, Bronte—any undue anxiety."

Max folded his newspaper neatly, then placed it methodically onto the seat of the unoccupied chair at their table and looked across at his impossibly elegant aunt.

"We are going to Dunlear for the weekend. Would you and Uncle Bertrand care to join us?"

"Oh, Max. You are splendid. Of course, we will be there. Amassing your army, I see. Are Devon and Abigail going to be there?"

"Devon certainly. I haven't been able to get ahold of Abigail for weeks. I think she's WWOOFing in Scotland or some damn thing and she doesn't return calls for weeks at a time."

"What in the world is *woo*-fing?" Claudia pronounced it so it rhymed with *goofing*.

"You know, volunteering on organic farms..."

Claudia shook her head slowly to indicate she had absolutely no idea what Max was talking about.

"Never mind, Aunt Claudia. Spending a month in New Zealand

on a worm farm is not something you should ever have to contemplate. Meanwhile, Abby's up north somewhere planting lettuce and talking to rabbits and upsetting Mother with all of her alternative lifestyle decisions."

"I was wondering when I was going to get the full précis on Abigail," Bronte added as the waitress refilled her glass. "You and Devon have been so busy bolstering me up that I haven't heard anything about her. Lady Claudia, please elaborate."

"Aaah, well you really must thank her when you meet her."

"Really? What for exactly?"

"For paving the way, of course." Claudia raised her glass in mock-salute to Abigail. "Abby has been quite naughty all her life, but she always managed to stay in her father's good graces for two very good reasons. She loves manual labor and, well, she's an idea person. A fair assessment, Max?"

Max nodded and mm-hmmed his tacit agreement.

Bronte looked to him, then back to Lady Claudia, prompting her to continue.

"So of course, her father adored her. The fact that she likes girls"—raised eyebrow—"didn't really matter to him one way or the other. She's more of a Vita Sackville-West really."

"Oh, Claudia. Please don't try to be hip," Max groaned.

"Your sister is a lesbian, Max?" Bronte asked.

"Does it matter?"

"Of course it doesn't *matter*. It's just odd that you wouldn't have told me." Bronte gave him a puzzled look then turned back to Lady Claudia. "Pray continue. I am clearly going to gather much more family lore from you than I ever will from Max. Go on!"

"Well, not much else to tell, really. If you've just come from New York, I'm sure you've already met prissy Miss Lydia, and Claire is just, well, the type of careless woman who would incubate just such a daughter: vain, self-centered, and utterly oblivious."

Max gestured to the waitress for the bill. "Please tell us what you really think, Claudia."

"Funny you should ask," she said with an eloquent smirk. "I really *do* think Lydia might, just might, be salvageable if we get to her soon. She's not cruel, really; she just does what her mother tells her—which isn't very much, mind you—and the rest of her brain has been stuffed with thoughts of frocks and shoes and purses and eligible husbands." Lady Claudia raised a hand in silent protest. "Don't say it! I adore frocks and shoes and eligible husbands—plural—but when I was her age, at least, I gave the occasional thought to the occasional personal opinion."

"I said the same to Max in New York, that she might not be all bad, but she is just so... so... impertinent."

"She is that." Claudia took her final sip of champagne. "But you may have an ally there. Her grandmother occasionally makes thoughtless comments at her expense and you'd be wise to trade on that."

"God. It all sounds so deeply Machiavellian. It's bad enough I am, well, I guess I need to practice saying it, *engaged* to a duke, but the family drama is just so totally out of my league."

"Come now, Bronte," Claudia chided. "We all have families."

"Of course, but Max and I really dated in a vacuum, wouldn't you agree, Max?"

Max had just finished signing the bill. He folded his receipt and replaced his credit card in its slim black leather card case, then returned the case to his pocket. His fingers glanced across Bronte's thigh under the table as he looked into her eyes.

"Yes, a fabulous vacuum. Exactly." Then he turned back to Claudia. "We will look forward to seeing you Friday evening for supper, then? You'll stay for two nights?"

"Wonderful. Absolutely."

"And please, promise me we will get to talk about *real* issues then"—Bronte spoke in a deeply serious tone—"such as that Chanel suit you are wearing and where you think the best Sarah James—"

Claudia was laughing as Max hauled Bronte away from the table. Bronte tried to continue on about clothes and shoes, but ended up laughing through her farewell. "It was a pleasure meeting you, Lady Claudia. See you Friday."

"Good-bye, Aunt Claudia." Max had Bronte's hand firmly clasped in his. "We have an appointment at Coutts in ten minutes. Have to run."

Bronte wasn't sure, but she thought her fiancé winked at his fiercely chic aunt just as the two of them left the café and went to the sidewalk to hail a cab.

"I'm sorry"—Bronte was still recovering from her laughter—"but there is just no way in *hell* that your mother can be that much of a pill if that fucking dame is her sister."

"You'd better watch it or I will tell her you called her a 'fucking dame.'"

"You wouldn't!"

"Well…"

"No, I take it back. Go ahead and tell her; she would know I meant it as a compliment." They were settled in the cab and Bronte was smiling as she looked out the window, Max's hand safely in hers.

She spent the next fifteen minutes drinking in the lush London scenery. She had only been to London once, in college, and she had stayed in the all-girl dorm section of a Piccadilly youth hostel for nine pounds per night. Bronte smiled despite herself.

Ten years later, here she was traveling in a taxi with the nineteenth Duke of Northrop, who was whisking her off to some mysterious destination, then whisking her off to his family estate for the weekend. She didn't even feel like the same person.

For better or worse.

She recalled how confident she had felt at twenty-one, with a backpack and a passport and five hundred dollars in traveler's checks tucked securely into her money belt. She had felt utterly free. As exhilarated as she was at the prospect of a future with Max, she could no longer deny that by marrying Max, she would also be forfeiting that type of utter freedom.

"What are you thinking about?" Max's voice was gentle and low.

"All sorts of things. The last—and only—time I was in London. Backpack, youth hostel, you get the picture."

"Hail the conquering heroine and all that?"

"Hardly. You are going to think I'm being maudlin or overly analytical or whatever it is you think I am being when I dare to question the wisdom of diving into the deep end of the relationship pool head first"—she paused for a breath—"but I was just bidding farewell to that level of freedom… carelessness, I suppose… that has no place in the life of a well-adjusted adult. Especially a well-adjusted adult duchess. And yet…"

"Aaaah. Yes. The little *yet*. I think I know a little bit about that *yet*."

Bronte turned from the window to look more closely at Max's eyes as he continued.

"I… well… I have wanted to talk to you more about what it was like for me when I came back last year. I thought I had a good twenty years left to shirk my filial responsibilities"—he smiled but without any real humor—"or, if not shirk, then at least to have had those years to adjust to the reality of one day having to assume the role. Despite my pep talk on the plane this morning, I am not really any more cut out for this than you are, as you will soon see."

"Cut out for what, exactly?"

"The inescapable responsibility, I suppose."

"But you were so responsible about your academic work in Chicago—"

"That's just it. I loved the pressure, the research, the

complications. I loved fighting to resolve the issues that seemed insurmountable. Because, in the end, the solution always presented itself." He stopped to think, very slowly trailing his thumb up and down each of Bronte's fingers that rested in his hand. "The problem with my family... obligation... well, the whole dukedom seems so entirely intractable. Unavoidable, really. Endless."

"Max... maybe I'm just playing devil's advocate, but you sound so ungrateful. I'm sorry to be snippy, but really. Cry me a river."

"Very well. Turnabout's fair play and all that, but, well, you and I will... it will all turn out splendidly, of course, but you must always tell me when it starts weighing on you."

She looked out the window and thought of the anvil on her chest. "Okay."

"I mean it. You will *see* what it's like. It is splendid and grand and ancient and brooding and can sometimes just be a bit heavy." He gave her hand an extra squeeze. "Right here, Driver, thank you."

The taxi came to a standstill in front of the highly polished, very discreet, guarded mahogany doors of the Coutts Private Banking offices on Cavendish Square. The digital clock on the taxi's meter read 1:59.

Perfectly punctual.

Bronte was starting to realize that her husband-to-be had perfected the art of seemingly casual precision. Not that she was incapable of staying on task or completing her work assignments in a timely manner; it was just that she never really liked adhering to a recognizable routine. She went to work and did her job quite well, really, but she always welcomed the unexpected intrusion—the last-minute call from her long-lost cousin saying she was in New York for the night and asking if she could crash on Bronte's couch, the friend down the street who was always losing her keys and kept an extra set with Bronte. Something about the unpredictable offset Bronte's latent fear of boredom. She dreaded repetition. She was going to need to keep an eye on Max's reaction to the unexpected.

The immaculately uniformed guard made very brief eye contact with Max, then opened the silent front door to the private bank. The door closed smoothly and they were alone in a small vestibule: solid wood doors behind them, solid bulletproof glass in front of them. A professional female voice came over an invisible speaker and asked Max to look into the retinal scanner to his right, which he did. A few seconds later, the glass wall in front of them split into two sliding doors that retracted into the immaculate walls.

A woman in her mid-forties, sporting a perfectly cut black bob à la Coco Chanel, a fitted charcoal blazer with matching stylish pencil skirt, and impossibly high, black patent-leather pumps that still managed to scream "your money is safe with me," strode confidently toward them across the deep gray carpet. Bronte momentarily wondered if everyone who worked here had to color coordinate their wardrobe with the muted gray color scheme of the interior design.

"Your Grace." She nodded slightly, extending her arm to shake hands with Max. "Therese Balderton," she said with what sounded like a hint of a French accent. "A pleasure. And Ms. Talbott, welcome to Coutts."

"Nice to meet you, Ms. Balderton," Bronte replied, no longer surprised that Max had orchestrated everything down to the last detail, that this woman would know her name.

"If you will follow me." Ms. Balderton gestured toward a door to the left of the entry. "I have the private room available with the items you requested."

"Thank you. I appreciate it." Max had recaptured Bronte's hand in his and was channeling some sort of crazy excitement.

Bronte tried to get his attention as they followed the immaculate Ms. Balderton, but he was smiling at some private joke of his own and refused to make eye contact with her. Bronte finally gave up as they turned down a narrow corridor with five identical, unmarked steel doors on either side.

Ms. Balderton stopped in front of the third door on the right, shook her wrist down to reveal a chain with a single key attached, inserted it into the lock that was sunk flush into the plane of the door (there was no doorknob), and pushed into the room.

The small viewing room was approximately ten feet by ten feet, painted in the same muted gray as the reception area, with a modern circular tulip table and two chairs in the center. In the middle of the table was a large, oblong, steel drawer with two sets of white archival cotton gloves placed neatly on top.

"Do you require any additional assistance, Your Grace?"

"No. Thank you very much, Ms. Balderton."

"As you know, simply press the red button here to the right of the door if you need anything at all or when you are ready to leave." Then she turned to go and closed the door silently behind her.

"Well, isn't this just a little James Bond-ish?" Bronte clasped her hands together in genuine delight.

"I am so pleased you are pleased. Are you curious?"

Bronte stalked slowly around the table and drew her hands up around Max's neck, feeling the frisson of contact when her fingertips grazed past his hairline, along the edge of his shirt collar. She touched the ends of his hair with the tip of her index finger and felt his response as she leaned in to take his lips. "Always curious," she whispered.

She was sure there were hidden cameras—the whole room was probably one big hidden camera, for chrissake—but all this cloak and dagger had her wanting to throw herself at Max.

"Good to know… for future reference…" he breathed between hot kisses, "if we are ever going through a dry patch… I will schedule a private viewing at the bank to get you back on track, eh, Bron?" He kissed her again with more strength than passion, then took her hands firmly in his and moved them away from his neck. "But not right now, my dear. I have some things I want to show you."

"Oh, all right," Bronte huffed in mock capitulation, dropping herself unceremoniously into one of the chairs and crossing her arms across her chest like a pissed-off teenager. "What have you got?"

"Put on the gloves, darling."

Max handed her a pair of the thin white cotton gloves and put on his own. She slowly put one glove on, trying to make it kind of sexy, but Max was having none of it, and the gloves were more Mickey Mouse than Grace Kelly anyway, so she gave up and rolled her eyes at him with a smile.

She was still smiling when she realized Max had opened the safety deposit box and he was taking out black velvet boxes in all shapes and sizes.

"Good God, Max! What the hell is all that?"

"Fear not, my duchess-to-be; it is all yours—or very soon will be—to do with as you wish, at least in this lifetime. Now close your eyes."

"Oh, Max. Please."

"I'm serious. Close them."

Bronte reluctantly complied. She heard Max opening and closing several of the jewelry boxes with quick snaps of the hinges. Some opened with a small unfastening snap; others creaked slightly as the little-used hinges were put into rare service.

"Aaaah. Here we are. Keep those eyes closed."

"I said I would. Don't push your luck."

"Patience."

After a few more moments, Max finished setting everything out and told her to open her eyes.

"Are you a pirate for fuck's sake? Is that pirate booty?"

He laughed and she felt the thrum of his pleasure rise up through her own body. There were piles of gems: necklaces, rings, tiaras, long chain-mail looking things, bracelets, earrings, collars, lanyards, cuffs. She had never seen anything like it, except maybe in the windows at Harry Winston and, well, not even then.

"Holy motherfucker."

"Yes, that pretty much says it. Welcome to the private jewelry collection of the Dukes of Northrop. I was going to choose a ring for you, and I *have* really, but then I thought it would be fun for you to see the, er, selection, as it were."

He was fondling a sinewy bracelet that looked like it was from the 1930s and consisted of eight rows of diamonds that were somehow meshed together with an invisible filament. The effect was diaphanous.

"Maybe we will choose the same ring in any case," Max continued, "and then I won't have to be seen as the stodgy old-fashioned control freak who bullied you into wearing something you didn't even like."

"You're not stodgy."

"I get it… old-fashioned, freakishly controlling bully? Yes. Stodgy? No."

"I'm not saying…" She stood up to get a better look at all the loot on the table. She tried to busy her hands with smoothing the fabric of her skirt down her thighs because what she really wanted to do was grab great clumps of jewelry and feel the weight of it as it cascaded through her greedy fingers. "This is just plain wrong."

"What is?" he asked with genuine worry.

"This… I mean, I don't think of myself as a greedy person—"
Max smiled suggestively.

"Well, I may be greedy in *that* way, but you know what I mean. I never thought of myself as having any sort of *lust* for objects. A great pair of shoes, some perfect little Valentino dress… okay. But even those were just diversions, really. Or comforts. But seeing all this… all this… I don't even know where to begin. It kind of makes my blood race."

"Hmm. I like this idea of your blood racing. Please continue."

Bronte reached one gloved hand across the table very slowly, picking up an enormous ruby pin. The weight was surprisingly heavy in her palm. She held it carefully in the center of her left hand and then lifted it gently with her right to examine it more closely. The finely worked gold looked medieval, with cabochon diamonds and tiny seed pearls forming the perimeter of a Maltese square cross around the walnut-sized ruby.

"Odd you should pick that first."

"Why? Was this the first piece that the first duke got from the spoils of war?"

"A little bit later than that. It was just a bauble, really. Family lore says it was a secret gift from one of the Tudors to his momentary favorite, Sophia Heyworth, who was the second duke's granddaughter. She didn't curry favor for long, but the wily duke managed to keep the more valuable trinkets of their short alliance."

Bronte's hand shook slightly as she put the five-hundred-year-old treasure back into its slightly faded, perfectly fitted, white silk cushioned safety.

"I think I might need to sit down."

Bronte went around the small table and sat down next to Max. Shell-shocked.

"I remember the first time my father brought me here," Max said. "Keep in mind we are sort of, well, the unintentional dukes of the family. My dad was a farmer really. It sounds ludicrous, and when you see the place in Yorkshire, you will accuse me of false humility. But seriously, none of this was ever meant to be ours. When my grandparents inherited the title in the sixties, that was absurd enough—the crusty ex-military man married to the shy, retiring princess, the unexpected second son of the second son and all that. And then when my father's older brother died and it was my father who took the title, well, equally absurd. So here I sit, still scratching my head to some extent. I am not complaining about my responsibilities, but the weight still bears down. Do you see what I mean?"

"I guess the... well... I... I don't think I would spend a lot of time in here, that's for sure. I get where you're going with the weight of history and all that, but it's also a wonderful, albeit notorious, history to be a part of." She smiled and the twinkle in her eye soothed him. "You are a part of all that," she added as she gestured toward the mass of gems.

"You're right. And now I have you to take half the burden, eh? Enough of my worry. It's a joyous occasion and I would like you to choose your engagement ring. I'll start to put away the other pieces, unless—" He was holding a particularly intricate diamond necklace that rested in the pleated white silk interior of a substantial black velvet case.

"There must be fabulous stories about each piece. We could be here all day."

"Is that what you would like?"

"I guess, one rainy day I would love that. But right now for some reason, Max, it's all making me feel a little overwhelmed."

"I suspected as much. Let's put everything away except the rings. That should help to narrow our attention."

The two of them sat for a few minutes, carefully refitting the larger boxes back into the steel safety deposit box. When they were finished, all that remained were six identical black velvet ring boxes, revealing six vastly different rings. The recessed halogen spotlights in the ceiling created a sparkling refraction off the various stones.

"May I?" Bronte asked, indicating the need to take off her left glove in order to try on the rings.

"Allow me."

Max came to her side and held her left wrist in his hand. Bronte thought he seemed like a kind, adept pediatrician getting ready to take her pulse. He removed the glove, placed it down on the table, then brought the center of Bronte's palm to his warm lips, just as he had that first time in the coffee shop in Chicago.

It had seemed so intimate that day, so unexpected. Now it was like a brand. Still intimate but such a part of their bond, so fortifying. Her eyes closed for a few seconds as she tried to savor the feeling.

"I don't know what I did to deserve you, Max," she whispered.

"Likewise," he agreed as he pulled his own gloves off. "So, why don't we try them all on for size, as a start."

The rings were arrayed in no particular order, so Max reached for the closest one.

"I'm pretty sure this is an emerald from India, from the mid-1800s."

The ornate setting was raised extravagantly high from her hand. The ring itself fit her finger perfectly, but the high setting made her think there was a secret poison chamber hidden beneath.

"I don't think this is for me." Bronte smiled, then took the ring from her finger and put it gently back into its box.

They continued trying on different options: a spectacular, enormous diamond solitaire (six carats? seven? she had no idea), alone and perfect in its four thin platinum prongs (it made her feel lonely somehow); another emerald, rectangular and set deep within a wide gold filigreed band (too Guinevere); two dark sapphires, nearly black, that twinkled almost malevolently, Bronte thought for a split second, in a sea of tiny pavé diamonds (she quickly returned *that* ring to its place).

The final two were a ruby the size of her thumbnail, seductive in its way, and then a canary-yellow round diamond that winked at her cheerfully between two diamond trillions. She put one ring on the ring finger of each hand, weighing them, turning over her hands, fingernails up, then fingers bent in toward her palms; hand resting loosely on her shoulder, hand stretched at arm's length.

"I feel like a goddamned hand model, for chrissake," she joked, but Max knew it was only a nervous attempt at levity, as he too felt the real intensity of the situation crackling between them.

"It's all right, Bron. Take your time."

"In this at least," she murmured.

"I heard that."

"Well, I think I've decided. Was one of these the one you chose?"

"Of course. You didn't think I wanted you to wear those sapphire headlights of evil, did you?"

She smiled into his eyes.

"It's got to be the canary diamond, doesn't it?"

His smile was brilliant. He knew she would choose it. Or, at least, he had hoped to the very edge of knowing that she would choose it.

She continued, "I mean the ruby is, well, so fucking sexy. I don't think I could see myself changing a diaper with that glowing ember winking at me." She met his eyes with a mock smolder. "That said, maybe it winks best at diaper-changing time as a reminder of what happens after all that sexy *foolishness*. I would love to wear it—and nothing else, mind you—for some little rendezvous, but for my humdrum everyday life with you, I think the priceless canary diamond carries the day."

Max felt simultaneously gutted and perfectly grounded. He couldn't believe this sexy, brazen, strong, tender, crass, winsome woman was going to be the mother of his children. "You have no idea how badly I want to say, 'you had me at diaper changing,' but I will refrain."

Max slipped the empty black-velvet box into his briefcase and told Bronte to wear the canary. She looked momentarily taken aback, then helped Max close up the rest of the small velvet boxes and put them snugly back into the oblong steel case. Max pulled the top of the safety deposit box securely closed, then got up to press the red button that would signal they were ready to leave. The efficient Ms. Balderton opened the steel door to the room and escorted them out to the reception area.

"Thank you for your visit, Your Grace. Ms. Talbott." She nodded toward Bronte. "Please feel free to contact me directly if you need any further assistance."

She handed Max her small, perfect business card as the bullet-proof glass doors slid open. "The guard will open the outer door once these doors are securely closed. Good day."

She stood with her hands clasped professionally in front of her as the glass doors silently shut. A few seconds later, the security guard on the street opened the heavy mahogany door and nodded in a genuinely respectful way as they walked out onto the sunny London sidewalk.

Max pulled Bronte toward him, his arm securely around her waist. "What's your pleasure, Bron?" Max took a quick look at his watch.

"I hate to admit it, but I'm a little tired. Do you need to go to your office? I am happy to hop into a taxi back to your place for a little afternoon nap."

Max looked both ways, then guided Bronte across the crowded street. "Let's walk for a few blocks and then I probably should head over to St. James's for a couple of hours. I'd love to go over some property details with my attorney. Are you sure you don't mind?"

"Mind? Why would I mind?"

"I don't know… romantic moment, our first day in London? I don't know. I guess I forget that you are not really the sentimental type."

She smiled then looked down at her left hand. "I think you've gone the distance in the sentiment department today, Max. Let me put my weary head down for a few hours and maybe it will fortify me for when I meet your mom later."

"All right then."

"Where are we going for dinner, by the way?"

"Mother wanted us to come to Northrop House in Mayfair—"

"Oh… a casual night at home?"

"Yeah, I thought it might be a bit of a drag, so I suggested Birches over in Kensington. Mother loves it and I hoped that our announcement might go over better in public."

"Aaah. Safety in numbers or something."

Max looked down at the sidewalk. "Or something."

"Will Devon be there?"

"Yes, I invited him. More safety in numbers, right?" Max was trying to stay cheerful, but Bronte could feel his mood sliding into an almost palpable trepidation.

"Max, you have finally started to chip away at my natural state of extreme skepticism. Don't blow it by going all panicky on me now."

He smiled thinly. "It will be over soon."

"Well, that was stirring. Now I feel really psyched." She rolled her eyes and gave him a quick peck on the cheek. "What time should I be ready to leave?"

"We are meeting at Birches at seven thirty, so I will pick you up at seven fifteen. The restaurant is near my place. Does that sound good?"

"Of course."

He hailed a cab and helped Bronte get in. Max held the taxi door open a little longer than necessary as he watched Bronte lean forward and tell the driver his address. He liked the sound of it: his address coming out of her mouth, with that American accent—all business. She was already riffling through her purse looking for her cell phone, then clicking on her email icon, before she tossed her hair aside, looked up, and realized he was still standing there.

"What?" she laughed.

"Out of sight, out of mind, I see."

"Well, somebody's got to get some work done around here, and it's still morning in New York." She held her phone slightly to the side.

"I know. I'm off to do the same, but I think I'll just stroll to the office and savor the memory of you and me alone in the vault."

She smiled and reached out her free hand to grasp his. "I love you, Max. I'll see you soon." He smiled in return and released her hand.

He shut the cab door, gave it a firm slap-slap, and watched the back of Bronte's head through the rear window as the taxi slid away and was swallowed into the heavy London traffic.

Despite his joking with Bronte about being out of sight and out of mind, he had to admit it was something they actually shared. When they had been together in Chicago, he had been at the height of defending his PhD work on his dissertation. As intense and exhilarating as their physical life together had been, they were always able to direct their attention squarely on their work when the time came. He had presented his oral thesis in front of some of the most discerning academics in the field of corporate finance. Initially, he had worried that Bronte was going to be too much of a distraction, but it proved to be a baseless concern.

He walked down to St. James's where he had set up the family offices after his father's death. His mother had pleaded with him to use the study at Northrop House, but he had absolutely refused. He treated the dukedom and its holdings as a serious financial business concern, and he wasn't about to run it by proxy from some Regency antique escritoire in Mayfair. Several private banks and family trusts had offices nearby, including the Rothschilds and the Guinnesses. It was a millionaire's ghetto of sorts.

He sat down at his immaculate, nondescript, brown institutional desk and was relieved to feel that the sweet memory of Bronte in the vault had receded considerably. He was going to be able to turn his full attention to a land dispute at Dunlear that was presenting a complex array of obstacles. Unfortunately, concentration was not the problem, but keeping track of the time once he was consumed by a particular mathematical problem was.

A few hours later, across town, Bronte had tried on every different outfit she had packed and still didn't like how she looked. It was five after seven and she was pacing around Max's bedroom in her slip and high heels.

Catherine Malandrino dress? Too frilly.

J. Crew mustard-yellow pants? Not respectful enough for dinner with the duchess.

Barneys navy suit? Too mannish.

Sexy silk tank top with Rick Owens back slit skirt? Schizophrenic.

Michael Kors beige drawstring dress? Brown bag.

Armani black tunic dress? Funereal.

Good God. These had been all of her best eBay, Bluefly, and Barneys Warehouse prime finds. What the hell?

Wrong. Wrong. Wrong.

Finally reverting to type, she opted for sexy schoolmarm. She put on her navy pencil skirt and a crisp, feminine but not too fussy, white button-down shirt. She tried to dress it up with a wide patent leather belt and a pair of black patent-leather peep-toe heels that Sarah had given her the day before she had left for London.

"For good luck!" she had said with a kiss.

Well, here she was wearing them, and the luck did not feel forthcoming. Mr. I'll-Pick-You-Up-at-Seven-Fifteen was still AWOL and *tardy* was not the first impression she wanted to give the Duchess of Northrop on their inaugural meeting.

Fuck.

Her cell phone started ringing; somewhere under the pile of her entire travel wardrobe was her purse, deep inside of which, presumably, rested her blasted cell phone. She dug it out on the last ring.

"This is Bronte."

She knew it was Max, but her mood was too peevish to give him a kinder greeting.

"I am so sorry, Bron. I got completely involved in the agricultural dispute and whether or not we are going to be able to move forward with the drainage works on the entire six hundred arable hectares or if we—"

"You know what, Max? I don't give a rat's ass about arable hectares right now. I am having a fucking meltdown here. Are you still at the office, because I am not going to meet your mother alone, I'll tell you right—"

"Of course, I am not still at the office, Bron. I am on my way to pick you up right now. I was just calling to see if you could meet me out on the Fulham Road in five minutes, at the corner of the entrance to the mews, and then you can hop in the cab and we'll be right as rain—"

"Enough with the chipper BS. I have worked myself into quite a lather. I'll see you on the corner."

She turned her phone off and stared at it for a full minute. Obviously she cared about the arable hectares... but, fuck, did she have to care about them right now?

She pursed her lips and took a credit card, some cash, and her passport out of her big day bag and slid them into the sleek, oblong Anya Hindmarch black patent-leather clutch that Sarah had coerced her into buying on sale last spring at Bergdorf's. At least with the belt, the bag, and the shoes, she felt properly armed to deal with the coming storm. She threw in a lip gloss and her cell phone, then walked downstairs, almost tripping on the second-to-last step.

Perfect, she thought. *I'll fall flat on my face.*

She grabbed the keys to the house off the mahogany table by the front door and headed out onto the cobbled mews. Obviously, no one in high heels had played a part in the urban development known as cobblestones.

How the hell was she supposed to look like all that and a bag of chips when her heels were catching in the cracks of the street? She made her wobbly way out to the Fulham Road at almost the exact moment Max's cab pulled up. He jumped out and gave her a quick woo-hoo whistle, followed by a peck on the cheek and the press of his hand on the small of her back to guide her into the cab. Almost before the door had closed behind him, the driver was on his way north toward the tiny restaurant in Kensington.

"I am so sorry, Bron—"

"Don't worry about it. I was a cow. I will always be late if I'm at work, I'll warn you right now. I'm horribly unreliable. I just—"

"You look great, by the way." He came in for a kiss.

"Watch the lipstick!" she cried as she pushed him away.

"For future reference, we are never going out to dinner again if I am not allowed to kiss you in the taxi." He fumed like a toddler and crossed his arms.

Bronte smiled and let her hand rest innocently on his thigh.

"Where's the ring?!" Max grabbed her other hand.

"Back at the house. Why? Did you want me to wear it?"

He leaned toward the hard plastic divider in the taxi without a second glance toward Bronte. "Driver, please turn back," he said with terse authority, then he sat back to look at her. "Of course I wanted you to wear it. I would have thought—"

"It's kind of huge, Max. I'm not really accustomed to it yet."

"Accustomed to it?" He laughed as if she were being ridiculous. "Get over yourself!" He was trying to make light of her modesty, but it came out as plain old arrogance. "I want the whole world to see that ring on your finger," he added as he looked out the window.

"The whole world? Or just your mother?"

"What the hell is that supposed to mean?" he said, turning to face her again.

"You know damn well what I mean. What did you think, Max? That if I walked into the restaurant with that headlight on my left hand it would take the edge off? Make it easier for you to introduce me to your mother as your fait accompli fiancée?" She pulled her hand from his grasp.

"Bronte. Why do you have to twist this all around?"

"Me twist it around?! Are you fucking kidding me? We are going to be totally late! And for what? So I can parade around with that ginormous diamond—"

"What are you saying? You were not planning on wearing it all the time?"

"Well, I mean, it's bordering on ostentatious, don't you think?"

Max silently counted to ten as he looked out at the anonymous parade of seeming normalcy that was sliding past his window. He tried not to explode in pure rage. He turned back to look Bronte in the eye and in very slow, very modulated tones, he continued.

"Bronte, it was my understanding—unspoken, I admit—that, yes, you would wear the ring *all the time* because you would be engaged and subsequently married to me *all the time*. I hadn't even thought of discussing it because it seemed patently obvious, to me at least."

"Max—"

"Bronte, we're here." He gestured toward the passage that led to his mews house. "Please go back into the house and get the ring. If you refuse to wear it, at the very least, I can carry it with me so we don't get burgled and lose a family heirloom."

She stared at him as if she no longer knew who he was. In a daze, she got out of the taxi and headed back across the infernal cobblestones, inserted the shaking key into the lock, walked upstairs to the bathroom, got the ring out of her makeup case, slid it unemotionally, forcefully onto her left ring finger, made her way back down the stairs, locked the front door, tripped on another cobblestone, swore, and then got back in the taxi with a firm slam of the black door.

By this point, it was seven forty.

Bronte was wiped.

Max was still fuming but trying not to show it. He reached for her hand and she pulled it away and folded her arms tighter than necessary, stuffing her fingers childishly under her arms.

"Bronte, this is ridiculous—"

"Ridiculous? *Ridiculous?!*"

"No need to shriek—"

"I will *shriek* any time I damn well feel like it, but especially when you act like a fucking Greek shipping magnate who wants his latest bimbo to sport the day's haul from the vault—"

"It is nothing like that, Bron." Max tried to keep his voice even. "This is all your crisis-building. Only you could turn this into my failure to appreciate your tender sensibilities. I just gave you one of the most precious—"

"Stop! Stop right fucking now." The taxi slowed abruptly. "No, not you, Driver. Sorry." She looked down at her knees. "I'm just not up for it, Max."

"What?!" His head whipped around to take her in. "What the hell are you not *up* for?"

"I am not up for sitting across the table from your mother so she can make snide remarks about how low brow I am, how delightfully *common* I am—"

"Bronte—"

"You know I'm right. The ring, the rushing around, everything in such a flurry. Where's the fire, Max? What's the point?"

The taxi started to slow as it approached the intimate, warm glow of the small restaurant. As the cab came to a complete stop, the driver sat perfectly still and looked straight ahead as if there were something of very particular interest on the glass of his windshield.

"Fuck it, Bron." Max slapped both his hands on his knees and held them there. "I don't care. You want me to walk in and tell my mother dinner's off? You want me to go in and have dinner with her alone? You want to wear the ring? You don't want to wear the ring?"

She looked out the window at the restaurant.

She was lost.

What was she doing there? Who were these people whose high opinions she sought though she'd never laid eyes on them?

And why?

Her heart started to pound so hard and so fast she thought she could actually see the movement through the fabric of her white shirt. She took a very deep breath and tried to collect her scattered thoughts and feelings.

"Everything is all mixed up, Max. I care what your mother thinks. I hate to admit it, but I care. And I'm nervous and I... fuck... I don't want to have to factor in your feelings and I know that's mean and selfish. But—"

"Bronte, I'm sorry, but we have to go in. I mean, you don't have to go in—I didn't mean it that way. But it's quarter to eight and she's sitting in there and, well, one way or the other, I need to go in there. Are you coming?"

The silence in the cab was popping and hissing in her ears. She wanted to pretend that it was another ultimatum, that he was just another man trying to manipulate her, but the truth was too obvious. She looked at him and her stomach heaved. The pain behind her eyes was a throbbing bruise trying to force its way out.

It was her own raw fear.

She whispered, barely audible, "Max, I am fucking terrified."

The back of his hand barely touched her cheek, then his warm fingers were around the back of her neck, pulling her toward him. He whispered in her ear, "You're with me now, Bron. You are going to get out of this taxi in those impossibly sexy high heels and you are going to walk into that restaurant and you are going to unseat the duchess. Now put your big-girl pants on and let's get our asses in there."

He kissed her on the cheek, very close to her lips, then let the tip of his tongue trace her bottom lip. "And please invest in some of that newfangled nonsmudge lipstick I've been reading about."

He laced his fingers through hers, grabbed his briefcase from the floor of the cab, and stepped out onto the sidewalk, helping Bronte step out behind him. The warm summer night's wind swept through their hair as Max leaned in to pay the cab driver. He kept one hand lightly around Bronte's waist as he took the change, pocketed it, and picked up his briefcase again.

"It's just dinner, Bron."

"I know."

"And Devon can't wait to meet you."

"I know."

"So we're good, right?"

"Yes."

But her voice was small.

They walked down the steps into the golden, welcoming light of the intimate restaurant. Max could feel the shiver of anxiety coming through Bronte and did his best to hold her in check. She was exactly like the young foal he had jokingly compared her to, flipping her chestnut hair nervously over one shoulder, tightening her grip.

"Careful you don't grind your purse into dust, Bron."

She looked down at her own hand as if it belonged to someone else and realized she was holding the slim black clutch so hard that her fingernails were white and she was probably leaving permanent indentations in the patent leather.

There were only nine or ten small tables in the restaurant. Devon stood up so quickly he almost overturned his chair in his enthusiasm.

"You're here!" He sounded as though his jovial excitement may actually offset Bronte's rapidly solidifying dread. He was a little bit shorter than Max, maybe an inch or two over six feet, but while his older brother's charm had a formal, chiseled quality, Devon's looks, though equally engaging, were marked with an open, frivolous ease.

His hair was thick and wavy like Max's, but a lighter, sandy hue. His eyes were gray and sparkling, like Max's.

Before Bronte had a chance to speak, Devon had wrapped her in a firm bear hug that seemed more suited to a college football tailgate than this excruciatingly difficult first family meeting. He gave her a brotherly pat on the back and whispered, "It's all good."

Max was air-kissing his mother without actually touching her as Devon began to sit back down in the seat he had been in when they arrived.

"No, darling, Bronte is sitting there."

The duchess speaks.

Her voice was, well, beyond description. Bronte had never heard anything like it. It was deep, almost to the point of husky, but somehow retained a piercing accuracy. It was like Lauren Bacall with a knife to her throat.

Bronte stood perfectly still, her hands clasped in front of her, holding on to her Anya Hindmarch for dear life and suppressing a momentary giddy desire to kick up one heel, grab a corner of her skirt, and spin like a marionette.

But she didn't.

Max stepped out from behind his mother's chair. He took Bronte's hand in his and formally (very formally) introduced, presented really, his mother to Bronte.

The formalities dispensed with, the four of them sat, adjusted napkins; Bronte straightened her silverware. Max sat opposite Bronte, thinking to himself that his mother had obviously set out to separate them, even here at the table.

Devon dove into the conversation.

"How was your first day in London, Bron? Lots to do? Business? Pleasure? What do you think of Max's little Fulham fixer-upper?"

Bronte was taking a sip of her water and looked quickly at Max before turning her full attention to Devon. She swallowed.

"Full… yes… no… yes… lovely." She smiled for the first time in what felt like hours.

"I know! I have a terrible habit of talking excitedly right over people. But I am excited to meet you. We all are, right, Mother?"

"Of course, dear," Sylvia intoned. "Thrilled."

Again with the voice.

Why hadn't Max warned her about the voice? It was perfectly unassailable. Of course, she hadn't just said "thrilled" in the most sarcastic, insulting tone imaginable—or had she? That was the villainy of it: the appearance of complete innocence forming an impenetrable shellac over pure malice.

Max watched as Bronte smiled genuinely and turned to his mother. "Likewise, Duchess, it is my pleasure to finally meet you." As much as Max had assured her that was the proper form of address, it still rang false to her American ear. She kept having to stop herself from calling her something totally inappropriate, like "Your Highness."

"Finally?" Sylvia said softly, turning to Max. "Has it been more than a week or two? I didn't know."

"Yes, Sylvia. It has been well over a year since Bronte and I first met."

"I am so far removed from the *Sturm und Drang* of your comings and goings these days, Maxwell." Of course her German accent would be perfect. "I must have forgotten you telling me about your new friend." Thin smile.

Devon put his hand on Bronte's forearm, willing her to devote the rest of the evening's conversation to him. *Let the two of them hash this out*, his confident touch seemed to say. "So tell me more about your day. The weather has been so unaccountably fabulous."

Max watched as Devon kept Bronte wrapped in a lively discussion of their lunch at Bluebird and the happy coincidence of seeing their Aunt Claudia there. At the mention of her sister, Sylvia's eye twitched, almost imperceptibly, but Max caught it and had a momentary vision of licking his finger and marking a point for his team on the imaginary scoreboard that was always near at hand when his mother was around.

"Yes, Mother. That's right, we bumped into Claudia walking Amis on the King's Road earlier this afternoon." He spoke in muted tones, trying to keep their conversation separate from Devon and Bronte's, to better delay any unnecessary fracas between the two women. "I've invited her and Uncle Bertrand to Dunlear for the weekend."

"Charming. You will all have a splendid time."

"We will. Won't you be there?"

"Why would I be there, Maxwell?"

"Because it is the first anniversary of Father's death and I had assumed you would want to be there to honor the occasion."

Devon and Bronte had just come to a pause in their upbeat conversation at the words "Father's death," so the syllables fell like bricks into the middle of the dinner table.

The waiter arrived—right as Max finished the rest of the sentence—and handed a stiff linen-white card with the evening's fixed menu printed in a beautiful pale-green script. After confirming that no one had any allergies and handing Max the wine list, the server headed back toward the well-lit kitchen at the rear of the subdued yellow dining room.

Devon tried to pick up the thread of their previous humor, but his attempt felt forced and vague. Bronte smiled weakly and tried to soldier on, describing her impressions of London and her reminiscences of her first backpacking visit many years before.

Max forged ahead with his mother, trying to maintain his patience as she spoke.

"Maxwell, dear, I am in possession of both a calendar and a memory, so, yes, I am well aware of the year that has passed since your father died. And no, I will not be going to Dunlear to participate in some sort of ritualized show of sentimental group affection."

"As you wish, Mother. I had merely hoped it would be a time for us to be together as a family. I am pretty sure Claire and Lydia will be there, as well as Abigail if I can get her to return my calls anytime in a given thirty-day period. And Devon and Bronte."

"Why would Bronte be there?"

At the mention of her name twice in rapid succession, Bronte could no longer feign jovial interest in Devon's chatter. She put her hand briefly on Devon's forearm to let him know she was turning her attention briefly away, and she stared meaningfully into Max's eyes.

The various shades of gray, steel, slate, and blue that she had seen there in the past were gone. His eyes were so cold, nearly glacial. She almost didn't recognize them, or him. He blinked, coming back to himself, smiled at Bronte, then turned to his mother.

"Because we are engaged to be married."

A beat of silence.

The glass of water that had been on its way to the duchess's lips was carefully put back. "Congratulations."

"Is that all you have to say, Mother?"

"Is that not the appropriate response, Maxwell?"

"Entirely appropriate, Sylvia."

"Very well."

"Very well."

The soup course arrived just then, and all four of them began eating simultaneously, with the focus and commitment usually reserved for open-heart surgery. The waiter pulled the cork out of the Pouilly-Fuissé that Max had ordered and poured a small amount into Max's glass. Max tried it, nodded, and then the waiter filled all four glasses with a generous pour. Bronte wanted to guzzle the entire glass and wipe her mouth roughly with the back of her forearm.

But she refrained.

Now that the cat was out of the proverbial bag, Bronte just wanted to make it through the meal without collapsing face-first into her baked cod with summer vegetables. Had she been able to fully appreciate it, she suspected the food would be really superb. The pea soup had been a whipped, foamy, spring-green concoction, unlike anything the muddy, clumpy name had formerly conjured in her mind. The dollop of crème fraîche on top tasted like it had come from a dairy farm that morning. The cod, what she could remember of it, was also rich and succulent, with a gorgeous, honey-brown sauté. Dessert was a spectacular fruit something-or-other. Bronte thought she would be able to enjoy all of it, but while every initial bite hinted at greatness as it entered her mouth, each mouthful turned to wet cardboard as it slid down her throat. The verbal lacerations that passed for Sylvia's dinner conversation were nearly enough to put Bronte right over the edge.

Bronte knew that this woman must have hosted state dinners for her husband and carried the weight of countless social engagements squarely on her shoulders; she was never at a loss to initiate a topic. But even Bronte could tell that the duchess's patience was being tried by having to devote hours of her valuable time to an American *working girl*.

"Please tell me about your family."

Bronte answered in robotic compliance: father died… mother retired… then she reached for her wineglass with her left hand and saw the color drain from Sylvia's perfectly preserved complexion.

"What a lovely ring."

"Thank you."

It took all the concentration Bronte had to continue the movement of bringing the wineglass to her lips and to actually take a sip of what might as well have been battery acid, then very carefully put the glass back in its place. Putting that glass back in its place, as the duchess's eyes were inexorably glued to the canary diamond, was a slow-motion hell that Bronte would relive for the rest of her life.

"Max, you didn't tell me you were going to the vault."

"I didn't think I needed to check with you before going, Mother."

"Of course not." Fake, tinkling, light laugh. "You are the duke and that vault is under your purview, as are all of your father's rights and responsibilities. No need to be defensive."

"I was hardly being defensive."

"Of course you were. I was challenging your authority, after all."

"Let's not verbally assault one another on Bronte's first visit, Sylvia. It's so unattractive."

"Maxwell, please don't be dramatic for the benefit of your"—slight turn, hint of a sniff—"affianced bride. No one is assaulting anyone. And you know I dislike it when you call me 'Sylvia.'"

"Yes, I do know."

"Fair enough. Let's try to enjoy the rest of our meal, shall we?"

"Yes, let us try."

Max took the final spoonful of soup, placed his utensil between the bowl and the charger, picked up his napkin, and wiped his lips.

From there on out, Bronte became quite adept at using her right hand only. Luckily, fish was the main course, so she could use the side of her fork to slice it and then stab at the food without having to resort to the use of her knife. By the end of two grueling hours, she was on the verge of breaking down. Not just sobbing—more like willy-nilly running through the streets with arms waving and teeth gnashing.

The duchess, on the other hand, managed to look as though she had just had a splendidly charming dinner from which she hated to tear herself away. Bronte had to confess a grudging admiration for the woman's ability to reflect absolutely none of her true feelings through her appearance.

Sylvia rose from the table and placed her napkin on her chair. Her sons both stood. Bronte froze. Her mother's voice was clanging in her mind: "A lady never stands." Was there a mother-in-law exception?

"Very well. I must be off. Thank you for inviting me to dinner, Maxwell. Devon." Slightest pause? "Bronte."

Sylvia glanced at each of them in turn as she said their names, nodded infinitesimally, then stepped away from the table and crossed the restaurant.

All three watched—Devon turned where he stood to see her—as she walked up the steps and out to the street level. When the outer door had shut firmly and several more seconds had passed, Bronte picked up her barely touched glass of wine (forming her *left* hand into an unwieldy fist around the stem of the delicate crystal), downed it in its entirety, then raised it as if it were a stein at Oktoberfest to intercept the passing waiter.

"Another bottle of the Pouilly-Fuissé, please."

Devon picked up his glass, smiled, and chugged in filial solidarity.

Max looked at both of them and shook his head in mock disparagement.

Devon started to laugh, slowly and in low tones at first, then unable to refrain, he had to put one hand over his mouth and one hand over his middle to keep from embarrassing the people dining nearby with his guffaws. Bronte looked at Max and smiled, then got up and walked around to his side of the table, took his face in her hands, and kissed him deeply.

She pulled away an inch or two to see the softness had returned to his gray-wolf eyes.

"That's better," she whispered.

She took the seat in which Sylvia had been sitting, scooted it closer to his, took hold of one of Max's hands, and laced her fingers through his. "I'm having second thoughts."

Devon stopped laughing instantly.

Max just smiled and started shaking his head again.

"What kind of second thoughts?" Max asked.

"Well, remember how I said I didn't want a prenup, except to say I definitely didn't want anything and all that, you know, putting everyone's mind to rest and all that? Well, I don't think I want to put her mind to rest. Is that wrong?"

Devon started laughing again and this time the people at the neighboring table smiled at Max and Bronte with a look of empathy that implied, "Aren't you nice to spend the evening with your mentally handicapped friend?"

The three of them spent another two hours together and enjoyed a few more bottles of wine, with Bronte helping them laugh over every bitter proclamation Sylvia had uttered. The restaurant was totally deserted and the chef-owner, Lucinda Birch, ended up coming out of the kitchen to see how their meal had been.

Bronte was rosy-cheeked and confessed she would have to come back for another meal because this one had been utterly lost on her bitter palate. Ten minutes later, Lucinda came out of the kitchen with a bowl of steaming pasta in a saffron sauce with three sautéed scallops placed elegantly on top.

"Try this. It's lovely with the Pouilly-Fuissé. The recipe is from one of my favorite cafés in Marseilles."

They invited the chef to join them and poured her a glass of wine. Bronte took one bite and thanked all points in the universe for the return of her taste buds, then turned to the woman-angel-chef who had prepared the dish and asked, "Will you be my mother-in-law?"

Lucinda smiled. "Would that I could! I think there's something in the books about mothers-in-law having to be the mothers of your husband, but maybe that's just a story I heard."

Bronte loved this woman. Something about the saffron and the wine and those three perfect scallops, and the wine. This woman was an earth goddess of some sort. A genius of love. The love of food perhaps, but still, love nonetheless.

"Are you enjoying the pasta, Bron?" Max was leaning on one elbow.

"Mmmm-hmmm. Why do you ask?"

"Just the fact that you are swooning with your eyes closed while you eat it. Other than that, no reason."

She opened her eyes and swallowed the last bite of saffron bliss. "I think you had better take me home."

Devon and Lucinda were enjoying a friendly debate about farm-raised versus wild salmon as Max helped Bronte get up. She wasn't slurring exactly, but her tongue felt a tiny bit too thick for her mouth, so she decided to wave her thanks to Devon and Lucinda.

"The best!" was all Bronte could get out as Max grabbed his briefcase and guided her up to street level, where he hailed a cab. Her head rested against his shoulder during the ride home, and she couldn't wipe the easy grin off her face. She vaguely remembered him helping her across the cobblestones, into the house—*their house?* she wondered—and up the stairs, where he undressed her in a gentle, matter-of-fact fashion, then tucked her soundly into bed.

Max went back downstairs, barefoot, with his shirt untucked. He went into the kitchen and poured himself a huge glass of ice water, then stepped out onto the cool, misty terrace at the back of the little house and turned to look up at the night sky. *No stars in London*, he thought.

He took a deep, satisfying swallow of water and sat down on the stone bench near the wall of climbing ivy. The city sounds were muffled by the moisture; a horn seemed distant and irrelevant. The slight squeak of a car's breaks nearly dissolved as it trailed over the garden wall. The unexpected ring of his cell phone in his pocket brought him back to himself.

Devon.

"So I'm just getting in a taxi and heading home… that went well tonight, don't you think?"

"You are either facetious or demented or blind… which is it?"

"Honestly, it was hardly a blood bath. Sylvia hadn't had time to assemble her army. She was a lone wolf. What could she do? And Bronte is, well, as you of all people know, the bomb. So what are you worrying about?"

"Who said I was worrying?"

"I did."

"It's nothing. I mean, it's everything, but it's probably nothing."

"Tell me the everything part."

"Well, dinner was, as you said..." Max breathed in. "Mother didn't have time to sharpen her talons beforehand so she didn't do too much damage, but on the way there, Bronte got a bit... *peevish*."

"I'm sure she was just nervous at the prospect of meeting the dragon."

"I guess, but it was the first time she really turned it on me. I mean, I was up against it in New York trying to get her to see the absurdity of letting another day go by, of worrying over the year that we'd already squandered and all that. But..." His voice trailed off and the cell phone cracked and gaped into the silence.

"But what, Max? You feel like you've done your pitch and closed the deal and now it's time to move on to the happy bit?" Devon's laugh was not cheerful.

"I get it, Devon. The party's just starting and all that. But I'm telling you, she's not the type to wig out, and she was on the flipping verge."

"Oh, this is rich. I'm pulling up to my flat, so I don't have time to congratulate you further, but suffice it to say I will be encouraging the very astute Ms. Talbott to wig out early and often. Priceless. I'll talk to you tomorrow." Max thought he heard Devon chuckle again and then the line was dead.

Max finished his water, set the glass down on the slate paver at his feet, and let his hands fall between his legs, elbows resting on his thighs, neck stretched as his head hung down.

Devon's mirthless laugh echoed in his mind. Maybe he was

being an idiot, expecting Bronte to be woven into the fabric of his life within a matter of days—although, to his mind, it felt like the year they had been separated had somehow been part of the progress of their relationship.

A friend of his at the University of Chicago had been a recovering addict, and when Max had asked him one time, hypothetically, why he couldn't just pick up a beer after twelve years of being clean, his friend had explained with a metaphor he had heard at a twelve-step meeting.

"Even though I am no longer using, my addiction is progressing at the same rate as if I were. So, let's just say I go for twenty years without, then pick up again? It will not be like I get a new lease on twenty spanking new years of do-over; it will be like the waterfall has been coursing full bore for twenty years, and within a matter of months—probably days, in my case—I will be right down there where the hardest sheets of water are crashing against the huge boulders at the bottom. It's always there… waiting, rubbing its hands together with despicable relish."

Max shook his head and tried not to compare his adoration of Bronte Talbott to Stefan Gebhardt's adoration of alcohol, but something about the analogy stuck. He was not going to let her baseless fears about how it would all turn out destroy the reality of how good it already was. Together, Max thought, they had momentum. They had staying power.

He stayed outside for a while longer, letting the rustling night air clear his thoughts of frantic women, arable hectares, and canary diamonds. Finally, he picked up his glass, went back inside the silent house, and headed upstairs to be with the woman he loved.

Chapter 15

THE DORMER WINDOWS THAT opened into Max's bedroom were clearly designed to convey the wrath of an evil god as the sun's rays beat down on the anvil of Bronte's pickled brain.

"So thirsty," she half whimpered, half croaked, one hand trying feebly to cover up her eyes while the other patted blindly for Max's arm, leg, anything. "Max?"

She opened one eye between her fingers to see the silhouette of Max's—spectacular, really—body leaning casually against the jamb of the bathroom door. Naked and brushing his teeth, he was quite the specimen. She tried to feel the tiniest stir of passion, but felt only the stir of impending nausea.

"I should make you get up and get the water and painkiller on your own, but I'd never forgive myself if you went ass over elbow across the loo."

He turned back into the bathroom. She heard him tap the excess water off his toothbrush with two brisk smacks against the side of the sink, then drop it into a glass. He filled a glass with water, shook out a couple of pills, and returned. He walked back to the bed and sat down with a cheerful bounce.

"You are hideous." Bronte felt the vibrations of the mattress pound through her skull like multiple fists.

"Just thought you'd want a gentle reminder that a third bottle of Pouilly-Fuissé is *never* a good idea. You know, for next time."

"Have mercy on me, *darling Maxwell.*" She smiled as she

imitated his mother's drawn-out, caustic tone of voice and formal full-name habit. He moved very gently across the bed, the smell of his freshly showered skin like a purifying balm as it reached her nose.

He looked down at his crushed angel: eye makeup smudged, hair in a state of complete confusion, cheeks red with the flush of alcohol.

"You are a beautiful train wreck. I shall be merciful."

"I don't think I can lift my head off the pillow."

"Even better."

"And I can barely talk."

"That would be a novelty."

"Hey!" But she couldn't even muster the energy to be genuinely offended.

He helped her get to a half-sitting position as he handed her the two yellow pills, then cradled her in the crook of his strong arm as she drank shakily from the cool glass of water. He took the glass when she was finished and put it on the bedside table, then lowered her back down onto the pillow.

She was groaning quietly. "I so hate myself at times like this."

Max wanted to talk to her about her mini freak-out in the taxi on the way to the restaurant, but figured this was not the best time. "Don't you have meetings today?"

"Holy crap. I am supposed to meet the estate agent about scouting locations for the Sarah James London boutique. What time is it?"

"It's only seven fifteen. What time are you supposed to meet?"

"She was going to pick me up here at ten. Fuck."

"You'll be fine. Just sleep for an hour or two more and you'll be great. I have to get ready for my meetings. Everything is coming to a head today. The land stewards, the agricultural engineers, the solicitors…"

He was talking more to himself than he was to her as he headed across the bedroom to his large walk-in closet. He had converted a useless, smallish bedroom into a pleasant fitted wardrobe. He hated to admit how much he loved the precise order of everything in there. A place for everything and everything in its place, as his father used to say.

He came out of the closet, giving each of his cuffs a firm tug out of his suit jacket, and looked down at his miserable fiancée. She had one bleary eye opened.

"Do you still want to go to David and Willa's tonight?" she asked feebly.

"I don't know, Bron. Can we play it by ear? I really need to focus on work and—"

"I am so sorry, Max."

He stopped worrying about his clothes and took a long look at her. "What for?"

"You know what for… I warned you it was going to happen," she croaked. "That I would get needy and demanding and petulant. I am a—" Her voice caught, and it wasn't just from a raging hangover. "I am weak with loving you and I hate that. You're going to pay."

"Aw, Bron. Don't. It's all good. Devon thinks you should keep up the petulance as much as possible." He was putting a strand of her mussed hair gently behind her ear. "We'll get it all sorted. And you were right. There's no fire." He kissed her sweetly on her temple. "But right now I absolutely have to run. I adore you. Have a wonderful day about town and text me if you need me."

He picked up his cell phone from his side of the bed. "I don't know when we'll be taking breaks from the negotiations, but I will try to stay in touch. You go on ahead to David and Willa's and I'll try to meet you there if I can."

"I love you, Max."

He was standing at the top of the stairs and turned back to look at her.

"I love you too, Bron."

Then he was down the stairs and out the front door within a few minutes, the sound of his strong stride on the cobblestones trailing into the dormer windows as Bronte drifted back into an agitated half-sleep.

Her cell phone rang at nine o'clock on the dot. As soon as Bronte said hello, Willa was off and running with her eager babbling before Bronte had half a clue who was on the other end.

"…and another couple that I think you will adore; he's some sort of French banker friend of a friend of David's and she's at *Harpers & Queen*, and—"

"Hel-lo…" Bronte's voice sounded like hell.

"Bronte?"

"Willa?"

"What's the matter with you?"

Scratchy voice. "Just your run-of-the-mill hangover. Had the pleasure of meeting the duchess last night—"

"And you got sauced?!"

"No, I mean, yes, eventually. I managed to hold it together while she was there, but by the time she left the restaurant, apparently it seemed like a very good idea to order two more bottles of wine…"

"Oh, Bron!" Willa said, more amused than critical.

"Whatever. I feel better than I did two hours ago. And I'm glad you called, since I'm supposed to be picked up by the estate agent in about an hour. What can I bring tonight?"

"Oh, just you and your darling husband-to-be—"

"It might just be me sans darling husband-to-be, since he's going to be sequestered for most of the day with this deal he's been working on for the past nine months. Do you still want me solo?"

"What kind of question is that? Of course we still want you. He'll turn up later I'm sure. And we've got plenty of food. I'm in the mood for a curry, so I'll probably make too much as usual."

"Oh that sounds—well, it sounds revolting right this second, but I know it will be just the thing when this fog of pain lifts from my stupid head."

"Bronte, you are hilarious. Oh, by the way, did you know that your old beau from Chicago is living in London now? That chap from Texas?"

Bronte had let her head fall back to the pillow after her failed attempt at sitting in an upright position earlier in the conversation, so there was no chance of her falling out of the bed.

"Uh, no, I did not know that."

"I think he's friends with the French guy who's coming tonight or something. David will fill you in; he's been in touch with him a couple of times. Come 'round about six thirty so we can catch up before everyone else gets here at seven thirty. You have our address, right?"

"Mm-hmm."

"Great. Totally casual. See you then, doll."

The line went dead and Bronte whispered, "Bye, Willa."

Why did she give a shit if that *person* from Chicago—who never gave a shit about her—lived in London? It was one of the biggest cities in the world, for chrissake. She lifted up the lead weight that did double duty as her skull and made her way into the bathroom to shower off her physical and mental fog.

She reached into the shower enclosure and turned on the water, dreading the cold spray on her arm. She tried to whip her hand out of the way and banged her elbow into the glass door.

"Fuck."

She shut the offending door while the water heated up and went over to the sink to brush her teeth and take stock of her hungover self. She reached into her dopp kit, realizing she had obviously forgotten to take her birth control pill last night, in her oblivious stupor. Actually, she hadn't taken one on the overnight flight either, now that she thought about it.

"Great…" she muttered as she dug deeper into the brown-and-white striped vinyl bag from Henri Bendel, a going-away present from Carol Dieppe when Bronte had first moved to Chicago.

After a few more seconds of digging around, she finally crouched down on the floor and dumped out the entire contents of the bag. Mascara, toothpaste, lip gloss, eyeliner, blush, dental floss, eye shadow, face cream, a few stray cotton swabs, eye makeup remover (could have used that last night, she thought), three tampons, and an earring that she thought she had lost months ago all rolled out onto the white bathmat.

"Fuck."

She felt like a poster child for idiocy as she turned the stiff bag inside out, like there was some magical secret compartment that she had never seen but had somehow managed to put her pills into without remembering. She could have Carol FedEx the pack, but fuck, even then it would be more like three pills missed.

"Fucking genius."

She shoved the contents of her dopp kit back together and took off the oversized white T-shirt that Max had apparently changed her into in her inebriated state last night. She stayed in the scalding shower longer than necessary, letting the steaming water wash away the residue of the previous night.

Sally Fenworth arrived at ten o'clock exactly. Her brisk knock on the front door jarred Bronte out of her coffee-inhaling reverie.

"What a pleasure to meet you, Ms. Talbott! I am really looking forward to showing you around the various options for a Sarah James boutique here in London! It's going to be a wonderful day! I am so glad that Mr. Mowbray suggested you call me!"

Her enthusiasm was utterly enervating. Bronte stood in the door, her coffee mug held stiffly in front of her, staring at the effervescent Ms. Fenworth as if she were a rare anthropological artifact at the Natural History Museum. The little description card would read: "Overcheerful Sloan Ranger, Early Twenty-First Century."

"Ms. Talbott?"

"Yes. I'm so sorry. I'm a little jet-lagged. Would you like to come in?"

"Oh, no, thank you. I mean, of course, if you'd like a few more minutes to get ready, but I have scheduled seven appointments over the next three hours and the first one is at ten fifteen at Brompton Cross."

"Perfect. I'm ready. Let me put my coffee cup in the sink and I'll be right out." Bronte gathered up her bag, took a quick scan of the kitchen and living room, then headed out for the day.

Max hadn't looked up from his desk from the moment he'd arrived at work that morning. When he finally took note of the time, it was four o'clock in the afternoon and he needed to touch base with Bronte. He needed some fresh air as well, and decided to step outside while he dialed her up.

"Hey, you!" Bronte snapped with a good dose of cheer.

"You sound like you are on the mend."

"Thanks to you. The seven a.m. water and painkiller—followed by two good hours of sleep—did the trick. How's it going over there? Are you whipping the arable hectares into submission?"

"Let's just say if anyone's getting whipped, it is probably me. But I'm taking a break from that for the moment. Tell me about your day and take me away for five minutes."

"Oh, all right. I'd rather hear you, but I will oblige since you were so… accommodating last night. The way-too-bubbly Sally Fenworth showed up at ten o'clock… precisely. We saw a slew of perfect little boutiques if Sarah has any real interest in this whole London thing. I stopped into a few stores and also went into Mowbray's… ooh la la… quite the Britishy situation over there—all that wood paneling and manliness everywhere. Then came home and—"

"You…"

"What?"

"Nothing. Go on."

"Well, all right, but you sound stressed."

"I am. But not about us. Go on. What else? You sound like you are panting."

"Very funny. I'm just walking down the Fulham Road where I picked up a couple bottles of wine for tonight. I know Willa said not to bring anything, but it seems a little rude to show up empty-handed."

"Time's almost up, love. I shouldn't be here for more than another hour or so. Do you want me to go straight to David and Willa's or pick you up at home?"

"I love that."

"What?"

"That… the *home* bit. I like the idea of you… of us… of a home. Which reminds me, ugh, so idiotic, but I forgot my pills at home in New York and had a little minicatastrophe on the bathroom floor this morning. I think we better, you know, be careful for the next few weeks."

Max felt the floor drop out from under him. "I have to walk back into the conference room now, Bron, so I can't really process what you just told me. I think you may be implying that there's a chance you are pregnant, but I am so unable to take that in at the moment, that, well, I am just going to pretend I have no idea what you are talking about."

"It's not that big a deal. I can get the morning-after pill—"

"Bronte."

"Max."

"Bronte—"

Simon Ramwell, Max's land steward, poked his head out of the front door of the townhouse and did a pantomime of tapping his watch.

"I'll be right there, Simon." Max waited for him to reshut the door, then tried to breathe.

"Max. Please. Don't get upset. Go finish your meetings and we'll talk about it later tonight. It's not a big deal either way."

"Bronte. It's a huge deal to me." How could he even begin to convey how huge, especially if it was a boy? An heir? The next duke? How could she be so cavalier? "I never would have… we never would have been so careless in New York and in the shower if you were *not* on the pill. I'm going to have to—"

"Please, Max. I'm sorry I mentioned it. Go back to your meeting and we'll meet up at David and Willa's. I'm not pregnant… I mean, it is hugely unlikely."

"Bron. I've written entire dissertations on statistical anomalies. I cannot have this conversation right now. I love you. Don't take the morning-after pill. I'll see you soon."

She whispered, "I love you too" on her exhale, then hung up.

Max slowly took the phone away from his ear, double-checked that it was set to silent, and put it back in his pants pocket. He let himself back into the shiny black-painted front door and headed back to the conference room like a robot.

Thankfully, the final hours were mostly minor line-item changes to the contract documents from the project finance team. Max was in no frame of mind to contribute anything of any real value, so he opted for complete silence. He sat through the remainder of the meetings in a state of hazy worry. When all of the documents were finally agreed upon and everyone had left, Max reached for his cell phone. He dialed Bronte as he put on his suit jacket and put the revised documents into his briefcase. His call went straight to voice mail.

"It's about," he said, then paused into the recording as he looked down at his wristwatch, "six fifteen and I am desperate for a shower. I am assuming you are already on your way to the Osbornes, so I will meet you there. Realistically around eight o'clock. See you then."

Bronte came out of the bathroom in white jeans and a fitted,

pale-turquoise T-shirt. She had added a big, chunky, turquoise necklace and flat sandals. *The cobblestones just outside Max's front door
have beaten me into submission*, she thought as she looked down at
her practical footwear.

She grabbed her big purse and headed out, stopping in the
kitchen to pick up the bottles of wine and stuff them into her oversized bag. She had a good fifteen minutes to get to Willa and David's
and decided to walk to their flat. She knew roughly where she was
headed, but as she got closer, she had to refer to her *A–Z* (she loved
that *zed*) repeatedly, stopping to get her bearings, looking at the
map, and then moving on.

"Bronte Talbott, as I live and breathe!" The deep, confident,
laid-back American drawl was unmistakable.

Please. No.

*There are—what?—seven and a half million people in this city,
and Mr. Fucking Texas has to be walking down the same fucking street.*

"Uh. Hello." That was about all she could come up with. She
couldn't very well walk right past him—them!—though the possibility crossed her mind… maybe she could later say she was partially
deaf… and blind.

"So. Pretty weird bumping into you like this. Outta the blue,
huh? Who woulda thunk it?" His accent sounded particularly ridiculous compared to all the plummy British English she'd been treated
to lately, but he sounded strangely sincere.

The too-cute blond standing next to him was like a golden
retriever puppy, practically wagging for attention.

"Oh yeah," he said, turning toward his eager companion; Bronte
almost felt sorry for the poor woman, the way he made her seem like
an afterthought. "This is my wife, Marianne Scully. Marianne, this
is Bronte Talbott."

Bronte had never thought she would wish to be anything like
Max's mother, but at that moment, she had a deep desire to have

that woman's mastery of concealment, to show no emotion whatsoever, not even the concealment itself.

His wife?! Fuck.

Willa should have mentioned that small piece when she'd given Bronte the heads-up that Mr. Texas was now residing on this side of the pond.

"Hi, Bronte! What a pleasure!" the blond bubbled.

"Bronte knows Willa and David," Mr. Texas elaborated.

Bronte was going to mention that she was on her way to their place when the blond dove ahead.

"Really?!" Titter-titter. "Willa and David have been such godsends ever since we got here. Wait! Are you dating Max Heyworth? I think I saw your picture in *Hello!* yesterday. Was that you?"

Bronte nodded and looked sheepish.

Mr. Texas looked intrigued.

Puppy kept talking. "I have been dying to meet him! What's he like? We were going to all get together tonight but Willa said there was some scheduling conflict or something so we'll just have to all get together another night. Are you just here for a visit? We are absolutely loving living in London. It's so great to be an expat… totally great! And newlyweds and all!"

He was still looking at Bronte. Really looking. Like he had never really looked at her until that very moment. She wanted to stand there all day—looking like hot shit, if she should say so herself— and let him know *this* is what she looked like when she was with the right man.

The pert blond, all of a sudden showing unexpected intuition, snaked her arm possessively through that brawny Texan arm. Staking her claim, as it were.

Suddenly, Bronte wanted to laugh. Riotously. Uproariously. She wanted to skip around the street and do a merry jig. How easily that could have been her being ignored on that man's arm! What a near miss! Holy fuck! She wanted to shake the little creature and yell, "Run, you idiot!"

Or possibly shower her in grateful kisses.

She'd always hated that holier-than-thou pedantic aphorism, "There but for the grace of God go I," but in that electrifying moment, Bronte actually felt as if her relationship with Mr. Texas had been a very narrowly averted collision with an oncoming train.

However, instead of showing said gratitude or even whispering a warning from the sisterhood (let's be honest, camaraderie like that was not in Bronte's repertoire), in a moment of what was probably nothing more than catty meanness, Bronte let her left hand (the one boasting the canary-diamond headlight) move slowly up to the side of her face, then carefully put a strand of hair behind one ear.

The little yipping thing was momentarily arrested by the sight of what Bronte now considered one of the best weapons in any woman's arsenal. The blatant, flagrant, nearly grotesque material display of how much another man loved her, right there for everyone to see.

Given the brief silence, Bronte took the opportunity to hammer in the final nail. "Yes, Marianne, that silly *Hello!* magazine piece kind of let the cat out of the bag. Max Heyworth and I are engaged."

"Oh…" She recovered, loosening her grip on her now-safe husband and switching gears almost immediately back to social-climbing pragmatist. "Oh! I can't wait to meet him. We all must go out some time. That would be so much fun."

Bronte took one more moment to look straight into those Texan eyes and telegraph every ounce of perverse gratitude that was coursing through her, then turned back to Marianne. "I'm sorry I have to rush off. I am actually on my way to meet him in a few moments and he's terribly prompt. Bye."

"Oh," Marianne said. "Oh. Okay then."

And then Mr. Texas smiled that big, generous (meaningless) smile and the pair watched as Bronte walked off.

Just like that.

Just like it was totally normal to have your fucking wife prattling on about this and that with the woman you were *fucking* before you met her. As if the time that he and Bronte had shared was nothing more than a few months with some random woman who turned out to be nothing more than… nothing.

Bronte stopped short at that.

She glanced at those memories, all that misery and depression about what a loser she had been for misreading every possible clue that he was a perfectly good guy whom she couldn't quite catch, and was struck by another wave of near-hysteria. Suddenly it was all so clear: what she had really needed all along, what she deserved—what every woman deserved—was *not* a perfectly good guy, but a really spectacular one.

In that stunning moment, on the quiet side street that led to Willa and David's apartment block, Bronte had the joyful realization that she wanted to drop to her knees and thank someone, anyone, for making sure that she didn't end up with that perfectly good man.

He never *got* her. He never would have gotten her in a million years.

But Max did. Max *really* got her.

A few minutes later, despite being distracted by life's little epiphanies, Bronte managed to find her way to the Osbornes' apartment building, a wonderful Edwardian terra-cotta mansion block in Kensington. She practically fell through the front door when David opened it.

"Bronte! You look delicious, darling! Let me take a proper look at you; it has been, what, two years? You really do look divine." Then he turned without missing a breath and shouted, "Willa!"

Thank God for people who talk too much, thought Bronte as she reeled a bit from her recent run-in. *They offer the most wonderful reprieve from the burden of speech.*

"Come see how fabulous Bronte looks! What are you doing? Get out here."

Bronte extracted the clanking bottles from her bottomless pit of a bag and handed them, double-fisted, to David.

"And she's brought two bottles of excellent wine, Willa!" He lowered his voice and returned his attention to Bronte. "Oh well, she's probably fussing with her hair or some damn thing. Come into the kitchen with me while I get these into the fridge. Damn, you look great, Bron."

After he put the wine into the refrigerator and shut the door, he turned to look at her.

"Are you all right?"

Bronte laughed and gave him a big hug. "Oh, David, I have missed you! You are such a talkative idiot!"

"Well, I'm not that idiotic—"

"Yes you are, darling!" Willa said as she swept into the kitchen, clearly having taken the curry theme from the menu and applied it to her dress code. She had a sparkly pink tunic with little gold stars silk-screened on it, matched with a pair of gold, shantung silk pedal pushers, and strappy little Grecian sandals in matching gold. "But you are *my* talkative idiot so no need to change on my account."

David gave Willa a sweet kiss on the neck and put his arm around her waist as she continued, "Have you been able to get a word in edgewise, Bron?"

"Why would I want to interrupt a veritable torrent of nonstop compliments?"

"Get the girl a drink, David. She's probably been counting the hours until she could remedy that hangover without seeming like a total lush."

"I hate to admit it, but an icy-cold vodka would really make my day."

David headed to the other side of the kitchen where he had set up a bucket of ice and some bottles of liquor.

Willa turned to Bronte. "It's not just the hangover, though; I can tell. What is it?"

"Oh, Willa. Am I so transparent?"

"Not to talkative idiots, but maybe to other girls."

"You're right. It was the damnedest thing. I was standing on the corner of Kensington High Street with my nose in a map, and who should walk by but Mr. Texas and his blushing bride."

"Good God! I totally lied and told her we had a scheduling conflict. Did you tell her you were coming here?"

"No, she said you had canceled so I just said I was on my way to meet my fiancé. Your lying, depraved ways are safe with me."

"Likewise, I'm sure! But, you know, it's the weirdest thing. It's like she wants to be friends and I don't know how to tell her that that is so *not* going to happen. She's like a…"

"Puppy!"

"Puppy!"

They both laughed as the word came out of their mouths at exactly the same moment, as if on cue.

David handed Bronte a frosty martini glass with a handsome yellow curl of lemon rind floating in the center, then handed the same to Willa.

"Here you go, ladies. Let me grab mine and I'll meet you in the living room."

"Is there anything I can do to help with dinner, Willa?" Bronte asked.

"Of course not. Let's get out of the kitchen."

Chapter 16

THEY WALKED DOWN A bright red hallway and then into a sunny yellow living room accented in bold mid-century fabrics on the impossibly tall curtains. The furniture was a smart mix of new contemporary pieces and several threadbare, worn-from-love side chairs. The painting over the fireplace looked like a Sonia Delaunay. The evening sun in London seemed to stay out forever. The rays stretched in long golden strands through the double French doors and across the blond wood floors.

"What a great room, Willa!"

"I know! I mean, thank you, because the rest of the flat is sort of naff, but this room is stupendous, right? The view from here out to the private garden in the back, the light streaming in. It's all a bit of all right."

Bronte smiled at the familiar phrase, now happily devoid of her own negative memories, and encouraged Willa to continue.

"The bedrooms might as well be mole holes, but who needs light for anything back there, anyway, eh?"

"Cheers!" Bronte raised her glass to Willa's, then took a welcome sip of the delicious, cool vodka. It trailed slowly down her throat. Nectar of the gods. "Jesus. This is tasting way too good."

David walked in and sat down in the hand-me-down, scuffed, green-leather armchair near the empty fireplace, raised his glass, then took a sip. "So tell us, Bron. What's the news?"

"Well, I suppose the old news is that Max and I are officially engaged, as you both know. And he gave me this fabulous ring." She held out what she now considered her weapon of triumph, or at least a heraldic trumpet.

"Good God, Bron!" Willa practically ripped her hand from her wrist.

"Is it gauche?" Bronte was momentarily embarrassed by the sheer size of the central diamond, especially because she had used it so cruelly to give that Marianne a proper set down.

"Are you kidding? If anyone thinks this ring is gauche, they are nothing but jealous liars. It is quite simply the perfect ring. David, come look at the size of it, darling."

"I can see it quite well from here, love," he said to Willa, then winked at Bronte.

"Very funny, David." Bronte heard her phone beep to alert her she had gotten a message. "Whoops. I'd better check that. Max wasn't sure what his schedule was going to be, but I talked to him just before four and he thought he was going to be here after all."

Willa's landline rang and she excused herself as she got up to answer it.

Bronte took her phone out of her bag and noticed that Max had left her a voice mail; she clicked on it, listened, then returned her phone to her bag, vaguely hearing Willa's half of her phone conversation.

Bronte took another sip of her vodka and Willa's words started to sift into her peripheral hearing. That fearless puppy-wife had actually called to check in.

"...I know, such a small world... truly... such a coincidence..." Willa held up her martini glass and widened her eyes. "Yes... of course... some other time, I'm sure. Sorry to cut you short, but I have to run... will do... you too. Bye."

Willa walked back to the sofa she was sharing with Bronte, sat down, and took a healthy swig of her martini.

"Holy mother of God, that woman leaves me gobsmacked!"

Bronte started laughing and David joined in.

Willa continued, "I mean, seriously, who invites themselves over to dinner with their husband's ex-girlfriend... what the hell? I know you are still friends with him, David, but really, his wife is like this bizarre combination of savvy businesswoman and idiot savant. What was he thinking?"

Bronte almost spit out the sip of vodka she had just taken.

Willa was on a roll. "You know we Brits live in abject terror of that pushy American who won't take no for an answer... I mean, we have been so conditioned to turn away at the slightest hint of rejection: 'Are you around tonight?' someone asks. 'Well... ' you answer. 'Oh, no matter! We'll get together another time!' For us, the hesitation *is* the answer, you fool. Not to be met with, 'I am happy to bring extra food if that's the issue!' Seriously!"

Bronte and David were practically snorting as Willa continued her stand-up routine.

"Stop! Stop!" Bronte was gripping her stomach, pleading for a break from the laughter. David and Willa had always made her laugh harder than anyone she knew. "Oh, God. Willa. You are too much. But don't forget that you were guilty of encouraging me to get together with him in the first place, remember? All that might and muscle?"

"Oh, God, Bronte. Don't remind me. I woke up the next day after that party with a splitting headache and the vague thought that I'd sent you down the wrong path. But look what he's saddled with in the long run, so now you must thank me after all!"

"Careful, Willa! You need to be nice when you talk about her!"

"Why on earth?"

"Because, as of tonight, she is single-handedly responsible for making me the happiest woman alive! Can you imagine if I had ended up with him? What a disaster! It was almost as if I needed to see him with another woman, actually ignoring his own wife, to see what I would have suffered."

"You're absolutely right, Bron. David, let us all raise our glasses in sincere thanks to the lovely Mrs. Texas, Bronte's unwitting savior!"

Bronte caught her breath and raised her glass in joyful agreement, then spoke after she took a sip. "By the way, that was a message from Max on my phone just now. He's going to swing by home and be here around eight, if that's okay."

"Of course it's okay! Etienne and Helena are going to be here after that. I'd intended to sit down around eight thirty or nine anyway. I forgot! I made some hors d'oeuvres. Hold on one sec."

With that, Willa was up and out of the sofa again, a rush of hot pink and gold flying across the room.

"Oh my lord, David, you two are the best."

"She's a keeper."

"Honestly. How long have you two known each other?"

"Forever. You know the story."

"Yes, childhood friends and all that, but when I met you guys in New York, you were already an old married couple. When did you actually get together, you know, as more than friends?"

David smiled at the memory, clearly enjoying himself. "Our mothers were best friends going back forever, always foisting us upon one another at every opportunity. All through our early childhood we were happy mates, then as teenagers it was the worst: she was too tall and horsey and bossy and loud, and I was nerdy and into math and shy, and it looked like the mothers were going to be utterly defeated."

He took a sip of his drink.

"Then, I think we were twenty or twenty-one, she'll remember of course, and I went to a party in London. Max and I were staying at his parents' place in Mayfair, came down from Oxford for the long weekend, and ended up at this ridiculous tea party at some old doyenne's house in town. Max's mother was there being all look-down-your-nosey at everyone, so Max and I spiked our tea with wickedly strong whiskey, and in walks this gorgeous, tall, confident girl."

"And?" Bronte prompted.

"Well, Max had no idea who she was and gave her a quick once-over and then turned to me with a little check-that-out wink. And I thought, quite matter-of-factly, really, 'Perhaps I shall murder Max tonight.' And then I thought, 'That's odd, why would I want to murder Max?' And I looked back, classic Bogie-Bacall double take, and saw it was Willa, and well… that's when I knew we were—how did you ask it? Oh yes, more than friends."

Willa was leaning against the frame of the wide entryway into the living room, listening to David tell their story. "Now do you see why he's *my* idiot, Bron?"

"I do, Willa."

They caught up on other mutual friends in New York, ate Willa's delicious artichoke appetizers, and were just starting their second round of drinks when the buzzer sounded and Willa let Max into the apartment. David and Bronte had leapt up to greet him as well, David with hearty nuptial congratulations and Bronte with a silly-schoolgirl-crush feeling in her stomach. They'd only been apart for the day, for chrissake, but she could see he wanted to connect with her too.

Badly.

He was still shaking David's hand and half-hugging him with his other when he locked eyes with Bronte and smiled the most delectable, melt-in-your-mouth smile.

"David. Willa. I am going to have to have a private word with my fiancée if you don't mind."

"Oooh, darling!" Willa trilled, locking her arm through David's. "Remember when you used to have *private words* with me, David? So romantic! Of course, off you go, you two. No hanky-panky, please."

Bronte was flushed and happy as she followed Max down the dimly lit hall and into the first room on the left, a tiny guest room with a small desk. Max shut the door quietly then turned and took

Bronte's face in his hands and kissed her so deeply, so passionately, that she almost tilted right back onto the bed that took up most of the room.

"Mmmm…" she mumbled between hot kisses. "I had the most wonderful epiphany on the way here…" She spoke with her eyes still closed, kissing him wherever she could, neck, cheek, lips.

"Mmmm… and what was your epiphany?" he whispered between kisses.

"That you *get* me."

He brought his hands down to her neck, then made a trail down her back, then along her hips and around her backside, all the while continuing to overwhelm her with those searing kisses.

"Do I ever!" he agreed. "I get you every chance I can!" He gave her a bawdy squeeze on her ass to make his point, then stopped suddenly, sniffed, and looked into her eyes. "Have you been drinking?"

"Of course I've been drinking!" Bronte laughed. "I'm with David and Willa and it's after five o'clock… what else would I be doing?"

"But, Bron, what if you're pregnant?"

She felt the tenderness leave as an icy, rebellious thread began to weave through her. "I beg your pardon?"

He whispered, almost reverently, "What if there's a baby?"

"Max…" She let herself sit down on the edge of the bed after all.

"Bron, if there's even a possibility, don't you think it's worth…" His voice trailed off as he saw through his incipient joy that Bronte may not hold out the same hope.

"Max… I don't know what to say… and that's saying something. I mean, is it really right to have a child—to make the most monumental decision of our lives—based on my having forgotten my pill pack? I mean, what—"

"Bronte, this is no longer just a matter of you forgetting your pill pack. We were always belts-and-suspenders when it came to birth control. I mean, who else in their right mind uses condoms *and* the pill like we did? When we… I mean, last week, when I stopped using the condoms, it was because we were together… *are* together… I mean, a family… not because I wanted to—"

"Look, how about this?" Bronte interrupted. She felt like she was drowning, the conversation spiraling away from her, into confusing and desperate emotional territory. "Let's use condoms from here on out. I'll go off the pill for the rest of this month. If I missed three pills, which in effect I have, or would have even if Carol FedExed me my pack, I am supposed to use alternative birth control anyway, but that's assuming… well, we'll just see what happens in the next few weeks. I'll probably get my period in a few days anyway, but—"

"So you won't drink until we know, then?"

There was something totally vulnerable and tender about the way Max asked, but something very deep in Bronte bristled nonetheless. He was treading carefully, but perilously, on the knife-edge of compassion and control.

If she feared the erasure of her psyche when it came to matrimony, she could only begin to imagine the total loss of self that accompanied motherhood. Especially when one was mothering the twentieth Duke of Northrop. How could he not see that?

"Max…"

"Please, Bron." If she was pregnant, and it was a boy, the ramifications were more than Max could begin to contemplate or convey. He'd spent his entire life downplaying the importance of the title, making a concerted effort to have a clear, humble view of what it really meant. His father had been a wonderful role model in that respect, always joking with Max not to take *himself* too seriously but to always take his responsibilities seriously. Bronte might well be carrying the twentieth Duke of Northrop. That fact fell quite plainly under the Serious Responsibility column. How could she not see that?

"All right, I won't drink until we know."

But she wasn't happy about it, and *that* Max could see. He gave her a tender kiss, tracing the inside of her upper lip with his tongue as he withdrew. He had to fight off the brief impression that her response had bordered on perfunctory.

"I love you, Bron."

"I know. I love you too, Max." She moved slowly past him and opened the door out to the hallway, the sounds of the other guests' careless laughter wafting down the corridor. *Fuck.*

Max spent the rest of the dinner party pretending to listen to his friends' cheerful chatter while he worried over Bronte. She had casually offered him her vodka when they returned to the living room, as if the thought had just crossed her mind to save David another trip to the kitchen to make one. She declined wine with dinner, easily explained because everyone already knew she had had more than her fair share the night before.

The other couple, Etienne and Helena, was charming and animated, but Max could tell that something about them was putting Bronte on edge. Her smile got a little too bright when Etienne was asking her about the time she had spent in Chicago. Max was trying to listen to Helena talk about a recent dustup at *H & Q* involving a young male intern and a married senior editor whose indiscretion was now the buzz of the office.

"...but now they've reached the dreadful crossroads: destroy her family and move ahead with their own new life together, or end the affair and move back to some semblance of the nuclear family."

Helena was an engaging dinner partner, and on any other night, Max would have been happily drawn into her sparkling account of the star-crossed lovers. He was distracted but tried to participate.

"Would it forever be a *semblance*, do you think?"

"Hard to say. I mean, you don't even need to know them to get the gist. You always hear the variations: the marriage breaks because it was falling apart to begin with—what I call the Petri Dish theory:

the environment was right for infidelity, everybody parts ways, pulls it together, stays friends, that sort of thing. Then there's the happy-enough marriage that is sabotaged by the idea of something better: the Greener Grass theory. That one usually leads to short-term hell for the abandoned party and serial relationship failure for the aban-doner, since, as we all know, the grass is never—or hardly ever—greener. Finally, there's the worst-case scenario, not even a theory, really; just a nightmare. One of you falls madly in love with someone else. This one has been my preoccupation recently." She reached for her glass of wine. "Luckily, I write about relationships, right?" She raised her glass to Max with a merry tilt. "I can never get enough."

"I, on the other hand, enjoy the occasional dinner-party conver-sation about it, but probably have some sort of irrational superstition about overanalysis when it comes to my own romantic life," Max replied. "For me, love is like that quote about laws and sausages: I really don't want to think too much about how it's made; I just want to enjoy it."

"Touché... it's primarily a women's game, the discussion and dissection of it at least."

They paused to finish their meals and Max looked up to see Bronte smiling weakly at Etienne, almost wistful, as she spoke. "It was such an odd coincidence. I mean, what are the chances that I would be standing on a street corner in the middle of London and they would walk by?"

"It is funny, because you are really his only failure," Etienne proceeded with his sexy Gallic accent.

Max tried not to strain too obviously to pick up the thread of Bronte's conversation. He saw her blink away her confusion... and maybe a touch of anxiety.

As if she could feel Max's concern across the narrow table, Bronte turned and gave him a sad, fragile smile. Epiphanies notwithstand-ing, she had no interest in dredging up miserable memories. She was just beginning to celebrate that her feelings for Mr. Texas had well and truly expired; that did not mean she now wished to dissect those feelings in the midst of a delightful dinner party.

"Failure?" she asked with a little chuckle as she reached for her water glass.

"Oh, you know how he is," Etienne said, "all Texan ease and laid-back camaraderie for all and sundry. And then you come along and let him know you never want to see him or hear from him again and he was just, well, disoriented."

Even though he hadn't been able to follow all the details, Max suddenly realized that Bronte must have crossed paths with her ex-boyfriend earlier in the day. He was overcome by a quick, fierce need to protect her from anything upsetting. He was almost out of his chair to suggest how jet-lagged he and Bronte were from their recent trip when she began speaking again. He held his place.

Her words were brittle. "I suppose you might say I am old-fashioned and even prudish in a way, Etienne. I find it nigh on impossible to have pleasant, bubbly conversation with former lovers. No spite really, just a clean slate and all that." She looked across the table and took strength from Max's gaze. "And now that I am happily and permanently off the market, it is not a situation I will ever have to reconsider." She raised her glass toward Max and took a fortifying sip of cool water.

Etienne laughed warmly and replied, "If that were the case in France, no one would be speaking to anyone!"

Everyone at the table laughed with both humor and a touch of relief.

Bronte looked at Max with intense gratitude.

Plain. Simple. Gratitude.

In that moment, she knew that her petty gesture, waving her engagement ring in that woman's face, was just that: a gesture. An empty gesture. The ring itself was nothing. She kept staring at Max across the table as the others started to pick up the threads of new conversations. The real weight and heft of their relationship was what passed between them at moments like this: his look of gentle confidence, her radiant trust.

She would take those looks over any jewels.

Later that night, Bronte was in bed reading one of the notebooks that her mother had given her, trying to understand how her father's written voice could be so bitterly hilarious while his real voice had been just bitter. She laughed at one particularly vicious line, and Max poked his head out of the walk-in closet to see what she was reading.

"Not as bad as you thought it would be?"

"I may be a bitch, but I am more than happy to admit when I am wrong… and I was. Definitely wrong. This is fucking hilarious."

Max finished getting undressed and made his way into bed, looking preoccupied as he crossed the rough, wide-plank floorboards. Carelessly naked. Bronte stared at him as he adjusted his pillows, turned on his bedside lamp, took his book off the bedside table, cracked the spine, and began reading.

Then he looked up when he felt the pressure of her gaze on him. "What?"

"This is good."

"What is good?"

"This." She gestured with a vague sweep. "The two of us reading in bed, home at a decent hour, curled up. I'm digging it."

He reached over and put his hand on the side of her hip, letting his caress float over her.

"Me too."

Whatever real or imagined isolation or belligerence she had experienced in that little guest room at the Osbornes' flat earlier had passed. The feel of his hand against her bare skin made her shiver and scoot down deeper into the consuming cloud of white linen sheets and the airy eiderdown duvet.

"I don't think I've ever slept on sheets as utterly delicious, by the way. How can they be so damned soft when they look like such a wrinkled mess?"

He put his book on the bedside table, face down, his other hand never leaving her side. He turned back to face her and stretched his legs out along the length of the bed, testing the sheets as if he had never thought about it, then let one leg climb up hers.

"Mmmm. Utterly delicious."

"Max... you are..."

His mouth came down onto hers and the weight of his body pressed her solidly—safely—into the cocoon of the feather bed. All she could do was release a half moan, half sob of pure delight. He pulled away from the kiss and let his hand wander across her lower abdomen, right at her bikini line. He ran a single finger just beneath the elastic of her underwear and ripples of pleasure pulsed through her and out to her fingertips.

"I am not going to get overly philosophical, Bron, but I have to circle back at least one more time to the potential baby situation."

"No fair."

"What do you mean, 'no fair'?"

"I mean," Bronte sighed with a glazed-over smile, "you know I will give you anything when you hold me like this. Babies. Capitulations. Empty promises."

"All good. But stay with me for a minute longer. I think there was a particular point that I was trying to make that... that I failed at making. When I was asking or worrying or what have you about the idea of you being pregnant, I wasn't saying anything about your independence or your rights, or anything along those lines. I meant it more that the paradigm has shifted for us. We are a unit. And not in that atrocious way that makes your skin crawl. In the most *delicious* way." He shifted his body closer to hers. "Whatever it is, we can figure it out, as a unit. Do you see what I mean? Do you agree?" He needed to hear her say it, to know that those real or imagined beasts of insecurity or independence that had threatened to sabotage her trust in their relationship were well and truly slain.

"I like that... a unit... easier to swallow somehow than all that cleaving and honoring." She squirmed under him and went to kiss his neck, right where his tendons strained invitingly, but he held her back.

"I mean it, Bron. If you are pregnant and feel really strongly about, well, not being—I mean, I'm trying to be open-minded here, but to be honest, I'd be devastated. But we will figure it out. Together, okay? Please promise me."

"Okay, okay, I promise!" she replied without any attempt to conceal her rising lust, straining to kiss his neck again.

"You are an impossible harlot," he said in a low growl.

She savored the taste of his skin on her lips.

"Mmmm. I am. And also,"—she taunted him with her tongue running slowly along her upper lip—"I can't think about, much less talk about, unwan—I mean unexpected, imaginary babies... it's just too implausible."

He finally gave up, or gave in. He wasn't sure which.

Chapter 17

THE FOLLOWING NIGHT, WHEN Bronte looked out over the large drawing room at Dunlear Castle and saw the cast of characters, she wondered if she were in a dream, or a Noël Coward play. The castle was closed to the public for the weekend and the main rooms were once again open to the family.

Despite the vast grandeur of the space—soaring ceilings with extensive, intricate plaster moldings; miles of rich brocade curtains; Venetian glass chandeliers; acres of Aubusson carpets; priceless French fauteuils and bergères; massive, carved-stone fireplaces at either end—the ease with which these people slipped into the over-sized sofas with a cocktail and a ready smile made it all seem, well, utterly normal. They had convened at the far end of the room and Bronte was enjoying the overview as she came in a little later than the others. The train out from London had been pleasant enough, but she'd collapsed for a brief nap and was just now making her way back to the land of the living.

Max had invited Willa and David to join them, and those two were talking animatedly with the duchess, who had made a surprise appearance after all. Apparently, the idea of her entire extended family under one roof, enjoying themselves and talking about her behind her back, was more than she could bear. She looked as frosty as ever, her spine like a steel rod as she pretended to be amused by Willa's inside tidbit of gossip from the latest royal fiasco. But there seemed to be something less predatory about Sylvia this evening. Her eldest, Claire, was sitting nearby, laughing at Willa's rendition of the idiotic chauffeur who had tattled to the press about his canoodling—unmarried to each other—passengers and his subsequent dismay at losing his position. Even the duchess cracked a small smile at that.

Claire had turned out to be a very pleasant surprise. Bronte had anticipated a carbon copy of the supercilious, arrogant mother-in-law-to-be. Instead, Claire was more like a very pale version of Devon, a very rigid, focused version, to be sure, but hardly the conniver that Max had painted. She *was* eager to gather as much information about Bronte as she could, asking myriad back-to-back questions, just as Devon had. Before retiring Friday night, Claire suggested they take an early walk together the following day.

The two of them met up at the kitchen door at eight o'clock the next morning and headed out onto the beautiful, sprawling grounds of Dunlear Castle. Claire started talking about her life in London, and her frustrating attempts at reining in her wild daughter, Lydia. Bronte tried to keep her facial expression bland at the mention of the little tart.

"I suspect, from your atypical silence and her version of things that I already received, that she was not particularly polite when she met you in New York."

"She was fine."

Claire laughed and caught Bronte's right upper arm in a quick, affectionate hold, then just as quickly let go. "I shall assume that she was not *fine* as in a fine bottle of Château Margaux or fine Connolly leather." Bronte smiled and Claire continued, "Let's just say I have been more preoccupied with keeping my marriage together than with parenting for the past few years and it has not been an easy time for Lydia. I adore her, of course—how could I not? She's mine after all—but she has been let alone for too long and my mother has begun to plant the seeds of righteous indignation that I have spent my entire adult life trying to shed."

Bronte was beyond surprised at Claire's intimate honesty. Their ten-year age difference had seemed vast when they'd first met last night. Claire's innate formality and firm posture gave a rather grim, haughty first impression. But after they had spoken for a few minutes, Bronte realized that, unlike her brother Max, who projected casual ease while harboring a very concise and particular view of the world, Claire was quite the reverse. Her rigid posture was perfectly at odds with her obvious desire to embrace the new.

"I can tell you are probably taken aback by my openness. Max has always lumped me together with Mother in many ways. Our age difference was more or less cataclysmic in terms of fostering sibling affection between Max and me. I was living in London with Mother by the time he was learning to walk. And then Devon and Abby came in rapid succession and the dynamic was pretty much codified."

Bronte's look begged her to continue.

"Basically, Mother made it clear to me that my place was with her and the 'others' were, well, *the others*. Father was periodically allowed into our private, special world on those wonderful occasions when he would come into London with us and take me to the ballet or the theater. I dreamed that we were a proper family, the three of us."

Bronte looked sad and Claire tried to clarify again. "That sounds cruel, I know, but it wasn't like that. I honestly did not resent Max or Dev or Abby… it was just, oh, it's so hard to describe one's perspective as a child. Well, actually, you of all people understand the simultaneous loneliness and suffocation of being an only child. That's how it was for me. Mother never encouraged me to play with the little ones, as she called them. They were a pack unto themselves… always being rough and tumble with Father… and Mother always made me feel that she and I were cut from a separate cloth."

Claire shook her head in a cheerful attempt to mentally clean the slate. "That all sounds utterly moribund. Of course, I could have been a more attentive big sister, but I was a vain, adolescent young girl with a doting mother, so I suppose I was just lazy." Claire regarded Bronte. "When I look at you, I see this confident, tall, independent, brash woman who has captured Max's heart. Maybe you don't *relate*… you seem the type who wouldn't be lazy when it came to expressing your own thoughts."

Bronte gave a self-deprecating smile. "I'm not sure that's an attribute I am proud of, but yes, it's probably true. And, being an only child, it is chilling to hear stories of big, supposedly bubbly families that are populated with siblings whose childhood memories are, in fact, as cool and isolated as my own."

They were crossing out of the kitchen gardens and walking down several beautifully worn limestone stairs into a formal parterre boxwood garden. Bronte looked around and wondered at the splendid, precise perfection of the design. She started to veer down one of the pretty lanes, then turned to Claire. "Do you want to get out and have a real walk for exercise, or do you want to amble?"

Claire tilted her head to the side, almost imperceptibly, just as Max did. She was fair, with pale blond hair, pale blue-gray eyes, and a very fine porcelain complexion. But the genes didn't lie.

"Max does that exactly."

"What does he do?" Claire asked, not aware she was doing anything.

"He tilts his head in exactly that tiny way when he is trying to memorize something or think of a reply. It's just a tiny gesture, but you are all alike in different ways. I enjoy seeing that."

The cool morning breeze was starting to warm, and the mild wind felt lush across Bronte's face and neck. She turned her face to the sun and closed her eyes for a few seconds as they stood in that beautiful, peaceful place.

"Max is a lucky man. Don't let him get all controlling on you. This garden is the perfect example. This is what the Heyworth men are all about. It's beautiful and peaceful, but it is also immaculate and still. This garden was laid out in 1746 and it has not been altered since. Maintained, refined, perfected, but never changed. Just a thought."

"It is probably for the best, since I am somewhat unpredictable and flighty and could use a good reining in."

The two women continued their walk through the formal garden then out into the main park, returning two hours later, flushed and happy with the exercise and the promise of an unexpected burgeoning friendship.

Bronte got back after ten that morning and was surprised to see Max was still reading in their bedroom. He was in a comfortable armchair by the window, and when he looked up, Bronte's heart gave a little leap.

"Aren't you a bonny lass? All rosy and fresh," he said. "Ready for a morning tumble?"

"You are just plain naughty. I am going to jump in the shower and then curl up with a book somewhere. By the way, your sister Claire is nothing like you described."

Bronte was changing out of the T-shirt and shorts she had worn on her walk and stepping into the en suite bathroom as she spoke.

"You don't even know each other," she called from the large white, tiled room. "Not that I do either—know her, I mean—but I think you might become friends somehow."

She turned the shower on and stepped into the torrential mid-twentieth-century waterworks: one shower head was directly above her, cascading down her back like a waterfall, and three side jets could be angled wherever she chose. The tiny, white-square tiling that lined the floor and walls of the entire room was immaculate, despite a half century of use.

She took a quick shower, dried off with one of the huge white Turkish towels that seemed to be in miraculous abundance, and then wrapped the bath sheet around her body and padded out to the bedroom. She picked up her train of thought as if she had never left off.

"She's pretty intense, I guess, but she's certainly not out to get anyone. I think she feels generally ill at ease. Your mother certainly hasn't given her a wealth of tools for dealing with people. It sounds like the duchess kept her daughter close at hand for her own personal amusement. Pretty grim, actually."

"Oh, Bron. Please. Spending endless months at a mansion in Mayfair, shopping, being taken to lovely suppers and parties and—"

"Look, she's the first to admit she had a spoiled adolescence. Even she knows it was perverse, but she's forty for chrissake. Give her a break."

"I'm not going to argue with you. I'm happy that you two hit it off."

He looked back down at the book he was reading and Bronte threw on her now-ironed beige linen pants and a loose smock shirt and sandals.

"I think I'd like to go read in the *library*." Bronte tried to say it in a haughty British accent, but it came out sounding more like "*lie-bree*." Max looked up from his book, put his index finger between the pages to hold his place, and got up out of the large leather armchair.

"I'd be delighted to take you there," he said as he offered her his arm. She picked up her book and threaded her arm through his.

They spent much of that day in happy silence, reading in the upper gallery of the spectacular Elizabethan room. The wood paneling had mellowed to a gorgeous chestnut over the centuries. Throughout the day, Bronte found herself trying to process the magnitude of the wealth and splendor that surrounded her, often retreating instead into visions of Max in his *More Cowbell* T-shirt in front of the Ferris wheel on Navy Pier. The idea of great-great-great-great-grandparents who had been painted by Holbein and van Dyck was almost instantaneously terrifying. The idea of that shy royal grandmother whose father and brother had been kings made Bronte weak. Much better to stretch her bare foot across the red velvet sofa that she shared with her perfectly normal fiancé and rub his leg instead.

The elegant smell of thousands of hand-tooled leather bindings surrounded them; the midsummer sun streamed in through the clerestory windows. Max smiled again as Bron's foot made casual contact with his. He was happy to see her happy, but his mind was momentarily elsewhere. In his attempts to ignore his unresolved feelings for Bronte during their time apart, Max had stayed mind-numbingly busy. He had spent numerous extra hours at the office and nearly all of his free time putting together all the arrangements for a memorial in honor of his father. The final product of those efforts was to be set in a secluded part of the rolling forest to the south of the castle and was ready to be unveiled. The one-year anniversary of his father's death was the next day, and he wanted to make sure everything was in order. He put his book down and reached into his pocket for his cell phone, scrolling through his emails to make sure everything was up and ready.

He had worked very closely with the head gardener and the consultant from the National Trust to make sure his idea was in line with the overall site plan at Dunlear. Then he had contacted a contemporary sculptor whose work he had long admired and commissioned him to create some version of the piece he had in mind.

Martin Ellsworth had graduated from Oxford several years ahead of Max, but his reputation had already been established within a few years of leaving university. He was trained as both an architect and a sculptor in the classical tradition, and his work ranged from large-scale abstract and figurative bronzes that were mildly reminiscent of Henry Moore to outdoor structures that were neither sculpture nor dwelling but evocative of both.

It was one of the latter that Max had commissioned. Something that would represent his father's love of the outdoors, but also express his firm attachment to structure and order. Max had been able to meet with Ellsworth on several occasions to describe his father through anecdotes and memory.

He had also found and forwarded several of his father's diaries, nothing personal, really, but a lot about the years he had spent at Dunlear and how the physical property and landscape had affected him so profoundly. Ellsworth had found those particularly endearing, and Max was certain the final piece would reflect both the artist's vision and his father's worldview. The unveiling would be tomorrow afternoon, and Max was very pleased that everyone would be there to see it. Abigail still hadn't arrived, but she had finally called to say she would join them sometime later today.

Max responded to two relevant emails, ignored a couple from work, then glanced up at Bronte, who was blissfully immersed in *Wolf Hall*. He smiled to himself and refocused his attention on his book. As much as he felt a fool to admit it, his heart beat faster when he looked at Bronte: sitting on a couch and reading a book with this woman was the equivalent of skydiving while drinking champagne with any other.

Bronte sat up a while later and pulled Max's hands into hers. "Please tell me more about what this all means." She gestured vaguely around the two of them.

He was momentarily confused; he didn't know if she wanted to talk about *Wolf Hall* or Dunlear or their relationship. "What exactly?"

"You know, the dukedom, this place... the reality of your life here at Dunlear—"

"Our life," he corrected.

"Okay, our life. But... what do you envision? How will it all work?"

They had spoken very little about what it would really mean for him to assume the full spectrum of his ducal responsibilities with her as his partner, and everything that simple, loaded word *partner* implied. He had no sexist notions of Bronte quitting her job to attend to their marriage, but he shyly confessed his own secret desire to give up his so-called real job and devote himself entirely to Dunlear and its numerous possibilities.

"It sounds so old-fashioned, I suppose," he continued haltingly, "but I think my father's love of this place… and what it meant to him, to us… represents something profound and worth… maintaining."

Bronte saw a shining glimmer of hope in that desire to carry on his father's legacy, but it was clouded, as if he had tamped it down or, at the very least, postponed it for months, or maybe years. She felt a sudden, deep sadness for those lost years, the ones he had taken for granted while his father was still alive, when he might have shared and formed new hopes and plans with his father's input and blessing. Those years he could never regain. "Of course it is worthwhile," Bronte encouraged. "Your father would have loved that. What do you have in mind?"

"Oh. I don't know exactly, but there are so many options… for agriculture and education and the arts and… making this place a teaching institution or think tank or a cultural center of some kind… it's all just silly ideas that probably—"

"Stop that. It sounds glorious." She rubbed the back of his hand. "You are allowed to make something beautiful, you know?"

He leaned in and kissed her; it felt like gratitude against her lips. He withdrew and continued speaking. "For so many years, my mother pounded all of that *weight* into my brain… the ponderous importance of it all, the weight of the responsibility, what it meant to be a Duke with a capital *D*, to live up to the title… that I still feel a whiff of dread and, oddly, shame about the whole enterprise."

Bronte felt the slow rise of sadness and then anger on behalf of that little boy who'd been made to fear and worry over his inevitable future. One day, when she was in full possession of her confidence and wits—and maybe even her own ducal son—she would take her mother-in-law to task for such a wretched parenting failure. Max may have been a duke in training, but he was still a boy in need of a mother.

"Why are you crying, Bron?" He smiled as he wiped the solitary tear from her cheek.

"Because I love you so much and I can't believe your mother—"

"Shhh. It doesn't matter. She's not worth fighting against… I promise. She thrives on getting a rise out of people."

"Then she must grow like a weed!" Bronte joked.

Max smiled, then stilled. "Seriously, I am not trying to avoid anything that needs to be addressed or to put off some confrontation between the two of you—I suspect it will come regardless—but she decided to show up this weekend, after all, and that has to be a victory of some sort. She's not heartless, she's just… a product of her misconceptions, I think."

"You are too good, for which I suppose I owe her some reluctant debt of gratitude."

He smiled again, but this time with a sweet, childlike innocence. Bronte had the fleeting desire to slip her entire body inside his shirt.

"I suppose I should be grateful," Bronte conceded, "that your mother, albeit inadvertently, taught you patience and tolerance… especially for those of us who are hamstrung by our own misconceptions of what we can or cannot be."

Max pulled her up along the full length of his body and stretched the two of them out along the soft red velvet cushions. "I think you are quite aware of your own capabilities, my darling lady wife."

"Oooh, I love it when you go all medieval—"

He pulled her face to his and kissed her before she could finish her sentence, and the two of them set about the happy task of necking like a pair of teenagers in the middle of their historic, learned surroundings. A few long minutes later, an unmistakably aristocratic "ahem" punctured their careless fun.

Bronte flew up to a sitting position and quickly looked down her front to make sure Max hadn't commenced unbuttoning her shirt, only to realize she was (thankfully) wearing a long-sleeved T-shirt. Max sat up more slowly, completely unperturbed.

"Hello, Mother."

"Hello, Max." Sylvia paused. "Bronte."

"Hello," Bronte replied, proud of the even tone of her voice, despite the fact that her flushed face, plump lips, and disheveled hair cemented every hideous prejudice the duchess probably held regarding the unsuitability of her future daughter-in-law.

The three of them stayed silent for a few seconds and Bronte was surprised to acknowledge that Max's mother didn't look particularly judgmental or angry. In fact, Bronte was the one most ready to pick a fight. On the other hand, the duchess would probably look equally beatific—pale-peach Chanel summer jacket, off-white trousers, perfectly unscuffed shoes—as she drove a stake into the heart of her sworn enemy.

Max sat patiently. Bronte turned toward his chiseled profile and marveled at the power of that patience. She had a split-second vision of him at some imaginary negotiating table in London, and feared for his pitiable opponents.

At last, the duchess spoke, her gaze resting on Max. "I was just looking for you since we didn't really get a chance to speak at dinner last night. I hope it's acceptable that I decided to come down for the weekend. I may have been a bit peevish on Wednesday."

Bronte thought she'd misheard. It almost sounded like an apology.

Max stared at his mother for a few seconds. "Of course it is all right. I was very much hoping you would change your mind… about everything."

"Well…" She looked from Max to Bronte—more of a flash of her eyes than an actual look—then back to Max. "Let's take it one thing at a time, shall we?" She nodded her head in a single, conclusive gesture, as if to answer her own rhetorical question, then turned on her heel and left.

Bronte marveled at the sheer audacity of the receding duchess. "I think I just got the cut direct... what say you?" She turned to challenge him.

He reached over and pulled her back into his embrace, then leaned both of them down and resettled her on top of him. He nuzzled her neck, and when he spoke, his words blew hot and seductive so close to her ear. "I say that was the closest she's ever come to penance since the dawn of time, and you should take it as a triumphant approval of our pending nuptials. She practically asked to help with the flower arrangements at our wedding reception."

That evening, just before dinner, Abigail finally arrived. Max was refilling his drink at a large sideboard between two grand windows and had just made a joke to Devon over one shoulder. He was still smiling to himself as he put fresh ice into his glass. Everything was looking up. Over cocktails, his crazy, frosty, difficult mother seemed to have undergone a slight thaw toward Bronte—she was able to look at her, for example—but Max couldn't help notice the return of the maternal ice princess when his younger sister Abigail made her rough-and-tumble entrance.

His mother often joked—if you could call it that—that she would have no gray hairs if she had stopped having children after Devon. No one really thought it was funny (at all), but Abby, through no real effort, *was* forever disrupting her mother's equilibrium. Bronte hated to admit that the duchess was partially right: Abigail could not have been more disruptive had she worn a Halloween costume and come into the room blowing a kazoo.

The youngest Heyworth sported a prehistoric pair of black, military Doc Martens, laced almost knee-high; a Yasser Arafat black-and-white keffiyeh wrapped carelessly around her neck; a mane of black, wavy hair flying in every possible direction; and her girlfriend clomping behind her in Birkenstocks. Both of them hauled multiple backpacks over their shoulders. The two young women entered the room like a couple of midnight messengers in the midst of a Napoleonic War. Breathless. Eager.

"Max! Where is she?"

Abigail Heyworth was like a compact superheroine brought to life. It was impossible to imagine her quaking with fear or even contemplating that she might be wise to acknowledge her fearsome mother. Apparently, she never paused long enough to let her mother—or anyone else, for that matter—pose a threat.

Lady Claudia and her husband, Bertrand Seeley, Earl Rothwell, had decided to come for one night only and had arrived that morning. Claudia spoke with conspiratorial tones to Bronte, who happened to be sitting by her side. "Can you imagine draping that stellar feminine figure in those rags? It's a couture tragedy of the greatest proportions!" Bronte laughed despite herself and then watched as Claudia schooled her expression into a benign smile. After years of seeing their wild niece fly into drawing rooms dressed like a terrorist, Bertrand and Claudia were perfectly accustomed to the ruckus that always accompanied Abigail's theatrical entrances.

Abigail smiled broadly, removed her neckerchief in a sweeping circular motion, and tossed it on a (probably priceless) side table. Her girlfriend, Tulliver St. John, better known as Tully, held a similarly blasé view of family pressure and casually dropped her backpacks, Birkenstocks, and worries at the door. The two of them traipsed down the length of the formal, Elizabethan drawing room hand in hand and proceeded to greet everyone as the unified couple that they, very obviously, were.

Any worries Max may have had about the arrival of his (sometimes needlessly rebellious) sister were put to rest when she and

Tully reached Bronte Talbott's side and gave her two warm, substantial hugs. The three of them exchanged a few words, and then Tully plopped down in a seat next to Devon and started laughing almost immediately.

Abby said she needed to clean up a bit and asked Bronte to join her. Max smiled as the two headed out of the room through a nearby side door and into the large hall.

Bronte was thrilled to finally meet the independent, hippie, lesbian sister who had defied the dragon lady. The two of them left the drawing room, smiling in a conspiratorial way. Bronte had been in the house only two days, so the general layout was still pretty mysterious. She deferred to Abigail.

"Where are we going?"

"Follow me," the younger sister chimed happily, grabbing Bronte's hand as she pulled her down the corridor.

They reached a small sitting room a few seconds later. The door was not immediately visible, and Abigail gave Bronte a mischievous wink over her shoulder as she pushed the hidden door into the nearly invisible hall paneling.

"This is too much," said Bronte.

"I know, isn't it the best?" Abigail smiled over her shoulder again as she shut the door behind her. "I'm so sorry Tully and I have been up in Scotland this whole time. We have been having such fun at Findhorn. You and Max have to come up. Or maybe not. I don't know if that is your thing. We love it, but it's not for everyone. But—" Abby grasped both of Bronte's hands in hers and looked into her eyes with the same slate-gray Heyworth wolf eyes.

"You and Max have exactly the same eyes," Bronte said slowly. "I don't know whether to kiss you or to run as fast as I possibly can in the other direction!"

Abigail laughed with wonderful abandon. "You should definitely run!"

Bronte laughed as Abby's grasp fell away and the younger woman turned to go into an adjacent dressing room.

Bronte spoke toward the open connecting door. "I know we need to go back to the drawing room, but just give me a little family history—some of the dirty stuff that I will never get from your brothers."

Abigail had changed out of her farm wear into nothing particularly festive: a clean pair of jeans and a white Oxford shirt. The Doc Martens were tossed into the closet, and she slipped on a pair of expensive driving loafers. Only someone who could afford to volunteer in New Zealand and wear keffiyehs could afford to leave a pair of five-hundred-dollar shoes in the closet at her parents' house for the rare visit. Bronte was shaking her head from side to side when she realized Abby was asking her a question.

"What was that?" Bronte tried.

"I asked if Max is demanding. I never thought he was—he dotes a bit on me, I think—but he has that tendency and I was just curious if he tends that way when he's, you know, in love…"

Bronte stared at Abigail Heyworth. She was, quite plainly, the female version of Max. Direct. Eager. Sure.

Bronte wondered if she should use Abby to plumb the depths of her own relationship or leave it alone, thus preserving her own privacy. A little of both, maybe.

"He can be, I don't know, a little controlling. But always with my best interests at heart, so how can I resist?" Bronte smiled at Abigail. The smile said it all: *every fiber of my being wants to resist him, but it's not a factual possibility. I am devoted.*

Abby looked at Bronte and tilted her head, as if to better acquaint herself with the shape and form of the woman who was Bronte Talbott. "He has that effect on people. I've never been able to lie to him. That's why I have to go for months at a time without returning his calls. How can I possibly let him know what I really think until I have had a few months to ponder the truth of my own feelings?" Abby, by that time, had finished adjusting her clothes and sat on the edge of the small settee alongside Bronte. "He has that quality that demands the best, right?"

Bronte hung her head and then turned to this young woman, with whom she felt unaccountably connected despite never having had a conversation before this one.

Exactly! Bronte wanted to shout.

"He… has that quality… yes." Bronte looked up at Abby and, thankfully, saw a friend. "It's not always easy since I, well, I don't always even *know* my own feelings. But he is so *sure*. Do you know what I mean?"

Abigail merely laughed, got up from the small sofa, and walked over to the dresser in the corner. As she brushed her hair, she turned to Bronte and continued, "He is a belligerent seeker of the truth. Don't let him bully you into rushing."

Bronte looked at her knees, then up at Abigail with a smile.

Abby continued, "The thing is, he's so totally *genius*. I mean, he's so *right* about so much, so much of the time, that it's hard to contradict him. But the truth is, deep down, he knows that he needs a good set down. And you are clearly the one to give it to him. He certainly won't take it from me. I'm just the little hippie-chick sister who doesn't know the first thing about personal responsibility. The thing he doesn't get is the thing he needs most of all: a little ambiguity."

Bronte looked up as Abby put the beautiful silver-backed brush down onto the antique armoire. Didn't these people realize that everything they touched emanated a historical, familial imperative? Everything about Dunlear Castle was steeped in centuries of it. Not for the first time that day, Bronte pushed away the subtle, corroding thoughts that skewed her vision of the very familiar, lovable Max into the vaguely threatening nineteenth Duke of Northrop.

Bronte stood up and Abby slid an arm into hers, patting Bronte's forearm in sisterly affection as the two headed back to the drawing room. "You can handle him."

—⁓—

The following day offered a glorious midsummer backdrop for the unveiling of Martin Ellsworth's folly. Everyone, even an appropriately somber duchess, trudged the exact mile from the castle to the site.

The slight rise where the structure had been built afforded a wonderful view of the surrounding hills and nearly to the sea, five miles to the south. Ellsworth had built a dovecote of sorts that incorporated a fantastic array of ironwork over six arched openings. Max was simultaneously pleased with the outcome and overwhelmed with the sense of loss that it evoked.

Rather than solidifying some idea of his father as he had anticipated, the folly seemed to stir up endless memories of careening through the woods of Yorkshire on his father's back or being thrown in piles of leaves or simply following him around for hours as he checked on various parts of this property.

Max's arm was firmly around Bronte's waist, his head leaning toward hers. They stood for many minutes that way, silently taking it all in. There was no service or organized speech of any kind. Max simply wanted everyone together, and as the sun started to wane, casting lovely crimson light through the lush, speckled cover of leaves, he felt he had done right.

Bronte stayed as long as she could, but after an hour, she had to go. She whispered into Max's ear that the Virgin Atlantic limo was going to be there in about twenty minutes, and she needed to throw the rest of her stuff into her bag.

Abby, Tully, and Devon waved them on, the three of them preferring to remain under the dappled canopy of trees until the indigo darkness came. All the others had already headed back to prepare for their own returns to London, the duchess even taking a moment to wish Bronte a safe journey. Max was going to meet with several of the Dunlear staff in the morning, so he was staying on an extra night.

When she was packed and standing by the limo, Bronte gave Max a warm kiss good-bye, then hugged him with possessive ardor. She was trying to let him know, beyond words, that very soon, she would always be there to alleviate some of that indefinable weight and to share in all of the new joys that awaited the two of them.

"I'll see you in three weeks," she said in a low voice as her lips trailed along his ear and down his neck. They were standing in the spectacular forecourt of the castle. She felt completely out of scale, like a speck on the map of someone else's life.

"I love you," Max whispered. Bronte wasn't sure, but she thought his hand may have lightly trailed across her abdomen when they pulled away from one another.

As the black limousine drove away and Max stood with his hands in his pockets watching her go, she looked out the back window until her neck cramped. When the long driveway turned and she could no longer see Max standing there, Bronte looked down absently to see that her hand was resting unconsciously across her womb.

Totally implausible, she thought again.

———

Two weeks later, when Bronte found herself standing alone and barefoot in her bathroom in New York City, staring dumbly at the very dark blue plus sign that indicated she was, in fact—however *implausibly*—pregnant, she was absurdly reminded of that line from *The Princess Bride*. Apparently the word *implausible* did not mean what Bronte thought it meant.

Had she purposely waited until ten at night to take the test so she could pretend that calling Max at that hour, three in the morning London time, would be inconsiderate? She didn't know what the fuck she was doing or why. She threw the offending plastic wand into the little garbage can to the right of the toilet and crawled into bed.

Tomorrow was Saturday, thankfully. She was exhausted.

And pregnant.

Brilliant.

~~~

Max knew it was impetuous to fly back to New York to see Bronte. They had only been apart for two weeks—and he was already planning on going to New York next week anyway—but his negotiations had finally come to a close, every last document signed, and all he wanted to do to celebrate was get ahold of Bronte and roll around in bed for a couple of days.

He had managed to go standby on the Saturday morning flight, which got him into JFK around one thirty local time. He had flown with only a small overnight bag as his carry-on, so he whipped through customs after he landed. Within twenty minutes of deplaning, he was in a taxi and making his way to Bronte's apartment.

Exhausted from the lengthy meetings with his tenants, the investment advisory board, and the irrigation engineers, Max was feeling satisfied and more than a little proud about the final outcome. After nine months of intense preparation, weeks of arbitration, and numerous sleepless nights, Max honestly believed he had structured the deal in a way that benefited everyone concerned. The current technology and attention to environmental responsibility offered a real opportunity to prove that it was possible to be green *and* profitable.

Max's mind started to clear and he was mesmerized by the arched, white tile walls of the Midtown Tunnel as the glowing reflections of the passing cars threw a repetitive pattern of strobed light across the curved surface. He smiled, anticipating Bronte's reaction to his stealthy, unexpected entrance into her tidy little apartment.

She had given him a spare key in early June, so if she wasn't there when he arrived, he could hang out and wait for her until she came back.

In the event, he made his way silently into the apartment, set his bag down near the front door, removed his shoes, and padded across the living room into the bedroom. He was surprised, then thrilled, to see Bronte still in bed at two thirty in the afternoon, a sleepy, sultry mess of sheets, bare shoulders, punched pillows, silky chestnut hair, and soft, even breath. His heart faltered for a second, then accelerated as he stood there, taking her in. Then he headed quietly into the bathroom to clean up and join her in bed.

As Bronte rolled over, she pulled the comforter down slightly from her upper arms and had the odd feeling that Max was nearby. She could almost smell him. Even though her sleep-addled brain wanted to believe it, she was starting to wake up enough to remember that she was back in her own apartment in New York, and he was far away in his own sweet mews house in London.

Her first incoherent morning thoughts floated through her murky brain. Seemed like a quick wedding wasn't such a bad idea after all, she mused, letting a sleepy smile cross her lips. As corny as it sounded to her jaded ears, she was starting to believe in antiquated phrases like "my place is with him," wherever that might be. In the week she'd spent with him in England, she had become perfectly accustomed to their homey routine, his brief touches in passing or as they sat together reading or talking. She closed her eyes and savored those memories, of the two of them winding themselves into each other's dreams on that velvet couch in the library or holding hands as they fell asleep in London.

A few seconds later, she rubbed her eyes and tried to force herself to wake up a little bit more, stretching her legs toward the foot of the bed and reaching for her cell phone on the bedside table.

No messages. Small wonders.

Then she saw the time. Half past two in the afternoon? This pregnancy was going to knock her flat on her ass.

She put her phone back down, then stretched her neck, turning it first toward the window to her left, then right, toward the bathroom door. She screamed and almost had a heart attack when she saw a man standing there, then caught her feverish breath when she realized it was Max.

It was Max all right, standing there in the flesh, holding the white pregnancy-test plastic wand between thumb and index fingers in pincer fashion, and staring at her with a look that somehow managed to combine rage and tenderness in a terrifying mix.

"Bron?"

"Oh my God, Max, you fucking terrified me." She scrambled to sit up, wrestling with the sheets. "What the hell are you doing here? I mean"—she smiled seductively—"I'm so glad you are here—"

"Bronte."

It wasn't a question. He raised the plastic test a few inches.

"I just took it a couple of hours ago. I swear. I had no idea, for sure, until this morning." And why was he making her feel all defensive? Why wasn't he hugging her and loving her up?

"Then why didn't you call me right then? Were you ever going to tell me?"

"Max. Please. That's such a ridiculous thing to say." But she felt the tiniest flash of guilt as she thought of her relief the night before, that she wouldn't have to tell him right away.

"You text me when you see a ripe avocado at the store for chrissake, Bron! Why wouldn't you—"

"Max, please!" Her voice was sharp.

She felt justified.

About something.

She hoped it wasn't merely postfeminist indignation. If she wanted to have a few hours, or days even, to herself to contemplate a decision that would have an infinite effect on the rest of her existence—not to mention on the existence of an entirely new being—then she was damn well going to take a day or two to be alone with her thoughts. She thought of Abby having to go to another country for months at a time to avoid that penetrating look from her brother that was skewering Bronte at that very moment. Why did he have to be so... so... formidable?!

He half-turned and threw the pregnancy test into the bathroom garbage can. The hollow sound of it hitting the metal bin resounded with a pathetic ping through the silent air. Max left the bathroom and crossed into the bedroom.

Bronte tried to think: if she stayed in bed, she may have a better chance of luring him in there with her. If she got up and put on her robe and made coffee and debated every last ramification of her... her what? What he considered her momentary duplicity? What she considered her right to a day or two of solitary contemplation? It had been mere hours since she'd discovered the fact—was that so criminal? She tried to staunch the flow of that righteous indignation again.

Max sat down on the opposite side of the bed. Bronte mistook his nearness as an olive branch and rolled toward him—wanting to smell him if nothing else—but he stiffened as she got close, and it made her feel like some sort of serpentine, biblical villainess.

"Enough!" she barked as she threw off the sheets, stepped stark-naked out of bed, and slipped into her kimono robe. She spun to face him while she tied the belt overroughly around her waist.

He winced.

"What *is* your problem?"

"Problem? *Problem*?!" He stood up but kept the bed between

them. He wasn't just irritated; he was livid. His handsome cheeks were gaunt and pale, his eyes furious. Or tormented.

She wanted to reach out to him, to crawl across the bed and purr up against his length, to console him… but for what? For misunderstanding her? For judging her harshly? For being a bully? Bronte had misread so many signals, had questioned her judgment for so long, but in this, she absolutely would not budge. She had done nothing wrong. A few moments before, she had been lying in bed thinking how her place really was by his side, always, and how she would probably spend the day packing and surprise *him* with an unexpected visit to London.

"You are making this into a big deal and it really isn't—"

"I know you don't mean that." His voice was ice.

"Of course I don't mean the baby's not a big deal!" She was flabbergasted. "What is with you? Obviously the baby is a huge deal, but this"—she gestured impatiently between them—"this is just a misunderstanding."

Please let him see this. Please.

He looked down at her left hand, looking for the ring. She followed his eyes, then waved her bare hand in his face. "Fuck you. This is so fucked up. I was cleaning the goddamn bathroom last night, with bleach, and didn't think the fucking heirloom should be subjected to my mundane housework. What is this really about, Max?" She wanted to reach out and… what? Kiss him? More like beat the crap out of him. It would have been so much easier if they could have had some physical battle to strip away all the confusion and anger. His confusion about her supposed ambivalence, and her anger about his supposed need to control her.

Instead, his look said it all: as far as he was concerned, she had become an unreliable witness. Nothing she said was going to ring true.

"I don't know, Bron. I feel like I am always the one who has to understand you, and maybe I need a little understanding right now."

"I just found out I am going to have a baby, and *you* need understanding?"

"Yeah. You can turn it around like that if you want"—his voice had softened—"but it is *our* baby. You know I'm right... or at the very least I am entitled to my feelings or whatever lame psychobabble you want to slide in there. You promised—"

"What did I promise?"

"Everything. You promised everything." He sounded more defeated than angry. "You said you would tell me right away, no matter what. You gave me your word that whatever happened, we would go through it together. No more of those emotional distances, those little compartments that you want to manage alone. That we were a unit, remember? But you are still, even now, trying to hold something back, some sliver of... independence or freedom or an escape plan..." His voice dwindled to nothing.

She hated him so much in that moment.

For being right.

"You should probably just go."

"What?" He practically dove at her. In a flash, he had rounded the foot of the bed and stood before her.

She tried to practice his brand of silent patience as conflict resolution, but her arms were crossed in defiance and she knew she looked like the warrior that crouched right beneath the surface of her calm.

"You don't get it at all, do you?" He started to reach out to touch her, then let his hand drop. "You think I want to control you or make demands on you or whatever, when that couldn't be farther from the truth. I am devoted to you, Bronte. I committed myself to loving you, unconditionally." He pointed at the disheveled mattress. "Right here in this bed, remember? I'm not giving up on you, but it's your turn. You need to figure out why you're still holding back. Something stopped you from calling me—right then—not a day or two later, but at that exact second when that blue cross appeared on that idiotic pee stick, and it was a moment that should have been a shared moment…" He was simply exhausted of words.

She kept looking at the floor to avoid making eye contact.

He reached out then and rested his hand over her womb. She was frozen. She had the fleeting, despicable thought that he was *already* paying more attention to the baby than he was to her.

He spoke low and near her ear. "I would never want my wife or my child to be uncertain about the depth of my commitment and love. Why would you want me to feel that?" He kissed her at that tender spot on her neck and the hot tears began to trail down her cheeks. She stayed stock-still. He tucked a piece of her hair behind her ear, lingering there for a few moments, then turned toward the front door.

"I guess I have to respect your wishes, right?" He had paused halfway across the living room and turned back to face her. "That's the modern heroic ideal? You ask me to go and I go, because I honor your wishes. Because the truth is, I don't feel modern or heroic or honorable. I feel barbaric. I feel like what I'd really like to do is strap you to that bed and never let you go. Never let you go until you believed, down to the last cell in your body, that we belong together. That you don't ever have to carry these burdens alone. That I want to love you through it."

Bronte knew this was the part where she was supposed to run across the room and throw her arms around his neck (and her legs around his hips), but she remained utterly immobilized. Emotional paralysis, she thought idly, feeling as though she were looking at herself from about three feet above her own body.

"Please don't ask me to leave, Bron."

"I… I just have to have some time alone. I feel… you are making me feel crowded. I am suffocating." But the words were almost meaningless to her own ears, as if she were losing her command of the entire English language right along with her grasp of their relationship. Did she secretly want him to hold her down until she too was convinced of the truth? Or was she too confused to recognize any truths? She felt so lost, about who she was and why he could even love her. His very presence confounded her. He filled up her apartment with his body and clouded her mind with his demands.

"Please go," she whispered.

And he did. Because he *was* heroic. Because he *did* want to respect her.

She fell back onto the bed and pulled the comforter up to her ears, trying to convince herself that if she kept her eyes shut long enough and tight enough, then Max would still be in London, safely tucked away in his wisteria-trellised mews house, waiting for her wake-up call (his afternoon call), sitting in his walled garden, drinking a coffee and rereading Trevanian.

But he wasn't.

And she was alone.

She lay there, staring blindly, just as she had stared out another window, in another city, frozen in place, for some unfathomable length of time.

Then she just cried and cried, not even bothering to wipe away the tears and wet mess that covered her face and pillow. She cried for Max. She cried for herself. She cried for the loss of her father. She cried for the very real possibility that she would be a terrible mother. A terrible wife. A terrible person.

Chapter 18

MAX SAT IN THE Virgin Atlantic first-class lounge at JFK, cell phone resting strategically on the bar, and proceeded to get slowly but surely tanked. *On the Waterfront* played across the muted plasma screen over the stocked bar, Marlon Brando silently mouthing off in the backseat of the car. Max raised his glass in a dismal salute and mumbled, "I coulda been somebody."

He welcomed how the alcohol slowed his powers of deductive reasoning and gave him a distance from his own feelings.

Did I just walk out on Bronte? he asked himself.

No. No, not at all, his relaxed, buzzed self placated.

She wasn't expecting him, didn't want him there, needed time to think. All totally rational. He was respecting her fucking wishes. He was not going to stand around like a mooning idiot and be her *piss boy*, for chrissake. They were either in it together, or they were not.

And if she did not see it that way, then there wasn't really anything to build upon in the first place. Sure, it was happening fast; sure, he was eager—since when was that a crime? (Hearty slug of whiskey.)

She had been driving this train for far too long and he wasn't going to sit there and follow her around like a goddamned dog for the next fifty years. *Like father, like son*, he thought with dismay. What an ass. She can come running after me for a fucking change. (Rest of drink polished off.)

Another drink ordered. *New drink, new attitude*, thought Max as the peat fire trailed down his throat. *I'm Max Heyworth. I am somebody. I have people who love me. I can have any woman I want.*

And I want Bronte.

Shut up, whoever said that. (Another swallow.) He reached for the paperback in his carry-on and tried to get his eyes to focus on the swimming letters. *Maybe if I just concentrate on something else entirely,* he hoped, rather than believed, *I can get my mind off things for a few hours.* He moved with an unstable wobble from his barstool to a more comfortable armchair and tried to read.

Next thing he knew, there was a very tan, sexy, little hostess-of-a-thing tapping him gently on the shoulder and letting him know his flight was ready to board. They hadn't been able to get him a seat on either the six-fifteen or the seven-thirty flight, so he'd been sitting, snoring probably, in the lounge for the past five hours.

He stared at her without the slightest indication of understanding a word she was saying.

"Mr. Heyworth?" she said, for what was clearly not the first time.

"Yes?"

"The ten-thirty flight is ready to board, sir. Please follow me."

"Of course… sorry… was I asleep?"

"Yes, sir, but not to worry. When you arrive and depart on the same day, it can be a bit tiring—if you're not used to it." She smiled with what could only be described as a come-hither look.

Lust and spite are a potent cocktail, Max thought momentarily. *How easy would it be to fool around with this woman, take her out for a fun night in London, mindless sex, no muss, no fuss? No meeting the mother. No complicated negotiations. Just plain old how-it-used-to-be, fuck-around sex.*

"Uh… thank you for waking me…" He looked down at her very full bosom, which happened to be located behind her nametag. "Diana. Which gate?"

"Oh, I am working that flight, so I'd be happy to escort you directly to the first-class boarding area. Right this way."

How convenient that she could lead the way and swing her ass all at the same time. He didn't know if he was still drunk or starting to get a hangover. *I am so fucked*, thought Max, hearing the words in Bronte's voice, inside his own head.

So fucked.

Diana the Dedicated Flight Attendant turned out to be a perfectly nice woman and not at all the shag-o-rific piece Max had briefly envisioned in his whiskey-soaked imagination. The bosom was undeniable, and she seemed quite happy to bend over to reveal it while pouring the copious amounts of water that Max requested. But that was about all.

Max fell into a dead sleep for the better part of the flight, realizing, as he nodded off, that he hadn't had a proper sleep in nearly two days. *One more reason Bronte is a pain in the ass*, he thought vaguely. But a few seconds later, he was falling into a happy stupor thinking incongruously about Bronte's ass—and nothing to do with her being a pain in his.

Bronte spent most of that rainy Saturday curled up on the couch. Did Max just walk out on her? Was it over? What the hell had just happened? She didn't even know where to begin. In her view of things, she was just trying to be honest about her fears and how overwhelmed she was at the prospect of having a baby. *And everything*, she added to herself lamely.

When she finally got off the couch at four o'clock that afternoon, she felt surprisingly refreshed. She stood in the shower for forty-five minutes, letting the near-boiling water scrape her body clean, and her conscience maybe, if she was lucky. She was starting to feel guilty about something, but she wasn't sure what exactly.

Not good.

She put on a T-shirt and shorts and walked over to the Union

Square market. A lot of the vendors had already gone home, but she found some gorgeous leeks, artisanal goat cheese, and organic pasta. She talked to a couple of neighbors she bumped into on the way home. She was going to cook herself a beautiful meal, relax, read, chill out. Be alone.

Forever.

Oh, shut up, she thought briskly. She was not going to wallow in self-pity when this was the very thing she had supposedly been craving. More time. More space. Get her shit together. Maybe finish reading her father's book. One week was not a very long time in the grand scheme of things, and she was going to take *her* week to figure out what the hell she was doing with *her* life.

She made what she thought was a mature decision to not speak with Max at all that week. It was all going to work out in the end; she just needed time to get her mind around the pace at which Max expected her to arrive at that end. He was giving her space.

She cooked a delicious, healthy meal, read a few more chapters of her father's manuscript, cleaned her baseboards, and was back in bed by midnight. Not tired. Not tired at all. The idea of going a whole week without talking or texting or emailing Max should have been easier—she had gone almost a full year after Chicago.

Obviously the rules of engagement had been revised somewhat since then. At this rate, she wasn't going to make it twenty-four hours, much less seven days. She wondered how it was possible that only a few weeks had passed since they'd reconnected. She was going to have to be the bigger person and pick up the phone. It was either that or battle insomnia for the next week, and she needed her sleep.

Because she was tired.

And pregnant!

She rubbed her hand back and forth over her abdomen as she contemplated sleep. She kept thinking of all those idiotic clichés for pregnancy: bun in the oven, knocked up, broody, with child. Good God.

With child? What the hell? That sounded like a side act in Las Vegas. The billboard would read, "Siegfried and Roy, with Child." Bronte smiled to herself.

Plain old *pregnant* was what she was.

And she had no idea why she was pushing away the one person with whom she most wanted to share it. The one person who knew her, loved her, adored her. She started to doze as she finally let go, metaphorically unclenching her fingertips and finally falling away from the cliff onto which she had been clinging for the past few weeks.

For most of her life.

The too-tight grip on her independence that was really just a weak excuse for her unwillingness to let herself be loved unconditionally. Even the phrase "unconditional love" was oxymoronic to her. Every thought she'd ever had was conditional. Or maybe just conditioned. She'd have to get over that.

In the meantime, she could just stay in charge of her own life and gradually own up to the fact that she was now part of a unit. A perfectly dreamy unit. She would call Max first thing in the morning to tell him what an ass she had been. How she wanted to get married as soon as possible. How she wanted to be with him. To wear his ring. *All the time.*

—∿∿∿—

By the time Max's plane touched down at ten forty London time on Sunday morning, he knew he was an idiot. After half a bottle of scotch and three hours passed out in the lounge, you'd think he would have come to his senses. But no. Of course he needed an additional seven hours traveling in the *wrong* direction over the Atlantic to realize his place was in New York. Even if she was too pissed to let him stay with her, then at least he could stay in a nearby hotel, simply letting Bronte know he was willing to wait as long as it took for her to come to terms with the pregnancy, the marriage, their life together. All of it.

Diana the flight attendant was his new best friend.

"You are not going to fly back a third time, are you?" she asked.

"I think I have to." He tried to turn on his cell phone, then realized the battery must have died hours before.

"Maybe you should go into town, you know, to freshen up a bit?"

Charming, Max thought. *I must look and smell like a beast.* "Isn't there a two o'clock flight I could get on? I can clean up in the lounge, right?"

"I like your enthusiasm. Of course, there are full spa facilities in the lounge, but I don't think you have a shot of getting on that flight. You are probably going to be sitting in this very seat again come five fifteen on the return flight to JFK after they clean and refuel this aircraft."

"Perfect. Serves me right, I suppose. I can't be the first idiot who has done something this ridiculous."

Diana raised her eyebrows. "The first that I've ever come across. I've seen the there-and-back a couple of times…but a triple? I don't know."

"Just one more feather in my cap, right? The things we do for love."

"Oh, but it is romantic. She will be so happy to see you. I'm sure."

Max wasn't quite so optimistic.

A few hours later, he did manage to wangle the last seat on the afternoon flight. He would have Bronte back in his arms by dinnertime in New York.

Bronte woke with a chilling start at four o'clock on Sunday morning. The light in her apartment seemed askew somehow, the streetlight casting unfamiliar shadows across her bed. She turned on her bedside lamp and realized her heart was pounding. She had been dreaming about something bizarre and amorphous and menacing, dark halls, someone chasing her, gunshots—but it was fading already as consciousness returned.

She sat up a little and reached for her cell phone out of habit. It was nine in the morning in London. Max was probably already on the ground. *What a waste of a perfectly good transatlantic flight*, Bronte thought. She could have been rolling over into his arms, his strong hands stroking her back, instead of coming awake with a jolt, quite alone and disoriented.

She scrolled to the preset for his cell phone number, then tapped it and waited for the now-familiar British call signal to begin. Her heart soared at the sound of his voice, then sank a split second later when she realized it was only voice mail. She heard the demanding beep, then the waiting silence, ready for her to record her shame.

"Hey. It's me. The idiot. Your fiancée. So… I'm calling you, obviously… duh. Anyway, I was… well, it was the pinnacle of horseassery. I was the horse's ass. You came to surprise me and I… well"—she almost laughed—"I was surprised all right. I can't have this conversation one-sided. I love you so much. Please call me when you get this."

She turned the phone off and tried to get back to sleep, then gave up after thirty minutes of tense rolling around and forced eye closing. She put on a big thick robe that her mother had given her for Christmas, then went into the living room and picked up the next notebook of her father's novel. She curled up on the oversized, mossy velvet sofa, thought momentarily of Max's first visit to that couch, then refocused her mind and started reading.

Six hours and one stiff neck later, she was finished with the book and shaking her head in a repetitive, slow *no*.

It was inconceivable.

She had clearly missed major swaths of her father's entire humanity while living under the same roof with him.

Had she been an overly self-centered adolescent? Blind to any intelligence or wit he might have tried to exhibit?

Or had he simply turned entirely in upon himself and, by the time Bronte was old enough to notice, removed any evidence of his true self?

The person who was capable of filling the notebooks that lay scattered on the floor next to her sofa had no resemblance to the person who had supposedly raised her. She was sure there were plenty of quotes about the life of the writer not being the *life* of the writer, but still. It was bordering on multiple personality disorder. Was it better, in the end, that he had something to show for it, that he had not pulled an all-work-and-no-play-makes-Jack-a-dull-boy after all?

She wondered.

When she allowed herself to feel like the selfish, needy teenager she had been, she hated that he had put all of his wit and charm into those lifeless pages instead of into a relationship with her.

Then, when she reread her favorite passages, she was grateful to have something eternal, concrete, and real to remember him by. To hold in her hand. Because even though it was fiction, and it was written in and from and about some secret interior world that they had never shared, it was definitely real.

And it was definitely him.

For Bronte, it evoked a strange combination of pride and loss. Her father had titled the book *Notes from Underwood (Pop. 712)*, in a gentle nod to Dostoevsky. Lionel's fictitious world was populated by characters that were nothing short of vicious: the cruel mother who was in a perpetual state of tormenting her four unwanted children; the worthless husband who lied to his wife, stole her paycheck, and occasionally slept with the waitress at the Waffle House over by I-94 on the way into Bismarck; the twelve-year-old daughter who wrote it all down in blistering, breezy honesty.

The mother's self-loathing, usually justified, was always subtly obvious to the reader and completely lost on her. The father's oft-spoken suicidal tendencies were laughably ineffectual; he never seemed to hate himself as much as he ought. The young, witty narrator (Becky Sharp meets Mary Shelley, Bronte thought at one point) was desperate to prove her life, like one might prove a geometry theorem. If she could just get it all down, she was certain the pattern would emerge and she would be, if not saved (never saved!), at least living a comprehensible life.

Bronte reread the final chapter, took a deep, halting breath, then reached for the phone and dialed her mother.

"Mom?"

"Hey, honey. How are you?"

"Good." (*Pregnant and panicking*, she thought, *but we'll leave that for later.*) "I just finished reading Dad's book and I am so overwhelmed. I have so many thoughts and conflicting… well, suffice it to say it has raised a lot of questions for me."

"Did you like it?"

"Like? I don't know. It was amazing and might sell millions of copies, but did I *like* it? Probably not."

"Yes. I know what you mean. A little too close to the bone sometimes, right?"

"I guess. Sort of. But not really. I didn't mind the graphic stuff. The moments of violence were almost a relief, a sort of action at least. I think it was more emotionally graphic—those passages where he veered into insanity, or on the edge of watching himself veer. Then somehow laughing it off. It was just so raw. And still somehow funny. How did he do that?"

"Well, your father was funny—"

"Mom. He was so *not* funny—"

"Bron, he was. You were so busy rebelling, you never took the time—"

"Stop. I don't want this to devolve into the usual if-I-had-just-tried-harder-to-understand-him conversation. I get that you loved him. I don't get why—maybe a bit more now, I guess—but I accept it. So if you could please accept that I was the child and he was the parent and it was *not* my job to 'take the time' to understand him better. That was *his* job."

Bronte didn't know if that was silence or the slightest "hmmph" she heard on the other end of the phone, so she decided to be positive and think it was silence.

She continued cheerfully, "I am trying to agree with you, Mom, so there's no need to browbeat me. We need to agree to disagree on Dad-the-father and move on to Dad-the-writer, about whom we can both agree... to agree. How do you want to move forward on the book?"

"Well, if you are quite finished."

"Oh, Mom, please don't go all Victorian on me. Of course, I'm finished. I just didn't want to get on the Dad-Bronte-Conflict-Resolution train, but if you really want—"

"Of course I don't want that. I just wish—"

For fuck's sake, Bronte had to give the woman credit. She wasn't just a dog with a bone; she was fucking White Fang with the goddamned brontosaurus ribs from the opening montage of *The Flintstones*. It was endless.

Bronte tried to steer the conversation back to the book itself, but her emotions were running dangerously close to the surface.

"Mom, there is so much in there that is just too... that I don't... that I don't want to understand. I kept forgetting that it was Lionel who had actually written the words. Even his handwriting seemed different sometimes, as if he were simply channeling some other creative impulse. And then, while I was reading, I would find myself thinking that you and I were right there, a room or two away, living in that house... real, live people... and he was so cold—" Bronte stopped to cover the rise of unexpected emotion with the semblance of a thoughtful pause.

"Oh, Bronte. Do you want me to come into the city and we can spend the day together?"

"No. I'm fine. I mean, I have a ton of stuff to do and... I'm fine."

"The thing about your father, Bronte, was that he was so disappointed. And I think if you take a second to see what you adored about the book, but what you seem unable to appreciate, even in an abstract way, about your father, is that disappointment in oneself is, well, debilitating."

"Mom—"

"I am not idolizing him, Bronte. Just try to listen to what I am saying without seeing it all through the lens of your own adolescent loss."

"All right," Bronte conceded. She figured she could give her mother a full hearing—for the hundred millionth time.

"You know the part in the book when that miserable creep of a father forgives himself... again... after he gets that woman pregnant, then, you know, well, that part."

"Yeah... I remember."

"Well, don't you think the real thematic goal there was to show how that type of forgiveness, especially of oneself, is truly the most despicable, the most contorted interpretation of the heroic ideal?"

"I'm listening."

"Your father was disgusted with it. With a society that encouraged people to forgive themselves without a hint of remorse. Without any real regret. At least that was a disillusion that you and your father shared, wasn't it?"

"Yes," Bronte answered quietly, feeling the fight drain out of her.

"Well, I guess there are two things at work, from my humble perch."

"Go on."

"I think the narrator of *Underwood* was obviously you, or some version of you that your father admired."

"He never admired me, Mom."

"Please, Bronte. Stop being obtuse. He adored you."

"Mom! Stop it! He was so distant, so brittle. Living in that house was like walking on the most fragile Fabergé eggs... day after day—"

"Think about it, honey. You were always enthusiastic, joyfully alive, exuberant. I think he felt as if his own failed ambitions were almost contagious. The last thing he wanted was to contaminate you."

"What are you even talking about?"

"Bronte. He was so afraid that whatever intelligence he had given to you would be tainted by the same paralyzing self-doubt, the same self-destructive jealousy that destroyed him. He basically forfeited his paternal rights out of fear. Then, of course, he felt as if he had failed at being a father as well."

Whether it was the pregnancy hormones or the gravity of what her mother was saying, Bronte started bawling.

"Mom. It's too fucked up. I don't want to"—she hiccupped through her words—"I can't handle this right now."

"Of course you can, dear. It's all good news, isn't it? He was your father and he loved you. Just not in any way that did you any good at the time." Her mother laughed a little. "Life just didn't turn out the way he thought it would, and some people are able to accept that and get on with it, and others..." Her mother's voice faded out to nothing.

Bronte let the tears come (*more goddamned tears*, she thought) and then collected herself enough to continue. "But the forgiveness thing is really the main bit, don't you think? In the book and with us. Was he looking for my forgiveness, or yours, for that matter? He never seemed to welcome anything of the sort from me. Did he see himself as having forgiven himself too easily? Or not at all? I think I might just be angry, most of all, that he never wanted to even get to know me, let alone befriend me." Bronte was half-laughing, half-crying.

"Oh, sweetheart. He always thought that once you were through with all the frippery of adolescence that the two of you would find a natural way to, I don't know, connect as adults. Let's face it, not *everyone* is cut out to crawl around on the floor with a baby and make goo-goo eyes at her."

Bronte did her best to dodge that bullet.

Her mother continued, "Look, I think the novel was his way of saying everything to you that he could never say, exaggerated of course, but beautiful too, didn't you think?"

"Yes."

"And, again, even though the very creation of the book tore him from your life then, maybe it will do you some good now, you know, after the fact? Maybe it already has. Don't you see how your relationship with Max is so unlike your others?"

"What?" Where the hell did that come from?

"What do you mean 'what'? Bron, it's obvious you hold everyone up to these unrealistic expectations, so everyone is bound to fail. Luckily, Max doesn't buy into your I-need-my-space-and-to-be-in-charge-of-my-own-life line of cock and bull."

Silence.

"Bron?"

Silence.

"Bronte. Say something. Has something happened with Max?"

Bronte felt the underside of her upper arms give that telltale shiver that was undoubtedly a precursor to a very unpleasant note to self. Fuck.

She needed a long, hot think.

"Mom. I need to go." Her words came fast. "I take it back, I loved the book. Carol Dieppe's brother is an editor and I'd be happy to pass it over to him. I also have a friend from Cal who is an agent. Let me know what I can do. Love you."

"Bron?"

"Yes, Mom?"

"Oh, nothing. Call me later. Maybe we can meet up for dinner one night this week."

"Okay, that sounds great. I'll see you soon. And thanks. For everything, really."

"Are you sure you are all right, honey?"

"I'm sure. Positive, even." Bronte laughed softly. "I love you."

"Love you too. Bye, sweetheart."

"Bye, Mom."

Bronte hung up the phone and stared stupidly out her apartment window.

Sunday morning in New York City. Light streaming.

E. B. White would have had something grand to say about it. Full of possibilities. World was her oyster bar and all that. And apparently she was a demanding bitch who placed unrealistic expectations on everyone she loved. Or, more importantly, on those who loved her.

Great.

She reached for her phone and dialed Max. She waited impatiently for him to pick up, and when she got his voice mail again, she was both disappointed and—she hated to admit it—a little pissed that he hadn't returned her apologetic call yet. She was the one who was supposed to play the role of wounded self-sacrificer around here—pregnant, confused, life coming at her too fast. Where did he get off letting her stew at a time like this?

She left a very brief message—"It's me... again."—then turned off the phone and bent over to gather her father's notebooks into a neat stack.

She thought she should probably take it upon herself to transcribe the whole manuscript into a digital document, but as she stared at the slightly worn edges of the nine classic black composition books, she felt that the medium was, at least in part, the message. She decided to wrap them in brown paper, tie them with old-fashioned string, and hand deliver them, as is, to Carol's brother. She found a brown paper bag from the grocery store under her sink and set about her little craft project.

When it was finished, it looked just like one of those favorite things from *The Sound of Music*. Brown paper package. Tied up with string. She set the trim parcel on her kitchen counter and headed into the bathroom to take a shower and then venture out into the wide, wonderful world of New York City on a hot, sultry Sunday in summer.

By four o'clock that afternoon, she had exhausted all of the possibilities for savoring how great it was to be a single, liberated, twenty-first-century female in New York City.

No baby stroller—*look at me all footloose and fancy-free; no hands!*

No bossy boyfriend—*see my arms swing with independent delight as I spin and laugh with eyes all a-sparkle.*

No bitchy duchess sitting in judgment—*watch me swagger like one of Flo Rida's backup singers in the baggy sweatpants and boots with the fur. Yo!*

No critical mother—*look at me embrace everything around me, humming "Imagine," with judgment for none; I am a fucking Zen master!*

Denial was exhausting.

She went home with more healthy food and prepared another meal fit for Alice Waters. And sulked.

She served up her late-afternoon entree with a heavy dose of Al Green and Lyle Lovett, damn them. Their sexy duet had her scrambling for the phone for what seemed like the hundredth time to call Max again. She had passed through the multiple stages of immature frustration and annoyance at his lack of a response and fallen face-first into full-blown panic.

Bronte dialed and got his voice mail again.

"Okay. Point taken. I'm starting to freak out. Please. Please call me back. You win. I was wrong. Mea culpa. Punish me. Seriously. I like the sound of that. You. Me. Some sort of little leather paddle thing that I've never heard of, of course, but maybe you have, and you'll teach me a lesson in obedience. Please call me back. I'm worried. I love you."

After the call ended, Bronte stared at the stupid device that kept her permanently entwined in the lives of millions of people and still left her utterly alone.

She went back into the kitchen to clean up, then decided it was time to *really* clean. Every surface, every corner, every shelf, on top of the refrigerator, under the refrigerator. She was almost finished when Mavis Staples started singing in that rich, deep, compelling, sexy voice of hers. The haunting lyrics of the song cut Bronte to the quick. She couldn't do it alone any longer. Moreover, she didn't *want* to.

Bronte let her back slide down the kitchen wall, then she sank to the floor in a self-pitying pile. She sat with her forearms on her knees and let her head hang there for a long time. She was finished crying. This was ridiculous. She got up and threw the kitchen towel she'd been using into the sink, leaving the counters strewn with the spice jars, soup cans, boxes of pasta and cereal, and bottles of oil that she had removed from the kitchen cabinets. She had somehow, there on the floor with Mavis, come to realize that her job and her life and her very self were all pretty useless if she wasn't with Max.

She had been a coward. She looked at the clock on the wall above the sink and saw it wasn't even seven o'clock yet. If she tossed a few things into a bag and got in a taxi right away, she could be at JFK in time to catch the ten thirty flight to London.

She started making calls while she packed.

She called a messenger service to have her dad's manuscript picked up and delivered to the publishing company the next morning.

She called her mother and thanked her again for the great talk earlier. Bronte let her know she had made the decision to send Lionel's book to the editor and that she was on her way to London to surprise Max. Her mother was happy about both decisions and wished her a bon voyage. (No point in upsetting her mother with the very real possibility that Max would want nothing to do with her now that she had more or less implied she might not want his firstborn child... his heir. Genius.)

She called Carol and Cecily and told them she was probably taking a leave of absence, or not, but that she was going to be missing in action for a few days until she ironed things out with Max, then she'd be back in touch.

She called Sarah James and let her know that Carol would be handling her account for a couple of weeks, but she could reach Bronte on her cell phone. Sarah pressed for details, but Bronte feinted with an urgent need to make other calls to tie up a few loose ends before she left for JFK, and quickly said her good-byes.

She left a message on James Mowbray's New York office voice mail, letting him know the same. All of her smaller accounts would be happily taken care of by Cecily and Carol for the short term, and she recorded a new outgoing message on her office phone explaining the situation. After that, she would just have to figure it out.

Bronte sat on her luggage to squeeze it shut, zipped it with difficulty, then took one last look around her little, orderly world. She felt like she needed to take it all in before letting it all go.

She took the elevator to the lobby of her building and handed her father's brown-paper-package-tied-up-with-string to her doorman. She let him know the messenger would pick it up first thing in the morning, then asked if he would please collect her mail and put it into her apartment until she returned.

She walked out to the sidewalk, the summer sun setting to her left, Lexington Avenue stretching away into infinity across the park to the north. Bronte made a frown at the sea of occupied taxis that passed by, then gave a little sigh of relief as one rolled to a slow stop in front of her building to let out a passenger.

She was in such a rush to get into the taxi that she practically pulled the door off the car. The guy inside was passed out, probably drunk, his head in shadow.

"Wake up! I need this taxi!"

She bent her head down to look into the far side of the cab and felt the tears of joy start streaming down her cheeks. She dove at Max, rubbing her hands against the three-day growth on his cheeks, grabbing at his glorious, disheveled hair, kissing his neck, his ear, his eyelids, and then, as he started to wake from his groggy, sleep-deprived, cramped, passed-out, back-of-the-taxi slumber, his happy waiting lips.

"I'm so sorry, Bron," he tried to get out between kisses.

"Me too. I was so... foolish." She kissed him again, loving the feel of his jaw, his muscled arms through the thin fabric of his shirt. Her hands were practically clawing at him.

"Hey! Are you going to pay me or what?" the impatient driver barked. "Lady, do you need a taxi?"

"No!" Bronte cried as she made an awkward attempt to extract herself from the cab, then leaned into the front window to look at him. "No, I don't need a cab after all!" She took a hundred-dollar bill out of her wallet as Max walked around to the trunk of the car to get his bag. "Here! Here's a tip since you have just made me the happiest woman on the planet!"

"Thanks." The taxi driver took the money with skeptical grati-tude, then shook his head as he heard the trunk slam and pulled back into the slow stream of traffic.

Bronte almost tackle-hugged Max right there on the sidewalk, but they managed to get up to her apartment and into bed in record time. Max was almost delirious with exhaustion, and Bronte thrilled at the chance to strip him naked and get him all tucked up in her bed. He was a gorgeous dilapidated mess as his eyes slid shut and he told her he loved her for the hundredth time since he'd come awake in the taxi a few minutes before. He fell, almost instantly, into the rhythmic, even breathing of a deep sleep.

She lowered her head next to his on the cool, white pillowcase. Bronte put her face into his neck, breathing him in, stretching out against the length of his body, reaching across his chest with one arm, and draping one leg across his thigh.

She had always been mildly disturbed by that iconic Annie Leibovitz image of a naked John Lennon gripping a fully clothed and seemingly ambivalent Yoko Ono. It came to mind now. She used to wonder how he could be so shameless. He looked so desperate, one hand framing her face, the other clenched in a fierce tangle of her thick black hair. Why didn't Yoko hug him back? She was practically ignoring him.

But in this moment, on this bed, with this man, Bronte felt a wave of recognition… and joy. John Lennon didn't give a shit about what he looked like or what Yoko was doing, or who saw, because he simply loved her. It didn't matter to Bronte whether she was an advertising executive or a duchess or naked—she simply loved Max. She wanted to hang on him like a toddler clings to his mother. She wanted to wrap her body around his like a shroud. She wanted him to wear her like a loose-fitting garment.

A few hours later, Max rolled over and awoke to see Bronte's gleaming green eyes staring back at him a few inches away. He whispered, "We don't have to get married if you don't want to, if it's all too much too fast. I don't care as long—"

"You don't have to talk. Let's just rest for a while. We can get married today if you want to. Today. Tomorrow. Whenever." She started steamrolling: "I almost called City Hall while you were asleep, but I figured it'll be Monday morning soon enough, and of course they must perform weddings on Monday mornings. This is New York City, for goodness' sake. And then I remembered Devon saying you might prefer to get married at the chapel at Dunlear, with the family vicar and all that—which is fine, by the way, if that's what you want—but I'm not sure I can wait that long. I mean, I don't want our first child forever wondering if he was responsible for some sort of loveless shotgun wedding! So I've got it all figured that this is how the story will go: I was in a doleful state of missing you after these past couple of weeks and then a near-panic when I hadn't been able to reach you for *days*, and then the moment you arrived in New York, I couldn't wait another minute, and we were careless, and I had my way with you, and then—"

Max's smile stopped her in midsentence.

"What?" she said through her own smile.

"I love it when you think you can manage everything."

"You love it? I thought it was merely *adorable*," Bronte teased.

"I loved you then too, but I figured if I came right out and said so, you would think I was being insincere, in the first blush of lust and all that."

"Well, I'll have you know that I am happy to relinquish control… of everything. Whatever you want to do, wherever you want to do it, however many times you want to do it. My answer is yes."

"Just like that?" Max echoed her skeptical reply from so long ago.

"Just like that."

Acknowledgments

Without the encouragement and support of the following people, this book would not be in your hands: Allison Hunter, Anne Calhoun, Bettina Young, Brenda Phipps, Cat Clyne, Conway Van der Wolk, Deb Werksman, Dorothy MacDiarmid, Elizabeth Mellon, Emma Petersen, Fecia Mulry, Janet Webb, Jeffrey Huisinga, Katharine Ashe, Laura Munson, Linda Edwards, Lisa Dunick, Magdalen Braden, Mary Whittemore, Mate Bonilla, Mira Lyn Kelly, Miranda Neville, Nonie Madden, Peg Mulry, Rachel Edwards, Regan Fisher, Susie Benton, Tom Mulry, The Bridge Ladies, and everyone in the #1k1hr Twitter feed.

About the Author

Megan Mulry writes sexy, modern, romantic fiction. She graduated from Northwestern University and then worked in publishing, including positions at *The New Yorker* and *Boston* magazine. After moving to London, Mulry worked in finance and attended London Business School. She has traveled extensively in Asia, India, Europe, and Africa and now lives with her husband and children in Florida. You can visit her website at www.meganmulry.com or find her procrastinating on Twitter.

Are You In Love With Love Stories?

Here's an online romance readers club that's just for YOU!

Where you can:

- **Meet** great *authors*
- **Party** with new *friends*
- **Get** new *books* before everyone else
- **Discover** great *new reads*

All at incredibly BIG savings!

Join the party at DiscoveraNewLove.com!

♥ ♥ ♥ ♥ ♥ ♥ ♥

Nadia Knows Best

by Jill Mansell

The bigger the mistake, the more tempting it is…

When Nadia Kinsella meets Jay Tiernan, she's tempted. Of course she is. Stranded together while a snowstorm rages outside… who would ever know?

But Nadia's already been together with Laurie for years—they're practically childhood sweethearts. Okay, so maybe she doesn't get to see much of him these days, but she can't betray him.

Besides, when you belong to a family like the Kinsellas—glamorous grandmother Miriam, feckless mother Leonie, stop-at-nothing sister Clare—well, someone has to exercise a bit of self-control, don't they? I mean, you wouldn't want to do something that you might later regret…

Praise for *New York Times* and *USA Today* bestselling author Jill Mansell:

"Mansell crafts a lovely story."—*USA Today*

"A master storyteller who creates characters with unique personalities that captivate the reader's imagination and heart."—*Long and Short Reviews*

For more Jill Mansell, visit:

www.sourcebooks.com

A Walk in the Park

by Jill Mansell

After eighteen years, she's back with a big surprise…

Lara Carson disappeared at the age of sixteen without a word of explanation to her boyfriend Flynn or best friend Evie. Now her father has passed away, and Lara suddenly reappears in her old hometown of Bath…just in time to help Evie with her own disaster.

For Flynn, the boyfriend she left behind, Lara's daughter is the biggest surprise. But as secrets from the past begin to reveal themselves, there's no predicting where Lara's feelings may take her…

For more Jill Mansell, visit:

www.sourcebooks.com

Coming Spring 2013...

Thinking of You

by Jill Mansell

When Ginny Holland's daughter heads off to university, Ginny is left with a severe case of empty nest syndrome. To make matters worse, the first gorgeous man she's laid eyes on in years has just accused Ginny of shoplifting. So, in need of a bit of company, Ginny decides to advertise for a lodger, but what she gets is lovelorn Laurel. Yet with Laurel comes her dangerously charming brother, Perry, and the offer of a great new job, and things begin looking up...until Ginny realizes that her potential boss is all too familiar. Is it too late for Ginny to set things right after an anything but desirable first impression?

Praise for *An Offer You Can't Refuse*:

"Realistic, flawed, and endearing, [the characters] make Ms. Mansell's book shine."—*Romance Reader at Heart*

"A finely tuned romantic comedy."—*Kirkus*

For more Jill Mansell, visit:

www.sourcebooks.com

Marrying Up

A Right Royal Romantic Comedy

by Wendy Holden

Beautiful but broke student Polly and scheming social climber Alexa may have grown up in the same place, but they couldn't be more different. Polly's just fallen for Max, a handsome country vet. But Alexa can't be bothered with love—any guy with a pedigree will do, mind you, as long as he comes with a title, a mansion, and a family tiara.

Alexa wiggles her way into friendship with Florrie, a clueless aristocrat who could support entire countries with her spare change. Suddenly the grandest doors swing open for Alexa, and a new life is so close she can taste it. Polly could care less about Max's money, but his mysterious habit of disappearing scares her. What's he hiding?

"A brilliantly juicy
Cinderella tale."—*Heat*

"Holden's tale of social snobbery
and bare-faced ambition is a
modern fairy tale that chimes
perfectly with our post-Wills
and Kate world."—*Glamour*

For more Holden books, visit:

www.sourcebooks.com